THE SORROWFUL GIRL

A LIAM BARRETT GILDED AGE NOVEL

KEENAN POWELL

THREE HOOLIGANS PRESS

To William Barrett and Ann Cadon, Edward Gannon and Mary E. Barrett, and Michael James Gannon. Had these brave folk not ventured across the sea, I would not have had the opportunities only found in America. To you, I am eternally grateful.

PRAISE FOR THE SORROWFUL GIRL

Part social history, part adventure, part murder mystery, part family saga, *The Sorrowful Girl* is a pacy and absorbing tale of rough men and flinty women carving out their lives despite sectarianism, injustice and corruption. The hurtle towards the final showdown is irresistible. CATRIONA McPHERSON, multi-award-winning author of In *Place of Fear*

Keenan Powell's *The Sorrowful Girl* takes us on a compelling visit to western Massachusetts in the last decade of the nineteenth century. Liam Barrett, honor-bound and decent lawman, battles anti-Irish prejudice, corrupt police, and scheming robber barons as he searches for answers in the murder of a young Catholic girl. Desperate to escape her humble origins and bleak future, Deirdre Monaghan dares to dream of a better life, but meets her tragic end in a dark wood instead. Echoes of Celtic myths whisper through the Berkshires in this powerful historical mystery. *The Sorrowful Girl* packs an emotional wallop. Damn good! —JAMES ZISKIN, author of the Anthony, Barry, and Macavity award-winning Ellie Stone mysteries

CONTENTS

CHAPTER ONE

A PRETTY GIRL

1895
The Berkshires
Western Massachusetts

C APTAIN GEORGE WASHINGTON STANLEY stood in the forest over a body.

It was late autumn. The ground beneath her was covered in red and yellow forest litter. Leaden heat made Stanley's woolen police tunic weigh heavily against his chest. He examined the scene, wondering what to make of it.

She had once been pretty. A young woman with china-white skin and coppery hair fanning across the forest floor. Her lips were parted as if she was talking the moment that she had died. Whispering the pureness of her love, perhaps.

She was sprawled across a narrow game trail. The path had become a highway for tramps living in the woods. The earth was dry so there were no footprints to show which direction she had come from. The dried leaves carpeting the ground were undisturbed. There had been no fight.

She was dressed in her church clothes. A white blouse buttoned to her throat. Her black skirt undisturbed, nothing to suggest it had been hiked, willingly or forced, but the coroner could tell him more about that later. She could not have been there for too long. Crows and foxes, much less worms and flies, hadn't got her yet.

Stanley squatted, grasped her chin, and turned her head. Cool to the touch, but the neck moved easily. She was just newly dead. It was then he saw the ugly crater in her skull.

The tramp who had reported the body was standing an arm's length away. He held the peaked cap in his hands, working the edge with his fingers.

"Did you touch her?" Stanley asked.

"No, sir."

"Then how did you know about this hole?"

"Well, maybe I did touch her just to see if she was alive. That's the truth of it."

Still on his heels, Stanley spied a rock partially covered by debris. He had not seen it standing over the scene but from ground level, he caught a peek of it hidden beneath the leaves. He rose and took a few steps to reach it, a distance that would suggest that it had not been dropped but thrown instead and then intentionally hidden. When he flicked the leaves off, he found blood, hair, and bits of tissue stuck to the ragged stone edges. The murder weapon.

He took off his police cap, wiped the sweat from his brow with the back of his hand, and fanned himself with his cap, thinking.

George Washington Stanley, police chief of Pittsfield, Massachusetts, was standing over the corpse of a girl he had never seen. It was strange that he did not know her. He was acquainted by face and name with every man, woman, and child in his town and those from the neighboring farms and estates. It was his job to know the folks passing through his jurisdiction: the crippled Civil War soldiers, immigrants, the tramps, and the captains of industry now building their "summer cottages" nearby.

Despite these comings and goings, his town had remained peaceful. It was his job to make sure it stayed that way. Those who would never find work in Pittsfield, the Irish immigrants and tramps, were moved on quickly, sent in the direction of Adams town a few miles north where the cotton mill would employ anyone, American or not.

Stanley's talent for handling the rowdy and lawless was why he had been hired to police Pittsfield. He was a large man, quicker than most, and enjoyed the exhilaration that came with brutality. The city fathers were happy to look the other way as long as he kept their town peaceful. And it was this special talent that had earned him Alistair Cunningham's attention. The Scottish industrialist had taken residence in Pittsfield. Immigrant or not, he was tolerated and pandered to because he was rich. Of all those in Pittsfield who wanted to stand at his elbow, it was George Washington Stanley he had chosen because Stanley could get things done. And who was to stop him? Stanley was the law.

Before today, a Sunday no less, there had never been a dead girl in his woods. There would be those who would say Stanley had missed something or else this murder would not have happened. It would look bad for him. Worse still if he didn't solve the crime quickly. The city fathers might replace him. Then what use would Cunningham have for him then, no longer the friendly police chief able to fix the Scot's problems?

Stanley scanned the woods. There was no one in sight, not another tramp, no Sunday afternoon hikers. "You live in these woods?"

"Aye."

"That's trespassing. I could arrest you."

"Please don't, sir. I mean no harm by it. It's just there's nowhere else to stay if a man has no coin in his pocket."

"What's your name?"

"Owen Sweeney, sir."

"You're not from around here."

"I am not, sir."

"Where do you come from?"

"Boston?"

That accent did not sound like Boston. "And before that?"

"County Donegal."

"That's in Ireland, right?"

"It is."

Stanley had suspected as much. "How long have you been here?"

"Just a few days, sir."

"Did you see anyone in the woods this morning?"

The fool frowned and pointed at the body with his cap. Stanley would have to talk slow to get through to him. "Anyone besides this girl?"

Sweeney shrugged.

Stanley raised his voice to get the tramp's attention. "Tell me again how you found her."

The tramp's face twisted with some deeply felt emotion. That was not the response Stanley would expect from a killer, unless of course he was a practiced liar. "Sure, I was walking through these woods, sir." He waved the cap in a direction behind him. "Going to town, looking for work, and found her like that."

Looking for work on a Sunday, the Lord's day of rest? Unlikely. "You found her here, like this."

"Just so."

Stanley did not have a grip on what had happened, but he was certain there were mysteries at work. A tramp, a stranger to this place, and a murdered girl, a stranger too.

Their paths crossing in this lonely spot on a Sunday made for another mystery. "Did you know her before today?"

Sweeney doubled over, heaving. Guilty-looking. The muttering, the refusal to meet Stanley's eye, the nervous play with his hat. An open and shut case if Stanley had ever seen one but no judge would hold this man over just because he found a body.

When he was done retching, Sweeney shook his head. "Never seen this girl in my life. I swear it on my mother's grave."

Stanley needed this murder solved in quick order. He needed to show the city fathers and Alistair Cunningham that he was in control, he was the keeper of the peace.

With that copper-colored hair, the girl at his feet could well have been another immigrant, or a daughter of one, yet she was well-dressed and clean. She had a home and a mother, had been taught to care for herself, to wash her face, brush her hair, and iron her dress. If she had been from Pittsfield, he would have known her. If she wasn't from Pittsfield, then she was the daughter of an immigrant who lived nearby.

"Sweeney from Donegal, have you ever been to Adams?"

CHAPTER TWO

SANCTUARY

L IAM BARRETT WAS THIRTY-THREE years old and his back hurt like an old man's. He stretched, stiff from hours of sitting, and gazed over the farmhouse roof to the valley below. It was afternoon now. The sun burned over Adams town, a quiet place on a Sunday in autumn. Leaves on distant trees flared in colors of russet, orange, yellow.

He sat on the milk stool and thumbed the corner of a book, making a soft whirling sound he found comforting. He had spent many evenings in this shed contemplating justice, truth, and reason. It was where he read, listened to the wind in the trees and the chickens in the yard, while the light turned gauzy as the sun slipped behind Mount Greylock.

In a dark corner, the heifer struggled to her feet. She lowered her head, face tense, eyes shuttered. Her back hunched. Her belly convulsed.

The evening before, he had seen the signs. Her tail twitching back and forth as bloody slime streamed down her rump. She had stomped her feet, licked her side, and kicked at her swollen belly. At times, her eyes were so wide, the whites showed. Soon after the sun rose, he lifted her tail to examine her progress and her waters broke, gushing from her and drenching his boots and trousers.

He spent the day squatting on this milk stool. He had brought with him a slender volume of Plato from the farmhouse but could not concentrate. From time to time, he found himself staring at the page, not comprehending the words – his mind on the little cow and her unborn calf.

The contraction passed and she lifted her head to face him. She looked more tired than frightened now, her large brown eyes sagging. Nothing to show for her labor but another dribble of loose dung. He set his book on a crossbeam, stepped over the chain coiled on the dirt floor, and walked toward her dark corner.

"Now, now, old girl," he said in a low tone, one arm extended in case she shied. She was not a nervous cow. A gentle beast, she usually followed him around the small farm as he worked, occasionally nudging him for attention with her muzzle. And he would comply, putting down whatever was in his hand, and giving her a scratch under the chin. But she had never calved before. Neither of them knew what to expect.

He brushed his fingers along her jaw. She tilted her head and brought her ear closer to him, asking to be petted. He cupped his large hand at the base of her lobe and gently slid his hand to the tip. He did the same for the other ear, then patted her neck.

"There now, Bridget old girl, you'll be fine."

But he wasn't so sure. The calf could suffocate inside its mother. And, the mother unable to deliver the stillborn, would die.

He retrieved a pitchfork leaning in a corner, cleared the muck, and laid out clean hay. A dusty cloud rose from the dried grass making his eyes itch. Blinking away the irritation, he returned the pitchfork to its place, then crossed back to the shed's opening where a fourth wall would have been.

In the yard, the chickens squabbled, ill-tempered at having been shooed away from the little barn. The afternoon had begun to cool. Liam felt a sudden chill.

The cow adjusted her stance. Her eyes widened – the whites glowing in the shadows of the little barn. She was suffering. Helping her might be the only way, but he had to be careful. Dragging the calf out could save her or it could kill her, and there would be no way of knowing what choice was the right one until it was over. He would wait a little longer.

In the distance, a door creaked open. A silhouette appeared in the doorway of the house. Beyond the darkened figure, Liam's mother sat at her window, gazing toward the road, waiting for the husband who would never return. Liam's sister Kate was roving about, stopped to tuck in the mother's blanket, then resumed her course from one room to another. Ever since the father died, she seemed to be in perpetual motion. The younger ones, Kevin and Clare, would have been sent to bed.

The door closed. A man separated himself from the house's shadow. He moved up the hill, his priest robes flowing in his wake.

"How fares our Bridget?" the priest asked. Father Francis O'Shea was the same age as Liam, early thirties, but otherwise they were as different as two men could be. Liam was over six feet tall, lean, with his golden hair combed into submission. He had scant trace of an accent, having come to this country as a small lad.

The priest was a head shorter, built like a bull, with a mass of cherubic brown curls. He'd came from County Cork and spoke in a manner of those parts which sounded more cheerful than other Irish. The ladies of St. Thomas church, the old hens as Liam's father had called them, thought he was entirely too merry. Liam liked him well enough even if he was a priest.

He had recently arrived to replace a priest unexpectedly recalled by the diocese. The parish families agreed to take turns inviting him to Sunday dinner. Tonight was the Barretts'. Liam had excused himself from dinner to stand vigil.

"Her time is coming soon, Father," Liam said.

"Frank," the priest said. "We're the same age, Liam. I can't have you calling me 'Father'."

"Frank," Liam said with a nod.

"You're a copper, your sister tells me."

"It's a policeman I am," Liam said, answering the priest's question. How quickly his accent came back to him when he talked with someone from the Old Sod.

"Unusual it is to meet a Catholic policeman. Back in Ireland, they are considered traitors for signing on with the crown and taking up against their own. Things would be done. The house might be burned down, your cattle slaughtered. You might be lured from your home during the night and set upon by masked thugs."

"My neighbors are glad to have one of their own watching out for them."

"Grand so," the priest said, signaling he was happy to move off that subject. "I didn't see you in mass today."

"You did not," Liam agreed.

"Your sister tells me you were busy with Bridget here. Perhaps next Sunday, then."

"Did she promise you that?"

"I just assumed when this crisis had passed, you would take your place with the family."

"Unlikely," Liam said, in a tone meant to convey he would not explain himself. The priest nodded. He appeared to have understood the message.

They considered the little cow. In that moment of Liam's distraction, she seemed to have lost hope. The previously frantic look in her eyes had dulled.

"You can't save them both," Frank said. "The calf has a better chance of surviving if you sacrifice the heifer."

The thought of cutting the calf out of Bridget's warm body repulsed Liam. "Learn that in seminary, did you?"

"I grew up on a farm before I went off to the priesthood."

"I lived on a farm my entire life."

"You'd risk the calf for a chance to save the mother?"

"I'll risk both to save them both. Help me or stand out of the way." Liam wrapped the chain around the calves' hooves peeking out his mother's backside while Frank rolled up his sleeves. They took position behind the cow, Liam bracing his foot against her hindquarters and Frank behind him. They pulled. With the next contraction, Frank muttered blessings and Liam silently cursed as they pulled, their weight thrown back.

The chain slipped in Liam's hands. The calf was stuck. It might be dead already and the cow could soon be. He was dizzy. Sweat stung his eyes. "A quick break."

"Grand so."

They laid the chain down and caught their breaths.

"If there's a prayer for calving, this would be the time," Liam said.

"I'll send up a word."

They both lifted the chain. "On three," Liam said. "One, two." They gulped a deep breath. Liam planted his foot on the cow's rump and arched his back. "Three!"

Frank was grunting, pulling so hard the chain was as straight as a rod. Liam's shoulder burned. He thought he heard his sinews tear. His temples throbbed. He wiped his sweaty palms on his pants, one at a time, and placed his hands up the chain closer to the calf.

His muscles quivered. He would not let go unless he collapsed.

The chain slipped, just a tiny distance. Had Liam imagined it? Or had they dislocated the calves' legs?

They stumbled backwards, Liam crashing into Frank, as the calf slid out of his mother and fell to the ground with a thud. Suddenly released from exertion, Liam felt weightless. His arms floated away from his sides. A whirling sound rushed through his head. He leaned against the shed with one arm, catching his breath.

The calf wasn't moving. It lay on the ground in a glistening gray sack.

Liam fell to his knees. He swiped the mucus from its nose and mouth. The slime squeezed through his fingers as he rubbed the body, willing the calf to live. The shed's dirt floor was hard and cold against his knees. "Live," he whispered. "Live."

The calf twitched, then bucked. Liam kept rubbing. The little bull lifted his head and stared wide-eyed at him.

Liam pushed back and stood beside Frank. Bridget swiveled her head around. Upon seeing her first born, she slowly, carefully moved her bulk until they were face-to-face. She nuzzled him.

"Amen," Frank said.

"Amen," Liam repeated, catching himself in the habit of repeating a priest's words. Out of the corner of his eye, he saw Frank smile.

∞

"OFFICER BARRETT?" A MAN'S voice called.

Liam and Frank turned to find two men in police uniforms sitting on the bench of a horse-drawn wagon. A sad-eyed fellow in a peaked cap sat in the bed. Liam hadn't heard them pull up.

One of the men was Captain Curran, Liam's superior at the Adams police department. He was short, erect, and mustachioed. The officer next to him, a big, ruddy, and well-fed fella, Liam did not know.

Captain Curran took off his hat. "Good evening, Father. Sorry to intrude."

"God and Mary be with you," Frank answered as he made a sign of the cross in the air.

Curran had never visited the Barrett home, much less on a Sunday. "Is there a problem, sir?" Liam asked.

Curran turned to the man next to him. "Captain Stanley. This is my finest officer, Liam Barrett." Besides the captain, Liam was one of two officers in the Adams police department. Clearly, Curran wanted to make a good impression.

Liam looked down at his mucky hands and searched for something to wipe them on before he offered to shake.

Stanley spit on the ground. "Never mind, Barrett. We're in a hurry. Do you know this man?" He jerked his thumb towards the man in wagon bed.

"I do not."

"Are you sure of that? He's one of your lot. Fresh off the boat from Ireland."

"I'm certain." Liam looked to Curran for an explanation.

"The body of a young woman has been found near Pittsfield. Captain Stanley believes she might be from Adams and has asked for help identifying her. I wouldn't bother you on a Sunday, but – " Curran left the sentence unfinished.

If there was a dead woman from Adams, that meant one of Liam's friends and neighbors was missing a daughter, a sister, or a mother. The family would have started worrying when she hadn't come home. Liam remembered sitting up all night wondering when his father had not come home. It had been the longest night of his life.

"I'll go and clean up. It'll only be a moment."

As he pumped water into the trough, he heard Frank say, "You'll be needing a priest."

"A priest for what?" the Stanley asked.

"Amongst the Irish, it is customary to call a priest to administer the Last Rites," Curran explained.

"Do what you need to do, Reverend," the captain said. "But hurry it up, we're losing daylight."

CHAPTER THREE

YON WOODS

"A FTER YOU, FATHER." LIAM gestured to the wagon. Frank climbed into the wagon bed with surprising agility given the robes he was wearing. After Liam hopped in, he reached out a hand to shake with the man in the peaked cap. "Liam Barrett."

The man took his hand. "Owen Sweeney."

"How did you get involved in all of this?"

Stanley shouted over his shoulder. "He found the body. Or so he says."

Owen winced. "I had nothing to do with it, on all that is holy I swear." He spoke in a heavy accent from the north of Ireland. "I was walking in the woods and there she was. I ran into town to tell the constable there," he said, nodding towards Stanley.

Captain Stanley snorted and gave the reins a shake. Clearly, Stanley was of the opinion that Owen had something to do with the woman's death.

The gray leaned into her harness. Liam and Frank grabbed the bed surround to brace themselves. Owen saw the move and reached but too late. The wagon lurched forward and Sweeney fell into the dirt and dried leaves skittering across the wagon floor. Liam held out a hand, Owen took it and pulled himself upright. He brushed the litter from his face and spit out dirt. Liam pulled a handkerchief out of a pocket. "Here, your lip is bleeding." Owen licked his lip. He waived Liam's offer away. "Sure, it's grand."

Owen then kept his distance, watching the trees and farmlands go by. Liam stretched his legs out before him. He had been a young man when he took over his father's role and wondered, not for the first time, what it would be like to have no responsibilities. Being the patriarch did not always feel like a blessing. Still, he concluded the alternative was unthinkable. Kate would have never managed it all on her own. The wee ones would have ended up in an orphanage. Their mother in an asylum.

"Where do you live, Owen?"

"Yon woods."

Frank spoke. "Did you go to mass today, Owen?"

"I did not, Father." Sweeney avoided meeting the priest's eyes.

"Are there other Irishman in the woods with you?"

"A few, Father."

Frank gave Liam a meaningful look then turned back to face the road. The priest would soon add a few more lost lambs to his fold.

After Stanley dropped Captain Curran off at the Adams police station, they each retired to their own contemplations during the ride to Pittsfield. The gray pulled them into a dark forest. The wagon's rattling was the only sound in Liam's ears.

Who was the dead girl found as she was near Pittsfield? Was she from Adams?

Owen Sweeney spoke, interrupting Liam's thoughts. "A lucky man you are, if you don't mind me saying so. A fine house you have."

Liam had never thought of their farmhouse as fine. Suitable, perhaps, since it met their needs. He didn't remember life in Ireland, he had been so small when they came over, but he recalled stories his father and Uncle Jack told around the hearth. How most cottages were one room where everyone lived, animals included, but the lucky villagers had two rooms, one for the animals and another for the people.

The little Barrett farm must have looked like a country estate to Owen. Even Bridget and her calf had their own house.

"Where's your family now, Owen?"

"My ma was too old for the trip. She's back home living with her sister. I send money when I can."

"Have you no brothers or sisters to care for her?"

Owen shook his head. By the looks of him, it would be a rare occasion that the Widow Sweeney got any help from her son. He barely kept himself alive.

DAYLIGHT WAS ALMOST GONE when Stanley halted the wagon in front of the undertaker's parlor, a store front in Pittsfield. Inside the parlor, the undertaker was waiting for them. He was exactly what Liam had expected, ashen faced, gray-bearded, tall, gaunt, sullen. He took in the sight of Liam in his police uniform, Frank in his robes, and Owen in his rags. "We're all here, I see."

Without another word, he walked into a darkened hallway.

"You wait right here," Stanley said, pointing at Owen.

"Just so." Owen took position against the wall, arms crossed over the cap clasped to his chest.

The undertaker and Stanley continued to the farthest door in the hallway. The only light that shone was a faint flicker beneath the door. Liam gave Owen a nod and headed into the gloom with Father Frank close behind. Liam stumbled. He paused to see what had caught his foot, a ripple in the rug.

Stanley huffed. "Get on with it, man. My supper's waiting for me."

The undertaker pushed the door open. Yellow gaslight poured into the hallway falling upon Stanley and the undertaker so that they looked like paintings, half their bodies lit, half shrouded in dark.

Liam and Frank stepped past them.

On a table in the middle of a windowless room was a figure covered by a sheet. The walls were lined with cabinets, basins, medical equipment and bottles, and tools Liam didn't recognize. The air stank of chemicals.

The undertaker slid his way between the men and the table, then pulled the sheet off the corpse's face.

At first, his mind could make no sense of it. The pale white skin. The stillness of her. A young woman. And then he knew. Liam's stomach lurched. He fought to keep his dinner down.

It was what he had feared during the drive to Pittsfield. Deirdre, the nineteen-year old daughter of Sadie Monaghan, laid upon the table. Her half-shuttered eyes was the first thing Liam noticed. Then he saw her hair matted with blood.

This death was no accident. Someone had crushed her skull.

"Pretty girl," Captain Stanley said. "Damned shame." He hocked and shot spit into a spittoon. A tinny ring sounded as the glob slithered out of sight.

Frank slipped closer to Deirdre. He placed a violet stole around his shoulders, crossed himself, and began to pray quietly in Latin. "*Per istam sanctan unctionem et suam piisimam misericoridam, indulgeat tibi Dominus quid quid per visum.*"

Liam translated the Latin prayers in his mind. "Through this Holy Unction, and through the great goodness of His mercy, may God pardon thee whatever sins thou has committed by evil sight."

CHAPTER FOUR

LET THE HEAVENS FALL

L IAM'S FIRST CLEAR MEMORY of Deirdre was five years earlier when she had grown big enough to notice. Before that, she had been another ginger-headed wee one running the streets with her schoolmates. By the time she was fourteen years of age, her form had begun taking a womanly shape. Her thick red hair framed watery blue eyes that looked directly up into his. She had noticed him too.

At the time, he was working at the mill. One evening, he had come home to find Deirdre reading to his mother, who was sitting in her usual chair by the window, rocking her baby doll. Kevin sat at Deirdre's feet, entranced by the visitor. No one noticed his arrival. He went into the kitchen looking for Kate.

"I went to the market this morning," Kate said, chopping carrots with a ferocity that would strike fear into an Englishman's heart.

He waited.

"It's Saturday. I always go to market on Saturday."

Clare was scrubbing potatoes. Her ears, stuck through the curtain of hair hiding her face, burned red.

"The mother wandered off. I came home, she was gone and this one," gesturing with her knife at Clare, "with her head in a book, had no idea."

"What about Kevin?"

Clare lifted her head. "He left with his friends right after Kate went to market."

Kate wheeled around on Clare, the knife still in her fist. "No one likes a tattle tale. It wasn't Kevin I told to mind her. It was you."

"Is there any tea?" Liam asked, hoping to distract his sister.

She put her knife down, much to his relief, and went in search of the kettle, talking over her shoulder. "Deirdre found her wandering near the river. The river! By herself! Thank

God, she did. She took the mother to Sadie's, gave her tea and biscuits and then walked her home. She's been here ever since reading to the mother. I've invited her for dinner."

"As well you should have." He would have agreed in principle but it was always best to go along with Kate when she was in this mood.

Since that evening, Deirdre Monaghan became another sister. Every Saturday, she arrived at the Barrett home not long after breakfast and read to the mother while Kate went to market. Even after Kevin and Clare were old enough to be relied upon, she kept coming. In the evening, after he came home from work, they all had dinner, a roasted chicken or a lamb stew, and talked about their days.

One Saturday, after he had walked Deirdre home and returned, Kate suggested the girl had an eye for him. "Nonsense," he said. "I'm far too old." In a few years, when the family wouldn't need him anymore and the pain from losing Eileen had softened, he might consider marriage, but Deirdre wasn't the one for him.

She only talked about leaving Adams and seeing the world, her large eyes sparkling as she spun stories about Boston, New York, and Paris. She wanted to see plays, work in a nice dress shop, eat exotic foods, hear the music of foreign languages. That girl would never have been satisfied with a life in Adams.

Now here she was, laying on an undertaker's table. She had only got as far as Pittsfield. It was a damned shame indeed.

The sacrament completed, Frank had gone silent, hands clasped and head bowed.

Liam had always found silence comforting, a repose from all the doing that went on from sunrise to long after sunset. In those moments, his mind was empty and his spirit calm. But this silence was different. It was heavy with loss.

"Well?" Stanley asked. "Do you know her?"

The man's voice tore Liam away from his reverie. His eyes still on the earthly remains, he said, "Her name is Deirdre Monaghan. She's an Adams girl."

Upon hearing the tone in Liam's voice, Frank looked up at him.

Stanley gave a self-satisfied grunt. "You'll notify the family?"

"I will."

"Saves me a trip." The Pittsfield chief and the undertaker disappeared down the hall-way.

The footfalls receded and silence was restored. The loss Liam felt was coupled with tragedy. This bright young girl had cherished her life as few had, and she had been robbed.

So too had her loved ones as anyone who would have met her in the coming years. Somewhere there was a person so evil he believed his world was improved by her death.

Liam had long ago quit praying to God. If a problem was too big, the components too unknowable for him to solve on his own, he would ask for guidance, not that he believed there was a supernatural entity who could hear and would grant his wishes, but because it was how he was taught to organize his thoughts. Prayer gave shape to the vague worries that sometimes snaked through the murky background of his mind. He'd hone his query until it was as sharp as he could make it. When he finally spoke the words, he was prepared to accept the answer whether it came sooner or later and whether it was what he would had hoped for or not.

This was not one of those times. Justice must be done. Liam would not accept any less. Sadie Monaghan would be ruined to learn her only child was dead. A widow, she was now alone, with no one to care for her in her old age.

The security Adams town folks felt would be proven an illusion. Neighbors would eye each other with suspicion. Parents would watch their children more closely. The children would sense the pervasive fear and cling to their mothers' aprons.

Liam dreaded breaking the news. He had known when he was first hired by the department, there would be occasions such as these. Something in his efforts to protect his little town had failed. Evil had torn through and had left tragedy in its wake.

He spoke his prayer aloud, "Let justice be done though the heavens fall."

"Amen," Frank said, crossing himself.

Liam pulled the sheet back over Deirdre's face, resting it delicately. Even though he knew she was dead, he watched the shroud for signs of breath. The slightest billow or sag would prove there had been a mistake, she could be saved. He counted three of his own breaths waiting.

"Liam?" Frank asked. "Do you need more time?"

"Time won't change anything," Liam said and he walked into the hallway before Frank could issue a priestly platitude. In the front room, they found Stanley, the undertaker, and Owen.

"Look here, Barrett," Stanley said, giving Owen a push. "Have you seen this man before?"

Owen threw out his arms to steady himself. His cap dropped to the ground.

Liam said, "I have not."

"You sure?"

"Certain. He's not from around here."

Stanley jerked a head in Owen's direction. "Funny he knew right where the body was."

"Not if he found it, as he said."

Owen's eyes were trained on Stanley. It was clear to see where the Pittsfield chief was going with this.

"You have no evidence to arrest him," Liam said.

"In my experience, the first person to see her dead is the man who last saw her alive. You want the killer brought to justice, don't you? It was an Adams girl, one of your own."

"I do," Liam said. "If you arrest Owen, the investigation will end. You don't have enough evidence to bind him over and the magistrate will release him. Meanwhile the true killer would escape."

"The magistrate won't be here for a while. I'm willing to bet this tramp confesses before then."

Captain Stanley was a thug. Although Liam had never met him before, his reputation was well-known in Adams. Because of him those who were most likely to get into trouble, young men with a few dollars in their pocket, were advised to avoid Pittsfield. And young women never ventured into Pittsfield unescorted, except for Deirdre.

"If you make the arrest, I will find him a lawyer. He has the right to an attorney when you question him." Unlikely Stanley would beat a confession out of the man with a lawyer sitting there. And it was more unlikely that Owen would suddenly have an accident if a lawyer could testify he had been in good condition.

Stanley glowered at Liam. The undertaker fell back into the shadows. Liam sensed the subtle movement of Frank's robes behind him. The only sound to be heard was Stanley's huffing.

"If I let him go, he'll get away."

"If we uncover any evidence to tie him to this crime, I'll find him myself and bring him back."

The undertaker coughed.

"It's on your head then, Barrett," Stanley said as he gave Sweeney another shove.

"Off you go, Owen," Liam said.

He didn't need to be told twice. Owen Sweeney swept his cap off the floor and lunged out of the undertaker's parlor, leaving the door wide open. Only a dark rectangle of night was visible beyond the threshold. Stanley's mare whinnied and stomped as Sweeney was heard breaking into a run.

"Savage," the undertaker said, closing the door.

Liam watched Stanley, willing him to stay in place. The man had a reputation for throwing an unexpected punch. Frank moved to Liam's side and asked, "When will Deirdre be returned for burial?"

"After the coroner is finished with her," Stanley answered, then to Liam, he said. "Now you answer my questions. What was this Adams girl doing in Pittsfield, Barrett?" He said it as if the only imaginable reason was scurrilous.

Liam knew her reason was honorable. In her quest to escape Adams, Deirdre had taken a job as a scullery maid for the industrialist Alistair Cunningham. She had joked that the scullery, a hole in the ground beneath the kitchen, was a strange place to begin her worldly adventure, but, she had argued, she needed to start somewhere before she was too old.

"She works," Liam started, then corrected himself, "she worked at Inverness. They allowed her a half-day on Sundays to go to mass with her mother in Adams."

☙

L IAM AND FRANK TOOK the train back to Adams after Captain Stanley declared he didn't have time for another trip.

They didn't speak as the train rumbled through the night. Liam watched the autumn Berkshire landscape roll by, the vivid oranges and golds dulled to muddy colors under the darkened sky. He thought about Deirdre, young and full of dreams and ambitions that had struck him as unrealistic for a girl.

The world was a dangerous place. She had no idea. And she was given to falling in love, as girls do. He was happy for her when she found someone her own age, Finn O'Brien. Finn wasn't a bad man but he wasn't the best choice for her either. He lacked her spark. Liam had hoped that in her travels, Deirdre would find a better match for an ambitious and dreamy girl as herself.

He could almost hear her laughter as he called into memory the last time he saw her alive, over dinner at the Barrett home some months ago. She had been nervous all evening. Something was on her mind. Liam thought that she was going to announce that the date had been set for her wedding to Finn.

Clare had been excused from the table and was reading quietly to the mother in the next room, a story from her book of saints. Kevin was scraping what was left of a ham onto his plate, his third helping, when Deirdre giggled. She was not a girl given to giggling.

"Out with it," Kate said, a smile playing on her face. A bit of good news was always welcomed.

"I've been given a job at Inverness. It's only a scullery maid but I can work my way up from there."

Liam and Kate exchanged looks.

"Inverness, Alistair Cunningham's estate," Deirdre said. "He's that rich Scot. He bought an old farm and is fixing it up, built a grand mansion, with gardens and stables."

Both Liam and Kate knew who Alistair Cunningham was. He had recently purchased Adams' cotton mill. There had been talk amongst the workers of how things would change under his management, rumors of longer hours, smaller wages, and working even harder to make the little money they could barely get by on as it was.

"Oh, look at the two of you," Deirdre said. "You'd think I'd signed my soul away to the devil."

"And what did Sadie say?" Kate asked.

"That I'd always have a home with her, and if something happened or if I changed my mind, I should come straight back," Deirdre said. She laughed then stopped abruptly when she saw Liam's frown.

"I love Adams. I do. It's been my home my entire life. But it's not our real home, is it Liam? It's not Ireland. We don't really belong here. We're only here because we were looking for a new place to live. You found a home in Adams. My mother too. But there's a great, big world outside this little valley, and I, for one, want to see it. You understand, don't you? Please tell me you understand, Liam."

He understood only too well why this pretty, vivacious girl wanted more out of life than taking over her mother's boarding house and marrying someone who might be the right age and the right religion but who was not quite her equal. She was afraid of turning into a bitter old hag.

"What about Finn?" Liam asked. "How will he fit into this scheme?"

"I haven't told him yet. It was a mistake to say I'd marry him."

"You need to tell him."

"He might get angry."

Had Finn bullied her into their engagement? "Has he ever hit you?"

"No, never. But Finn acts like a spoiled child when he doesn't get what he wants. The only reason I said I'd marry him was because he kept crying. I felt sorry for him. He's an orphan, has no one, but does that mean I should give up my life to take care of him?"

"The sooner you tell him, the sooner he can find someone else."

"So that's why it makes sense that I leave Adams. Don't you see? It's easier that way."

It was just as well that she didn't marry Finn. Soon, she would have become bored, and with a baby or two in her charge. It would be tragic if she aged into a shrew, embittered because she had missed out on her dreams. Liam knew how it felt to be cheated out of his destiny and he didn't wish it on anyone.

So when Deirdre asked him if she understood, he had said, "yes."

Now he wished he had warned her. Don't talk to strangers. Don't go walking alone. Don't believe what men say to you, watch them, find out where they came from, see how they treat their mothers.

BY THE TIME THE train pulled into Adams, squealing and groaning, the moon had risen. Its watery light flickered through naked tree branches looming over the streets Liam and Frank walked.

Sadie Monaghan's boarding house was a hundred years old, a clapboard home with a covered porch on a tree-lined street. She had five bedrooms besides the room she shared with Deirdre, enough to house up to twenty men at a time, most of them mill workers. Father Frank had taken a room while the new rectory was being built.

"Who's living there now?" Liam said as they walked up the path.

"Sadie, Deirdre, Finn O'Brien, a few of the boys, and myself," Frank said as he opened the front door. He led Liam into a parlor lit by a low-burning oil lamp. The room seemed smaller than Liam remembered. As a boy, he'd visited many times, making deliveries for his mother. She had taken in laundry to save up for the farm. Even after they'd bought the place, she kept it up with more than enough work of her own. She was like Kate, in perpetual motion, until the time she wasn't.

The parlor was empty.

Normally Liam would have looked for Sadie, but as this was an official call, he and Frank waited for her to notice their arrival.

She came out of the kitchen, her short, square body rolling like a sailor's, wiping her hands on her apron. As she adjusted the lamp's flame, shadows leapt up the walls. She took in Liam's expression.

"What ails you, agra?" she said.

"Will you take a seat, Mrs. Monaghan?" The weight of Deirdre's death had settled upon Liam's heart during the train ride. Her sparkling future wiped out, her joyfulness lost to those who loved her, leaving behind a widow who had dreamed for grandchildren, a son-in-law, and a happily married daughter.

Sadie studied Liam, who returned her gaze. She appeared to know that the sorrow he brought was not his to bear. It was hers.

"Deirdre," Sadie said, her voice breaking.

"Please, Mrs. Monaghan, take a seat." Liam remembered the men who had come to tell them his father's body had been found. The strange way the priest and the other men spoke, weighty and almost embarrassed at the same time – he could not remember what they said. His mother fainted. The men fell away and the women appeared, cooing over her. The doctor was called. He gave her laudanum and she fell into a stupor, staring out the window in her rocking chair.

Sadie Monaghan would not need drugs. She was strength itself.

She perched on the edge of the horsehair sofa, posture erect. "Tell me," Sadie said.

"Your Deirdre was found in Pittsfield, in the woods."

"Had someone..."

"No, no, nothing of the sort," Liam said quickly. He could not be sure until the coroner was done with his work but there was no reason to worsen this woman's anguish in this cruel moment.

Frank sat next to Sadie. He held her hands in both of his own.

Liam took in a deep breath and went on. "She was struck down. We're not sure who or why."

Sadie pulled her hands away. She stood, wobbled. Liam was beside her, a hand under her elbow. He eased her back down to the couch. Her gaze skittered around the room as if she was searching for something.

"I knew no good would come of it, working for the Scots. Her seeing all those useless things they had, the pretty clothes they wore. But my Deirdre was headstrong. She wanted to see the world. How much of the world can you see from a rich man's scullery, that's what I wanted to know. But you know how she was. She got ideas into her head. She thought she could work her way up to ladies' maid, travel with Miss Victoria, someday get a job in a nice shop. Or maybe, if Miss Victoria married and had children, she could become a governess. No one tells the governess what to do, my Deirdre said, she tells them. The governess is as important as the housekeeper in a big house like that."

Deirdre had been protected and cherished by the small Adams community. She'd never any reason to worry about the men she met walking down the street, no reason to fear for her own safety, surrounded by people watching over her. In church, in their yards, on the street, people looked out for everyone's children. As a boy, it meant the occasional clubbing on his ear by a nearby adult if Liam misbehaved. For girls, it meant they had no idea there were bad men in this world. Ignorant of how she had been protected, Deirdre was fearless. If only Liam had warned her of the dangers.

He wondered if she had broken her engagement. "What about Finn? How could she manage a position if she was married with a family of her own? Would they allow her to stay on if she had?"

"Of course not," Sadie nearly spat the words. "There was no room for Finn in her plans. I was hoping marriage would settle her, that she'd see her place was here, that she'd want a family as she saw her friends having babies. I have plenty of room. They could have stayed with me."

Sadie choked. Frank left the room and came back with a teacup filled with water and offered it to her. She refused it and reached for her apron hem, wadded it up, and scraped at her eyes.

"Is Finn here?" Liam asked.

"You can't be saying Finn had anything to do with this. He loved my Deirdre. He went with her and me to mass every Sunday, then we had breakfast and he walked her to the train station. They were to take the train to Pittsfield together – was that today? It seemed so long ago now. She was going back to work and he was going to the horse races."

Finn hadn't been on the train with Liam and Frank. "Did he return?"

Sadie frowned. "He should have been home by now. You don't think anything happened to him, too? Has anyone looked?"

Chapter Five

A Big Man

GEORGE WASHINGTON STANLEY WALKED into Alistair Cunningham's study and found the big man himself sitting behind his massive desk, feet atop, cigar in one hand and brandy snifter in the other. Big he was too, not in a gone-to-seed way but square in the shoulders and with a pug nose as if he'd once labored, and fought, for a living. Now he was dressed to the nines, in a pinstriped three piece suit, gold pocket chain tucked into his vest, snowy white hair combed just so over his balding head and a neatly trimmed white beard. As usual, he had that look on his face. The cat that got the cream.

In a chair opposite sat Malcom Dunbar, Cunningham's right-hand man, in working man's clothes, bristly shaved head and a full red beard. He focused on his cigar, tapping it on the edge of a massive brass ashtray on the desktop.

Gas lamps mounted on the walls filled the room with a soft yellow light. Behind Cunningham, red velvet curtains were drawn and made the room look smaller. As Stanley walked across the carpet, the squelch of his boots was the only thing he heard. The two of them had to know he was there but they didn't look in his direction. Something was watching him, though. It was a bust of some Scottish poet, Stanley didn't remember his name, whose blank eyes seemed to follow him. The long walk from door to desk reminded him of a recurring nightmare. He'd walk and walk but never arrived; the further he went, the further away he was from his destination.

He remembered the last time he had been there in daytime. The view behind Cunningham's desk was of an old farmer's field, some woods beyond and mountains in the distance. Cunningham mentioned that he was building a garden, copying a place he'd seen "on the continent" meaning Europe. He had said "the continent" as casually as Stanley would have mentioned a local brothel.

Stanley's stomach lurched at the sight of Dunbar. He acted as if he knew everything there was to know about Stanley and had the power to manipulate Stanley's life as he saw fit. If he didn't like a man, that man would not prosper. Nor would he tolerate anyone threatening his position with Cunningham. Stanley knew Malcom Dunbar had taken an instant dislike to him and with each interaction, his disgust had grown.

If Stanley was to make a place for himself in the Cunningham organization, the furthest he'd ever get was directly underneath the boot of Malcom Dunbar. That is, as long as Dunbar was around. And if he wasn't? That would be George Washington Stanley seated before that desk, puffing on a cigar and drinking expensive booze.

Both men ignored him. It was a ploy. Dunbar didn't need to look at you to know where you were. By not looking at you, he made that point. But with Cunningham, it was a different point being made. He'd look at you if he wanted to and not before.

Sometimes Stanley wondered who the biggest dog in the room was: Cunningham the rich man or Dunbar the enforcer. Cunningham had said that they had known each other since Scotland, when he was still poor. Now here they were in America, one rich and the other in his service. Why hadn't Dunbar gotten rich too? Despite their years together, there was a distance between them, like an old married couple who despise each other. What secrets bound them together?

He came to a halt before the desk and outside Dunbar's arm reach. Cunningham took a puff from his cigar, then tilted his head and watched the blue smoke curl out of his mouth and dissipate over his head. "What news have you, Captain?" he asked. Despite all his years in this country, he still talked with a thick Scottish burr.

It was their weekly meeting when Stanley reported what progress had been made on his tasks. Cunningham wasn't the mayor of Pittsfield, but he might as well be its king. As rich as he was, the real mayor and town council bowed and scraped to him. He had made friends with the local powerbrokers by promising to employ their feckless sons and nephews, in management of course, after his second mill was built. Anything he wanted from them was his for the asking.

"Harry Gallagher's booze shipment got lost," Stanley began, knowing this was the first thing on Cunningham's mind.

"Too bad," the old man said, swirling the snifter. Dunbar jammed the cigar between his bared teeth and glanced at Stanley, snarling like a wolf. That was his smile.

"And how did that happen?" Cunningham asked. He always did the talking.

"The bills of lading were switched. On accident. No one will ever figure out how that happened. Harry Gallagher will be picking up an order of ladies' dresses Monday morning."

Cunningham lifted an eyebrow. "Then there will be no booze in Adams come Friday."

"None, sir."

When Cunningham had mentioned he wanted the shipment waylaid, he'd said it was the habit of the Molly Maguires to congregate in local pubs where they would freely buy drinks for working men, preach their sedition, and enlist followers. He feared labor organizers the way other men feared syphilis. He was obsessed with the Mollys, that Irish clan of scallywags he called them, afraid they would take over his cotton mills. Given the large Irish population in Adams, and how many Irish were working in his mills, he insisted that the plague of the Pennsylvania steel mills would soon find its way into the Berkshires carried by one Paddy to another.

So while Cunningham had not exactly said he wanted Stanley to interfere with the shipment, so much as said he wished the liquor would disappear, Stanley took the hint. He needed to prove to the old man how valuable he was. If he could impress Cunningham, Dunbar would have to accept him because above all else, he was loyal. The trick was making himself valuable before Dunbar got in his way. And then find out what the enforcer's weakness was and get rid of him.

So, it wasn't the first time Cunningham had said he wanted something done and Stanley filled his wish. Sometimes he wanted one of his men released from jail, charges dismissed. Stanley saw to it. Sometimes he wanted someone else hauled to jail for a few days. Stanley saw to that too. Sometimes he wanted someone convinced that being his friend was better than being his enemy. Those were Stanley's favorite jobs.

Good things came along every time he did one of those little favors. A box of cigars. A case of fine whiskey. A ham or a turkey. Even that gray mare he drove and the wagon that came with her was delivered by one of Cunningham's lackeys.

Stanley had tried explaining the Mollys had been wiped out twenty years back, their leaders and followers arrested, tried, convicted, and hanged. And the ones who'd escaped legal hanging got lynched. Swinging one way or another, with or without trial.

But the old man insisted that if they weren't called Mollys, then they worked under some other name. It was the Mollys or their spawn at work, and he did not want them getting a foothold in Adams. The heart of those gatherings was the local bar, so it was that place he wanted attacked first. If there was no booze, there would be no gatherings and no insurrection.

Labor unrest had not died off, the old man said. The news, he pointed out, was filled with reports of strikes and riots. That was why Stanley started reading the paper. He wanted to know what Cunningham knew, the better to anticipate his needs and be ready with an answer before the question was spoken.

The governor's visit had only been reported in the newspaper that morning, but Stanley had known already. He'd heard about it from Cunningham himself. The old man did not want the rabble roused at the Adams library dedication in a few days. He had donated the land and would construct the building out of his own pocket in a show of charity. Stanley knew better, of course. He gave with one hand as he took with the other, but it was never an even trade. The old man always got more than he gave.

"This is good news," Cunningham said. He eyed Stanley through the smoke of his cigar. "Anything else, Captain?"

The maid. Stanley had almost forgot. "A tramp reported a body in the woods. Turns out to be an Adams girl. She worked for you, as a matter of fact."

"How do you know that?"

"I could tell by looking at her, she was Irish, so she had to be from Adams."

Dunbar's neck thickened with tensing muscles. He stared at Stanley. The man was small but fierce and Stanley didn't want Dunbar looking at him at all, much less in that way. Stanley didn't know what he had said wrong.

"How do you know she worked for me?" Cunningham spoke the words slowly as if he was speaking to a dim-witted child. Stanley felt knocked off balance.

"I fetched an Adams officer. He said her name was Deirdre Monaghan, one of your scullery maids."

In one move, Dunbar stood, slammed his snifter down, and tossed the cigar into the fireplace. It was so sudden, Stanley jumped back. Dunbar stalked out of the room, leaving the door open.

"Mrs. Ramsey!" Dunbar yelled from the hallway. His Scottish accent was rougher than his employer's.

Why was Dunbar so excited about a scullery maid? Stanley looked at Cunningham for an explanation, but he got no hint in return. Instead, the old Scot considered the ember of his cigar, pulled a wooden match from a vest pocket, struck it, and puffed until the cigar produced a solid plume of smoke that burned Stanley's eyes.

"Mrs. Ramsey!" Dunbar hollered again.

The tapping of a woman's shoes came from somewhere deep in the house, not at a run, but in a steady motion. Stanley had to give the crone her due. Any man Dunbar yelled for would have come running, but not this old bird.

Mrs. Ramsey, Cunningham's housekeeper, stepped past Dunbar, giving him a sidewise glance, and took her position in the middle of the study. She could have been in her fifties, but her skull-like face made her look older. She was dressed all in black. Her bony fingers were intertwined at her waist.

Cunningham pulled the cigar out of his mouth. "Mrs. Ramsey, do we have a Deirdre Monaghan in our employ?"

"Indeed we do," she replied, her speech more heavily accented that Cunningham or Dunbar's. "She's the girl who takes her half day on Sunday to go to church with her mother. The one I was telling you about."

"The one you suspected of stealing jewelry?"

"The same."

By now Dunbar was in the room again, standing behind Mrs. Ramsey, his face almost purple, a vein throbbing in his forehead. "Where is she?"

Mrs. Ramsey flinched at the sound of Dunbar's voice, but she did not turn. She spoke to Cunningham instead. "Run off, it would seem. Left last night but never came back."

Dunbar stalked out of the room.

Cunningham stood. "First thing tomorrow, Stanley, bring me that Adams copper."

LIAM'S BONES ACHED AS he walked up the road to the Barrett home. It had been a long day with the vigil over Bridget, pulling the calf, seeing Deidre dead, and then the visit to Sadie. When he left the boarding house, she and Frank were on their knees praying.

He checked on the cow and calf, curled up next to each other sleeping, then let himself into the house. He paused next to the holy water font the mother had nailed up by the door. Good Catholics would dip their hand in the basin and bless themselves. It had been years since Liam done so, but he couldn't shake the habit of stopping only to resist the urge to perform the ritual.

As he approached the parlor, he heard soft crying he recognized as his mother's. He found Clare sitting at her feet, talking to her softly.

"Stop crying, Mommy, please stop. It's going to be alright. Please stop crying, Mommy, please."

There was no point in asking what disturbed the mother. She never answered. She went on weeping, staring out the window, cradling her baby doll, to all appearances having not heard Clare. For all he knew, she didn't recognize her own child anymore. Deirdre had been the only one who could calm her. Not that his mother knew who Deirdre was either, but there was something about her manner the mother liked.

It had been years since their mother drifted "away with the fairies", as the old hens called it. As a grown man, Liam realized that she had been different all along. At times, she seemed to be elsewhere, humming old tunes, drifting through the house. But with his father's steady comings and goings, his sister Kate assuming the household duties, and Liam's own preoccupation with his studies, his mother's problems didn't seem so serious.

All that changed the night his father had died. She was gone now more than she was with them. Most of the time, she sat by the window, waiting for the father to come home. He didn't know if the tears she shed were for her husband or some other terrible thing from her past. Things had happened in Ireland that were never discussed.

Liam went into the kitchen, found Kate on her hands and knees scrubbing the floor again, although she'd done it that morning too, her long auburn hair knotted behind her head. He poured himself a cup of cold tea and leaned a shoulder against the wall. "Where's Kevin?"

Kate shrugged. "How should I know?"

The front door opened and shoes shuffled towards them. Kevin, the boy-man, paused in the threshold of the kitchen. They both resembled their father so much that people sometimes called each of them by his name, Patrick: broad-shouldered, straight brows, square jaws. Kevin's body was lean and gangly and a soft red down grew on his lip. Liam felt himself stand a little straighter, measuring the difference in their heights as he grew taller and his brother seemed to shrink away. Then Kevin pulled himself to his full height. They were nearly eye-to-eye.

"Off my floor!" Kate said, flourishing her scrub brush.

"Why does he get to come in?" Kevin jerked his head at Liam.

"Because she likes me better," Liam said.

Kevin stumbled on his comeback. He went to the doorway and leaned against the jam on one shoulder as Liam had been doing when he came in, "I want to get a job."

"We've talked about this before," Kate said. "Your schooling is your job."

Kevin's education was an investment of the entire Barrett family. Liam had to give up his dreams of becoming a lawyer. It was Kevin's chance now to take his place in the professional class and help the people who had created a safe community for him to grow up in. Irish-Americans needed doctors and lawyers as much as they needed farmers and mill workers.

"It's boring. I know all the stuff they're teaching. I can read. I can write. I can do numbers. All they want us to do is read books and sing songs. If I had a job, we could buy things. We could buy a horse."

Maybe the boy was too smart. Maybe a challenge would force him to focus. "Where would you work?" Liam asked.

"Hogan's. I was over there talking to Tom Gillespie and he offered me a job. They're building a new warehouse. Tom has big ideas. He says Adams is growing and Hogan's will grow with it."

"And that's your ambition?" Kate asked, now sitting back on her heels, pushing her hair out of her face with the back of her hand. "To be a grocery clerk? You could be an accountant. Or a lawyer. Or a doctor, even."

"Have you never heard of Marshall Field's, the big department store in Chicago?"

Kate barked a laugh. "A department store in Adams! Never. We make the cotton they sell in those stores, and we can't afford to buy it back again."

"I'll think about it," Liam said.

"Liam!" Kate threw the brush into the bucket.

"But no missing school. I'll consider it only if you keep up your schoolwork and your chores on the farm."

Horror washed across Kevin's face. "Oh, Jaysus, Liam! You and this farm."

"Language!" Kate yelled.

Kevin snorted and stomped his way down the hall.

"Our farm," Liam called out even as Kevin disappeared. The bedroom door slam and the house juddered from the shock.

"What has gotten into your head, William Patrick Barrett?" Kate asked, pushing herself to her feet. Liam extended a hand to help her. She batted it away.

"I said I'd think about it, that's all."

Liam put his cup on the table. "We need to talk."

Kate was roused for a fight. She crossed her arms and stood her ground in the middle of the kitchen. "Then talk."

"It's Deirdre Monaghan."

"That cracked girl, running off like that to work for the Scots, leaving her mother behind. That woman did everything for her. What was she thinking?"

"She's been murdered."

Kate crossed herself. "Oh, bless that child. What happened, Liam? Does Sadie know?"

"She does. It seems Deirdre was walking from the train station to Cunningham's estate and someone attacked her. That's all we know so far."

"Is there someone with Sadie now?"

"Father Frank."

"I'll call around in the morning."

"What about the mother?"

"She can come along. Staring out this window or another, what does it matter?"

CHAPTER SIX

A RED, RED ROSE

THE NEXT MORNING, LIAM found himself standing in a long, sunny room in Inverness, Alistair Cunningham's mansion. He wasn't sure why. An hour before, he had stepped out of the house and had found Stanley sitting in his wagon, the mare dozing.

"Get in," Stanley had said.

"Where to?" Liam asked.

"Mr. Alistair Cunningham wants to see you, Barrett. I've cleared it with your captain. Get in."

Liam climbed into the wagon and sat on the bench next to Stanley. "What's this about?"

Stanley shook the reins and made a clicking noise. The horse's ears rotated towards the sound. Then she pushed against the harness and the wagon lurched into motion.

"It's not for me to say." Stanley did not look at Liam as he spoke. Instead he stared forward, not that the gray needed supervision. Liam wondered if Stanley's coyness was intended to conceal the fact that he had not been told. Was the Pittsfield police captain an errand boy for Alistair Cunningham? Couldn't Cunningham find someone else to deliver his messages? Or was he making a point: by dictating to law enforcement, he was the law itself.

The morning fog burned off as the gray trotted southward. The few yellow leaves left on the trees seemed to glow. It would be sweltering hot today but soon winter would be upon them.

At Cunningham's mansion, a woman old enough to be Liam's mother answered the door. Her dark hair, streaked with gray, was pulled into a severe bun at the top of her head. The bodice of her high-necked black dress was so tight, Liam wondered how she breathed. Her face was tight as well, heavy eyebrows pushed into a frown, lips pursed. She peered up at Stanley, clearly not intimidated by the large man.

Stanley cleared his throat. "I've brought the Adams patrolman, as Mr. Cunningham requested, Mrs. Ramsey."

She eyed Liam slowly, gave a short nod, then stepped back to allow them entry. "Wait here."

The foyer floor was tiled in black and white. Overhead was a large chandelier with tiers of crystal droplets that cast across the walls. A wide staircase swept upwards to a landing. There the family would gather as guests arrived for a party, pausing to look down, to say a few words perhaps before promenading down the stairs.

Liam had never been in a house so grand as this. It was fit for a king. But there were no kings in America or so he had been told in school.

The foyer in which they stood looked down the long hall where the old woman had gone. To one side were closed double doors. To another side, the doors opened to a sitting room.

"In here," Stanley said, then walked into the room.

"But, Mrs. Ramsey said we..."

"You let an old crone tell you what to do? What kind of man are you?"

Liam followed Stanley into the room. The ceiling was so high a man would need scaffolding to reach it. More chandeliers sparkled in light streaming through tall windows. Chairs and settees were upholstered in bright yellow silks, their wood painted gold. Gold everywhere on everything you could possibly cover in gold. A marble mantle stretched across a fireplace big enough to roast a small pig.

At one end of the room, the furniture had been pushed aside to accommodate a portrait artist. He was working on a canvas eight feet tall. Before him, with her back to the window, was a young woman in a low-cut gossamer blue gown and glittering jewels. The painter had framed her against a window overlooking the estate. One long red curtain split the background.

The Roman-style gardens the painter had imagined in his composition did not exist. Instead, workmen crawled along bare earth, digging, planting, laying tile, hauling statues, fountains, and balustrades.

Stanley watched the painter's progress, clearly enraptured by the subject.

The sitter was tall and slender, her dark hair pulled high upon her head in an elaborate design. She stood with the fingers of one hand barely touching a table. Liam had never seen so much of a woman exposed before. The old hens would be scandalized at the sight of that milky skin spreading downward from her throat. The gown was barely high enough to cover her breasts.

Holding that pose, with one arm outstretched, would be tiresome. The sitter noticed him watching her, and said, "Oh!" as if she was surprised. Then taking a second, longer look, she added. "My apologies, sir. I thought you were someone else."

Liam hardly registered her words. He realized he was staring, holding his breath. The girl gave him a wicked smile. Even as she did so, a blush rose to her throat. Then she lifted the perfectly posed hand and brought it to her heart in a mockery of embarrassment.

He scanned the room, searching for something else to fix his eyes upon and settled on his own dusty boots. He thought about brushing them off and then decided against it, not wanting to attract any more attention.

The painter threw his brush into a jar. "Victoria, how many times have I asked you not to move."

"That's enough!" Mrs. Ramsey said as she walked into the room. She set a tray on the same table upon which the young lady had rested her fingertips.

"Madam, I must protest," the painter said. "Mr. Cunningham wants this portrait finished in two days."

"Looks fine to me," she said. "The child needs her nourishment. Look at her, she's about to faint. And what will you paint then, Maestro, a young lady sprawled across the floor? A pretty picture that would be."

With Mrs. Ramsey commanding the room, Liam felt it safe to look up from his feet.

"I'm sorry, Mr. Sargent," the girl named Victoria said to the painter, in an American accent that bordered on British. Liam had never heard that manner of speech before, which reminded him how limited was his experience. Deirdre's short time at this estate brought her closer contact with the outside world than his reading could. Victoria broke her pose and stroked the old woman's arm. "Ramsey has been like a mother to me since we were very young."

"Go on with you, child. Drink your tea. I made it sweet, the way you like it."

The painter, pacified somewhat, pulled his brush from the jar and wiped it on a rag. "Five minutes, then, and no longer."

Victoria locked eyes with Liam, cocked her head. "Have you come to see Poppa?"

"Good morning, Miss Cunningham," Stanley interjected. "That's right, we're waiting for your father. Beautiful picture. It would have to be with you in it."

"This?" She gazed at the portrait. The blush had spread to her cheeks and faded to pink. Her earlobes were now a deep rose. "This, Captain Stanley, is nothing more than a flagrant advertisement. Poppa has hired the finest artist money can buy so this painting will be displayed in New York, then London, and then Paris in hopes of attracting a *suitable match.*" She had dropped her voice into an imitation of a man's baritone, affecting a strong Scottish accent. In her own voice, she added, "It seems I am to be peddled off to the highest bidder like horseflesh."

Mrs. Ramsey huffed.

"And why wouldn't he be proud his daughter is such a beautiful woman?" Stanley asked.

"Perhaps you're right." Victoria Cunningham's mood changed in an instant. She placed a light kiss on Mrs. Ramsey's cheek, then floated out of the room, the dress train trailing behind her. As she passed them, she gave Liam a quick glance and smiled again, as if she was enjoying a joke he didn't understand. He was sure he hadn't imagined it.

"And you two," Mrs. Ramsey said. "The Master will see you now. Follow me."

The woman led Liam and Stanley into a wood-paneled room. Clustered around a great stone fireplace were a deep leather couch and armchairs. Beyond that, an ornately carved desk was set in a bay window overlooking the same garden view Liam had seen from the sitting room. The room smelled of leather, paper, and cigars.

Books with gold-etched titles lined a wall. Liam would have liked to run his fingers across the spines, pull out the occasional book that struck his fancy, read a few pages or the whole thing, then select another one. If he had as much money as Cunningham, he would spend his days reading.

Two men were bent over a scroll open on the desktop, ignoring the interruption. Liam and Stanley stood in the middle of the room while Mrs. Ramsey hung by the door, apparently waiting to be dismissed. The larger of the two Liam recognized as Alistair Cunningham. The shorter, a red-bearded man, was dressed in working man's clothes.

In an alcove was a bust of Robert Burns. Liam heard the poem begin in his head: *Oh my love is like a red, red rose,* lines he had once memorized to impress Eileen Hogan. He had recited it to her one Saturday afternoon. Through the machinations of old Doc MacPherson who knew powerful people, he was bound for Harvard in a few years, accepted on scholarship, and would return to Adams a lawyer and ready to begin a family. He wanted that family with Eileen Hogan. His destiny had been written.

He had picked a bud from his mother's rosebush by the door and kept it in his pocket all afternoon. They were sitting on a bench in front of her father's store. He recited the poem and when he pulled the limp little rose from his pocket, he was mortified. He wanted to hide the silly thing but she had already seen it.

"Oh, Liam, how sweet!" She said as she plucked it from his opened hand. "All it needs is a little water." Then she looked quickly over her shoulder to see if her parents were watching. They weren't. She gave him a kiss on the cheek that was soft and warm.

Stanley cleared his throat and the kiss faded away.

"Who do we have here?" Cunningham asked.

"Officer Barrett from Adams, sir," Stanley said. "Barrett, you are in the presence of Mr. Alistair Cunningham and Malcolm Dunbar, his right-hand man."

"Stanley, why don't you go to the kitchen with Mrs. Ramsey and see if you can find something to eat." Cunningham said.

"But..."

"Dunbar will find you."

Stanley lingered, looking from Cunningham to Dunbar and back again. Dunbar coughed into his fist, one cynical eye on Stanley, then moved towards him as if to usher him out. Stanley's shoulders sagged as he seemed to realize arguing was no use. They wanted him gone. He followed the woman out of the room and Dunbar closed the door behind them. He then took one of the chairs near the hearth and waited.

Cunningham strolled to a carved wood sideboard, selected a crystal decanter, and poured two fingers of whiskey. "Will you have a drink?" He said as he lifted the glass in Liam's direction.

"I will not," Liam said.

"Taken the pledge, have you?" The old man's eyes twinkled.

"I don't care for it." Liam said, which was a truth of sorts. He was beginning to wonder why he'd been brought to this house. It certainly wasn't to keep the old man company while he drank in the morning. He had Dunbar for that. "Captain Stanley said you needed to see me."

Cunningham took a sip. He rolled his lips in, sucking the residue from them, then put the glass down on the sideboard.

"So he did, young Barrett, at my request." He stabbed the scroll spread across his desk with a stubby finger. "Did you notice the men working on my grounds? We're preparing for a very important visitor. The governor himself is arriving Thursday, three days hence.

He will be the guest of honor at the library dedication on Friday. You are aware of the library I am building for your town?"

How could Liam have missed it? The library that was to be built was the talk of the town. Who would get jobs building it? Who would work in the library once it was built? Where would the books come from? Rumor had it that Cunningham was paying for it but the townspeople whispered amongst themselves "What is this going to cost us?"

"I am aware of the library," Liam said.

"The governor's safety is my paramount concern. His safety and that of my household, of course. This wretched killing of that poor lass has everyone in an uproar. I can't have a murderer running loose near Inverness. What are you doing to apprehend the culprit?"

Liam would like nothing better than to find the man who killed Deirdre Monaghan. "I'm afraid, Mr. Cunningham, that the murder falls within Capt. Stanley's juris—"

"But the girl was from Adams, was she not? And her lover from Adams too?"

Liam felt his neck tighten. He didn't care for Cunningham's implication. He had never known Deirdre to disgrace herself. "She had a fiancé, that much is true."

"You are aware that the girl was stealing from my household? We hadn't caught her red-handed, mind you, but it had to have been her. She was confronted and denied it, but what would you expect her to say? No doubt she'd made off with more jewels and was murdered by her accomplice. That lover of hers."

Deirdre was not a thief. Liam was certain of it. Granted, there was not much worth taking in Adams. But this picture her employer painted was so far from the truth, thievery and loose morals, Cunningham seemed to be conjuring arguments for reasons of his own. If Liam were to take the case, he wanted to be certain the investigation was fair and the right man was accused. Justice for Deirdre and for her loved ones, and the protection of public safety, demanded no less.

"There's been no mention of thievery to me," Liam said. "I've known Deirdre Monaghan for a very long time and she has a fine reputation. You must be mistaken."

"Jewels are missing."

"Then perhaps someone else on your staff is the thief, but it wasn't Deirdre. She was not running away from Inverness. She was killed on her way back."

Cunningham watched the workmen's progress outside the window. A horse-drawn wagon pulled into view, the bed filled with young trees. A man dragged one of the trees off the wagon and dropped it near a large hole. There were two lines of these holes, one on either side of a walkway that led from the patio to flower beds in the distance.

Cunningham went back to his desk and settled in the chair behind it. "Perhaps we were mistaken. It's a good thing we have you, with your knowledge of the girl and her associates, to guide us. We might have wasted time looking in the wrong places. You see how important you are in finding the killer. I'll clear it with Stanley and your superior. What's his name?"

"Captain Curran."

"Curran, that's right. I'll send word."

The night before, Liam had lain in bed, staring at the dark ceiling as Kevin snored in the next cot, when the answer to the prayer he had said over Deirdre's body came to him. He would find Deirdre's killer and bring that man to justice. Stanley, who had no connection to Adams, would not be sufficiently motivated to find the responsible man. He was already more interested in pinning the crime on the most convenient suspect, Owen Sweeney. Now it appeared Cunningham had chosen Deirdre's fiancé, Finn O'Brien, for the scapegoat instead.

"I'll do it, Mr. Cunningham, as long as I have authority to arrest and charge the man responsible."

"You will. I'll see to it."

"And no interference."

"No interference." Cunningham winked at him.

Liam had no doubt that Cunningham would manipulate the prosecution later if he so chose. He was the kind of man whose promises were transitory things made only to elicit a bargain and easily taken back. The trick would be to make the arrest, and build a case exonerating the innocent, before Cunningham had a chance to intervene.

His first task was to find Finn. Liam would have been working toward that end had not Stanley diverted him from the task this morning. He hoped Sadie was right, for her sake as well as the townspeople. He couldn't imagine what life would be like in Adams if one of their own had murdered another. He would see if Finn could prove his innocence. Perhaps he had information that could lead to finding the killer.

Cunningham came around the desk and stood close enough for Liam to smell the peaty scent on his breath. "I have children, did you know? A daughter and a son. My heart would be broken if something happened to either of them. Nothing, absolutely nothing, is more important than family. You're a family man. You understand."

Liam took in the heavy wood furniture, the silk rugs, the books and the bust, the twitchy Dunbar, and the imperious Cunningham. Whether or not solving the crime benefitted these men was of no import. If he could find out who killed Deirdre, he could put Sadie's mind to rest. And if there was a killer hiding in Adams, it was indeed Liam's problem.

He was about to speak when the heavy door was thrown open. Victoria Cunningham entered, outfitted in a gray traveling ensemble, fitted jacket, long dress, jaunty hat, lace collar, and a large sapphire-studded brooch on her lapel.

Dunbar, who'd made no sound during the interview, was suddenly on his feet.

Cunningham frowned.

"I am sorry to interrupt, Poppa, but I'm off to catch my train to Albany."

"What train?" Cunningham asked.

Victoria shook her head with an indulgent smile. "I told you all about it. Remember, Poppa? I'm going to stay with the Spencers. We have fittings for Constance's bridesmaid dresses. I'll be home in a day or two." With that, she gave him a peck on the cheek and floated out of the room.

Cunningham watched her leave with an enchanted look. "My daughter, Victoria," he said. "There is nothing I would not do for her." He cleared his throat. "Where were we?"

"I will find the man who did this," Liam said.

Cunningham slapped Liam on the shoulder. "There's a good lad."

"I need to see Deirdre's room."

Later, much later on the train back to Adams, he wondered how Alistair Cunningham knew Liam had a family.

Chapter Seven

The Servants

L IAM FOLLOWED MRS. RAMSEY up narrow backstairs to the third floor servants' quarters. As elaborate as the rest of the house had been, it was a shock to see plain white walls and plain wooden floors. The hall was narrow, with barely room for two people to pass.

"The girls are in this end," Mrs. Ramsey said.

"There are men living on this floor?"

"A few. Most of the staff is in New York but they will arrive later this week. Follow me."

She opened a door to a small room with a slanted ceiling accommodating the pitch of the roof. A narrow bed was in the corner, a nightstand beside it. A window overlooked the woods. Over the bed hung a crucifix.

Mrs. Ramsey pulled a satchel out from under the bed, dropped it on the mattress, and opened it. She then pulled open a dresser drawer, took out the neatly folded clothing, and packed it in the satchel. She motioned at the crucifix. Liam took it down and handed it to her. She placed it on top of the clothes.

"That's it," she said, snapping the bag closed.

"I need to examine the room," Liam said.

She stepped aside, as if waiting from him to leave the room ahead of her. "You've seen all there is to see."

Liam didn't want this woman deciding what was important and what was not. "This room is small, Mrs. Ramsey. I need to move around. If you would stand in the hallway why I make my inspection, I will soon be done."

The woman seemed to argue with herself.

"You can watch, if you like, from the hallway."

She looked at him keenly, then made her decision. "Very well."

As she looked on, Liam opened the dresser, pulled out all the drawers, and examined each. He found nothing. He checked the nightstand and only found a bible, St. James version, which the household must have provided. He put it back. He lifted the pillow of the neatly made bed, pulled the pillowcase off, and found nothing. He pushed on the mattress, systematically pressing one area and then another. After a few pushes, he felt resistance.

Liam slipped his hand beneath the mattress, found a slim edge, and slid the item out.

It was a silhouette portrait of a young man, unframed and mounted on heavy board. He had an aquiline nose, firm chin, no mustache, and neatly combed hair.

Mrs. Ramsey was by Liam's side. "What's this?" She grabbed for it.

He pulled it away, not far enough to start a wrestling match, but enough to let her know he would hold onto it until he was ready to let go.

"That's my question," Liam said.

"It's one of Mr. Cunningham's nephews back in Scotland," she said. "The cracked girl must have found it and taken it for herself. She's a thief you know. Always taking things that don't belong to her."

"Had she known him?"

"Never. He hasn't been to this country since long before she came to work at Inverness."

"Then why would she have it?"

"Thievery is a crime of opportunity, Officer, you should know that. She saw it, she wanted it, she took it. There's no explaining why some people think they're entitled to what they aren't or what makes them think they're better than they are."

Deirdre Monaghan had never been a thief. But Liam understood why Mrs. Ramsey would be critical of her ambition. She probably felt threatened by this pretty, vivacious young woman in her house.

"But isn't that why we are all here? You from Scotland? My family from Ireland? To improve our lot? And look how well your employer has done for himself."

"That's different. Alistair Cunningham is a clever man. Hardworking. He didn't take advantage of his acquaintances."

"And you're saying Deirdre did?"

"I don't like to speak ill of the dead, Officer." She reached out her hand. "Now, if you'll hand the picture to me, I'll see that it's returned to where it belongs."

G EORGE WASHINGTON STANLEY SAT at the servants' table in the middle of a large drafty kitchen. A cup of tepid tea was on the table in front of him. He'd been sent downstairs like a rowdy brat. On every other visit to Inverness, he had been invited into the study by the great man himself, given a drink and a cigar, and listened to Cunningham's problems. These meetings were Stanley's chances to show how useful he could be, the answers always so clear Stanley didn't know why the old man hadn't thought of them himself.

Not this time. He had been dismissed. And in his stead, Liam Barrett was having that drink and cigar.

Dunbar was the key. If Stanley played his cards right, Dunbar could be his ally. The nasty little Scot hated him, but he knew Stanley was dependable. The trick was to learn his secrets, his weak spots. Why did Cunningham trust Dunbar so much when they seemed to hate each other? That Ramsey witch would know all their secrets, what bound those men together and what they hid from each other. And at this moment, she was showing Barrett the servants' rooms.

This was the first time he'd been in the kitchen. He had sat where she pointed and she set a cup in front of him.

"What's this?" he asked.

"Tea."

"I don't drink tea."

"Then you'll drink nothing," she reached for the cup.

He picked it up before she did. He sniffed. Took a sip. It tasted like warm water at first, then bitter and sweet at the same time. A woman's drink.

"It's good. I've never had it before."

"Your mother didn't make you tea? You Americans, you're in such a hurry to build your big, new country. What's the point if you're going to live like savages?"

He hardly remembered his mother. When he was a boy on the farm, he worked all day by his father's side trying to make up to the old man for the loss of the oldest son, his brother, the favorite. When they came inside to eat, she wouldn't look at him.

"Will you sit with me for a spell? Finish your cup?" Stanley asked. He sounded like a kid begging for attention.

She regarded him warily, then drug her cup over to the chair opposite and took a seat.

"Have you worked for Mr. Cunningham a long time?" he asked.

"A fair bit."

"You came from Scotland with him?"

"Aye." She peered at him over the rim of her cup.

"This morning, Miss Victoria said you were like a mother to her."

The crone's face softened. She almost smiled. "She has no memory of Mrs. Cunningham, poor girl. The mistress passed away shortly after Edward was born. Childbed fever. Very sad."

"And you've no children of your own?"

"Did someone tell you I had? Who said that?"

She was upset. He had said something wrong.

"I figured as much, because your married."

She barked a laugh. "Married? Me? No, not me, Captain Stanley. In the big houses, it's custom to call the housekeeper 'missus.' I've never been married to a man and if I were, I wouldn't be allowed in service here or any other place. I've said it often enough, I'm married to this job. The Cunninghams are the only family I know."

"Dunbar too?"

"Bah," she said. "Don't speak that man's name in my kitchen. The way he acts, he thinks he's one of them. But he's a servant, as are we all, and he does what he's told like we all do."

"Seems like he's been with Mr. Cunningham a long time."

Mrs. Ramsey took a sip of her tea, her big fishy eyes staring over Stanley's shoulder.

Behind him, Dunbar said, "Who has been with Mr. Cunningham a long time, that's what I'd like to know." Stanley hadn't heard him come into the room.

"Felix," Mrs. Ramsey said. "He was asking after that Irish fella who works in the barns, Felix Malone."

Dunbar eyed the old woman, then looked Stanley over. "Never you mind about Felix Malone."

She had lied. She didn't give a rat's tail about Stanley, she had lied to protect herself. It would be trouble for her if Dunbar knew she was talking about the family. Her lie was a secret between her and Stanley. They were conspirators now.

Dunbar said, "You're wanted."

Stanley made to get up.

"Not you, Stanley," Dunbar said. "You wait here."

The hag carried her teacup to the drainboard where a bucket of potatoes was sitting. She dropped the bucket and a paring knife in front of Stanley. "Make yourself useful," she said.

Stanley pushed the bucket away with his foot. "I don't work for you."

"You work for his lordship like everyone else under this roof."

Dunbar snorted at her joke. They left and Stanley was alone with cold tea and a bucket of potatoes. He dumped the potatoes onto the table, picked up one, and slid the knife down one side of it. A brown curl of skin dropped into the bucket between his feet.

Maybe Cunningham had a plan for him, something he'd talk about later out of Barrett's earshot. Something special. Something that finally got him inside Cunningham's trust.

A rich man needed protection. That anarchist nearly killed Henry Frick in Homestead a few years ago. If Cunningham was right and Mollys were coming, there would be violence. And what about kidnapping? They'd want Miss Victoria. Everyone knew Cunningham spoiled her and would pay a fortune to get her back. Stanley could guard her on her trips. Boston, New York, London, Paris. Maybe she would like a man like him, big, rough. Some women do.

Stanley had once been married. For all he knew, he still was. She was a soiled woman, a few years older than he, and he was a young copper, the cock of the walk. The first time he met Gabriella was on a visit to the house she worked in. He had been there many times before and had been serviced by many women, old, young, toothless, dim-witted. She was new. She was special.

She had wild dark hair and eyes that sparked like fire. Strong and fragile at the same time and with a temper on her. On those Saturday night visits to that house, he never knew if she would dance for him or try to tear his face off. But it always ended the same. And a few hours later, George Stanley left that house feeling like he was a real man.

He never knew why she married him. He had asked because he wanted to rescue her from that life. But as soon as she moved into his home, it was like the spirit had gone out of her, and without her fire, he had none of his own. He'd come home from a long day at work, the house a mess, no food cooked, cockroaches crawling across dirty dishes in the kitchen and Gabriella asleep. She said she was sick. Always sick.

He was stupid. She was an addict. He had believed her because he loved her and she had lied to him. Finally he realized the laudanum wasn't her cure but was the thing making her sick. He stole her tincture as she slept and poured it down the latrine. When she woke, she cried and moaned until he went to the doctor and got more. He told her he had enough, she had to quit. The first few times, she said she would and promised she'd be a good wife. They talked about children. And then a few days later, he'd come home finding her in a bed, stupefied, stinking of sweat and urine, her hair oily and matted.

Why didn't she love him enough to quit? All day, he did his job, arresting people, locking them up, because they were drunk or violent. Night after night he came home to more of the same. His only joy was hitting someone. So he started hitting her. She made him do it. If she had been a good wife like she promised, he would have never hurt her. Instead of fighting back, she would laugh at him, spit on him, hiss profanities.

One night, he came home and found her gone. Her clothes, her perfumes, and her valise were gone with her. Later, the girls at the whorehouse told him that Gabriella had been seeing a man in his own home while he was at work and that man had taken her away. Her real name wasn't even Gabriella. It was Melanie. Most men would have hunted them down and killed them both, but Stanley didn't. He should have. No one would have blamed him.

Victoria Cunningham was not that kind of woman. She was pure. He wanted to touch her. When he was rich and powerful, she might let him.

He imagined he was following Miss Victoria at a respectful distance from ship to shore in a foreign land when a swarthy character stepped alongside her, matching her gait, and spoke to her. As he distracted her, another man reached into the purse hanging from her crooked elbow. With one lunge, Stanley would knock the first man away and grab the thief's arm, twisting it into the air. She would swoon into his arms.

Movement outside the kitchen window caught his attention. Stanley stood, knocking over the bucket. Potato skins scattered across the floor.

His wagon, drawn by his mare, was moving down the lane. Dunbar was driving with Barrett riding along side.

Old Mrs. Ramsey came into the room. "Look what you've done, you stupid lout," she said. She noticed Stanley's stare and followed his line of sight. "Look ye there! Isn't that your rig?" And then she cackled.

CHAPTER EIGHT

SHATTERED DREAMS

L IAM KNOCKED ON SADIE Monaghan's boarding house door and waited. From inside he could hear shuffling and the murmur of voices. The women of Adams had arrived.

The door opened. Inside, the air was warm, heavy with the smell of baking bread. The women's voices were clearer, a soft musical blanket of several conversations going at once. "The tea needs warming. I'll get it." "Little Timmy got a new tooth." "The baptism is next Sunday." "Is there anything I can get you, Sadie?"

The door was being held open by a woman whom Liam had not seen in a very long time. His heart squirmed.

Eileen Gillespie, once Eileen Hogan. She looked much the same as she had when they were courting. She was shorter than most. The Hogans were known for it. When they had worked together in her father's general store, she'd enlist his help, asking for something to be taken down off a high shelf or put back up. Her father, Joe, would admonish her for taking Liam away from his duties. Then he would find something that needed doing elsewhere and leave them alone again.

That was a long time ago. Liam's own father was still alive. Liam had been allowed to continue in school instead of going to work in the mill at the customary age of fourteen years. Joe Hogan had given him an after-school job so he could save money for his education. He would have been the first Adams son to attend Harvard.

It wasn't difficult to avoid her the past few years despite how small Adams was. Liam quit school after his father died and went to work in the mill. In the evenings and weekends, he worked on the farm. If the family needed something from Hogan's, Kate made the trip. The only other place he would have seen her was church, a place Liam had not visited since his father's funeral. He should have known she would be at Sadie's with the other women.

"Liam?" Her hand rested on the doorknob lightly.

The once pretty girl was now a striking woman. Her face was leaner, making her blue eyes seem even larger. Her long straw-colored hair that once hung loose about her shoulders was pulled back into a bun. And, her figure was round with pregnancy. Liam felt sick.

"Are you alright?" Eileen asked. She took his sleeve, a familiarity they would have thought nothing of before. He looked at her hand on his arm and she withdrew it. But not before he caught a glimpse of her gold wedding band.

"Come in, would you?" she asked. "There's bread in the oven. It'll burn if I don't see to it."

Liam stepped inside the door. He and Eileen faced off like uncertain foes. It only took the smallest shift in the universe for the dearest person to cause a man pain. What had happened wasn't her fault.

"Deidre's things," he said, offering her the satchel. She took it from his hand.

From the depths of the house, Father Frank's voice called out, "Is it yourself, Liam?"

Liam closed the door. When he turned back, the space in front of him was empty. From the sitting room, he heard an older woman say, "Eileen darling, there you are. Would you..." Her words then faded into the music of feminine voices.

Frank appeared from the shadows of the long dark hall that led to the back of the house.

"How is Sadie?" Liam asked.

"Brave enough until the women arrived. See for yourself."

Liam followed Frank into the sitting room. The women hushed as the priest entered. It seemed all the mothers and grandmothers of Adams were there. The older ones sat on the horsehair sofa and kitchen chairs, cradling babies. The younger ones, having a moment with their arms free, maneuvered through the room with tea and biscuits. They all halted upon the priest's entrance. After one long hushed moment, he was greeted with a chorus of "Father, father, father."

"Ladies," Frank said as a path cleared between him and Sadie seated on the couch. A small child ran through. A woman caught him by the arm and swung him to her hip.

Sadie was different than she had been the night before. Heavy dark circles hung beneath her eyes. Her round cheeks were deflated. The hem of her apron was clutched in one fist. She was wearing the same clothes. Indeed, she was sitting in the same place that Liam had last seen her. He wondered if she had moved at all. Upon seeing him, tears welled in her puffy eyes.

There was no need to ask how she was. Liam could see for himself.

"When is my Deidre coming home?"

More than anything, he wanted to give this woman, now alone in the world, something to ease her pain. After Dunbar had driven him to Pittsfield, he didn't think to stop at the undertaker's parlor before taking the train. He had been preoccupied with questions. Had Finn killed Deirdre and then run away? Had she resisted a tramp, a friend of Sweeney's, so he killed her and Sweeney was covering up for him, distracting the police while he got away? Could Sweeney have killed her? Or was there some other unknown person who wanted her dead?

He should have known Sadie wanted her daughter back. He could have easily detoured to the undertaker's office to ask before coming home. Pittsfield might as well be the far side of the moon for those who had neither the time nor the money to take the train and he had been there only an hour ago.

Frank took in Liam's hesitation, and said in a soothing voice. "We shall go to Pittsfield today and make the arrangements." Liam wondered if they taught that voice in seminary.

Sadie stared at Frank as if he was speaking a different language. It seemed she didn't want an answer. Instead she wanted to occupy the unknown, a waiting station between what had been and what was to come, her own purgatory. Her mind was trapped, or hiding, in that other world. Her eyes darted about the room, not settling on anyone, as panic began to skitter across her features. She would have to come back to reality sometime when she was ready. It wasn't a kindness to rush her.

"Let us pray," Frank said, crossing himself deeply. The women in the room followed and bowed their heads. What a handy trick for commanding a roomful of people, Liam thought as he bowed his head.

"O sweet mother Mary, who knew the sadness of mourning those your heart loved most, Jesus, your Son, and Joseph, your devoted spouse, pray for us in our time of loss. Amen."

"Amen," the women repeated as they blessed themselves. They lifted their heads and looked about the room, inventorying children.

One of the women handed Sadie a glass of whiskey and they closed round her again. Frank walked out of the room so gracefully his robe barely made a sound. Liam followed.

On the stoop, Frank pulled two cigars from the folds of his cassock, handed one to Liam, and struck a match on the porch post. After their cigars were lit, Liam said, "I've been seconded to investigate Deidre's death. Old Cunningham wants someone in jail before the week is out and has a mind that Finn O'Brien is the culprit."

"Finn? That's nonsense. The boy is in love with Deirdre, follows her around like a besotted Shakespearean fool, so he does, with no mind of the way she treated him."

"And how was that?"

"Ah, it's not my place to gossip. I am the village priest, after all."

"I could save a lot of time if you'd just tell me what you know, and," Liam nodded toward the house, "much less disruption. I'd as soon leave Sadie alone if I can."

"Right you are. It's not fair to burden her. I should have thought of that myself." Frank struck another match and relit his cigar. "It goes like this. Deirdre came home Saturday evening on the train, as she usually does. She went straight into the kitchen to help. She left the poor boy sitting in the parlor all evening waiting for her. He tried going into the kitchen once to see her only to get barked at. A couple of hours later, she came out, gave him a prim kiss on the cheek and went up to her room. Well, I don't need to tell you the boy didn't dare follow her upstairs, Sadie would have had his head.

"The next time I saw them was after Mass. As they left, Finn maneuvered close to Deirdre's side and tried to take her hand. She batted him away. That's the last I saw of either of them. It looked to me like Deirdre was ready to be shut of the poor boy but hadn't told him. Or, if she had, he didn't believe her, hoped he could talk her out of it."

"You didn't mention this before."

"It didn't seem relevant."

"Let me decide what's relevant or not. For the time being, I need to know everything there is to know about Deirdre, Finn, anyone else in their circle."

"You should know more than I do. You've lived here all your life."

"And you're new so you have fresh observations. Do you know why they recalled the last priest?"

"Father O'Brien? Needed elsewhere, I assumed."

"He buggered a boy. It had been going on for years. Drove the lad to suicide. No one saw what was going on. The mother went mad with grief and he killed her to protect himself. Secrets, Father. Villagers wrap themselves up in secrets, only showing their neighbors what they want them to see. And those secrets have power of their own. They twist people's thinking. They drive people to do things they would have never done in their right mind."

"You're not suggesting I should violate the sanctity of the confessional?"

"If justice is to be done, if Deidre Monaghan's murderer is to be brought to account, I will need to unearth the secrets. So don't presume to know what is relevant and what is not. The first thing I need to do is find Finn. Cunningham has a mind that Finn is responsible. And that Captain Stanley has me worried. This case is his jurisdiction and why he let Cunningham interfere is beyond me. He has a reputation for rough justice. I'm worried that if he finds Finn before I do, something bad will happen, an accident while resisting arrest perhaps. And then Finn will not be around to answer our questions anymore."

"If Stanley is happy to do Cunningham's bidding, why do you suppose they involved you?"

"Cunningham is rattling Stanley's cage, wants him to feel uncertain, like there's possible competition for Cunningham's favor."

"I wouldn't have taken you for someone who'd jockey up to anyone."

"I would not. But Cunningham doesn't know that yet. And I'd like to keep it that way until this is over."

But that wasn't the real reason Cunningham had seconded him, Liam suspected. The rich man was shooing the investigation away from Inverness. Perhaps to protect secrets of his own. Or, he is worried about scandal ruining his attempts to impress an even more powerful man.

As helpful it might prove to have someone to talk through his thoughts, Liam wasn't sure how far he could trust this talkative priest. For the time being, Liam would keep his suspicions to himself, secrets of his own.

"Then we best be off," Frank said, stepping from the porch. "Where first?"

"I am the police officer, Father, not yourself."

"Who best to obtain the release of Deidre's body than a priest?" Frank said. "I'll tag along, keep you company on your travels."

Liam considered Frank's offer. The priest was a boarder in Sadie's house which was now filled to the rafters with women and children, coming and going. Like any man would, he must have felt overwhelmed. Even a priest needed a moment to himself from time to time. And he could prove useful.

"First to Deirdre's room," Liam said.

"Do you need to violate their privacy? Surely, the answer isn't to be found in this house when she was murdered so many miles away."

Deirdre had hidden the silhouette in the servants' quarters. She was not a thief as Mrs. Ramsey claimed. Someone had given it to her but her reason for owning it was secret. "Is there something you're not telling me, Father?"

"If there was, I couldn't tell you. But as it happens, Deirdre hadn't been to confession in months."

"Clearly something was going on in her life, something we don't know about. There was a reason Deirdre was murdered in those woods. She met someone or someone followed her. I don't believe it was a random attack. I need to know everything, all those things a young woman doesn't tell her friends or family."

Liam stubbed out his cigar and left it cooling on the porch rail. When he stepped back inside, he felt the spirit of the room had changed. A pall had fallen over the women. Even the children were still. Sadie was sitting on the horsehair couch, a cup of tea on her lap, her expression distracted. She started when Liam spoke.

"Mrs. Monaghan, I need to look at Deirdre's things."

The women turned as one towards Liam, astonished by his boldness. How could Deirdre's privacy, Sadie's or any woman's, be so easily cast aside? He could hear them thinking, "has he no respect?"

Sadie frowned. By the look of her, she had heard his words but she was holding on to that other world where her child was alive. There was no telling when she'd come back. If Liam waited too long, the murderer could escape. "It's important," he said.

Frank was beside him. "I'll come along, so there will be no accusations of impropriety."

Sadie nodded. A small girl, about two years old, with long blonde ringlets, pulled herself up onto the couch. Sadie handed her teacup to a nearby woman and pulled the child onto her lap. The spirit of the gathering shifted. Children began moving about again. The women returned to their conversations.

The room Deidre shared with her mother was nearly as spare as her quarters in Inverness. Two beds pushed against opposite walls, tidily covered in quilts. Over one bed was a framed picture of the Virgin revealing her immaculate heart. Another framed picture, this of Saint Patrick, hung over the second bed beneath. A rosary was pooled upon the pillow.

Liam knelt next to the bed. He gathered the rosary and placed it in Frank's cupped hand. Then he slipped his arm beneath the mattress, as he had done at Inverness when he had found the silhouette. If her bed was Deirdre's favorite hiding place, it only made sense there may be something secreted here as well. This time, his fingers touched something hard. He clasped it and slid it out.

It was a slim book. He opened it. It was a book of poetry by John Keats. There was no inscription.

"Keats," Liam said. "Have you seen it before?"

"Never," Frank said. "Why would she hide poetry?"

Liam fanned through the pages slowly. Midway, the book fell open to a dried flower, a violet, pressed flat by the weight of the mattress.

"Because she didn't want Sadie to know she had it," Liam guessed. Then he hit on a better reason. "Because she didn't want Sadie asking how she came by it."

"What is wrong with poems?"

"It's not the poems that are the problem," Liam said. "It was who gave it to her. It wouldn't have been Finn. If he had, there was no reason to hide it. Besides, Finn doesn't strike me as the poetry-reciting type. I'm not sure he can read, for what that's worth. This book was a gift from an admirer, someone special she wanted to keep secret from everyone."

"Who?"

"That is the question. Is it someone in Adams or someone at Inverness? My guess is the latter. This violet would have bloomed in the spring. About the time Deirdre went to work for Cunningham."

CHAPTER NINE

THE BLACK ROSE

LIAM AND FRANK FOUND Harry Gallagher behind the bar, his massive arms folded across his broad chest. He was watching three young gents playing cards, his only patrons. By the looks of them, they'd been at it for a while. Sweaty, laughing uproariously, backslapping.

"Good afternoon to you, Padre," Harry said, then to Liam, "and to you too, a chara." Harry, a bear of a man, had come over from Ireland as a child. Originally from Ulster, he had black hair, a full black beard, and his rolled-up sleeves revealed arms as thick as mutton legs covered in black curly hair.

The Black Rose was the favorite gathering place of the local Irishmen. Harry's father, now long gone, purchased the bar from a Civil War widow. It was a fine establishment with an ornately carved backbar and gleaming bar top. Liam caught his reflection in the mirror: the brass-buttoned wool police tunic, thick wavy red-gold hair. Maybe it was time to grow a mustache as was the fashion. There was no denying he was a man now. And had been for quite some time. He suddenly felt tired.

"A pint for myself and my friend," Frank said.

"Liam doesn't take drink, Padre," Harry said. "I'll put the kettle on."

Harry wandered down the bar with one eye on the cardplayers.

"Taken the pledge, have you, Liam?"

"It's a long story."

"Listening to long stories is my job."

The last thing Liam wanted right now was to have Frank lead a room in prayer for his tortured soul. "And perhaps I'll tell it to you some day."

"Fair play to you, then," the priest said, eyeing Liam curiously. To Harry, he called out, "Two fingers would be grand."

Harry returned with Liam's tea and poured a whiskey for the priest and one for himself, then placed the priest's drink in front of him as daintily as a man had ever moved. When Frank reached into the depths of his cassock, Harry held up a hand, "Your money isn't good here, Padre."

Liam suspected Frank's offer to pay was only a gesture. He would have known Harry wouldn't take money from a priest.

Frank saluted with his drink. "Sláinte."

"Sláinte," Harry said, lifting his own drink.

Liam raised his teacup. "Sláinte."

Frank and Harry knocked back their drinks in one throw as Liam took a sip of his tea.

"That's about the end of it, don't you know," Harry said.

"The end of what?" Liam asked.

"The whiskey. Only one bottle left. The shipment didn't arrive this morning. There was some mix-up at the railway. Bloody shame it is, with the big to-do this Friday, the Governor coming and all. Plenty of thirsty people visiting Adams to see the goings-on."

"Can't you order more?" Frank asked.

Harry shook his head. "Before they send another shipment, they need to get paid for the one that's lost. Without whiskey to sell, I can't pay the bill. There's the rub of it."

Mean-spirited laughter erupted from the gents' table. Before them were empty and half-full bottles, small whiskey glasses, and beer mugs.

"Have they been at it long?" Liam asked.

"They came in right after I opened, drunk as lords already. Looks like they made a night of it." Harry jerked his head in the direction of young men. Each wore a long frock coat and fancy vests. With shadow of beards starting, hair in disarray, and their expensive clothes wrinkled, it looked as if their celebration had begun a day or two before. Each had a shine on his face and the gloss in his eyes.

Close in age, two of them resembled each other enough to be brothers. "Who are they?" Liam asked.

"Never seen them before. Claims they're in town looking to buy horses, but they been here all day." Harry polished the bar top. "Not a horse in sight, mind you."

One man slammed his fist on the table. Cards flew in every direction. Half-full beer mugs toppled spilling their contents. Another man, taller and sturdier, pushed his chair away from the table, but not soon enough. His trousers were soaked. He stood, toppling his chair, and grabbed for the shirt of his still laughing friend, who, upon seeing the attack coming, tried to dodge and tumbled into the lap of the third who then pushed him to the floor with a loud profanity.

"Here now!" Harry slapped his rag on the bar top. The gents took no notice.

Harry splayed one hand on the bar and was about to vault over when Liam moved to block his landing. He finished his tea and placed the cup between them, then strolled to the table. "Good afternoon, gentlemen."

The one on his feet wheeled around. "Constable!" He stumbled back, caught his balance and with as much dignity as he could muster, pulled himself to his full height, almost as tall as Liam's own six feet two inches. To the others, he said, "We have a guest, sirs."

"Visiting Adams, are you?" Liam asked.

The man extended his hand in an offer to shake. "Abraham Lincoln, at your service. Allow me to introduce my comrades, Secretary of State William Seward and the gentleman on the floor is none other than General Ulysses S. Grant."

The man introduced as Seward guffawed. Grant tried to mule-kick Lincoln and missed.

Liam had stopped at a distance too far away to shake hands. He looked for weapons. Guns were not common in Adams town, but it's best to be careful with angry drunks in a bar. There were no firearms at their sides, nor were there any laying within in arm's reach. He doubted Harry would permit an armed man to enter his bar, but it was always prudent to check.

"My name is Officer Barrett," Liam said. "What brings you to our fair town?"

"Horses," Seward said. "We'd like to purchase a stud or two for our farm."

"Where would that farm be, sir?"

"Why Albany, of course. Home to the finest horse racing in the great state of New York."

The other two gave a tired cheer.

Liam cast his eye over the three. Rumpled and sweaty from a day or two of drinking, they appeared sufficiently well-healed to invest in horses. Certainly, they weren't working men. At this time of day, most men were laboring at their jobs. But in a couple of hours, they'd stop in at the Black Rose on their way home, thirsty and in no mood for drunken gentry.

The one identified as Grant was nodding off and dangerously close to toppling out of his chair again. Lincoln, still standing, shifted his weight, the momentum of his good cheer dissipating quickly. "Perhaps you could recommend a breeder?" he asked.

"Not today, Mr. Lincoln. I suggest you take your comrade back to the hotel for a good night's sleep. Try again tomorrow."

Lincoln took notice of Grant, folding slowly over the arm of his chair. Lincoln grabbed Grant's upper arm by the tender inside and dug his fingers in until Grant came to life. "Time to go, General. You too, Mr. Secretary."

"What?" said Seward, who had been staring numbly at an empty bottle in front of him.

Liam went back to the bar, leaning on an elbow as he and Harry and Frank watched the three men stumble out the door.

"Works every time," Harry said. "The fight drains out of them as soon as you walk into a room. What wicked spell hast thou cast upon those blackguards?"

"It's my natural charm."

Harry guffawed. "What blather is that? I've been standing here all afternoon as charming as a butterfly on a warm spring day and that didn't work."

"You great hairy lout! A butterfly on a warm spring day? Where do you get this stuff?"

"I make it up," Harry shrugged. "For the out-of-town visitors, like yon gents. They love a bit of Irish poetry to take home to the little woman. It's good for tips."

"I can see how it's improved your custom," Liam said glancing around the empty barroom.

Harry ignored the comment. "Not that it matters with nothing to serve," he said. Then, poured the last of the bottle for himself and the priest. "There you go, Padre."

"Long life to you," the priest responded.

After they downed the second round, Harry put the bottle away and reached beneath the bar.

"Will you'll not have a cigar, fellas?"

Liam held up his hand. "This isn't a social call, Harry. Have you heard about Deidre Monaghan?"

"So I have, poor lass. Found murdered in the woods. She would have been on her way to the big house in Pittsfield Sunday afternoon."

"That's right. We're looking for her young man, Finn O'Brien. Have you seen him?"

"Last I seen him was Saturday after he got off work at Hogan's. Practically dancing around like, so happy he was that he would see Deirdre. Said something about setting a date for the wedding. He's a good lad, Finn, but not the brightest, if you know what I mean. It was plain to see she had other ideas. Come to think of it, I did see him in Mass on Sunday with Deidre and Sadie. It was before you came in, Padre. When they were stepping into the pew, Deirdre managed it so that poor Finn had to sit with Sadie between them. My heart broke for him, so it did. Nothing harder on a young man than to love a girl who doesn't love him back. He spent the entire service trying to catch her eye but she just ignored him. Not that I wasn't paying attention, Padre, you understand, it's just that I happened to be sitting a couple of rows behind them and couldn't help but notice. You might want to check with Tom Gillespie, he might know something I don't. Maybe he said something to Tom about their plans for Sunday afternoon."

Tom Gillespie, Eileen's husband and the father of her unborn child, was the last man on earth Liam Barrett wanted to see.

CHAPTER TEN

A BIRD WITH ONE WING NEVER FLEW

I N ANOTHER SALOON MILES away, Captain Stanley stood inside the door as his eyes adjusted to the gloom. A handful of men were bellied-up to the bar, eyes on the mirror or on their drinks, and none looking friendly, farmers who'd come into town for supplies and stopped in for a few before the long drive home. Stanley took his usual stool near the cash register and raised a hand for attention. The barman approached, put a glass in front of him and half-filled it, slammed the bottle down next to the glass, then went back to washing dishes, all without a word. The barman knew Stanley didn't tip, much less pay for booze. He never did.

Stanley scanned the faces in the mirror, looking for anyone that might be of use to him. What luck! There, two stools away, was the scrawny little rat of a man from Inverness, Felix Malone. Stanley had never seen him in the saloon before, only at the estate, but he had heard that Malone had lived in Adams.

Stanley sidled up to him, the fifth of whiskey in hand. "Buy you a drink?"

The little rat-man peered at him as if he was searching through a fog. His face and hands were darkened by the sun, his thinning hair the color of the earth. There was a fine web of broken blood vessels across his cheeks. The whites of his eyes were red.

"Suit yourself."

Stanley topped off the man's glass, filled his own, and settled onto the next stool.

"Haven't I seen you around the Cunningham estate?" Stanley asked.

"So you have."

Stanley reached out his great mitt of a hand. "Captain George W. Stanley."

Malone took a healthy swig from his glass, wiped his mouth with the back of his hand, took Stanley's and shook. "Felix Malone," he said in a faint accent.

"Too bad about that maid. Did you know her?"

"Aye," Malone said.

"Looks like murder."

"Aye."

"I bet you see all the comings and goings. Maybe you got some idea about who could have done it, working out there on the estate and all. The boss man would be thankful for any help you can give."

"Isn't Liam Barrett in charge?"

Stanley polished off his glass and carefully placed it on the bar top. The whiskey burned his throat. Malone's glass was empty. Stanley lifted the bottle and shook it. "Another?"

"Sure, a bird with one wing never flew."

Stanley didn't understand what that meant but figured the sot wasn't refusing. He filled their glasses again and took a swig. "So you know the Barrett lad?"

"Well enough."

"Where can I find him this time of day? Is there a bar in Adams?"

"There is, the Black Rose. You may or may not find him there. He stops in on his rounds. Liam doesn't drink but Harry's a friend."

Stanley barked a laugh.

"No, sir, our Liam doesn't take drink. He promised his mother, don't you know." The accent grew thicker as Malone's speech became sloppier.

Patience was said to be a virtue, but not one Stanley wanted badly enough to learn. Still, he knew there was no pushing a drunkard, only leading and listening. He'd have to give this little rat-man room to wander in his own thoughts. What Stanley wanted was everything about the man who had pushed him aside in the Cunningham world, Liam Barrett. It should have been Stanley brought into the study, sharing brandy with the big man himself. It should have been Stanley's murder investigation.

Not only had Stanley been reduced to women's work, peeling potatoes, Dunbar took his wagon and drove Barrett to the train station. Stanley waited the entire afternoon in the kitchen with that dried up old woman laughing at him, until his wagon was returned and he could go home. That's when Dunbar came into the kitchen and said Barrett was investigating the murder and Stanley was to stay out of it.

Despite all his hard work, the most important job he'd been given was waylaying an order of booze while Liam Barrett was out looking for a murder suspect.

George W. Stanley needed two things. He needed to solve the murder first to prove himself. And he needed to know where Barrett's weakness was. He'd make sure the Adams cop never got in his way again.

"His mother made him swear off?" Stanley asked.

"One day, there he was, bound for Harvard with a sweetheart who'd wait for his return. He was going to be a lawyer, a great man, maybe even a judge or a senator someday." Malone finished his whiskey, looked at Stanley's bottle and waited.

Stanley poured. "And?"

"The next day, he's taking his father's place at the mill, backbreaking work it is, six days a week, fourteen hours a day, to keep food on the table."

"His old man skipped out?"

Malone slapped the bar top. "Never was there a finer man than Patrick Barrett. May God have mercy on him. The poor soul fell off the bridge one night on his way home from the Black Rose. Must have hit his head and drowned. Left a widow, the two half-grown children, and two wee bairns."

"What do you mean he worked in the mill? Barrett's a cop now."

"Liam has the gift of peacemaking. There's something about him that men respect. One day he walked into the Black Rose as a couple of his mates started pushing each other around. He came up behind them, nice-like, not acting the big man at all, at all. Wisht, they were calm. Strangest thing I've ever seen. The police captain was walking by and he heard the noise. He seen what Liam done and gave him the job. Out of the mills and keeping the peace. Best thing that ever happened to Adams. Mind you, it'd been grand too if he'd gone to law school, like he was supposed to, but one way or another, Adams is a better place because of Liam Barrett. His family too. They're lucky he was around when old Paddy died. He took over the farming. His sister took over the wee ones. If it hadn't been for Liam, they'd be in the poor house."

"What about their mother?"

"Ah, a beautiful woman she was with a voice like a linnet, Mary Barrett. Loved her husband, a good mother to her children, but that's over now," Malone said, his voice softening. "Away with the fairies."

What the hell was that supposed to mean? She was dead too? "The fairies." Stanley said.

Malone twiddled his fingers near his own head. "Gone, you know. Here but not here. Doesn't know what's going on around her."

∞

B EHIND HOGAN'S GENERAL STORE was a half-finished warehouse. There were no carpenters about. Laboring at the mill full-time, the only chance they had to build was during long summer evenings and Saturdays. Now that the days were shorter with not enough light to work after the whistle blew, the warehouse would not be finished until next year.

Wooden floorboards creaked as Liam and Frank stepped onto the store's porch. Through the window, Liam spied Tom Gillespie behind the cash register, staring absent-mindedly out the window. With all the womenfolk attending to Sadie, his store was empty. Their eyes met.

Seeing Tom always made Liam uneasy. A long time ago before everything changed, they had been good friends.

Tom, smallish for a man, was clean-shaven, his thick brown hair cut short, neither handsome nor ugly. His parents had both died of consumption when he was still young. Joe Hogan had taken him in and treated him like a son. And so, the three of them, Liam, Eileen, and Tom Gillespie, were quite the merry band at one time. Liam had to admit there was much about Tom that would attract a woman's interest. He was hard-working, loyal, and kind. Despite the pain of losing Eileen, Liam was grateful that she had found a solid man to marry.

Tom had a gift. He could anticipate the needs of the townspeople and stock the shelves to meet those needs ahead of time. As a consequence, Hogan's General Store prospered. Satisfied that the store and the family's future were in good hands, Joe Hogan had given the day-to-day running of the place over to Tom.

When they entered the store, Tom greeted them. "A good afternoon to you, Father O'Shea, and to yourself, Liam."

"Good afternoon, Tom," Liam said. "How is business?"

"Quiet, but I need to mind the till with Eileen over at Sadie's. It's a good thing you stopped by, I've been meaning to have a word about your Kevin."

"He says you offered him a job."

"I know, I should have spoken to you first. He's a hard worker and never makes trouble. We need to get the roof on the warehouse before snowfall. Right now, it's only me, and old Joe, and Finn when he shows up. We were hoping to get some of the lads to help out."

"As long as he goes to school every day, Tom. You'll make sure of that?"

"Promise."

"And he needs to be home for his chores by dinner."

"Of course."

The two sized each other up. "I need to ask you a few questions."

"About Deirdre, I expect. I don't know that I can help you. I only knew the girl to say hello."

Liam sensed Tom felt inadequate in his presence. In school, he was good with figures but was not the student that Liam was. No one expected much out of him. Liam had accepted their differences as a natural thing, not realizing that in doing so, he may have been thoughtlessly dismissive. It had not occurred to him that Tom may have loved Eileen too.

If Tom resented Liam, he had earned it. He hoped in the coming years, he would find an opportunity to make amends. But now, he needed to focus. "Have you seen Finn O'Brien?"

"That's a curious thing. I had expected him to come in Monday morning. He knows I need to get the warehouse finished. I'm quite cross with him about it, I don't mind telling you."

"Cross about him not coming to work?"

"About being so foolish, man, in Pittsfield."

Had Tom seen something between Deidre and Finn? "What are you talking about?"

"At the races. I always go to the races Sunday afternoon. Nothing as invigorating as a good test of horseflesh."

What Liam knew is that Tom enjoyed betting. It was said he won some but lost more. But from the looks of the store, it would appear that his habit had not diminished the family's resources too badly.

"There I was watching the horses and having a beer, when a great knot of humanity came crashing into the crowd. Knocked me over, spilt beer all over my suit. My Eileen didn't like that, I'll tell you. When I dragged myself off the ground, and the men were pulled apart, there was Finn, langered, arse over tip he was, and looking for a fight. And he found one. The last I saw him, he was being hauled away by the police. He's probably still in jail for all I know. Like I said, he didn't turn up Monday morning or since. I wonder if he knows about Deidre."

CHAPTER ELEVEN

AN UNSTAINED SOUL

WHEN LIAM AND FRANK walked into the Pittsfield police station, Captain Stanley was standing in the hallway leading to the cells.

"Back here so soon, Barrett?" Captain Stanley asked. "And with your little friend, I see. "Have you found the killer already?"

"You're holding Finn O'Brien," Liam said. "I need to speak with him."

"You mean the drunk and disorderly we picked up at the races? What business do you have with my prisoner?"

"It concerns the death of Deidre Monaghan."

"You're out of your jurisdiction, Barrett. Pittsfield is mine. Why don't you go back to your town and snoop around there? Isn't that why you were put on this case, because you're the one who knows Adams so good?"

"I'd be happy to tell Mr. Cunningham that you refused to allow me to speak to the last man who saw Deidre alive," Liam said, turning to walk out.

"Good day to you," Frank said.

"Wait! Last person to see her alive or first person to see her dead? Are you telling me that I had the killer locked up in my jail all the while?"

"There's no proof he killed her." Liam waited. Men like Stanley needed turmoil to assert control. They fed on other people's anger, justifying their own violence and overpowering the weaker. To Stanley, the heaviness of silence would smother his fury and render him impotent.

The Pittsfield captain jammed his hands into his beltline. "Maybe I'll have a little word with him first."

The news of Deidre's death should not be delivered by this man, who had no sympathy for her or Finn. It would be cruel and dangerous.

"Shall I tell Mr. Cunningham you took over the investigation?"

Stanley looked over his shoulder, then gave his attention to Liam and Frank.

"And what's the reverend for?"

"I have come to offer consolation," Frank said.

"Finn doesn't know his fiancé has been murdered," Liam pointed out.

"If he did it, he does," Stanley said.

He appeared to be calculating. If he had the culprit in this jail without knowing, he would look foolish. He had to know that. Liam had no desire to visit shame on this man. Perhaps he could make a friend out of Stanley yet if he offered him a way out.

"You had no reason to know Finn took the train with Deidre," Liam said. "Imagine Cunningham's pleasure if he finds out that you've taken a murderer off the street. That is, if it turns out to be Finn."

Stanley appeared to make his decision. "You can talk to him," he said. "But I'm watching."

Stanley motioned for Liam and Frank to follow down the hall. He unlocked and opened a cell door. On the cot was Finn O'Brien, curled up in a tight ball facing the wall.

"O'Brien, you have visitors," Stanley shouted, jerking Finn awake.

He rolled over in his cot slowly, then struggled to push himself upright. The left side of his face had been savagely beaten, his eye was a purple pulp, his lips as fat as leeches. Dried blood blackened his shirt and his nose was crushed. His face looked like a grotesque mask on his small, lean body.

Liam moved to Finn's side and helped him to sit up. "What happened to you?"

Stanley snorted.

Finn scowled. "Honest to God, Liam, I don't know. I was at the races and the next thing I know, I woke up here." His speech was muffled by the bloated lips and flattened nose.

When he noticed Frank, his confusion became panic. "Are they hanging me?"

"Why would you say that, boy?" Stanley asked.

"Why else would Father O'Shea be here?"

"So then you admit it," Stanley said.

"Admit what? I don't remember what happened."

"Before the races, Paddy."

Liam faced Stanley. "His name is Finn, not Paddy."

Stanley made a gurgling sound, like a forced laugh that had failed.

Liam said, "Captain Stanley, I heard what Finn said, as did Father O'Shea, and we'll testify that there was no confession. You're putting words into his mouth."

"Very well, Barrett," Stanley said. "You talk to him. See what you get."

"What's going on?" Finn asked.

Liam motioned Finn to be quiet.

"Thank you for showing us to the prisoner, Captain. We can proceed from here."

Liam stared at Stanley, intending to convey that there would be no talk until Stanley left them alone. Given the ferocious beating Finn had suffered, it was unlikely that he had received it in a drunken brawl. More likely that Stanley's men or Stanley himself had inflicted the injuries for sport.

If indeed Finn killed Deidre, he would pay the price. He had promised Sadie he would find justice for her. But Liam wanted to be sure first.

"I'm a busy man with things to do," Stanley said as he shut the cell door and locked it. He began walking down the hall, stopped, and pointed at Liam. "And I want a full report before you leave the station, you understand?"

Liam understood that Stanley was a suspicious and brutal man. There must have been some reason Cunningham insisted that Liam investigate this murder that by all right should have been Stanley's case, since it occurred in Stanley's jurisdiction. Until Liam understood why he'd been selected to investigate, and who was responsible for the murder, he would keep his counsel to himself.

Again, he thought of secrets, powerful motivators. Once made, the holder will go to ever-increasing lengths to hide them, bending their morals to vindicate the sins accumulated along the way. A man like Cunningham would have many secrets, that was how he exploited men and markets. One of those secrets could have cost Deirdre her life. Had she seen or heard something she shouldn't have? Given his slavish devotion to Cunningham, if Stanley knew what that secret was, he would protect it as a dog protects his bone.

"I understand," Liam said.

Stanley walked out of the cell block. His footfalls stopped when he was just out of sight. He was eavesdropping.

Finn was gulping air in panic. Liam put a loose arm around his shoulder. "It was merely a brawl at the races, nothing more. You're in jail for drunk and disorderly. The judge will release you for time served when you're arraigned. They kept you long enough to sober up."

Finn's breathing slowed. He sat on the edge of his cot, weaving his fingers around each other over and over.

"But I have sad news for you," Liam continued.

Finn glanced at Liam, then looked up at Frank who was standing quietly in the corner. "Someone's dead. It must be Deirdre."

"How did you know?"

"Why else would you come here to tell me?"

"I'm sorry, son," Frank said.

Finn tried pushing himself off the cot and fell back again. "I have to get out of here. This can't be true. My Deirdre dead? How can that be? She was on the train. Tell me it isn't true, Liam. This is a mistake. It has to be. It can't be, not my lovely Deidre."

Liam had never seen so much pain in a man's eyes before. Finn crossed his arms over his stomach and started rocking. Panicked gasps grew into sobs.

From the front office, Liam heard footsteps moving away. Through the small barred window of the cell, the world went about its business. A bird flew by. Passersby called greetings to one another. Horses clomped down the street. A baby cried.

All Liam could do was look on as Finn fell into despair. He didn't know the young man well, as Finn had arrived in Adams a couple of years ago with neither kith nor kin, another drifter looking for work. He wasn't the smartest of the lot but he was always ready with a helpful hand.

After a long time, Finn's crying ebbed.

"Tell me about the fight at the races," Liam said.

Finn shrugged. "It was a fight. Honest, Liam, I don't remember much. I said something. Or someone else said something. Someone got mad. The next thing I know fists were flying."

Finn looked down the hallway where Captain Stanley had disappeared.

"And they think I hurt Deidre?" Finn said, his voice bordering on hysteria. "That I killed her?"

Frank stepped closer.

"And you're here to grant me absolution, Father? Well, I didn't do it, I'm telling you. I shouldn't even have to say that. Everyone knows how much I love Deidre."

"Tell us what happened," Liam said.

"We went to mass, me, Deidre and Sadie. I took communion, Father, you know that, with no stains upon my soul. That should tell you something, shouldn't it? Then we all went back to Sadie's and had a grand breakfast, and then me and Deidre took the train to Pittsfield. She was going back to work and I came down for the horses. All morning, she wouldn't have nothing to do with me. Didn't want to talk to me. Didn't want to be seen with me. After the train pulled out of Adams, she got up and moved to another seat. I followed her and she kept moving. I asked what I had done. She'd been standoffish all morning but we hardly had time to talk. I didn't think anything of it, but not to sit with me? This was different than her usual pouts. So I asked her, why are you so mad at me? And she said it was over. She wasn't marrying me and that was that. She wasn't going to spend her life chained to a working man in Adams, making just enough money to get by, then one bairn after another, always worried that any minute there wouldn't be enough. Did she meet another man, I wanted to know. How can you not love me anymore? She wouldn't answer. And now you're telling me she's dead? Where, when? Who did this to my lovely girl?"

"She was found in the woods between the station and Inverness," Liam said. "Did you see her with anyone else?"

"She was standing on the platform, searching for someone. I tried to stay with her, make sure she got safely home. But she stomped her foot and told me to go away. I was to leave, she said, or she would scream for the police. She scared me, she'd never done anything like that before, so I left. Last I seen her, she was still there on the platform, by herself."

"And where did you go after that?"

"I headed for the racetrack. Felix Malone drove up in a wagon, leading two racehorses. He said they were running and would I like to help him get ready? I was glad for the ride and happy to help Felix. He's an Adams man, you know, working at Inverness. I think he got Deidre the job."

"At mass, you took communion," Frank said. "I remember."

Liam looked at Frank, wondering what his point was.

"But Deidre did not," Frank added.

"She hadn't gone to confession, had she?" Finn answered too quickly. "How could she, working six days a week at Inverness?"

Easily enough, Liam knew. There was a Catholic church and a priest in Pittsfield. She could have gone to confession there in the evening after her work was done.

"Had she missed communion before?" Liam asked.

"Ere these past few weeks," Frank said, weightily. He seemed to be implying that there was something which Deirdre should have been confessed but wasn't willing.

"She's been working at Inverness longer than that," Liam said.

"Lookit, Liam," Finn said. "I know I wasn't good enough for her. Anyone could see that. She was an angel sent down by God straight from heaven. I was surprised as anyone when she let me take her out for strolls. I didn't have any money. But I loved her. I wanted to make her happy. When she said she'd marry me, I thought she had put aside those silly ideas about leaving Adams, seeing the world. We could have been happy. We could have..."

And then he started crying too hard to talk.

Frank laid a calming hand on Finn's shoulder. Liam sensed a prayer coming. He rose from the cot and looked out the window upon the alley between the station and the courthouse. Dust floated through shafts of sunlight. Rats scurried in the shadows of the courthouse's brick wall. The sounds of the busy city drifted away as he listened to Frank speaking in low, soothing tones to Finn.

This man was surprised to learn his girl was dead. Finn O'Brien did not kill Deirdre Monaghan, of that Liam was certain. He needed to confirm the alibi before anyone had a chance to get to Felix. And then he would start looking for the killer.

When the prayer was over, Liam said, "I'll be back for you when you're released."

"If they let me go," Finn said.

"I'll see to it they do." Liam gave Finn a squeeze on his shoulder. "I promise."

As they walked through the police station, a young officer behind the desk said, "Captain Stanley stepped out for a minute. He said you should stay until he returns."

"You can tell him you gave us the message," Liam said. He stepped out onto the boardwalk with Frank behind him while the officer was saying, "But, but..."

"Are you forgetting you promised to give him a report?" Frank said.

"I'm forgetting nothing. I didn't promise him a report. I merely stated that I understood he wanted one. But, you, Father, promised Sadie you would look into having Deirdre brought home and you shall keep that promise. After that, we have one more visit to make before we return to Adams."

"You would have made a fine lawyer," Frank said.

Liam hadn't told Frank about his law school plans. He must have heard it from someone else, Sadie most likely. It wasn't a secret. But it was so long ago, it felt like someone else's life.

"The undertaker is this way," Liam said, stretching his legs into an easy gait.

They found the undertaker sitting in a chair in front of his parlor, exploring his mouth with a toothpick. "Afternoon, gents," he said.

"Good afternoon," Liam said. "We've come to inquire about the release of Deirdre Monaghan's remains."

"Her mother is in great distress," Frank added, "as you would expect."

"Seen it often enough, you don't need to tell me," the undertaker said. He stood, tossed the toothpick into the street, and pulled himself to his full height, nearly as tall as Liam. "Unfortunately the coroner hasn't performed his examination yet. As you know, Officer Barrett, the remains cannot be released until he does so."

"When do we expect that to take place?"

"Not today," the undertaker said, opening the parlor's front door. "Check back tomorrow."

CHAPTER TWELVE

DOWN BY THE WILLOW GARDEN

LIAM AND FRANK SAT opposite Felix Malone at Inverness' kitchen table. His chair pushed back, he was worrying a grubby cap held between his knees. He reeked of whiskey. His eyes were bloodshot, the skin beneath them sagged, and he kept wiping his nose. He was sweating out last night's whiskey.

The last Liam had seen Felix, it was to deliver the news that his wife had died. They had been separated, she in Adams, a woman tortured by the loss of her only son, he at Inverness tending to Cunningham's livestock. He'd taken that news in stride, unsurprised. She had been spiraling downwards ever since the death of their son. Despite his history for intemperance, his eyes were clear. There was no sign he'd taken drink in a very long time.

But now he was drunk.

"I should never have brought her here," Felix said. He covered his face with one gnarled hand. "It's all my fault."

A thousand questions flooded Liam's mind. Was that a confession? Why would he kill Deirdre? She was like a daughter to him. He couldn't possibly have killed her if Finn's timeline was correct. Finn had her standing on the platform when he met Felix. Or did he know beforehand that she was in danger? Could he have prevented her death?

Liam could smell hay and grain in the stockman's clothes beneath the stink of whiskey. Outside the window, workers toiled on the grounds, shouting to each other in angry voices. Meat was on the cooker boiling, filling the room with a moist gamy air.

"Go on," Liam said. Having chastised Stanley for putting words in a man's mouth, he was loath to do the same.

"It was my fault she was here." From beneath his brow, Felix dared a look at Liam. "I got her the job. She wanted out of Adams. And she was such a lovely slip of a girl. That village was too small a place for her."

Malone raised his head, lost in a memory. "One time when she was a little girl, I was working on Sadie's roof. A few shingles had come loose in a storm. Deirdre could not have been more than five or six. It was hot as Hades." Malone stole a look at the priest. "Sorry, Father. It was hot. I'd been up there half the day, sweating like a –," another glance at Frank, "and I hear this little voice. I look down and there's this tiny mite of a thing on the ground there calling up to me. The sun lit up that baby hair, it was more orange than red, and she looked like a little angel calling my name."

"Mr. Malone, Mr. Malone, she says," Felix said in imitation of a child's small voice. "I brought you something to drink."

"So I come down the ladder and there she is, holding a tall glass of water with ice in it. Can you imagine that, ice? With those tiny little hands, she'd gone into her mother's ice box and chipped off enough to fill the glass, then poured water on top of it and brought it out to me. Sadie was on the other side of the house, hanging the laundry. She would have been gobsmacked if she'd known Deidre was chipping with that ice pick. The bairn could have hurt herself."

Liam let Felix revel in the memory. Little stories like that bonded one person to another. When told to another, it became that person's story too. These little stories were the closest thing to magic Liam could think of, simple words building communities.

"No one ever did that for me before," Malone said. "Why would they, I'm nothing special. But Deidre was."

He sighed. "What was I to do? She asked me to say a word for her, help her get a job here at the big house. I was so proud of her I was, working her way up from the scullery to a maid so quick-like. She was going places, that one."

"Mr. Malone," Liam said. "Where were you on Sunday?"

"Fed the horses, same as always, then Dunbar told me to ferry two of them to the races."

"Did you see Finn O'Brien?"

"I did. He was walking along the road so I offered to give him a lift if he promised to help me. Moody he was, not wanting to talk much. At the track, we got the horses saddled and ready to go. Then he got himself something to drink. I saw him here and there, wandering around, until he got into a fight with some big fella, got the stuffing knocked out of him and then the coppers picked him up."

"You saw all that?"

"I wasn't watching him, if that's what you're asking me, but I saw him from time to time right up until he got pinched."

"Did you see the fight?"

"Only heard about it."

"How badly was he injured, do you know?"

"He went down on the first punch, so I heard. Our Finn isn't much of a fighter."

"Before the fight, could he have followed Deidre into the woods and come back to the races?"

Malone shook his head. "He couldn't have gotten to the woods and back that fast. Whist, you can't be saying he did this! To Deidre? He loved her. Mind you, he wasn't good enough for her and he well knew it. And none of us understood what she saw in him, but you know how it is for the pretty girls, all the boys are afraid of talking to them. Maybe she thought she could change him. But that lad wasn't going anywhere. You could see that. No ambition. No imagination. He was content to work at Hogan's all week and drink and gamble on the weekends. But he never did anyone harm."

Liam and Frank exchanged looks. Finn's alibi was confirmed. What's more, Felix had nothing to do with the murder either. It was time to move on. Liam stood. "That'll be all for now, but if there's anything else you can think of, would you get word to me?"

Malone nodded, then he shifted in his chair as if he was working the courage up to say something.

"Is there more?" Liam asked.

"Only that when I was in town, I ran into that scut Captain Stanley. He was asking me questions too."

"It's his turf," Liam said.

"But that's the thing," Malone said. "His questions weren't about Deirdre. I don't understand, but figured you should know, Liam. He was asking about you."

Mrs. Ramsey appeared in the doorway. "His lordship will see you now."

MALCOM DUNBAR WAS SEATED behind Cunningham's desk, head buried in a stack of bills, writing in a ledger. There was no fire lit. The room felt cold. Dunbar lifted his head from his paperwork. His stare settled on Frank then slid over to Liam. "Need your confessor, do you?"

"Father O'Shea is making the funeral arrangements."

"Oh, aye?" Dunbar said. "Mr. Cunningham is a tolerant man. He indulged the lass so she could go to church with her mother but we'll have none of your papist claptrap around here."

Liam wondered how Alistair Cunningham could have indulged Deirdre when he seemed unaware of her existence. Perhaps it was Dunbar himself or Mrs. Ramsey who was so generous in Cunningham's name and without his knowledge. It couldn't have been Ramsey. If there was any kindness in her, it would not have been spared for Deirdre. It was apparent she disliked the girl. It must have been Dunbar who arranged the special accommodation but was making a good show of being disinterested. Why would he do her a favor?

Dunbar put his pen down. "I'm busy, man. Do you have any news? If not, be gone."

"I found Finn O'Brien, Deirdre's fiancé. But I have not found the man who murdered Deidre. They are not one in the same. Finn has an alibi. He parted company with her at the train station and was picked up by Felix Malone who was ferrying your horses. Finn was at the races the rest of the afternoon until he was arrested for drunk and disorderly."

Dunbar lifted a shaggy eyebrow. "Of course, he was."

"Look, Dunbar, I know Finn O'Brien. I can tell you at no time before Sunday has he ever disturbed the peace." Drink to excess was another matter.

"This day was special for what reason, do you suppose?"

"Deidre had broken their engagement."

"Good lass." A faint smile crossed Dunbar's face, then disappeared. He thumped the ledger with a thumb. "What makes you think he didn't kill her and join up with Malone later?"

"There wasn't enough time for Finn to follow Deirdre into the woods and be picked up at the train station if Malone is to be believed. In Adams, Felix is known to be an honest man."

"Here as well," Dunbar conceded. He leaned back in his chair and looked down his nose at Liam with one eye as if he were lining up a shot. "If not the hapless suitor, then who, Officer Barrett? Who killed the lass?"

"I don't have another suspect at this time."

Dunbar stood suddenly. "There's tramps in the woods, or Molly Maguires disguised as tramps. Same either way if you ask me. My men have seen them coming and going for days. If memory serves me correct, the lass' body was discovered by one of their lot."

The place where Deidre was discovered should have been the first place to look for evidence. Liam assumed Captain Stanley had. Cunningham was in such a hurry to hang Finn that Liam's first priority was to secure his alibi, if there was one, and he hadn't had time to examine the scene. Now, as Dunbar said, they were starting over. The best place to start would be the beginning. "I'll search the woods. The men living out there may have seen something."

Dunbar peered out one of the tall bay windows. Mount Greylock was in the distance, hazy because she was so far away but still recognizable. Beyond the mountain laid Adams town and the Barrett farm where Kevin would be cleaning Bridget's stall and giving her fresh food. The sky darkened as the afternoon light waned. "Too late to make a start of it now," Dunbar said. "First light."

"You're coming?"

Dunbar spun around. "Time and tide wait for no man, Barrett. The Governor arrives Thursday afternoon and already you've wasted an entire day on a wild goose chase."

"It was your boss who sent me looking for Finn O'Brien."

"When a pretty, young girl like her is killed, an affair of the heart is behind it," Dunbar said. "She wouldn't give him what he wanted, or she did and he didn't want the responsibility."

An old ballad came to Liam's mind, *Down by the Willow Garden.* A boy was hung for murdering a pregnant girl named was Rose Connolly. There were many versions amongst the Irish. Liam suspected a similar song had been sung by the Scottish and Dunbar would have known it.

"Neither was the case," Liam said. "Deirdre was leaving Finn."

"Jealousy, then. She told him she's done with him. He lashed out. It's an old story."

"He didn't have the time. She only told him on the train. He met up with Malone while she was still waiting on the platform."

Dunbar's head jerked forward, his stare locked on Liam. "Waiting for who?"

"That's the question."

"Shouldn't you be asking around town, finding out who'd seen her on the platform, who she met there?"

"Do you want me to find who did this or don't you? I'd waste my time if I stood around on the platform all week. The weekday travelers are unlikely to travel on the weekend. It'll be Sunday before we'll find someone who saw her on last Sunday, someone who routinely was at the train station on that day."

"It'll be too late by then. As I said just a moment ago, the Governor is coming Thursday. You were listening, weren't you? Mr. Cunningham wants this over before then."

"Your boss will have his arrest as soon as I find the man responsible and no sooner. I'll start at the beginning, with the murder scene, tomorrow morning. First light."

Dunbar looked at Frank, who had been standing quietly. "Have you nothing to say, priest?"

Frank lifted his right hand and made the sign of the cross in the air. "Dominus vobiscum. The Lord be with you, my son."

"None of your Papish nonsense here." Dunbar waived a hand in the air as if he was clearing a bad smell and hollered, "Mrs. Ramsey!"

❧

O NE OF THE INVERNESS workmen drove Liam and Frank to the train station. The driver did not speak when he pulled the rig to the mansion's front door, merely motioned for Liam and Frank to board. He drove the horse at a brisk pace, apparently eager to deliver his load. Along the way, each retired to his own thoughts.

After a wide turn leading away from the mansion, the drive opened onto a road that wound through heavy forest. From time to time, Liam noticed game trails in the woods. He recalled Captain Stanley had said Deidre was found on one such trail. If it had been a random attack, then anyone she met in the woods was a suspect. But if she was the intended victim, then the killer had selected that time and place because he knew she would be traveling that way. Perhaps the person she was expecting to meet? Had that person failed to arrive at the station, knowing that she would head out onto the trail alone, then lain in wait, and set upon her in a remote spot?

The driver pulled the wagon to the train station, slowing long enough for Liam and Frank to dismount, and pulled out again without a word.

"Nasty bugger," Frank said.

"The driver was in a hurry, I reckon," Liam said. "Wants to get home before the other hands finish off Mrs. Ramsey's stew."

"Not him. That Dunbar fella. That one --," he gestured toward the wagon pulling out of sight, "is a sullen bugger. There's a difference."

"Learn that language in seminary, did you?"

"Bugger? Nonsense. I learned that language at the knee of the great aunt who raised me, God rest her soul. First words out of my mouth were 'bugger all!' I had dropped my biscuit and the dog stole it from me."

Liam suppressed his smile as they boarded the train. He wondered if there had been a great aunt, or if she was a convenient fiction.

They found a seat apart from the other few passengers.

"What next?" Frank asked. "You found Finn. He couldn't have done it. Do you really think Mollys are congregating in the woods, waiting to accost a young woman? Is that what they do in this country? Back home, they fought for farmers' rights."

Liam tapped the window glass with his finger as he thought. The Molly Maguires were known for a lot of things, insurrection and reputed murder included, but he had never heard of them preying upon women. In America, they were working men, fighting for the right to earn a living wage so they could care for their families. They were miners, factory workers, laborers and they were all settled in industrial communities. It had been nearly twenty years since the trials in Pennsylvania. After the hangings, the Pinkertons claimed to have broken the movement. The likelihood of a resurrection of the Molly Maguires was small.

No, if there were tramps in the woods, they were single men. Immigrants, like Sweeney, who had landed in New York City or Boston, in need of work and started walking, hoping to find day labor deeper in the countryside working on farms or a building site.

The train pitched forward. As it gained speed, the carriage settled into a rocking motion. A baby cried until his mother put it to her bosom.

"It well may have been a tramp who did this," Liam said. "I would have started my investigation at the scene, but I'd been dispatched to find Finn first. By tomorrow, two days will have passed since the murder. I'm not so sure what, or who, we will find there, but the place where Deirdre was found is as good a place as anywhere to start."

Chapter Thirteen

Our Fair Valley

S ADIE'S PARLOR WAS EMPTY. In the adjacent dining room, several men were sitting down to dinner at a large table. Sadie stepped out of the kitchen, wiping her hands on an apron. She had gone back to work. The women of Adams had returned to their own families. "When is she coming home?"

"Can we speak privately?" Liam asked.

She came into the living room, pulling the sliding doors shut behind her. "When is she coming home?" She asked again.

"Not tonight, I'm afraid," Liam said. "But soon."

"How am I to make arrangements? You think things like this happen by themselves? There's cooking to be done, and..."

"And it'll happen in God's time," Frank said. "Is that lamb stew I smell?"

"Sorry, Father, where's my manners? Liam you'll stay for dinner, won't you?"

The stew smelled rich and meaty and Liam could feel hunger gnawing at him. But what he really wanted was to sequester in his room, away from people, for a few sweet hours in the dark alone or as alone as he could be with Kevin snoring in the next bed.

"Kate's expecting me," Liam said.

"Then you best be off before she takes you to task, William Patrick Barrett."

W HEN LIAM WALKED INTO the Barrett yard, he found Kevin sitting on a stool in the shed watching Bridget and her calf.

"How's she looking?" Liam asked.

"Good."

"And the calf?"

"Nursing well."

"How was school?"

"Boring," Kevin said. "Tom Gillespie says he talked to you."

"So he has."

"And?"

"And, your sister's against it."

"Since when is she the boss of you?"

Challenging Liam's authority was a clumsy strategy. Alas, Kevin would never have Clare's persuasive abilities. He should have realized by now that Liam was offended by the presumption that men ruled the world and women were little more than hand servants. The ebb and flow between men and women was far too elegant and subtle for such graceless, rigid labels.

Ultimately this had been Liam's decision, not because he was the head of the family but because Kate appreciated that Liam knew best the tragedy of a derailed future. Despite the reassurances from Tom Gillespie that the job wouldn't interfere with Kevin's schoolwork and Kevin's own promises, the boy lacked the tenacity to focus on two goals at once. He would work very hard on the one pursuit that gave him the most gratification in the moment, not appreciating that his education would open doors he could not immediately imagine. His grades would suffer and eventually he would drop out. He would unwittingly have corralled himself into a life of back-breaking labor. He was capable of so much more.

Liam squeezed Kevin's shoulder as his own father had done. The gentle strength and the manly affection had made Liam feel special and Liam wanted Kevin to know that his primary concern was the boy's welfare. "You have to pick your battles, my lad."

"But—"

"Give it time. Keep going to school, doing your chores, and we'll see what happens. But you can go over to Hogan's and help out in your spare time. Show me that you can keep up your own work as you take on new responsibilities and we'll talk about it again."

Kevin nodded. He leaned against the shed, arms folded.

"You're not coming in?" Liam asked.

Kevin shot a look towards the house. "Think I'll sit here with Bridget and the calf for a bit longer."

"Is there something I should know?"

"Go see for yourself."

The Barrett home was deathly quiet. The mother was snoring quietly in her chair in the sitting room. Kate was at the kitchen table, leaning towards the window for better light as she sewed. She rose and put a kettle on, without speaking. A door opened in the back of the house and Clare could be heard shuffling towards the kitchen. She appeared in the doorway and looked up at Liam, her face blotched red from crying. She looked accusingly at Kate.

Kate spun around, a fist on her hip. "The duchess here wants to join the convent."

This was nothing new, she'd been talking about it for a couple of years. Liam waited.

"Now," Kate said.

"We don't have the dowry."

Clare sniffed. "I could make the money. I could work in the mill or take in laundry."

"You most certainly will not," Kate said. "You're going to school and I'll hear nothing more about it."

What was it with these children, both in such a hurry to become adults? Was the life Liam and Kate provided them so miserable they needed to escape?

Clare looked up at Liam, a pleading expression in her eyes. Liam's much longed-for rest would have to wait.

"Take a walk with me," he said.

By the time they reached the road, the sky above them was deep blue and a thin strip of violet hovered in the west. Tiny pricks of starlight sparkled. Liam and Clare walked down the road until they came to a knoll. In the distance, yellow light burned brightly in mill's windows, one of the first buildings wired for electricity. They hadn't spoken since leaving the farm. As they walked, Clare's sniffles had slowed down and she had calmed.

Liam pointed to a place in the grass flattened along the roadside and settled onto the ground. Clare sat down beside him. A door in the mill opened. Silhouetted shapes of men, women, boys, and girls merged and undulated as they poured from the building and disappeared into the night shadows.

"You used to work in the mill," Clare said.

"I did."

"And Da did too, I heard you say. And Kate too."

"True enough."

"Why can't I go work in the mill?"

"You'd have to quit school."

Unlike Kevin, Clare loved her education. She read all the books she could and excelled in class. Her teachers reported that with her inexhaustible patience, she had a gift for helping other students.

"I hear the calling."

"It's a big decision. It would mean leaving us and never coming back again. If you went to Boston, we wouldn't be able to visit you. It's too far away. We would miss you. The mother, Kevin, me, Kate."

"All Kate would miss is me doing chores."

"Ah, Clare darling, you hardly know your sister at all."

Crickets chirped. The voices of tired workers drifted up to them. Liam waited for Clare's natural curiosity to take over. She was one who easily accepted answers once she had cleared a place in her mind for them, but strongly resisted any facts which were forced upon her.

"What do you mean?"

"You're too young to remember but when Da died, Kate took over raising you and Kevin. You were still a bairn, didn't even have a name yet. We named you after the mother's favorite sister back home. Kate's twenty-six years old now, unmarried with no suitors in sight. She's been so busy taking care of our family that she hasn't had the time to start one of her own and soon she'll be too old. In her mind, you're the closest thing she'll ever have to a daughter." Liam bumped Clare with his shoulder and whispered, "I think she's hoping you'll have a family and give her more babies to care for."

"Like their gran?"

"Just so."

Clare gazed upon the field, the grass, the line of bare-branched trees along the road.

"But I want to do more. I want to make a difference, help people."

"You can, macushla. If you finish your education, you can teach. Show children the joy of learning. You have a talent for it; your teacher has said so often enough." Liam gestured at the mill. "Most of the people working in there can't read, did you know that? And that's why they're doomed to working with their backs."

"What if I get married? Wouldn't I have to quit teaching?"

"Things are changing all the time. You can make your own future. Mind you have found a man who is worthy of you. That's all I ask."

A long time passed with Clare staring into the night and Liam hoping that something he said had taken root in her imagination. Finally she gave a little jerk of her chin. "I'll think about it. Let's go home."

∽

S TANLEY PAUSED ON THE boardwalk in front of the Black Rose, the bar Felix Malone mentioned. If Barrett caught him visiting his haunt, Stanley would need a story to explain himself. He couldn't say that he went there looking for Barrett because he knew where the man lived and had been to his home. Why would he look for the Adams cop in a pub when everyone knew that he didn't drink?

He needed a better story. If Barrett was inside now or arrived before Stanley left, he'd say he was on his way to Barrett's home but decided to stop for a drink first. If he was asked why he was looking for Barrett, he'd think of something.

He pulled open the door and crossed the threshold. The pub was empty except for a big man behind the bar with messy black hair, a long black beard, and furry arms sticking out of rolled up sleeves. The man was as big as Stanley himself and no doubt was the owner of the establishment. A man didn't get muscles like that standing behind a bar unless he exercised them tossing drunks into the street.

The bartender eyed his badge. "It's a fine evening we're having, Officer, what will you be drinking?"

Stanley bellied-up to the bar. "Whiskey."

"No whiskey tonight, sorry to say. I have beer and sarsaparilla. Or tea. Would you care for a cup of tea?"

Stanley had nearly forgotten. This was the place that was expecting the shipment he waylaid and they were out of whiskey already. Cunningham would be pleased if Stanley told him the plan had worked, but he felt hesitation. Admitting that he'd visited Adams seemed like a bad idea. He wasn't sent here by the old man so the old man might not like that he had come.

"Beer, then."

The hairy man pulled a mug of draft with too much foam that came nowhere close to the top and planted it in front of Stanley, a clear message that he expected the cop to have his drink and leave in short order. "If it's Captain Curran you're looking for, he's gone home to dinner."

"Stopped in to wet my whistle," Stanley said. He chugged half the beer, then stared into the backbar mirror, aiming to look like he was making small talk. "You lived here long?"

"All my life." The bartender ran his hand over the glossy bar top with a rag as lovingly as a man might stroke his favorite horse's neck. " 'Tis my place, this, the Black Rose. And I am Harry Gallegher, at your service. It's been my great good fortune to grow up in this town after my parents brought me here as a wee lad, and not a finer place could you find to make a home. Fair weather, good hardworking people, a strong sense of community although most of us are from different places in Ireland and, sure, there's some here when we came not Irish at all. The Quakers, for instance. A peace-loving people. And you'll never hear a day's – . "

Harry the bartender was warming to the sound of his own voice but Stanley had enough. "Got anything else to drink?"

"Thirsty, still, are you, Officer? Well, let me take a look around." Harry made a show of examining the back bar where bottles should have been kept. There were none. Then he took Stanley's mug and held it under a tap. A dribble of beer sputtered into the mug. The stream stopped and he let the tap go. "Got a splash here for you, if that'll do the trick."

Stanley grunted. The bartender brought the mug back to him. "As I was saying, the Quaker folk are a fine people. There used to be more of them living here but they've mostly moved on, looking for better soil than the rocky stuff we have here. They're farmers, you know, much as ourselves. Rocks are no problem for us. You can always build a fence or a wall, or even a castle, with enough rocks."

Stanley held up a hand to stop the blathering. He drunk the beer and pushed the mug back at Harry.

"Who else lives here besides the Quakers?"

Harry took a step back, eyes wide, in feigned surprise. "Did I not mention that? The Irish, of course. From all parts of Erin's fair isle, we came to this valley."

It was going to take all night to bring this man around to talking about Liam Barrett.

"Yes, yes, the Irish. You mentioned them. And you're farmers."

"Aye, farmers, mill workers, Hogan owns the general store, me myself this bar here, a few other shopkeepers, the blacksmith."

"I met Liam Barrett the other day, a policeman here."

Harry slapped the bar. "My friend Liam, not a better man alive. In fact I remember the time..." Harry spotted something over Stanley's shoulder and stopped talking. "Well, lookee here, it's your man now."

Stanley felt a rush of cold air enter the room before he turned to see Barrett walking toward him.

"Stanley," Barrett said.

"Barrett."

"I'll put the tea on," Harry said.

Stanley winced. "Tea?"

"Officer, you drank the last of my alcohol. It's tea or nothing." Harry went through the curtain at the end of the bar.

"You're the man I was looking for," Stanley said.

"You know where I live."

"I didn't want to interrupt your supper," Stanley said, then congratulated himself silently for the quick lie that had come to his lips.

"Kind of you," Barrett said.

"That Finn O'Brien rotting in my jail. He's done his time for drunk and disorderly. I wouldn't want to make a mistake and release a murderer. Will you be charging him? I need to know." Another quick story. Stanley was playing the game well. "You were supposed to wait at the station and report to me but by the time I got back, you had gone."

"His alibi checked out. Felix Malone, up at Inverness, verified his story. So I'd appreciate it if you'd let him go."

That was news to Stanley. "When did all this happen?"

"Late this afternoon."

"And why wasn't I told?"

"I was instructed to report to Dunbar. Figured he'd let you know."

"And now what? If O'Brien didn't do the girl in, who did?"

"Dunbar and I are going out into the woods first thing tomorrow to examine the scene."

"Dunbar and you? What for? I already went over the scene. Nothing to be found there. You're wasting your time."

"Not faulting you, Stanley, you followed your nose."

"You won't know where the body was found. You'll need me to show you the way."

"The game trail between the railroad station and Inverness. Clear enough. We'll manage."

Stanley didn't like this. Barrett had made him look stupid again. First, he found O'Brien, the man they had been looking for, sitting in Stanley's jail. Then Barrett got someone to alibi him, and O'Brien would go free. And now, Barrett was working hand in hand with Dunbar. It should have been Stanley. He should have found O'Brien and got him charged before Barrett interfered.

George Washington Stanley didn't like what was happening one damn bit.

Chapter Fourteen

The Golden Crucifix

D RIED LEAVES CRUNCHED BENEATH their feet as Liam and Malcom Dunbar walked down the game trail. The air had a snap to it that had not been there before. Little gusts of mist blew from their mouths.Several hundred feet into the woods, the leaves had been disturbed. A large dark stain had spread across the earth. Liam bent on one knee and dug his finger into the dirt. It came up moist with blackened liquid. He held it to his nose and smelled the coppery tang of blood.

Dunbar had progressed further down the trail. He stopped and turned. "What is it, man?"

"This is the place."

Dunbar walked back slowly, halting six feet away. He stared at the blood-stained earth and the churned dirt where Stanley and the tramp would have picked Deidre up and carried her back to the road. "The place where she died?"

Liam nodded.

"What makes you think the attack began here? It could have well begun at the road, the attacker chasing her into the woods, she takes the short cut hoping to reach Inverness before he caught her. Or he came out of yon woods and chased her back to this spot." Dunbar pointed deeper into the forest.

Liam thought it a waste of time. It was clear where the struggle, what there was of one, had occurred. But Dunbar would need to be pacified before they could continue. "You go up the trail, I'll retrace our steps. See what you can see."

Liam moved back towards the road, one careful step at a time, sweeping leaves in the trail away with his boot, looking for signs of scuffed dirt, long strides, someone running. All he found was the trod of men who'd traveled this way and an occasional impression of a dainty heel.

"Look here!" Dunbar shouted from several yards into the woods. Liam couldn't see him because of the trees in between. Another man's voice was raised in alarm. Dunbar swore. The other man cried out in pain.

Liam ran as fast as he could on the lumpy earth, jumping over fallen trees along the way. Dunbar was on top of a man, twisting his arm and shoving his head into the dirt. "Dunbar!"

The Scot lifted his head. "Took you long enough, Barrett. I found this tramp. He was watching us. I spotted him and he tried to get away." Dunbar wrenched the man's arm and the man cried out again.

"Let him go."

Their eyes locked. Dunbar was beyond reason, as feral as a fox falling upon a rat in the woods, his only concern was extinguishing this man's life.

"Dunbar, I said, let him go!"

"You'll arrest him, then?"

"I'll talk to him. After you let him go."

The man on the ground had quit fighting. Dunbar jumped from his back, far more agile than Liam would have expected of a man in his middle years. He dusted his hands on his pants and brushed at the dirt and leaves that had clung to his knees.

The tramp pushed himself up tentatively, with his eyes on Liam, appearing thankful for the rescue. It was Owen Sweeney, the man in Stanley's wagon the night Curran and Stanley appeared at Liam's farm. As Sweeney rose, Liam noticed a gold chain dangling from his neck. A fine gold Celtic cross hung at the end of the chain.

Liam had seen one like that before. It had belonged to Deidre but he couldn't be sure it was hers. Many Catholics wore crucifixes, men and women alike. Hers was an expensive cross, a high quality of gold, which had attracted the attention and comment of her acquaintances, but that was all he recalled. It had been a gift from Sadie's husband who had died when Deidre was an infant. Sadie had passed it down to the daughter for her confirmation gift.

If Sweeney had been wearing a cross like that when they first met, Liam would have noticed.

Dunbar spotted the necklace and lunged at the man. "Where did you get that?"

Liam stepped between the two men. "I am the law. I will ask the questions, Dunbar. Remember that."

Dunbar stopped his attack but did not step back. He held his ground, now staring at Sweeney over Liam's shoulder. "Oh, aye, laddie," he said. "Oh, I shall."

Liam turned back, making sure he blocked the path. "Owen, where did you get that crucifix?"

Owen's eyes widened. "It was my mother's." He was filthy with sweat and dirt smeared across his face and his nose bled.

"Can you not see he's lying?" Dunbar was nearly yelling. "It's too fine a thing for this lout to own. He stole it. A thief. He killed her for the gold." Liam could feel Dunbar maneuvering behind him. Liam raised his arm to block Dunbar's path.

"You said your mother was back home in Ireland," Liam said.

It was then Owen took off running deeper into the woods. Dunbar drew his gun and aimed. Liam batted it away and it fired into the ground.

Liam ran after Owen. The man ahead of him darted through the trees like a deer while Liam tripped on roots and slipped on wet leaves. What Liam lacked in agility, he made up for with conviction. If he didn't catch Owen, Dunbar would shoot him in the back.

Liam caught him by the collar and set his weight, letting the other man's momentum pull his feet out from under him. He fell to the ground. Liam knelt and spoke into this ear. "That man is ready to shoot you in the back, Owen. Do as I tell you. It's the only way you'll come out of this alive."

Owen stopped fighting and allowed Liam to handcuff him. The only sound in Liam's ears was his own heavy breathing and pounding heart. The birds and small woodland creatures were silent, hiding. They knew better than to show themselves when predators hunted.

Dunbar arrived, his pistol pointing at the two.

Liam blocked the shot. "Put that away, you fool! You will not kill a man in my custody."

Dunbar holstered his pistol. Liam braced himself against a tree. Spit poured into his mouth and for a moment he thought he was going to be sick. "You weren't wearing that cross last time I saw you, Owen," Liam said. "Where'd you get it?"

"I found it back there in the woods."

"Look how easy he lies," Dunbar said. "First it's his mother's, now he's saying he found it. He stole it from the girl. Can you not see that?"

"You're saying you found the cross in the dirt?"

Sweeney nodded. "Just so."

"Then why did you say it was your mother's?"

"I thought you wouldn't believe me if I told the truth."

Dunbar reached for Sweeney. "You filthy scut!"

"Dunbar, get a hold of yourself!" Liam pushed him away. To Sweeney, he said, "you wait here." Then by stepping in close to the Scot, he forced the smaller man a few feet away. "Listen to me. It looks like the cross Deidre wore, but I can't swear to it, can you?"

Dunbar, his head tilted back, locked eyes with Liam. "I cannot."

"Then we'll take him back to Adams. If Sadie identifies the cross, then I'll charge him with robbery."

"Oh, aye? Robbery? That's it? He clearly murdered the girl for her gold. Explain me this! How did the cross come off her neck with the chain unbroken? Not ripped from her neck? It's because he killed her first and then took the necklace. You don't believe this story about him finding it in the woods, you can't be such a fool. I think not, laddie. Or have I got you wrong? Anything to protect a fellow countryman?"

"Or someone took it from her after she was dead and dropped it running away."

"Or that someone hid it until he could come back for it later. And there's your man," Dunbar said tossing a gesture at Sweeney.

"Look, Dunbar, there's no point in arguing the possibilities. What we need is evidence. We have barely enough to hold him on the robbery charge. I'll keep investigating. If he committed the murder, I'll find the evidence and then I'll charge him, I promise. But not before."

Dunbar stared at Liam.

"He isn't going anywhere. He'll be in the Pittsfield jail."

Dunbar looked back at Sweeney, still panting on the ground. The Scot sucked on his long mustache, frowning.

"As you wish, Constable. We'll do it your way." He stepped around Liam and gave Sweeney a vicious kick in the ribs. "You'll know justice, yet, lad. Let judgment run down as waters, and righteousness as a mighty stream."

L IAM WAS GUIDING THE handcuffed Sweeney down the trail, Dunbar behind, when a rock whizzed past Liam's head, and then another. He pushed Sweeney to the ground and crouched with one hand shielding Sweeney's head.

Dunbar squatted beside him, his pistol raised. "Where's it coming from?"

Liam pushed Dunbar's pistol down. If the rock thrower had wanted to hit them, he would have. All three of them had been out in the open. The birds had suddenly gone quiet, aware of the danger too.

Something rustled in the undergrowth that could have been a frightened hare. A man stepped out from behind a tree, held a finger up to silence them, and hurled another rock over their heads. It hit something with a thud. A bird fell out of a tree.

Liam stood. "You could kill a man throwing rocks like that."

"If you aim it right," the man said. He was dressed like Sweeney, dirty trousers, dirty shirt, a kerchief tied at his throat, but he was tall and lanky, and had hair so red it was almost orange. Liam reckoned he was in his early twenties.

"Ho, what's this?" the man said as he approached and saw Sweeney on the ground, handcuffed.

"He's under arrest," Liam said.

The man took a close look at Liam and Dunbar. "He's done nothing wrong."

"And how would you know that, laddie?" Dunbar asked.

"Owen, what they get you for?"

"You know this man?" Liam asked.

"I do. Owen Sweeney, as good a friend as any man could have."

"You'll not interfere with the law, laddie," Dunbar said. "Your man Sweeney is a thief and a murderer. And you are a poacher."

Liam said to Dunbar. "This isn't Cunningham's land."

"No it isn't, but it's someone's. "

"Well, someone isn't here to complain so I won't arrest him today," Liam said, then spoke to the stranger, "I'm Officer Liam Barrett with the Adams police force. What's your name?"

"Timothy Hennessey."

"And you're a friend of Sweeney's?"

"I am, Officer Barrett."

"Do you camp near here?"

"I do."

Hennessey considered Liam for a moment, then walked directly through the cluster of men and picked up the bird he had killed by its feet.

"Get anything?" another man's voice called from several yards away.

Liam followed the voice and saw another man emerge from the woods, the spitting image of Hennessey. His brother, no doubt. Perhaps his twin.

"This fine bird," Hennessey said holding up his catch. "And what's that in your bag?"

"Your bird is nice, as little bony hens go." The brother was holding a bag, filled with something lumpy. "But I've caught this hare."

"And you are?" Liam asked.

"Denny Hennessey, his brother," the newcomer said with a nod towards Timothy. "Hey, what did you nab Sweeney for? Is it against the law in America to be a great fat eejit?"

"Robbery and murder," Dunbar said.

"Nothing of the sort." Liam scowled at Dunbar. "Did the two of you see a young lady walking through the woods Sunday afternoon?"

"We did not," Timothy said.

"Did Sweeney here tell you about finding her body?"

"He did."

"Have you seen this cross he's wearing before?" Liam asked.

"Of course we have. He wears it all the time."

Timothy Hennessy might be a great shot, but he was a terrible liar. He had answered too quickly.

"Where are you taking him?" Timothy Hennessy asked.

"First to Adams, then back to Pittsfield jail," Liam said. "You can visit him there if you like."

Timothy gave Sweeney a meaningful look, and a nod, and then as if by cue the two Hennessys trotted back into the woods.

DUNBAR DROVE THE WAGON while Liam rode beside him and Sweeney was in the back. Detritus from previous loads skittered across the boards as Dunbar pushed the horse. A wheel struck a rock. Liam had to grip the rough wood sideboard lest he be thrown out. A fog of hay dust from the wagon bed burned his eyes as bits of hay lanced his uniform. He could hear Sweeney choking and coughing. The wagon hit another rock. Liam felt himself levitate in the air long enough to realize that he was helpless to control where he landed. When he crashed, he landed sidewise on his leg and nearly slid off to the road. It was the wheels he thought of, how he would be tangled in their axle if he fell beneath the wagon.

"You'll get us all killed," Liam shouted to Dunbar over the clatter of the horses' hooves and the wagon's banging. He had been called to the scene of an overturned wagon once before. The horse's leg was broken and it had to be put out of its misery. Liam, the only man armed at the scene, shot it in the head. What had been the wagon was a long trail of shattered wood. After the horse had been dispatched, the bodies of two teenagers were found. They had been thrown clear of the wreckage. From a farm, they had been sent into town for supplies.

Liam accompanied Captain Curran to the farmhouse. When the farmwife opened the door, Captain Curran pulled off his hat and Liam did as well. She could tell, just by the fact that there were two policeman on her porch, hats in hand, that the news was bad. It was the first time Liam had witnessed a mother learning of her child's death. He thought of that now and how the woman had broken down, her husband at her side, catching her before she fell to the floor.

Dunbar kept up the pace until they fell into traffic approaching town. He slowed the horse to accommodate other wagons but he refused to stop for shoppers crossing Columbia Street. People panicked. Some scurried back to the safety of the boardwalk, others rushed directly in front of the wagon. One young mother was part-way across the street when she saw the wagon coming. She lifted a little boy by his arm and ran, holding him suspended in the air, a look of terror on his face.

"If there's an accident, I will be a witness against you," Liam said.

"No one got hurt," Dunbar said. "You've nothing to testify to."

Liam pointed Dunbar down a side street to Sadie's boarding house. When they arrived, Liam climbed off the wagon and brushed his uniform clean. His thigh was tender where he had crashed back to the wagon bench. His face burned. He touched it and felt a scrape, not knowing how he'd gotten that.

Dunbar leapt down, seized Sweeney and wrenched him out of the bed.

Liam grabbed Dunbar's arm. The Scot froze and looked at the offending hand. He lifted an eyebrow.

"I am the law, Dunbar," Liam said. "You are not. He is my prisoner."

Dunbar shoved Sweeney, causing the prisoner to stumble backwards. Liam caught him before he fell, then he took Sweeney's elbow and pointed him towards the house.

They were half-way up the walk when the front door opened.

"What's this?" Sadie said. She seemed annoyed. If she had the second sight as people said, she should have known they were coming. Liam doubted she, or anyone else, had that ability. He suspected her reputation was built on a cunning knowledge of people's nature and a swagger that made her sound authoritative. Yet he did not challenge her. She was a respected member of the community and had never perpetuated a fraud or done anyone harm with her predictions.

Liam brought Sweeney to the bottom of the porch steps. With his height, Liam was still the taller of the two even with her standing on the porch, but with the stance she took, barring entry into her home, she was formidable.

She looked over his shoulder. He turned to see what had caught her attention. Dunbar was hanging back by the wagon.

"That's Malcom Dunbar," Liam said. "Cunningham's man."

Sadie grunted in response.

"Something has come up, Mrs. Monaghan. We found this man in the woods near where...," Liam paused to reframe his sentence. He didn't want to say they had visited the spot where Deirdre was murdered. It was too harsh a thing to say to her grieving mother, "where we were investigating this morning. His name is Owen Sweeney. It was he who found Deidre."

Sweeney's breath sped up.

"He is wearing a cross that looks familiar to me," Liam said, watching Sadie as he spoke. "I wondered if you have seen it before."

Sadie was stony-faced, her eyes shuttered as she stared over Liam's shoulder. "What's that, Liam? What did you say?"

"Do you recognize the necklace this man is wearing?"

She stepped off the porch and stood in front of Sweeney.

"It's hers," Sadie said in a defeated voice. "How did you come by my daughter's crucifex?"

"I found it in the woods, ma'am," Sweeney was no equal under the glare of a childless mother. He began to cry. "But I swear, that's all that happened. I found it. I never touched her, or any other girl, you can ask anyone."

Liam held out his open hand. "It's evidence now, Owen." Sweeney unhooked the necklace and dropped it in Liam's palm as Sadie watched. To Sadie, Liam said, "I need to keep this for the time being, but I'll return it to you. I swear."

"It's just a bit of gold," Sadie said. "It can't bring my daughter back. But I'll be glad to have it returned." She adjusted her head minutely to look over Liam's shoulder. "You're one of the Scots from the big house, are you? Where my Deidre worked?"

"Aye," Dunbar croaked.

"This would not have happened if she had a father looking out for her, the way a proper man should," Sadie said to him.

She stared at Dunbar. He said nothing in return.

Rose bushes flanked the porch. Sadie reached her hand to one of the shrubs and pinched a dead flower from its stalk, then tossed it onto the ground.

"I am a widow, Scotsman. I came to Adams to start a new life alone with no husband by my side and only an infant in my arms and I worked as hard as I could. You have no idea. Day and night. All I had was this house. Tending a colicky baby myself, walking the floors with her at night. As soon as she settled, I went back to scrubbing the kitchen for the next morning's breakfast. At times, not enough food for the boarders and myself, I was grateful I could put the babe to breast. At least she ate. Filthy working men staggering in drunk all hours of the day and night, thinking I was convenient to them, bursting into the room I shared with my little girl, expecting I would welcome their filthy urges in front of my daughter. There was no man to protect me. I protected myself."

Liam had never heard her speak like this before. She had always seemed so strong, fearless, and he never imagined she could have felt threatened. The color in Dunbar's face drained. He chewed on his mustache, transfixed in her stare.

"I did the best I could. But a child needs a father. And there was no father to tell her how men are." She spat on the ground and walked up the porch steps. Before she entered the house, she stopped and spoke to Liam. "It's her necklace. But this Irishman didn't kill my Deirdre. I know it. I can feel it. Go find the man who was responsible, Liam. Do it for my little girl who had no father to protect her."

Chapter Fifteen

Primogeniture

LIAM, SWEENEY, AND DUNBAR climbed back into the wagon. Dunbar directed the horse back to Columbia Street, heading out of town. He drove the horse at a trot.

When they arrived at the Pittsfield jail, Liam escorted Sweeney into a cell, unlocked his handcuffs, and walked out. Stanley slammed the cell door shut and turned the key. Dunbar hung back in the shadow of the hallway.

"Is he our man?" Stanley asked.

"I'm charging him with theft. He had Deirdre's cross." Liam handed him the necklace. "I'd like to see that get back to her mother after the case is over."

"He killed her for this bauble?"

"I never hurt her," Sweeney said, a wheedling note in his voice. "Why are you arresting me? I told you the truth. I found the cross."

Finn O'Brien, in the next cell, was on his feet. "What cross?"

"Never you mind," Stanley said to Finn. Liam gave Finn a cautioning frown.

"This man has been arrested for theft," Liam said. "He has Deidre's crucifex. Sadie identified it."

"I found it in the woods, I told you," Sweeney protested.

"Here's the thing, Sweeney," Stanley said. "You're the man who found the body."

"What?" Finn said.

Liam remembered the sight of Deidre on the undertaker's slab. Every time he closed his eyes, he saw that image. The blue cast to her face. How young she looked. There was no wound that would have been caused by a cross being ripped from her neck. Indeed, it could not have been if the chain was still intact. Sweeney hadn't taken the cross from her by force. She must have already been dead when he took it. His story of finding it in the woods sounded contrived.

Finn threw himself at the bars between the two cells. "You murdered my darling girl!"

Captain Stanley whacked Finn's cell door with his baton. "Not another word out of you!"

Sweeney was crying now. "I swear to you, I did not."

Dunbar, who Liam had forgotten about, grunted. He was standing in the threshold between the cell block and police station, gauzy sun lighting him from behind so that he was nothing but a blackened figure. For a moment, Liam thought he looked like a shade, as the old women described them, an otherworldly creature come to wreak havoc upon humans.

"One of ye did it," Dunbar said. "And I'd be happy to see ye both hang." The two prisoners grew still.

Stanley joined Dunbar and they walked through the threshold, disappearing into a flare of light.

After the door closed, Finn asked, "What's this about hanging? Have they found something? Hang me for what?"

"Neither of you are hanging just yet," Liam said. "No, Finn, there's nothing new. All we have is this necklace Sweeney says he found in the woods. Sweeney, we don't have enough to charge you with murder – yet. I don't know if you did it, but I won't see you hung on so little evidence. Trust me, I'll get to the bottom of this. But if I do find out you murdered Deidre Monaghan, I'll see to it you're prosecuted to the full extent of the law, do you understand?"

Sweeney nodded, slid down the wall, and rolled into a cocoon.

S TANLEY WANTED TO HIT someone. Barrett had showed him up again. First, he found O'Brien in his jail. Then before Stanley had a chance to charge him for the murder, Barrett found him an alibi. And then, Barrett arrested the tramp that Sweeney had in his wagon Sunday night. Stanley didn't see that cross and if he had, he'd known the tramp had stolen it. He stole it from the girl and then killed her, plain as day. And Barrett was getting all the glory.

Stanley left the police station, walking in long strides, kicking at the dusty earth as he went. Dunbar and Barrett would go back to Inverness together, leaving Stanley behind to babysit the prisoners while they drank brandy and smoked cigars. And that was another thing. It was Barrett riding beside Dunbar on the wagon, not Stanley. Barrett who reported to Cunningham, not Stanley.

With all distraction of the Adams girl's murder, Stanley had missed going to the racetrack Monday to collect his fee. He'd go now. With any luck at all, the trainer would have spent it all and Stanley could give him a licking for coming up short.

The walk was two miles in the hot sun. When he arrived at the track, he heard the cackling of half-grown boys coming from behind one of the barns. He found two kids bent over dice, shooting craps with the stable boy, their backs to Stanley when he rounded the corner. One of them jumped up from his crouch with a yelp, his fist held high, gripping money. It was easy enough to slip the bills out of his hand.

"Hey!" The kid whipped around. He was skinny and gawky, maybe fourteen years old, with shorn hair and green eyes. "That's mine!"

"Not anymore, boy. Gambling is illegal in Pittsfield."

"We're not in Pittsfield, the city line is a mile down the road," the kid said.

"Well, I'm the Pittsfield captain and I say there's no gambling."

The kid grabbed for the money. Stanley cuffed him on the ear, knocking him back against the barn wall, and set him yowling. The other two, the stable boy and some other kid Stanley didn't know, watched. They looked like they were going to piss their pants.

"Who are you brats? Shouldn't you be in school? There's a truancy law in Pittsfield. Maybe I'll run both of you in."

The second kid grabbed the yowler by the sleeve. "Come on, Kevin, let's get out of here." He pulled until they both broke into a run. Stanley didn't go after them. He didn't need to. He didn't want two kids rotting in his jail, what he wanted was someone to hit. To the stable boy, he said, "Where's your boss?"

❦

"**B**EFORE WE GO BACK to Inverness, there's something I need to check on," Liam said to Dunbar.

"Make it quick," Dunbar said as he climbed into the wagon. "I've work to do."

Liam found the coroner and the undertaker standing on the boardwalk, smoking cigars and watching the world go by. Small flies were making the most of their last days of summer, buzzing around piles of horse dung in the street, nipping at exposed flesh.

Liam had met the coroner before. Doctor Hawthorne was a portly man, but nearly as tall as Liam. He wore a fine suit with a gold watch and chain draped across his broad middle. One hand was shoved in a pocket as he chatted with the gaunt undertaker.

"Officer Barrett," the undertaker said. Doctor Hawthorne jiggled coins in his pocket and nodded.

"I've come about Deidre Monaghan," Liam said. "Is the examination finished?"

The expression on Dr. Hawthorne's face shifted. "You'd better step inside."

Liam followed the doctor into the undertaker's parlor. Despite the sunniness of the day, heavy drapes covered the windows. The acrid stink of chemicals floated on heavy air.

"When can I bring Deirdre home?"

"Tomorrow will be fine," Dr. Hawthorne said. He glanced at his shoes and cleared his throat. "Look here, Officer Barrett, did you know the girl well?"

"She was like a sister to me, a good friend to my family."

"Did she have a young fella, a suitor?"

"Indeed, why do you ask?"

"A responsible young man, would you say?"

There was no need to answer. Hawthorne was not curious about Finn, it was obvious. He was slowly preparing Liam for shocking news.

"She wasn't wearing a wedding band. I'm told she did not have a husband." The doctor cleared his throat, considered the polish of his shoes for a moment, then looked directly into Liam's eyes. "I'm afraid the young lady was in the family way. Three months gone, I'd say."

D RIVING BACK TO INVERNESS, Dunbar seemed more relaxed now that Sweeney was in jail. He allowed the horse to set the pace. He shifted a bit in his seat, leaned out of the wagon, and spit on the ground. He sat up again, facing the road. "Did you have a word with the coroner?"

"Doctor Hawthorne said he'd release the remains."

Liam didn't want to share the news of the pregnancy with Dunbar first, so that he would have time to spread the word. Liam wanted to tell Cunningham himself and see the expression on his face when he learned that not one, but two lives, had been cut short.

Dunbar dropped him off in front of the mansion's portico, then drove the horse and wagon to the barns. Mrs. Ramsey opened the massive front door. Upon seeing him, her face tightened into a mask. He stated his business. "I'm here to see Mr. Cunningham."

She made a low guttural sound and stared at him in silence for a few moments. "Follow me," she said, and led him to the morning room.

"I'll tell them you're here." She closed the double doors behind her as she left.

The room was bright. Shafts of gold-tinged light drifted across the ornate furnishings. The unfinished painting had a cloth draped over it and the tableau Victoria Cunningham had occupied was now vacant.

In some other part of the house, Liam could hear the clatter of dishes and occasional bark of Mrs. Ramsey's voice. The smell of warm meat grew stronger as he imagined dinner was being prepared.

This was the place where Deirdre Monaghan had met the father of her child, Liam had no doubt about it. She had been living here for months yet only stopped taking communion several weeks ago, about the time she became pregnant. He was certain that Finn had not been the father. As determined as she was to leave him, she would never risk being tied to him for the rest of her life because of a child. Nor did anyone else in Adams strike her fancy.

It had to be one of the men in Inverness. It was doubtful she would carry on with a working man, wanting to rid herself of the one she already had. No, it was far more likely she had taken up with someone more interesting, educated, monied. Someone like Alistair Cunningham himself, or his son, Edward, who Liam had yet to meet.

The strains of that sad ballad came back to him again. Rose Connolly had been murdered because she was carrying an unwanted child. The boy who killed her had not made her pregnant, his father had.

Outside, a few men bent to the task of planting shrubs and flowers. The grounds had progressed since he was first there. A patio had been constructed, covered in white tile and surrounded by heavy stone railings that opened on all three sides. Beyond the patio, an oblong rectangular pond had been constructed with a central fountain. Tall conical-shaped shrubs dotted the scene, leading the eye from one small garden to another, laid out on a precise geometric pattern. Liam imagined that wandering the garden would engender a peaceful continence in an otherwise troubled mind, if one had the luxury of wandering gardens. Yet the men laboring and sweating to create this retreat did not seem tranquil.

Liam found himself next to the painting. He carefully lifted the tarp from the easel with two fingers. The image of Victoria Cunningham's face glowed in the shadow of the cover.

"Get away from there," Mrs. Ramsey said sharply from somewhere near the door. "The painter will have your hide if he finds you disturbing his work."

"I didn't touch it." But he had wanted to.

"That's not what it looks like to me. Mr. Cunningham will see you now." With that, she disappeared into the hallway, her wooden heels clattering away, apparently confident that Liam would follow her.

And so he did. She led him back to the study he'd visited before. Cunningham sat in one of the large leather chairs near the fireplace, chugging on a newly lit cigar, with a book in his lap. Dunbar was standing in the window, watching the workmen.

"I hear you've arrested a tramp," Cunningham said, snapping the book shut. "But you haven't charged him for the murder. What is the delay? I told you I needed this crime solved in short order."

"We've only circumstantial evidence of the robbery," Liam said. "It's barely enough to hold him. A murder case wouldn't stand up to a judge or a jury on this evidence."

Cunningham squinted at Liam. "I don't want this Fenian character released for lack of evidence and him gadding about when the governor visits. And I can't let Victoria out of the house with danger in our midst. What kind of evidence do you need? What are you going to do to get it?"

Liam had enough. Tact was useless with the old man. "Did you want the right man charged or would any man do?"

Still by the window, Dunbar met Liam's eye. His hostile look was gone. It had been replaced by curiosity.

"Tread carefully, Constable," Cunningham said as he put his book aside. He pushed himself back in the chair. "What are you suggesting?"

"In the beginning, you insisted that Deidre's fiancé was responsible and since I was best acquainted with the people of Adams, I was dispatched to find him. But Finn had an alibi. Then your theory was a tramp in the woods had killed Deidre. And now you're pushing for charges against Sweeney on the thinnest of evidence. The question is, do you want the murderer apprehended, or do you want the case closed quickly?"

"The safety of my household is my first concern, Barrett. Need I remind you that a major event is to occur here this weekend? Do you understand the governor will be staying with us at Inverness. He is here to dedicate the new library site in Adams, the library I am building for your people, giving them free access to books, so they can educate themselves and improve their lot. I cannot have an unsolved murder clouding the festivities."

"Sweeney had no reason to hurt her," Liam said quietly. "But another man may have." Cunningham's pose collapsed ever so minutely. Dunbar's big mustache twitched, his eyes locked on Liam. Did that man ever blink?

"I need to interview the male householders," Liam said.

Cunningham forced a small laugh. "What's this about, man?"

"Your son Edward lives here as well?"

Dunbar's mustache twitched again.

There was nothing more to say, and nothing more was said, as the three of them stood considering each other. The ember of Cunningham's cigar had turned to ash. Dunbar cocked his head, his eyelids narrowed. They must have understood Liam's implication.

"There's been a development," Liam said.

It was then the French doors opened and three young men entered, the same rowdy gents Liam had quieted in the Black Rose the day before.

"Poppa!" one said, pretending that he was surprised to find Alistair Cunningham in his own study.

Cunningham shifted his attention. "Edward, I'm in a meeting."

"Sorry to bother, Poppa. We've been riding and thought a splash of brandy would be just the thing."

"Greetings lads," Cunningham said to the two men in Edward's company. "The brandy is on the sideboard. Help yourselves and then if you would excuse us, there are matters to be discussed."

"Of course, of course, sorry to have interrupted," Edward said mockingly, then he took notice of Liam and laughed.

"Mr. Lincoln," Liam said. "We meet again. And I see you have Secretary Seward and General Grant with you."

Cunningham frowned. "What's he talking about, Edward?"

"Oh, a little joke, really," Edward said with a laugh. "We met Officer Barrett in Adams yesterday." He swept his arm and bowed deeply. "I apologize, Officer. No harm done, am I right?"

"Perhaps introductions are in order, Edward," Cunningham said.

The young man patted his chest. "I am Edward Cunningham, scion of Alistair Cunningham, at your service, and these are my friends, Benjamin and Nathanial Mitchell. It is true that they are in the area looking for horses to purchase, and I am their host."

With that, the three young men sidled to the sidebar where Edward poured brandy into cut-glass snifters.

Alistair Cunningham struck a match on his thumbnail. "Have you any children, Barrett?"

Liam didn't answer. Cunningham already knew. He hinted as much when they first met. Why that was any of his business, Liam didn't know. But it was the second time he had brought it up. A threat, perhaps. Or was he making sure Liam understood that Cunningham knew more about him than the other way around. He had made himself rich not in the trade of goods or securities but ultimately in the exploitation of knowledge. Secrets, who was buying land and where, who was forming alliances with whom, were his stock in trade. What he knew or thought he knew about the Barrett family didn't matter. Liam had nothing to hide.

Cunningham puffed on the cigar, bringing the ember to life again. "A man would do anything to protect his children." He allowed a cloud of blue smoke to billow from his open mouth and squinted at Liam through the hazy curtain. "If you have something to say, Officer Barrett, then say it."

"Edward, did you know Deirdre Monaghan?"

The younger Cunningham's eyes flicked between his father and Dunbar. He shook his head and frowned, "Not quite sure, isn't she that scullery girl? Why do you ask?"

The leather beneath Alistair Cunningham's bulk squeaked as he crossed his legs. He flicked ashes in the direction of the fireplace. They fell short, settling on the stone hearth, which he pretended not to notice. This is a man who did not clean-up after himself. He had someone do it for him. He returned Liam's gaze.

Dunbar crossed the room, took a cigar from a large humidor on the mantle, and was now occupied with lighting it.

Liam looked at Edward. A sheen of sweat had developed across his face. "Are you saying you never had contact with the girl?"

"What are you playing at, Constable?" Cunningham interrupted. "Are you suggesting my son and this servant girl were intimate?"

Edward snickered. Liam spiked him a look, instantly silencing him.

"Mr. Cunningham, someone had. If not Edward, then who? Yourself?"

Cunningham snorted. "Surely, you jest. A servant girl at my age."

Liam faced Dunbar, "Was it you then?" Dunbar didn't answer. He had resumed his stance, one shoulder against the mantle, braced on one leg, the other crossed casually in front, but every muscle in his face and body was tense.

Liam turned to the young men. "Where were the three of you Sunday afternoon?"

Edward scoffed. "Why should it matter?"

"The girl is dead," Liam said.

"What?" Edward looked sick.

"Deirdre Monaghan was murdered Sunday afternoon in the woods not far from here."

Edward frowned at his father. "Why didn't you tell me?"

Cunningham shushed his son.

"So, again I ask you, Mr. Cunningham," Liam said to Edward, "Where were the three of you Sunday afternoon?"

A moment passed without answer. A light glinted in Alistair Cunningham's eyes, now locked on his son. Edward's boots scraped across the silk carpet as he shifted his weight.

Alistair Cunningham cleared his throat. "Edward was with me. As it happens, all three of us were here, in this very room, making plans for the gala Friday night. My son has a bright future in politics. Don't be surprised if you see him in Washington DC one day."

"When did you first arrive in the area?" Liam asked Edward.

"They rode in late Saturday night," Alistair said before Edward had a chance to answer. "We had some brandy and then the boys slept in Sunday, exhausted from their journey."

"Were you all three here all day Sunday?" Liam asked Edward.

"They were indeed," the older Cunningham answered. "Under my roof, all day long."

"Why did you not attend the races? Wasn't that the purpose of your visit?"

Again Alistair Cunningham answered for his son. "The lads were too tired, so they decided to wait until next week."

To Benjamin Mitchell, Liam said, "Have you been to Inverness before?"

Benjamin laughed and gave Edward an astonished look. "No."

"And yourself?" Liam said to his brother, Nathanial.

The younger Mitchell shook his head.

"I'd like to speak with you further, Mr. Edward."

Edward laughed again. "What about?"

"It's a sensitive matter."

"Edward, perhaps you could show your friends to their rooms?"

Benjamin Mitchell raised his hand. "No need, sir. We'll be on our way. You'll find us in the stable, Edward." Then he led his brother out the French doors again.

"Why all the mystery, Barrett? What's this about?" Cunningham asked. Liam was certain Cunningham understood why Liam was asking these questions. Dunbar did as well. But Edward seemed to be half a step behind them.

"I spoke with the coroner, Doctor Hawthorne. It seems Deidre Monaghan was expecting. Do you gentlemen have any idea who could have fathered her child?"

"What? What are you talking about? Was she going to have a baby?" Edward asked, the color leaching from his face. "But—"

Dunbar coughed, apparently a warning to Edward to hold his tongue. Edward gave a quick smile, then a shrug of his shoulders. "I don't know what this has to do with me."

Cunningham's face set into a grave expression. "So you want to know if one of us had taken advantage of the poor girl."

It had to be Edward. He was the right age for Deidre, the others too old for her taste. "I must ask, you understand."

"You're doing your duty and I'd expect no less," Alistair Cunningham said. "But I warn you again, be very careful where you tread. As for the suggestion, it is ridiculous. No doubt it was the Adams boy who sired her bastard, the one you let go. Edward, go and see to your guests."

Chapter Sixteen

A Day in Court

Dunbar showed Liam to the portico, wished him a nice walk back to Pittsfield, and went back inside, closing the heavy door again with unnecessary force.

Liam walked away from Inverness, lost in thought. After each of the men had denied fathering Deidre's child and claimed they were together on Sunday afternoon, Dunbar insisted his laborers were innocent as well. They had no interactions with Deidre, and further, they could not have killed her because they were in the bunkhouse, sleeping off hangovers when she died.

Liam remained unconvinced by the denials. He was certain Finn and Deirdre had not had relations. Deidre, working and living at Inverness six and one-half days a week, did not have an opportunity to meet any men other than those who lived or visited the estate. Edward was the mostly likely candidate, a rogue youth, one who had little concern for the consequences of his actions. Yet Dunbar, or Cunningham himself, could have easily seduced the girl with the lure of financial security and travel to exotic new places.

A fatherless girl, like Deidre, was susceptible to the attention of an older man, Liam only knew. On one of her visits, she had crept up on him mucking out the shed. When he looked up from his task, she seemed to have suddenly materialized in front of him. Aware of how he must have smelled, he took a step back so as not to offend her. She responded by taking one step forward, occupying the space he had vacated. "Are you afraid of me, Liam?"

She was barely sixteen years old. He was ten years older. Yes, he was afraid of her.

"Certainly not, child," Liam said. She wrinkled her nose when he said the word, *child*. "I'm merely concerned about your delicate sensibilities. Can you not see I'm covered in dung?"

"You smell of the earth," Deidre said, spinning slowly side to side, twirling her long skirt. "I like pigs. I like how they eat and sleep, how they couple right there in the open for anyone to see." She smiled. "I like how they make babies and how the little piglets suckle at their sleeping mother's tits."

"What a funny girl you are," Liam said, quickly side-stepping her. He went to the basin, worked the pump, and splashed his face with cold water. She followed him and was standing so close, water droplets were soaking into her skirt. He looked into the kitchen window, hoping to catch Kate's attention. She was watching. Liam frowned and jerked his chin toward Deidre, then ducked his face into a basin of cold water. He stayed under for as long as he could. When he came up for air, Kate was standing on the porch.

"Deirdre, I need more hands in the kitchen."

A look of disappointment flashed across Deirdre's face. "But..." she began.

"Hurry up now girl, the water's nearly boiling."

Deirdre gave Liam a side-long glance. One corner of her mouth was curled into a salacious smile. It disappeared so quickly, Liam thought he might have imagined it.

After that, he volunteered for Saturday patrol and left the mucking to Kevin.

He thought of all this and how difficult it had been not to notice that Deidre had grown into a young woman. Her hair was thick and full as she flipped it over her shoulders. Even under the cover of her dress, her budding young breasts had shocked him. Sadie was right. She had no father to teach her about men and no way to understand the wild urges she felt. If Sadie had said anything, she would have told Deirdre the same thing that generations of good Catholic Irish women had told their daughters: whores behaved like that, ladies did not, you shall speak of it no more.

At the undertaker's parlor, Dr. Hawthorne had assured him that there was no mistake, Deidre was with child. She was far along enough that she would have known. Soon anyone who looked at her would have known as well – had she lived. Whoever had fathered that child had done the deed three months earlier – when she was working at Inverness.

A horse's whinny caught Liam's attention. Victoria Cunningham was mounted upon a black stallion, holding back the reins as the horse danced from side to side, frustrated its run had been interrupted. She wore a dark red velvet jacket, a white bow tied at her throat, and a long black skirt. Her dark hair was pulled up under a cocky little hat. She seemed to be laughing at him. "Looking for breadcrumbs, Officer Barrett?"

The stallion spun in a circle. His nostrils flared and his front hooves stomped like a demon from the other world. Liam didn't like horses. Too much power and not enough compassion for mankind. "Pardon?"

"You were staring into the woods. I thought you may have become lost, like Hansel and Gretel, and that you were searching for your way home."

"Ah," Liam smiled, in an effort to be pleasant despite the threat of being pummeled to death. Perhaps the horse would understand that he wasn't a threat. "Not that, only occupied in thought. We were never properly introduced, Miss Cunningham. How do you know my name?"

At this she laughed. It was a musical sound the likes of which he never heard before. He wondered if she'd been taught that laugh in training to find a suitable marriage. "With all your comings and goings, how was I not to notice you?" She leaned forward in her saddle, then spoke *soto vocce*, "Mrs. Ramsey tells me everything, you know."

"Everything?"

"Why certainly! You're investigating the poor scullery maid's death. Yes, I can see by the look on your face that I'm right. And, that's not all I know. The poor girl was pregnant and you think my brother took advantage of her. You practically accused him!" She shook her head theatrically. "Not quite sure you're on the right track, Officer Barrett."

How could she possibly know that, Liam wondered. He'd barely left the mansion. "How do you know I spoke to your brother?"

"Mrs. Ramsey listens at doors."

"That conversation was barely half an hour ago."

"I was on my way out. Goliath was already saddled and he's badly in need of a run, as you can see."

The horse was stomping his front legs. Liam didn't take a step backwards, as much as he wanted to, because he did not want to show fear in front of this woman. At the same time, he was baffled about why her opinion of him mattered. He'd sort that out later.

"Does your father know you left the mansion?"

"Poppa? As if he could stop me."

"Are you not worried, a young woman alone in the woods?"

"How silly!" Again, the chime-like laugh. "Goliath is faster than anyone or anything. And I have my whip." She flicked the nasty looking thing in her palm.

Suddenly Felix Malone's comment made sense to him. Malone had assumed Deirdre had been promoted to upstairs maid. Yet the others still referred to her as a scullery maid. Malone must have been told that Deidre was seen in the family's private quarters.

"You think it's unlikely that Edward could have fathered Deidre's child? She had been seen on the second floor, Miss Cunningham. Is that not where the family bedrooms are located?"

"Indeed. And above the kitchen would be strange for a scullery maid to be...unless she was on a personal errand. But Edward is not the only man with a bedroom on that floor, Officer Barrett."

"Go on."

"My father has a room there too. A man is a man, after all, and she was an attractive girl. I understand you knew her?"

"I've known her since she was a child but I didn't notice her looks," Liam lied.

"Of course not," she laughed again and the horse circled. "Not only that, I saw Malcom Dunbar talking to her in the kitchen garden last week." She dropped her voice again. "It looked serious."

"Did you hear their words?"

She shook her head. "I wasn't that close."

The horse had a savage glint in his eye, as if he was planning murder.

"And I'm in your way," Liam said, stepping aside.

"You're in Goliath's way," Victoria said. "I, however, am pleased to see you again." With that, she flicked the reins. The front hooves of the beast reached into the air level with Liam's head, then he stretched himself out and leapt, galloping away with Victoria seated so snuggly upon his back, it seemed that she and the horse were one.

B EFORE CATCHING THE TRAIN back to Adams, Liam stopped at the Pittsfield courthouse. He wanted to find Finn O'Brien and bring him back home. The judge would convict him of disorderly conduct, give him time served, and let him go. There was no reason to keep a now sobered-up man from going to work.

His Honor wasn't on his bench yet. A couple of anxious farmers sat on opposite sides of a pew glowering at one another. Probably another wandering bull at the heart of their dispute. One thinks the other stole it. The other thinks the first encourages the bull to graze on his land for free. The real issue was who owned the calves it had sired.

A courtroom always brought church to mind. The pageantry. The solemnity. Ripe with expectation. People lined up in pews, dressed in their best, praying something monumental would occur and they wanted to soak up their bit of grace or justice. Their absolute faith that divine intervention was attainable, even if some declaimed they didn't get enough, unified them into neat rows, hushed and staring forward.

God hadn't been fair to Liam, or to his family. After he quit the church, he found a new religion: justice. Where God cheated people, Liam did his best to right the wrong. He couldn't restore a stolen life, but he could hold a wrongdoer accountable.

The jury box, where prisoners were sat, was empty. Stanley had not brought Finn to the courthouse yet. He would be waiting in his cell. Liam could catch him in private to ask him about Deidre's condition.

As Liam opened the police station door, he heard the unmistakable sound of brawling coming from the cell block. The desk was empty and the hallway door was open. Liam strode towards the noise, expecting he would need to help Stanley subdue a violent prisoner.

But what he found was Stanley bashing Finn's face into the bars. Finn's hands were cuffed. The desk sergeant was watching with a smirk on his face. Sweeney was in the hall, cuffed, and shackled, ready to be transported.

"Let go of him!" Liam yelled, pushing the sergeant aside. He grabbed Stanley's shoulder and spun him around.

Stanley, still holding onto Finn with one hand, threw Liam off with the other, slamming him into a brick wall. Stanley tossed Finn across the cell, where he crumpled to the floor. "The prisoner doesn't want to go to court."

Liam stepped in between Stanley and Finn. "Stop it, right now. I'll…"

Stanley slammed both hands onto Liam's shoulders and tossed him aside. He jerked Finn off the floor and shoved him out the cell. The sergeant stepped out of the way and let Finn crash into the wall. Stanley spun on Liam. "You'll what?"

Liam had stumbled into the cot. He pulled himself to a stand. "I'm charging you with assault, Captain Stanley."

"You just do that, Officer Barrett." As Stanley pinned Finn to the wall, the sergeant slapped irons around his ankles. Stanley opened the back door. "Get a move on, prisoners."

Sweeney shuffled outside first, blinking in the sunlight, and held his arms up to shade his eyes. Finn staggered into the alley and fell into Sweeney, his eyes swollen so much he couldn't see. Liam followed them out into the alley and next door to the courthouse. The sergeant unlocked the courthouse back door. Stanley shoved the prisoners into the building and the sergeant pulled the door closed behind them. Liam pulled on the handle. It was unmovable, locked.

Liam stared at the door, his head spinning with what had happened. He'd never seen someone abuse a prisoner like that. Not Captain Curran, and certainly not Liam. Stanley belonged in jail. At the very least, he should lose his job.

Liam strode to the courthouse's front door and jerked it open so hard that it slammed against the building. Inside, he found the pews had filled. With only one judge hearing every matter on the calendar, civil and criminal, a variety of citizens had crammed into the courtroom. The two farmers Liam had seen earlier were standing next to the railing, hoping to be called first.

Sweeney and Finn were sitting in the jury box with Stanley standing a few feet away. Finn flinched every time Stanley moved. The desk sergeant was planted in front of the door he had closed on Liam, arms crossed.

The judge entered from a side door. He leaned heavily on a cane and was helped up the few steps to the bench by his bailiff. It was old Judge Nathan Trimbley. Behind his back, lawyers called him Old Trembling because of his shaking hands. Liam had once overheard a lawyer say that appearing before Old Trembling after lunch was hell. His gut always gave him problems after a meal. Short tempered, he leapt to conclusions first and then justified his decisions. Sympathies and loyalties drove him, rather than truth and fairness.

Liam pushed past the farmers.

"Hey now, I was here first," one farmer said.

"You weren't, I was," the other said.

"Police business," Liam said. "Sorry, lads, you'll have to wait." They eyed him, his uniform and badge, and grumbled. He took position, standing at a counsel table, the supplicants behind the bar, leaning forward, hoping to be called. But no one was getting heard before Liam was.

This is where Liam's destiny had lain before his father died. He would have come to court wearing a suit instead of a uniform. He would have argued cases on behalf of clients, winning justice for them, or at the very least, fighting for it.

"Your Honor," Liam said.

"Officer Barrett, I did not see your name on the docket. To what do we owe the pleasure?"

"I am filing charges against George Washington Stanley for assault." Out of the corner of his eye, Liam saw Stanley swell as if he was preparing to fight. But he was rigid too, afraid.

Judge Trimble pushed his small round glasses to his forehead and rubbed his eyes. The chatter in the room stopped. The judge took an extra moment to pinch the bridge of his nose, then slowly lowered his glasses into place, and folded his hands on the bench. "Whom do you allege he assaulted, Officer Barrett?"

"His prisoner, Finn O'Brien." Liam swept his hand in their direction. "Look at the man. He's barely conscious."

Finn was leaning against Sweeney, his head lolling. A thread of bloody drool spilled from his mouth.

"This is a serious charge, Officer Barrett. Captain Stanley is a sworn peace officer and has appeared in my court many times. Many times. Have you a witness?"

"Myself."

With a boney finger, the judge motioned for Stanley to move in front of the bench. Stanley did so, and struck a stance, legs spread apart, hands clasped behind his back. He was playing soldier.

"Captain Stanley, Officer Barrett has accused you of assaulting a prisoner without provocation. How do you respond?"

"What does 'provocation' mean?"

The bailiff cleared his throat.

"Your Honor," Stanley added.

" 'Provocation' means that you had a reason to use force. If, say, you were attacked first, then you were defending yourself and you could not be guilty of this charge. Self-defense is an absolute defense against the charge of assault."

Stanley thought for a long moment, then said, "I don't know what the right answer is."

Jesus wept. Trimbley was leading Stanley like a tethered dog. How much more did he need?

A sour expression crossed Old Trimbley's face. "What is the prisoner charged with?"

"Disorderly conduct," Stanley said. "He got drunk at the races and started a fight."

"A violent drunk, then. Did you have trouble arresting him?"

The judge was leading Stanley again. A child would know how to give the desired answer.

"Your Honor!" Liam said.

Trimbley held up his hand. "You've had your say. Now let Captain Stanley explain the facts and circumstances."

Stanley had finally picked up the judge's hint. "We had a terrible time arresting him. Took me and a couple of other men to hold him down long enough to get him cuffed. Scrappy son-of-a-bitch."

"Stanley!"

"Sorry, meant no disrespect." A moment passed. "Your Honor."

"The scuffle at the races must be how he got those facial injuries," Trimbley said. "Am I right?"

Finn was bleeding from his nose and mouth. Fresh blood.

"Your Honor!" Liam said.

"Officer Barrett, you'll speak when you're spoken to and not before. So, Captain Stanley, Officer Barrett claims to have observed some sort of brouhaha at the jail before you brought this violent prisoner to court. Tell me what happened."

"This prisoner was scheduled for the docket and he refused to leave the cell. When I went inside to cuff him, he attacked me."

The judge gave a wry smile. "I see. Do you have a witness, Captain Stanley?"

"Briggs, my sergeant."

"Is he with you in this courtroom today?"

"Here, Your Honor." The desk sergeant, still guarding the back door, raised his arm. "It's as the Captain said. The prisoner attacked him. I was standing right there and I saw it all."

"I have a good picture of the events." Judge Trimbley faced Liam. "How do you respond to this evidence?"

Liam knew where the matter was going. Old Trimbley was relying on Liam's honesty to destroy his case. He hadn't been there when the fight started. He didn't see who threw the first punch. Even if Finn had resisted, beating him to this extent was an overreaction. Stanley was going to get away with it, but before he did, Liam was going to have his say. Sometimes fighting was the right thing to do even if loss was inevitable.

Liam glanced at the prisoners. Finn seemed unconscious. Sweeney was scared. He have seen the whole thing. He was being arraigned today too but he wouldn't be released because of the seriousness of his charges. The judge would order a bail that was too high for him to make and he would stay in jail until the next time the judge came to town. Meanwhile, he was vulnerable to Stanley's brutality. If Liam asked him to testify, and if he testified as Liam expected, saying that Finn hadn't provoked Stanley, he would suffer the same fate. He'd be lucky to live long enough to stand trial. If he lied to protect himself from Stanley's wrath, Finn would be no worse off than he was now. It wasn't fair to ask Sweeney to take the risk when it wouldn't help Finn's case if he did.

Liam spoke. "Your Honor, I witnessed Stanley beating Finn, who was already handcuffed. I didn't see the fight start. That is true. But the prisoner was cuffed. Stanley could easily have controlled him. There was no reason to beat him."

"You admit you didn't see the fight start?"

"Finn O'Brien is a peaceful man. He would have never attacked a police officer. Or anyone for that matter."

The judge flipped through papers laying before him on the bench. "Yet he was arrested for doing that very thing at the races last Sunday."

"Yes, Judge," Stanley shouted more loudly than was necessary.

"I see," the judge said. "Having considered the charges and testimony of Officer Barrett, the not guilty plea of Captain Stanley and the testimony of his witness, the sergeant, I hereby dismiss the charges Officer Barrett lodged. And I warn you, Barrett, you need to be careful in the future about bringing spurious charges against a fellow law officer. Your credibility as a law enforcement officer is at risk."

Liam had known he'd lose but he was stunned anyway. What Stanley had done was wrong.

"You're dismissed, Barrett," the judge said. "Next case."

Liam remained standing at the counsel table.

"You're dismissed, Officer. Make room."

"I have another case on the docket, Your Honor."

"Very well. Stand aside while the real lawyers have their say."

Liam stepped next to the jury box while two besuited men walked up to the counsel tables and opened their briefcases.

A court clerk read from his list, "Pittsfield versus Finn O'Brien."

"Officer Barrett's friend?" Trimbley asked.

"Yes, Your Honor," Stanley said. "Drunk and disorderly at the races on Sunday."

"Anyone injured?"

"Himself, that's all."

"Any damages?"

"None."

"Time served," Judge Trimbley said. "You're free to go, O'Brien."

Briggs, the sergeant, unlocked Finn's chains as the bailiff called Sweeney's case. He was charged with robbery of Deirdre's necklace. As Liam expected, the arraignment was over quickly and he was held for trial. Briggs pushed Finn out of the jury box and Liam caught him.

"What's going on?" Finn mumbled through swollen lips.

Liam wrapped an arm around his shoulder, moving him to walk through the people lining the walls. "We're going home," he said. He looked over Finn's head to Sweeney. "I'll be back, Owen."

Owen Sweeney's eyebrows rose doubtfully.

"I promise."

CHAPTER SEVENTEEN

A MOTHER ALWAYS KNOWS

A T THE STATION, LIAM found a bench for Finn to sit on while they waited for the next train. The damage to Finn's face was worse than before. Both eyes blackened, a nose that bled off and on, reddened welts where he had been slammed into cell bars, bruises darkening and scrapes scabbing. People stayed well away from both of them.

Liam let Finn doze until the train came, then helped him up the steps and into a carriage. There were few passengers, two women who sat as far away from Liam and Finn as they could. Finn stared out the window, deep in his own thoughts, then wiped his eyes.

"What set Stanley off back there in the jail?" Liam asked.

Finn blinked a few times, pulling himself out of his reverie. "He said I'd made him look like a fool, hiding in his jail. I wasn't hiding, Liam, honest. No one asked my name that I remember. They kept call me 'Paddy'. The longer he talked, the madder he got. Honest, Liam, I didn't do anything. He put the handcuffs on and the next thing I know, he's whaling away at me. I didn't start anything, believe me."

Liam wasn't surprised. Stanley was a bully. He was the kind of man who beat women, children, and disabled men. "I believe you."

"Have you found out who killed my Deirdre?"

"Still working on it, Finn. There's a lot to sort out."

"You think that Sweeney fella did it? The one who stole her cross?"

"I don't know. He says he didn't."

"Well that's what he would say, wouldn't he?"

"He doesn't strike me as a man who'd kill a girl he'd never met. An insane man might, but I spoke to him long enough to know he has sound mind. I can't see him striking a woman at all."

"Then why did he have her cross?"

"He says he found it. Sure, if you saw something gold laying in the woods, you wouldn't leave it there, would you?"

Finn returned his gaze to the window, not answering.

Liam had talked to the Inverness men and he was fairly sure they were all lying. Edward behaved the most suspiciously. Most likely, it was he who seduced Deirdre with flowers and poetry about noblemen falling in love with beautiful shepherding lasses. Still, he had to be sure.

"I have a difficult question," Liam said.

"What's that?" Finn asked. Liam could see Finn's reflection in the glass. Tears streamed down his face. He wiped his nose with his palm, then rubbed his hand on his trouser leg.

"It's about you and Deidre."

Liam remembered that Finn had taken communion but Deidre had not. No Catholic would have taken communion if he, or she, had broken the seventh commandment unless he, or she, had received absolution.

"You took communion Sunday, is that right?"

"I did."

"And you went to confession on Saturday."

"I did. What does this have to do with my lovely Deirdre?"

"You don't have to answer this next question. Is it possible that you were absolved for something that happened with Deidre but she hadn't gone to confession and that's why she didn't take communion?"

"What are you getting at?" Finn was beginning to look suspicious.

"I'm sorry, Finn, I have to ask. Did you and Deidre engage in marital relations? You wouldn't be the first couple who hadn't waited. You were going to be married, anyway."

"What do you mean? You mean me and Deidre? You want to know if we...?" Finn's suspicion flared into anger. "What do you think I am? What do you think she was? I don't believe you're asking these questions. She was a friend of yours, your family. How many times did she go to your house to help with your mam? She was nothing but kind and now she's dead. I would have never."

"She was going to have a baby, Finn."

Finn stopped talking. He seemed to have stopped breathing too. He gazed out the window for a long time as the trees and hills rolled by. Liam sensed movement in the aisle. The conductor had entered the car and was making his way to the back of the train.

"Oh my poor beautiful girl," Finn said. "It wasn't me, Liam. I swear to our heavenly mother, it wasn't me."

Two lives snuffed out. Had Deidre lived, there would have been a baby for Sadie to coo over. Deidre would have settled down, moved back home with her mother, married Finn. Liam pictured Sadie chasing a giggling toddler through sheets drying on the line, Deidre with a baby on her hip and another tugging at her skirt, a houseful of grandchildren for Sadie to dote upon. But that was not to be.

Liam cocked his head to one side, watching Finn, waiting for his story to shift. When confronted with facts, the guilty would try to weave the evidence into their story. Even an inept liar knew that abandoning the first story was an admission of telling falsehood. No one lied if they were innocent but the question was, what were they hiding? Finn may not be the greatest thinker who'd ever come to Adams, but even Finn O'Brien would know that an unplanned pregnancy would be cause for heated argument that could end in violence. Liam only had the word of Felix Malone giving him an alibi.

If Finn hadn't fathered the child, someone else had. Had Deirdre been carrying on with someone no one knew about? Or had someone forced himself upon her, someone from Inverness. It was Edward, one way or another. Certainly, her pregnancy would explain her mood change, the sullenness, her temper.

"Do you have any idea – ," Liam begun.

Tears were pouring down Finn's face now. "Must have been someone at the big house. She's there six and a half days a week. They'd let her go long enough to take the last train to Adams Saturday night so she could go to mass, have breakfast with her mother, and come home again. Who could have –," Finn couldn't finish the question.

It would have been cruel to speculate in front of Finn, so Liam held his tongue. Yet those were the same questions rolling in Liam's mind: who fathered the baby, was she in love, had she planned to marry another, could she have been secretly married, did someone force himself upon Deidre, why hadn't she told her mother, why hadn't she told Finn, what had she planned to do.

Secrets and intrigue were not the Deidre Liam knew. The only secret Deidre had ever kept was a bundle of wildflowers behind her back, a present for Liam's mother. She was the perfect loving child, something that had gone missing in their own family. Their da gone, the mother drifted away. Kate, too young for such a burden, took over not only the household but minding her own mother as well. The long hours and toil sometimes made her shrewish. Liam worked until he dropped, with only the occasional moment to observe his family. Kevin was growing into an angry young man. Clare was remote, finding solace in prayer and the occasional jab at Kevin.

Then Deidre became a fixture in their family. They'd known her all her life, growing up only a few streets away, but until that day when she brought the mother home, she was just another child in the pack that ran around Adams.

On her weekly visits, she came only to shine some light into their lives. Liam could see her even now, a book on her lap, and a light coming from her face. Deidre Monaghan had become the heart of the Barrett family.

Her murderer must be found. For Deidre, her baby, Sadie, Finn, the Barretts and himself. There would be a great hole in the lives with her gone, an inexplicable gash in the life they had built in Adams. Sense must be made of it. Justice must be done.

FRANK HELD THE DOOR as Liam and Finn crossed the threshold into Sadie's boarding house. "Good evening, lads."

"Good evening, Father," Finn said. He dipped his hand in the holy water font by the door and blessed himself. Liam had forgotten it was there. Frank closed the door as Liam walked in and pointedly watched him slide by the font without dipping his hand.

"Mind the door," Liam said. "Sadie won't thank you for letting the hot air out."

The house smelled of roasted chicken and potatoes. Liam suddenly realized he was hungry, having not eaten since early that morning. So much had happened since then. The arrest of Sweeney. The trip back to Adams where Sadie had identified Deirdre's crucifix. Learning from the coroner that Deirdre was with child. Confronting the men at Inverness. Victoria nearly running him down on that demonic horse. Her suggestion that her own father may have dishonored Deirdre. Finn O'Brien's adamant denial that the child was his.

"Who's letting the hot air out?" Sadie asked as she rounded into the parlor from the kitchen, wiping her hands on her apron.

"It was myself," Frank said. "I'll be more careful next time."

"Oh, well then," Sadie said. "No harm done." If it had been Liam, he'd had gotten a clout on the head. Frank gave him a clandestine wink as she turned away.

"Finn, my boy, what have they done to you?"

"It's nothing. I'm fine."

"You most certainly are not. Liam, did you see the state of him? This boy is as thin as a rail. Did they feed you at all? Come along, lads, I'm about to put dinner on."

Sadie looked like she was back to business, none of the tides of grief he'd seen only the day before. A woman who toiled all her life, she would find solace in work. No doubt she had shooed the other ladies out, reminding them their own broods needed attention. But she would have sorted the dishes they would bring to the wake before closing the door behind them.

"Perhaps you'd like to sit down, Mrs. Monaghan," Liam said. "We need to talk"

She seemed to consider it, then shuffled into the parlor, sitting slowly on the edge of the horsehair sofa. Liam took a chair opposite.

"I have some bad news," Liam said. "I'm sorry to have to tell you this."

"Spit it out, Liam. What could possibly be worse?"

"The coroner believes Deidre was with child."

Finn came forward and fell to his knees before Sadie. "It wasn't me. I swear it. But I'd have done right, I'd have made an honest woman of her."

"Poor lad," Sadie said. "Poor, poor lad. I know you would have."

"You're not surprised," Liam said. "Had she told you?"

"A mother always knows," Sadie said. "A girl can't hide a thing like that from her mother. That glow. It was like someone had stoked a fire in her soul – it shone that bright. It made her look....holy." Quickly she added, "I understand, Father, under the circumstances, it's sacrilegious to say so, but that's how my little girl looked to me. Pure."

Liam had no idea what she was talking about. Eileen Hogan, Gillespie, was with child now, but she had always looked holy to him. He wouldn't have known there was a baby until his sister Kate pointed out her swollen waistline. It made Liam sick to think about Tom's child growing inside her.

Maybe Sadie had the second sight after all.

"It had to be one of those Scots who took advantage of her. I would not have approved so she wouldn't have told me. No sir, I would not have approved. Did she think the bastard who did this would marry her? If she did, she had another thing coming."

Indeed she did.

"When will they release my little girl?" Sadie asked.

"Tomorrow, Mrs. Monaghan."

"YOU SAID YOU WERE out of beer," Liam said when Harry set a foaming mug down in front of Frank. The three were alone in the bar.

"Whisa, I held this back from that Pittsfield gobshite. I'll be bollixed if I serve the last of my beer to the likes of him, a chara. Hold on, I'll be back with your tea."

Father Frank took a long draft and set the mug down on the table. "A bairn, are you sure?"

"I have no reason to question Doctor Hawthorne. He said it would have been obvious soon."

Harry returned with a cup of tea and set that in front of Liam. "The coroner. You cannot be serious. Deirdre? She was having a baby? Does Finn know?"

"I told him. He had no idea. He wasn't the father."

"Do you think someone at Inverness beguiled her, as Sadie said?" Frank asked.

"I'm leaning towards the son, Edward Cunningham. He was distressed to learn about the baby, but the other two, his father and Dunbar, were not."

Harry took Frank's empty mug and doused it in a bucket of suds. "Who's Edward Cunningham?"

"He's one of those young gents who was here Monday."

"Said they were horse breeders?"

"Those are the ones."

"Ah, Liam, none of those fellas looked to be her type. They're useless, rich men's boys throwing around the family money. She was a more sensible girl than that, our Deirdre."

"I found a silhouette portrait hidden in her room of a young man. It could have been Edward Cunningham. The housekeeper claimed it was some distant cousin and that Deirdre had stolen it."

"Deirdre never stole a thing in her life," Harry scoffed.

"A gift, I'd wager. And then there was the poetry book she'd hidden at Sadie's. John Keats."

"Shepherd boys, Greek goddesses, and such like?"

"Just so."

"Bah, they call that poetry. Those people have no gift for the language and it was theirs to start with. But I tell you what," Harry slammed his open hand down on the bar top, "I can see one of those gits reading that rubbish to a young girl like Deirdre, beguiling her, as you say, Father."

Liam remembered his own experience with Deidre, how she wielded her allure, the power of which she couldn't possibly understand, and her fascination with the exotic. She would have easily been impressed with a few lines of idyllic love. "I can't be sure. It could have been him or it could have been someone else at Inverness."

"What about Felix Malone?" Frank asked.

Harry laughed. "Felix? Poetry? Can he read?"

Felix was drinking again after years of having sworn off, guilt ridden by Deirdre's death. He felt responsible for bringing her to Inverness. He didn't seem the likely candidate for romancing a girl young enough to be his daughter.

Liam shook his head. "He loved Deidre, in his own way. And, he was free to marry. If she was carrying his child, surely he would have known. He would have married her the instant he'd learned of the baby."

"Liam," Harry interjected. "I've known Felix Malone all my life, as have you, and I can swear to you that he wouldn't take advantage of a child like Deidre."

"I didn't say that he would. Besides, Malone was at the races that afternoon with Cunningham's horses. Felix Malone has the strongest alibi of them all."

"Sometimes people lie for their friends," Frank said, "believing they couldn't have done the evil deed."

"Nah, Father, you can't be serious," Harry said. "I don't like how this murder is making us turn on our friends. You're the most suspicious priest I've ever met."

"We're men like everyone else, Harry."

"What's that mean, Frank?" Liam asked, thinking about his sister Kate, her fascination with Frank, and the old priest O'Brien who spent too much time giving lessons to altar boys.

"It means we have eyes and ears, minds and hearts, like everyone else. What did you think it means?"

Harry cleared his throat. He, too, knew the story about the old priest O'Brien. Most everyone in Adams did. "A chara, if it wasn't Finn O'Brien and it wasn't Felix Malone who took advantage of Deirdre, then it's got to be one of those filthy bastards at the big house who did and killed her to cover up his sin."

"Stanley doesn't think so. He's in a big hurry to charge Owen Sweeney, the man who found her body. Stanley's convinced that Sweeney killed her so he could steal the cross or trying to have his way and took the cross afterwards. He has no alibi."

"Is Sweeney from the Old Sod?"

"Just off the boat. Took off walking, looking for work so he could send money back home to his ma."

"Do you think he took the cross from her?" Frank asked.

"If he found her dead already and saw something valuable like that, he may have taken it, thinking she wouldn't need it anymore. I can't see someone wear it if they killed for it. More likely he'd hide it as a keepsake."

"Did he –," Harry started.

"She wasn't ravaged. The coroner confirms it. No signs of a fight. It seems as if whoever killed her snuck up on her and bludgeoned her with a rock."

"Could it have been some other kind of weapon? A club or a brick?"

Liam remembered the half-moon shaped hooves of Victoria Cunningham's stallion clawing at the air. If a horse had run her down, there would have been other wounds. And the damage to her skull would have been much more severe. "Perhaps, but there is no one who carries a club and no bricks were around."

"So of all the men at Inverness, Cunningham, Edward, Dunbar, who do you think is the most likely suspect?" Frank asked.

"Most likely suspect of what?" Liam asked. "Despoiler or murderer? It's a mistake this early to think the two are one in the same."

"Either," Frank said, shrugging. "Both."

"Deidre had no father. She was attracted to older men. A girl like that would be vulnerable to a man who represented financial freedom and sophistication. That puts Alister Cunningham squarely in the box. His own daughter thinks there was something going on between the old man and Deirdre. If he used her, I cannot see him killing her. He's built an empire, and violence was used no doubt, but he wouldn't sully himself. He has more finesse than that. No, he would encourage her to give the baby up for adoption, maybe suggest she go away for a while and then promise her some kind of reward when it was over. Or even set her up in a dress shop like she dreamt about, somewhere far from here, and let her pass herself off as a widow."

Liam warmed to the subject. "Dunbar, however, has a short fuse. She might have been attracted to him. He's powerful in a more primitive way. Some women like that. And Victoria said she saw them having a serious conversation in the kitchen garden. He has a bedroom on the second floor, where she had been seen according to Felix Malone. But why would he kill her? He could have married her. Dunbar might enjoy having a young wife even if she was Catholic. We're a long way from Ireland or Scotland. Things are different here."

"What about Edward?"

"Young, handsome, impetuous, a great admirer of himself. He'd be more likely to pursue her than the others would with no thought as to the consequences. His father has plans for him, big plans. He couldn't be saddled with a Catholic wife, a scullery maid at that, who was clearly expecting before they married. The scandal would destroy his future."

"It would be alright for Dunbar but not for Edward to marry her?" Frank asked.

"Oh, Father, you're just off the boat yourself," Harry said. "There's no room amongst the rich and powerful for a man with an Irish Catholic wife. Down here, where the common folk live, some care but not enough to stop a determined man."

"He could always work for his father," Frank said.

"But that's not what Alistair wants," Liam said. "He's using Edward to expand his influence. He's trying to line Edward up for a post in the government, to enter the inner sanctum of the powerful – the heart of which Alistair could never breach because he is an immigrant. Say what you will, Alistair Cunningham is smart and hard-working. He built an empire and a palace, lined his shelves with books, recites poetry. But he isn't quite accepted by the old money types as he so badly wants."

"He'll never rid himself of that accent," Frank said.

Harry laughed. "Have you ever met a Scot that would? They're fiercely loyal from whence they came. And that's the very thing that is scares those native-born Americans in the halls of power. They're afraid he'll steal everything they have. All they see is a predator. Well-dressed and educated, but a predator. But here's the question, Liam: do you really think that foppish boyo has what it takes to kill someone?"

Edward was spoiled. If Deirdre made demands of him, he could have lashed out at her in anger. And his alibi was weak. "Cunningham senior, Dunbar, and Edward all claimed they were together at Inverness when she died," Liam said. "But they're lying."

"Aye, but where's the proof?" Harry asked. "If you're coming up against the likes of Alistair Cunningham, you'd better be armed."

Chapter Eighteen

An Unwelcomed Guest

"W̲H̲A̲T̲ B̲R̲I̲N̲G̲S̲ Y̲O̲U̲ H̲E̲R̲E̲, Stanley?" Cunningham asked.

The crone had told him to go around to the back, that was where he'd find the old man. Cunningham was standing near a fountain, smoking a cigar, gazing at the mansion.

Stanley rubbed the bruises on his right hand, gotten when he drove his fist into the horse trainer's face. "I heard something, Mr. Cunningham. Something I thought you'd want to know right away."

He didn't want to blurt out his news all at once. He wanted to savor it, make the big man ask for it.

"Get on with it, Stanley. What is it?"

"Liam Barrett, that Adams cop who's working for you."

"He's not working for me, lad, but I know who you mean."

Stanley was confused. He worked for Cunningham. Barrett was getting the jobs he should have. Barrett must be working for Cunningham too.

"His uncle is a Molly Maguire."

Cunningham flicked an ash from his cigar. He wasn't impressed with the news. "And you know this how?"

"Old Felix Maguire let it slip."

"What's your thinking?"

"If the uncle is a rabble-rouser, maybe the nephew is too. I thought you'd want to know who was working for you."

Stanley felt like the earth was crumbling beneath his feet. He'd brought a choice bit of news to the old man which should have proven his value, his ability to find out secrets and his loyalty in reporting them. Now told, not only was the old man not impressed but Stanley had lost his advantage.

"He doesn't work for me, I told you that." Cunningham tried to puff on his cigar but it had gone out. "What, if any, is the relationship between Liam and Joe Hogan, the storekeeper? Have you found anything that links them?"

"Barrett was sweethearts with Hogan's daughter."

"Joe Hogan is a problem. I have long suspected that he was involved with the Mollys. It's too convenient, his little store. His wagons going in and out of Adams for supplies. Guns could come and go through there and no one would be the wiser."

"You think they're planning something for the dedication? A riot?"

"They very well could be, with old Joe Hogan in the thick of it. Here I'm trying to improve their lives, their minds, by giving them a library filled with books. And I'm bringing the governor to visit their little hamlet. That's no way to repay my generosity, is it, Stanley?"

"No, sir, it is not."

"Hogan is building a new warehouse. That's where they would be hiding their arms, don't you think, Stanley?"

"Yes, sir, I do."

Cunningham examined the blackened butt of his cigar. He pulled a match from his pocket, struck it on the fountain's stonework and it flared to life. He put the cigar in his mouth, tilted his head, and held the flame beneath the tip as he puffed until the ember glowed again. He held the burning match aloft.

"Behold fire, Captain Stanley. It gives us light and warmth. Turns water into steam to power our engines. Cooks our food. And, yet, unharnessed, it has the power to destroy. Do you know your history, Stanley? They say Nero fiddled while Rome burned. The city was destroyed. London too, in 1666, gutted by fire. Yes, Captain Stanley, fire can be a terrible thing."

With that, the Scot spit on two fingers, clenched the cigar between his teeth, and clamped his fingers around the burning phosphorus. The ember hissed, then went silent. He opened his fingers and held the match up again for Stanley to see. The tip was gray. "A terrible thing, fire is. A terrible thing, indeed."

⤫

THE NIGHT HAD COOLED as Liam walked up the drive to the Barrett home. He was keenly aware of a hollowness inside him. During his walk from Adams, the eastern sky had darkened from a shimmering violet to a crystalline deep blue. He would not have made out the shape of the Barrett home were it not for the bright yellow windows burning in the night.

As he approached, he saw his mother in her chair staring outward. He stopped. She would not be able to see him out there in the dark. She wasn't watching for him. She was still waiting for Liam's father. Or at least that is what the family told themselves. For all they knew, she was waiting for the faeries to take her back home.

Behind her, he could see movement. Young Kevin scuffed his way through the parlor on his way to the bedroom he shared with Liam, then a light bloomed in their window. Clare was settled upon the sofa working on embroidery. She had heard that in some convents, nuns were employed doing needlework which was sold for charity, so she practiced her stitches to present to Mother Superior.

As he grew closer, he saw Kate coming out of the kitchen and going back in. It was unusual for her to be scurrying around at this hour. Then he saw a large man in the parlor sitting near the hearth, the image of his long-dead father. His mind was playing tricks on him; he knew who it really was. He lengthened his stride.

By the time he stepped inside, Kevin had taken a seat on the floor, and Kate had settled on the sofa next to Clare, their backs to him.

"The year was 1789," the man's voice said. "Young Daniel O'Connell stood on the stone ramp with the other bright boys watching the little ship bob towards them in the dark of night, about to carry them away to France where they would be educated. In those days, a Catholic was not allowed to learn letters or numbers in Ireland, don't you know, but the priests taught them anyway. You know what hedge schools are, don't you?"

It was the voice of Jack Barrett, his dead father's brother. Liam stopped inside the threshold. No doubt they had heard him come in, he wasn't hiding. No, he was preparing himself to see his uncle again. Liam hadn't seen him since the fateful trip to Pennsylvania. The thought of it made Liam's heart clench.

That was not the only reason Liam prepared himself. Jack and Patrick Barrett, eleven months apart, had looked so much alike growing up that people thought they were twins. Liam was not prepared to look upon the image of the father he missed so much quite yet.

A career in the police is not what Liam's father had wanted for him. When Patrick Barrett died, Liam could not leave his family and go to law school. Someone had to put food on the table. Kate was already working in the mill but her one income wasn't enough. Kevin and Clare were babies. So Liam took his father's place in the mill and a few years later, he was recruited to work for the police – an Irish officer being badly needed in an Irish village in the middle of America.

Liam straightened his tunic, brushed the dirt of the road from his boots, squared his shoulders, and took the few steps down the hall into the parlor.

"Liam, my lad, look at you!" Jack said, in a mocking voice. "When last I saw you, you were just a lad, no bigger than Kevin. And now you stand before me: trussed up in a copper's uniform?"

"What are you doing here?"

Clare picked up her needlework and processed through the room in her nun walk. Kate slumped into the sofa, propping her head on a fist. Kevin's eyes lit up. The fight was on.

Jack stood. Liam had remembered him as a giant, like Finn McCool of the old stories. But even drawing himself to his full height and filling his chest with air, Jack wasn't quite as tall as Liam anymore. His shirt and trousers were old and tattered, but clean. No doubt there was a woman somewhere looking after him.

"Outside," Liam said. He walked out the way he'd come, hearing his uncle's footsteps behind him, and led him to behind the shed where their voices would not drift back to the house. "I'll ask you again, what are you doing here?"

"Passing by," Jack said. "Thought I'd see how my brother's family is doing."

"Grand without you," Liam said. "Why didn't you come when Da died?"

"It was nearly a year before I'd heard the news. I'd been traveling. You know me, son, always on the move."

"Don't call me 'son'."

"By the time I heard the news, so much time had passed, I reckoned best to leave things well enough alone. I heard you were in the mill."

"That's right."

"And now I come here to find Adam's finest strolling into my brother's home."

"It's my home now."

"So it is, so it is."

"There are tramps camping near Pittsfield. What do you know about them?"

"Pittsfield?" Jack laughed. "Why should I know anything about Pittsfield?"

"They're rumored to be Molly Maguires."

Jack stepped in. "Who says?"

"Alistair Cunningham. I need to know if something is being planned. Cunningham's itching to clear them out."

"Ha! We've put the fear of God into them. Ironic, don't you know, since all our plans came to naught."

The house door slammed. Liam and Jack stepped out from behind the shed to see who was coming. Kevin, with his long loose-jointed arms and legs, stumbled in their direction. Liam wondered if he looked so awkward at that age, when he'd last seen Jack. Probably he had.

"What are you talking about?" Kevin asked.

"Uncle Jack here was telling me he needed to leave soon."

"Did you talk to him?" Kevin asked Jack.

"Relax, son, I'm not leaving quite yet. We're getting to that."

Kevin shoved his hands in his pockets and looked at Liam. "Uncle Jack says I'm old enough to get a job."

Liam had stopped in at the Black Rose before going home. Harry mentioned he'd seen Kevin walking towards the school not long before the end of the day, no doubt so he could fall into the mob of kids walking home. "You cut school today," Liam said. "We talked about this, you need to keep up your schoolwork and chores if you want to take a job."

"School is stupid. I know my letters and my numbers. All they got us doing is reading old stories and singing songs. It's time I made a living. All my friends are working in the mills already. I'm the only one left. I'm the oldest boy in the class. It's full of little kids, Liam. I spend half my day teaching them."

The same argument, yet again. The boy was relentless.

"You're not quitting school. You're lucky to have a future. It's not to be squandered. I'm making enough money for the family."

"I'm a man, Liam," Kevin said. "I'm almost as old as you were when you went to work. There is no future for us, not in this country. Working for someone else, earning less and less all the time. We organized in the mines and they started killing us outright, not slow like they were doing before. Starving us with their wages. We're getting further and further into debt at the company store. If I start working now, I can get ahead, make something of myself someday. I'm not going to the mills, I'm going to Hogan's. Tom's making it into something. If I start with him now and show him how smart I am, he'll let me work in the office. Someday I could own my own store."

"I already talked to Tom," Liam said. "You're not quitting school. And I have to talk to Kate, but if you stay in school and get good grades, I'll think about letting you work part-time."

"Part-time?" Kevin yelled. "You don't understand." He turned his back and lurched his way down to the house, slamming the door again after he went inside.

Liam spun on Jack. "I have you to thank for this."

"Whoa, whoa, whoa! What have I done?"

"Putting political ideas into his head. The company store? We don't have a company store. He's talking about the coal mines. That never came out of him before you showed up. And how is it your place to decide what's good for him and what's not?"

"Good seeing you too, Liam. Say good-bye to the girls for me." With that, Jack slapped his cap on the top of his head and strolled down the drive.

"Where are you going?"

"Off to Sadie's."

"You heard about Deidre."

"I did. I'm going to offer my condolences, right after I look in on my old friend Harry Gallagher."

"He's out of whiskey."

"What's that you say?"

"His shipment was lost in route."

"Was it, now?"

Chapter Nineteen

A Ghost in the Window

IN THE WOODS OUTSIDE Adams, Stanley had settled on a fallen tree, biding his time, watching stars flicker overhead. Papery leaves beneath him crunched every time he moved. He took a swig of whiskey from his flask and felt the warmth fill his head and throat and ease down through his body. Nearby the grey mare stood asleep in the shadows, her head hanging.

With a moon bright enough to cast shadows, the movement of an opossum scurrying out from its hiding place caught his eye. "Boo!"

Stanley laughed, expecting to see the critter hightail it away, or better yet play dead. Instead, it froze in place and turned its pointy white snout in his direction. "Boo, dammit! Didn't you hear me?"

The demon opened its mouth and hissed with its fangs gleaming in the moonlight. Stanley picked up a rock and pitched it. The rock flew over its head, the whole time its beady black eyes locked on Stanley's. It must be rabid. Why else would it act that way? Do opossum get rabies? Stanley wasn't sure but he wasn't risking a bite. He drew his revolver from its holster. He must have looked away for a moment – by the time he went to aim at it, the thing was gone.

He'd waited long enough. The moon had traveled across the sky and now seemed to hang directly over him. It must be midnight, or close to – the townspeople should be asleep. He woke the horse with a slap, mounted her, and skirted the town, keeping the horse in the dirt so her hooves would make less noise.

The place was easy enough to find with the sign hanging over the door, "Hogan's General Store". Behind the store was a half-built warehouse, framing finished, siding going up. Stanley decided to start there. He dismounted and dropped the reins, leaving the horse on the road for a quick getaway.

Lucky for him, there was a kerosene barrel on the store's back stoop. He pried the shop door open, grabbed an empty jug, took it back out, and filled it. Then he splashed the kerosene along the foundation of the warehouse, emptying the jug. He went back for more, and did this over and over, filling from the barrel and emptying on the warehouse until every wall was soaked. Then he struck a match, tossed it at the building, and stood back. In an instant, the structure exploded into an inferno. The fire ran towards him, following the trail of kerosene that had slopped out of the jug while he was working. He threw the jug away but the flames kept coming. He ran past the store and onto the road, as he felt heat on his boots, then on his trousers. The horse whinnied when she saw him coming and took off running, hooves thundering. He threw himself on the ground and rolled.

He heard shouting. He pulled himself up, made a quick check, and saw his boots were charred and pants legs eaten away by fire, then ran back into the woods. There wasn't any pain so he figured the burns weren't that bad. Someone was coming out of the house next door, an old man and a young man. A young woman came out too, heavily pregnant.

He had planned to torch the store too but there was no time. He needed to get out of there quick before they saw him. He worked his way through the woods a quarter mile and then came back out on the road where he couldn't be seen from the store. The mare was nowhere in sight.

He ran. He was a big man and he hadn't run in years, not even to run down someone he was about to arrest. It wasn't long before his breathing came hard and his heart pounded in his chest. He was behind the town, skirting along the foot of Mount Greylock, when he saw lights flicker on across the valley. The alarm had been raised. He stopped for a moment to catch his breath. His calves, where the pants had burned away, felt warm. He was burned but not so bad, he hoped. There was no use in worrying about it now, he had to get home first. The hag could doctor him up if needed.

Cunningham would be pleased. There would be something special in Stanley's future, thanks for doing a good job. He was one step closer to joining the crew.

But Cunningham hadn't said anything about burning down the warehouse. Was that what he wanted? Did he want the store burned instead? Or did he want something bad to happen to Joe Hogan? He hadn't exactly said. What if Stanley was wrong? What if the old man was babbling and didn't mean anything by it?

∞

L IAM DRIFTED IN AND out of sleep with Deirdre's poetry book splayed across his chest. He was vaguely aware that his bedside candle had guttered out, of Kevin's snores from the next cot, and outside the window, the hoots of an owl.

He dreamt he was going to a law school exam and he didn't know where the lecture hall was. For some reason he couldn't remember, he hadn't attended class all term, nor did he know the professor's name. There were students hurrying across the campus and then they disappeared. Exams had started. He would not be admitted late and he would fail the course. His life was in ruins. He didn't know how he would face his family and friends who had counted so much on his becoming a lawyer.

The creak of a floorboard woke him. When he opened his eyes, he first saw a blurry vision of the window, the tree beyond where the owl lived, moonlit clouds, and the floating figure of a woman dressed in white. He must still be dreaming. He rubbed his eyes and scanned the room. That was when he saw his mother in the doorway, dressed in her white nightgown, watching him. It was her reflection he had seen, no ghost at all.

Suddenly, the moonlight brightened and Liam saw terror on her face.

He clambered out of bed and went to her side. Her eyes flicked to him then went back to the window. There was a strange light in the distance, an orange glow reflected against a few clouds scattered across the sky.

Fire.

Liam grabbed a boot, pulled it on, and kicked Kevin's cot. "Wake up!"

Kevin pulled his cover over his head. "Leave me alone." Liam kicked the bed harder, nearly knocking it over. Kevin pushed himself up onto an elbow. "What?"

Liam pulled on the other boot. "Fire!" He pointed out the window and ran out the door. He was halfway to town when he realized he hadn't put trousers on over his long johns. He kept running. A few moments later, he heard Kevin racing up behind him.

Liam pointed to Summer Street. "Wake them up!" Kevin peeled off as Liam pounded north towards the fire. At first, he thought the cotton mill was burning. Fires were common, usually occurring during work hours, and the workers managed to put them out. Liam had seen a few during his years at the mill. But with no one in the building when it started, there was little hope of controlling the flames before the entire mill was gutted. Half of Adams would be out of work overnight. The other half of Adams, businesses like the grocer, the butcher, Joe Hogan's dry goods and Harry Gallegher's pub, dependent on workers' wages, would have no income. The town would go to ruin when folks left looking for work. Liam stretched out his legs and ran harder.

As he came around a bend, he saw the mill was dark. The orange glow was closer, near Hogan's store. Flames leapt into the sky, revealing the store intact but the warehouse behind it burning. Sparks drifting out of the sky fell on Hogan's store and the Hogan home next door. Did they know? Was Eileen safe?

Liam felt like he was flying. His foot barely touched the porch and then he was inside the house, in the dark parlor. All was still. He realized the door had been open when he came in.

"Joe?" Liam shouted.

No answer.

"Tom? Are you awake? The warehouse is on fire. We need to get you out."

He felt the emptiness of the house. Everyone had gone.

Back on the porch, he shielded his eyes, and looked into the flames. No one was close to it. Out of the corner of his eye, he saw a white night dress, ethereal in the gloom, carrying a box of goods from Hogan's store across the road. Eileen. She was followed by old Joe Hogan, in his long johns and barefoot, carrying another box. Tom Gillespie appeared in dungarees and shirtless. His arms were full. They had seen the warehouse couldn't be saved, had forsaken their home, and were trying to rescue the merchandise.

Liam ran to the water faucet next to the house, grabbed the bucket, and pumped. He ran to the store and threw as high as he could, splashing the roof. He ran back and forth as he was aware of being joined by men, women, and boys who had brought buckets of their own.

Soon there were two lines, one watering down the Hogan house and the other watering down the store. The fire crackled and roared as they worked. Animal-like groans came from deep within the warehouse as if the building itself was in pain. Beams crashed to the ground, scattering embers that landed on the workers' clothes. A woman's nightdress caught fire. She didn't say a word as she batted at the flames. A man ran to her, pushed her onto the ground, and rolled her back and forth until the fire was out. Another woman helped her limp across the street and sat her on one of the crates carried out from the store.

After the warehouse's last timber fell, the men began dousing the fire. Liam was in the front of the line, pouring buckets of water handed to him by the man behind him. He caught a glimpse of Kevin shoveling dirt onto the flames, shoulder to shoulder with grown men, moving as much earth as the largest and fastest of them.

The pain in his chest was sharp as he wished their father could see Kevin now. How proud he would have been. For a moment, it felt as if his spirit crumbled. Nothing he could do would replace Patrick Barrett for Kevin. Liam didn't want to be the head of the family anymore. He didn't want to make the decisions and try to guide the wee ones. He wanted to be the son again.

He raised an arm to wipe his face, hoping that if anyone saw him, they'd think he was merely wiping away sweat.

The sun was rising by the time the last of the flames had gone out, embers still glowing in the blackened hole that had once been the warehouse. Men shoveled dirt onto the hot ashes but moved more slowly. Captain Curran came through and told the water brigades they could quit now. The house and store had been saved.

Liam stretched, his back and arms aching, and now his legs too. He stood with the other men, women, and boys watching the fire, not wanting to leave lest it breathed new life. Many of the men and women had to go on shift soon. They began drifting home to ready for their day.

Joe Hogan walked through the clumps of stragglers, thanking them, calling each person by name, shaking the men's hands, patting the women's shoulders. Tom Gillespie followed behind, doing the same.

When they reached Liam, Joe said, "Thank you, lad. Kevin told me how you woke him up when you saw the flames. If you hadn't roused the alarm, my house and store would have been lost."

Joe Hogan had given Liam an after-school job so he could finish his education. When his father's body was found, Joe was one of the men that came to the house to tell them.

"You'd have done the same for me," Liam said.

Joe, Liam, Tom, and Kevin walked around the ruins but there was little information to be gleaned. The blackest of the destruction was in the front of the warehouse. There were kegs of kerosene on the store's porch. Hogan was lucky the fire hadn't sparked those kegs, the store would have been lost as well.

"What woke you to the fire?" Liam asked Joe.

"Eileen saw it," Tom said. "She's been getting up in the middle of the night lately – you know – with her condition."

"Did she see anything, anyone?"

"A man running away, his clothes on fire, but she didn't know who he was. All she saw was a figure, no face."

Liam would search the woods. It was possible someone had taken refuge in the warehouse for the night and had built a campfire that got out of control. But first he needed to make sure Eileen was safe.

"Is she alright?" Liam asked, looking around to see if he could find her.

"Sadie and Eileen went into the house to start breakfast," Joe said. "Eileen's a strong girl, no need to worry about her."

A silence drew out.

"I'd better go see if I can be useful," Tom said, then headed towards the house.

Kevin shuffled his feet. The boy was hungry. He was always hungry.

"I'd invite you to stay, Liam, but it's still a delicate thing you know. Best not to make problems between a man and wife if it can be avoided."

Liam pictured Hogan's kitchen, the table he'd sat at so many times while Eileen and her mother served Joe and himself. The big cooker was the pride and joy of Mrs. Hogan, who had died shortly after Liam's father. Now Eileen was the woman of the house. As he watched Tom Gillespie open the kitchen door, he imagined her frying bacon and eggs, an apron tied around her ribs, covering her round belly. Liam peered into the door opening and saw a sliver of the kitchen he knew so well. He tried to catch a glimpse of Eileen. Gillespie seemed to have sensed him. Before Tom closed the door, he turned, blocking the view, and looked directly at Liam, an anxious expression on his face.

"Not to worry, Joe. We need to be getting home. Kate will have something on the cooker for us already."

∽

AFTER LIAM HAD SEARCHED the woods across from Hogan's store and found no man, injured or otherwise, hiding there, he and Kevin walked down East Road towards home in silence. Mist hovered over the ground and Kevin, still sometimes a boy, kicked at it, delighting in how he made it swirl. The sun hadn't crested the mountains yet and the sky was colored in pastel pinks and blues. As they walked, Liam could feel his body cooling, the sweat drying into a thin, brittle veneer. A chill moved through him.

The sound of a horse-drawn wagon approached, bumping and clattering, hooves clomping on dirt. As they rounded a bend, they came face-to-face with the horse and wagon Liam recognized as Joe Hogan's. It was driven by his uncle, Jack Barrett, with a young fella sitting close beside him. Tethered to the back of the wagon was a big, black horse.

The wagon pulled to a stop. "Jack, what are you doing here?"

Jack and the young fella stiffened. The boy had his hands in Jack's pockets, warming them. He quickly pulled his hands out and jammed them into his own pockets.

Liam didn't recognize the passenger until he smiled. It wasn't a boy at all. It was Victoria Cunningham, dressed like a working man, a cap on her head and kerchief at her neck.

"Fine morning to you!" Jack said. He took in the appearance of his two nephews, their clothes grimy and wet. "Rough night?"

"Hogan's warehouse burned down."

Jack leaned forward in his seat. "Why? How?"

"An accident, perhaps. Not sure. Eileen saw a man running away. I'm thinking a tramp snuck into the warehouse for the night and made a campfire that went out of control."

"Who?"

"She didn't see him well enough to identify him."

"Hey, Uncle Jack," Kevin interjected, "how'd you get Joe Hogan's wagon?"

"We're old friends, lad."

Kevin walked to the wagon bed and peered in. "But why? Where'd you go? What's that in the back?"

In the bed of the wagon were beer kegs and whiskey crates.

"What are you up to this time?" Liam asked, remembering how Jack had filled their wagon with guns, disguised as food, on their trip to Pennsylvania.

Victoria Cunningham scrubbed her hands on her trousers. "I best be off."

Her face drew close to Jack's for a moment as if they were about to kiss, paused, then they both pulled back. She laughed and stood. He slapped her on the rump. She whirled around and pushed him but not so hard he'd fall off the wagon, both of them smiling. "Get on with you, now," Jack said. "before someone notices you're gone."

She leapt down from the bench, walked to the black stallion tied to the back, stroked his neck and spoke into his ear, then untied him. Kevin watched awestruck.

She led the horse a few paces away, then mounted him astride like a man, and loped away, the cap pulled low across her face.

"Are you insane?" Liam asked. "If Cunningham gets wind his daughter was traipsing around the night with the likes of you, there's no telling what he'd do."

"Harry ran out of whiskey, we can't be having that now, can we? So I had a word with my friend Joe who lent me the wagon and took a little drive to Albany. Adams shall not suffer from thirst any longer."

"Who is she, Uncle Jack?" Kevin asked.

"A friend."

"You must be out of your mind."

"Hardly," Jack said, self-satisfaction tugging the corner of his mouth into that crooked smile women found so charming.

"Do you know what they'll do to you if you're caught?" Liam asked.

Jack leaned forward and lowered his voice. "That's the point, isn't it, lad? I don't intend to get caught. Now, why don't the two of you climb aboard and we'll get you home. Say, Kevin, I've been driving this wagon all night long and could use a break. You want to take the reins?"

"Do I!" Kevin said, climbing onto the bench before Jack had finished asking the question.

∞

WHEN THE WAGON RATTLED up to the Barrett farmhouse, Kate was standing on the porch, fists on hips. "What in the name of all that is holy?"

Jack leapt down from the wagon and gave Kate a kiss on the cheek. "Is there any chance that these fine firefighters can find a warm breakfast?"

That was Jack all over. Charming when he needed to be. Secretive the rest of the time. Liam knew only too well that Jack Barrett was scheming and plotting, seeing where his advantages lay, how he could line up his contacts – all for the cause, he would claim shrouding his chicanery with nobility. But underneath it all, he was another blowhard politician. He'd found a way to avoid an honest day's work, by claiming his true vocation was fighting for the working man, and they loved him for it.

Kate batted him away. She scowled at her brothers. "The state of you." Then she went inside while the men cleaned up at the water pump, and Kevin released the horse from her harness, gave her hay, and tied her near the trough.

In the kitchen, they sat around the table while Kate served a breakfast of hot tea, bread, sausage, and eggs. Liam and Jack ate in silence. Kevin, still excited by the night's events, filled her in on the fire at Hogan's while she went back and forth from the cooker, making sure their plates and cups were full.

"And Eileen, is she alright?"

"Why wouldn't she be?" Kevin asked, his mouth full of half-eaten food.

"Don't talk with your mouth full and why wouldn't she be, you ask? She's having a baby. There's all manner of things that can go wrong."

"She's fine," Liam said.

Kevin's plate was clean, again. "Is there any more sausage?"

Kate huffed, picked up the plate, and filled it. "That's the lot. It'll have to do you."

After they were done eating, Jack pushed away from the table, pulled out three cigars, passed one to Kevin and another to Liam, and struck a match. Kevin's face glowed.

Kate took the cigar from Kevin's hand. "What are you thinking, Jack Barrett? Kevin's far too young to be smoking."

"I'm almost fifteen!"

"You're barely fourteen!"

Liam didn't often disagree with Kate in front of Kevin or Clare. "He's done the work of a man, all night long, Katie. This once won't hurt."

She slammed the cigar down on the table. "Then I'll leave you to it," she said, untied her apron, hung it on a hook, and left the room, dishes and pans unwashed.

With his own cigar between his teeth, Jack lit Liam's cigar, then Kevin's. "Don't inhale, lad."

Kevin sucked and puffed. After a few moments went by, the color drained from his face. He ran out the front door, retching. It was the same when Liam smoked his first cigar with his father and Jack at that very table. The mother had given the men a tongue-lashing, embarrassing Liam even more.

"He's a man now," Jack said.

"You're an arse, you know that?"

"He lasted longer than you did."

"No one told me not to inhale."

The front door banged with Kevin's return.

"Not a word in front of the boy," Jack said.

Kevin paused at the threshold of the kitchen, his face waxen.

"You worked all night, Kevin," Liam said. "One missed day of school shouldn't set you back. I'll have a word with your teacher. Go on back to bed." Kevin nodded and dragged himself away.

"So how is it, Jack Barrett, that if you aren't up to something, there is a group of Irishmen living in the woods behind Pittsfield when you appear."

"They're not with me, I swear it. The countryside is full of Irish just off the boat, looking for work."

"Then why are you here?"

"Visiting, like I said. Haven't you become the suspicious one now that you're a copper!"

"That's the thing. You aren't just visiting. You show up once at dinner time and then I find you sneaking through the night with Victoria Cunningham and a wagonful of liquor."

"You're better off not knowing, son. Leave it alone."

"I told you, don't call me 'son.' You're not my father. What happens in Adams is my business. And those Irishmen in the woods back of Pittsfield are my business too. Alistair Cunningham insists that they had something to do with Deirdre's murder. One of them found her body and he had her crucifix, claimed he found it in the woods. Cunningham thinks the lot of them are Mollys and they're here to start something when the Governor visits. He's pushing for an arrest. Now, with this fire, he's going to say there's even more evidence that they're trouble. One of them started the fire on accident. Or it was part of a plan they'd hatched."

"That doesn't make sense. Why would they burn down Hogan's warehouse? You say that man was on foot. Adams is a long walk from Pittsfield."

"He could have hidden a horse somewhere."

"A tramp with a horse?"

"Stolen, Cunningham would say."

"Has anyone seen them in Adams? Is there any reason to think they'd crossed paths with Joe, maybe had been in his store, and something happened? Had he kicked one of them out for stealing?"

"If old Joe Hogan saw someone stealing from his store, he'd look the other way to save their dignity. He'd figured they needed it more than he did. Tom Gillespie too."

"Just so. No one would believe Hogan's was burned down for revenge."

"It doesn't have to make sense to a mob ginned up by the lord of the manor. He wants the case closed before the Governor arrives and he doesn't care who swings for it."

Jack stubbed his cigar out in his plate, bare but for some smeared egg yolk and a few breadcrumbs. He stood. "I know a safe place where they can hide for a few days."

"Where will that be?"

Jack reached into his coat pocket. "What's this?" In his hand was the brooch Victoria Cunningham had worn when Liam last saw her at Inverness. She had returned from Albany the same day Jack had arrived. He never said where he had last been, always maintaining that air of mystery. "It seems my friend left a gift behind."

Jack Barrett would burn in hell if he seduced that young woman to get at her money. "She's funding you?"

"I know what you're thinking. But Miss Cunningham is a big girl and perfectly capable of making her own decisions."

"How will it work between the two of you? You, who you are, she, who she is? Marriage? Family? Children?"

"You cannot be that naive, Liam. There are things that happen between men and women that don't necessarily end in marriage." Jack reached into his pocket again and pulled out a key. "What I meant to show you is this. It opens the Black Rose's cellar. We'll run by there, unload the liquor, fetch those men out of the woods, and bring them back to Adams. They can stay under the bar for a few days until we think of something."

Liam didn't have any better ideas. Until he solved Deirdre's murder, those men weren't safe.

"But first, answer me this," Liam said. "How is that you have Joe Hogan's wagon and Harry Gallagher's key?"

"Because we're all old friends, Officer Barrett. Me, Joe Hogan, and Harry's father. When he died, Harry took his place."

"His place in what?"

Jack tossed the key into the air and caught it. "At the whist table. You'd know that if you didn't spend all your time with your nose in a book."

Chapter Twenty

Striking the Fiddle

I T WAS STILL EARLY morning when Liam and Jack pulled the wagon into the alley behind the Black Rose, having first secured a fresh horse from the livery stable.

Harry lived in an apartment on the second floor, accessed by a fire escape. As Jack was unlocking the cellar door, Harry clambered down the stairs, rubbing his eyes. The last Liam had seen him was at Hogan's a few hours before, slinging water with the rest of them. There was still soot on his face. "Jack Barrett, you old scoundrel, is it yourself? What's that you brought? It's not often I catch someone breaking into my cellar with a delivery. And a fine good morning to you too, Liam."

"Can't have the Black Rose running dry, can we?" Jack handed Liam a crate and nodded towards the cellar. As Liam walked down the steps, he heard Jack and Harry talking, their voices lowered.

Soon the three had unloaded the crates and kegs. Harry locked the cellar as Liam and Jack climbed back into the wagon. "Happy to have the lads to keep me company. We'll be seeing you later today."

"It's a solid man you are, Harry Gallegher," Jack said.

"I'll be digging out the cards. Steel yourself for humiliation yet again, Jack Barrett."

"From the likes of you? That'll be the day."

The conversation sounded rehearsed. "Since when do you play whist, Harry?" Liam asked.

"Learned it at my father's knee. It's one of those things you don't forget."

"Why am I only hearing about this now?"

"Your father wasn't much of a card player. Maybe that's why you never learnt. Slán, lads." With that, Harry entered the bar. There was something unusual about his behavior. The bear of a man had never broken off a conversation. His success as a barkeep was dependent on being sociable. For that matter, Liam had never seen Harry close a door.

Everyone came into the Black Rose where Harry could be found standing behind the bar, wiping down a table, or sweeping the floor. There he always was, not going in and out of places, and certainly not shutting someone out.

How was it Harry was so familiar with Jack when Liam hadn't seen him in years? Could Jack have visited Adams without stopping by the farm and without Liam knowing he was in town? If that was the case, more people were in on his secret comings and goings. Who else? Joe Hogan who had gladly lent his horse and wagon to Jack the night before. Liam didn't know they knew each other. What about Sadie? Could they all be involved in Jack's causes? Were the Molly Maguires really gone or had they only faded into the scenery like the Finn McCool's flying columns, ready to return?

When they arrived at the camp, the men were beginning to stir. A fire had been lit and the smell of burnt coffee and beans hung in the crisp air. The Hennessey twins were there, as were few more skinny, ragged, just-off-the-boat Irishmen.

Although he looked to be the youngest at the camp, Timothy Hennessey stood and greeted them. "A fine morning to you, Officer Barrett," he said, then glanced at Jack. "Is this your da, is it? The apple didn't fall too far from the tree, did it?"

"My uncle," Liam hurried to explain. "Jack Barrett."

By then, the men had stopped what they were doing and were watching the conversation.

"I'm afraid we've no food to share, but there's coffee," Tim said. "Care for a cup?"

Liam wouldn't take food from starving men. "Don't mind if I do," Jack said, taking a seat on a fallen log next to the other Hennessey twin, Denny. A tin cup was produced and Jack helped himself, filling it half-way from the pot. Then he pulled a hip flask and poured a splash from that into the cup as well before passing the flash around.

"Sláinte!" he said holding the cup aloft before he drank it down in one gulp like a shot of whiskey. "Sláinte!" was repeated back to him as each man in turn took a drink from his flask.

"Is this official police business?" Tim asked, he and Liam still standing, not quite squared-off for a fight, but at a distance where they could sense each other's moves quickly enough while Jack had taken a seat at the fire and was passing the bottle around to his new-found friends.

"Yes and no," Liam said. "I need to know one thing first. Are any of you involved with the Mollys?"

Tim barked a laugh. "Not here, not back home. We're looking for work with no heart for trouble. Who says we're Mollys?"

"There's been talk in town. You're being blamed for anything that happens."

"Such as?"

"The girl who was murdered."

"Owen Sweeney didn't have anything to do with that. He told you. He found the body and thought he'd do the right thing and tell the police. And look at him now, in jail for his troubles! He could have walked right past her, never told a soul and none of this would be happening. But that wouldn't be the right thing to do, leave the poor girl out there to all manner of creatures. And if he had, no one may have ever known she died. We didn't come here for trouble. We heard there was work building the new big house but they turned us away the moment we asked. We're just hoping to get a few days' labor, farming or construction. We'll take whatever we can get. Then we'll be on our way to Pennsylvania where there's plenty of work for the likes of us."

"You went to the big house? Inverness?"

"That's the one. Got chased off by an old Scottish hag and a dour little man with a big read beard."

Mrs. Ramsey and Malcom Dunbar.

"When was this?"

"A few days before Sweeney found the body."

"Then some farmer came around here waving a gun, accusing us of stealing his chickens. Said he'd call the law on us."

A couple of the men around the campfire shifted in their seats at the mention of chickens.

"Did that farmer have any witnesses?"

"None I saw," one of the men shouted setting the others to laughing.

"I didn't hear that," Liam said. It wasn't his jurisdiction. Any farmer in Adams would have gladly fed the men for the extra help. Besides, he didn't have the authority to make an arrest for a misdemeanor he hadn't witnessed.

"Have any of you been to Adams?"

"Where's that? Is there work to be had?"

"A few miles north of here. A warehouse was burned down last night. With all this agitation against you, I'm worried you'll get blamed and somebody might take the law into their own hands."

"Time to move on, is that what you're saying, Officer Barrett? No Irish need apply? We've heard a lot of that but didn't expect to hear it from a son of Erin. Who's side are you on? Aren't you the one who took Owen Sweeney away and we've never seen him since?"

"He's safe in the Pittsfield jail. He stole that necklace and needs to answer for it."

"He says he found it."

"Like your friend found that chicken?"

Jack spoke. "Liam means you no harm. We have a nice safe cellar for you boys to camp out in the next town over. And here's the thing, it's under a pub."

The men were kicking dirt into the fire before Jack finished speaking.

On the ride back to Adams, the newcomers talked freely. They were from all parts of Ireland, potato farmers, a smithy, a carpenter, and a bricklayer. They would come in handy, rebuilding Hogan's warehouse, Liam thought. He'd speak to Tom Gillespie about it once everything was settled.

It was late morning when Jack pulled the wagon behind Gallagher's, having led the horse down the back alley to reduce the likelihood of being seen. Liam and Jack led the men into the cellar and helped them move crates around to make room for their bedrolls. Jack took out the hip flask and passed it around again. "Mind you, lads, stay out of the bottles. This is Harry's livelihood and it's a kindness he's doing letting you stay here. No drinking him out of house and home."

Liam took the stairs up to the pub and found Harry pulling chairs down from the tables. "Thanks for taking the lads in."

"I have some cold meat and potatoes upstairs," Harry pointed to his apartment overhead. "I'll get the lads fed. You look dead on your feet, a chara. Go home, get yourself some rest. We'll be seeing you at the wake tonight, just so."

∞

THAT EVENING, LIAM FOUND himself wedged against a wall in Sadie's guest-filled parlor. The open coffin was in the middle of the room with furnishings pushed to the walls. Liam caught a glimpse of Deidre's brow and her copper hair. He resolved not to go closer, he'd seen her already.

Old women sat on the sofa and stuffed chairs. Old men were clustered on wooden chairs in a corner, smoking cigars, and drinking from tankards. Young and middle-aged men and women filled the floor space. The ceiling was hazy with smoke.

A fiddler Liam couldn't see in the crowd struck a note and the din ebbed. He began one of those old, sad tunes that no one ever sang to. Before he finished the first phrase, the room had gone silent. Even the children stopped running.

Liam edged his way through the crowd. He spotted Kate's long red hair bent over an old woman, listening politely with one ear. She moved her head aside and Liam realized the old woman was their mother.

Seeing her away from home, he was struck by how much she had aged. Her hair had thinned. Her lids sagged around large round eyes. But she was still the most beautiful mother in the room. She had a mildly confused expression.

Nearby Clare was handing another old lady a cup of tea. Kevin would be hanging around the men out back. Father Frank, standing near the fireplace, held court with a number of young ladies. He'd struck his priestly pose, hands clasped in front of him. As Liam edged by, Frank gave him a wink. It'd appeared that the children of the parish were safe enough in his presence, but Liam wasn't quite sure yet about those young women.

As he passed through the parlor into the dining room and made his way toward the kitchen, he spied the fiddler seated in a corner next to the dinner table laden with breads, sliced beef, stews, and cakes.

The musician was the newspaper man who'd recently moved to town. James O'Herlihy was a gaunt, serious fellow and a few years Liam's senior. The lenses of his round wire rim glasses were opaque as he dipped his chin to his instrument. Liam had hoped for a chance to talk to this man, having read his articles. His writing was that of an educated and impassioned man. But now was not the time.

A small boy, two or three years old, darted between legs and crashed into Liam. A woman's hand grabbed the child by the upper arm, stopping him in his tracks, bent, and spoke into his ear. He wasn't sure if that child was hers, but it didn't matter – all the women were expected to marshal the wee ones. Liam remembered being collared by Sadie when he was five or six years old at some other gathering, a harsh warning whispered into his ear intended to put the fear of God into him. He couldn't remember what she had said but he did recall the sudden emptiness he felt in the pit of his stomach.

He found Sadie in the kitchen, sitting on a bar stool Harry had brought from his pub, marshalling the younger women and older girls in the making of sandwiches. As long as Liam had known her, Sadie worked. She worked when she was happy and she worked when she was sad.

A steady stream of men, carrying empty mugs on their way out and filled mugs on their way in, snaked through the door leading from the kitchen to the backyard. Kevin was in line holding two empty tankards in each hand. Liam gave him a frown. "It's for the old gents," Kevin protested, animated. It was the first time amongst a collection of their friends that he was being treated no longer as a child, but instead as that half-thing between boyhood and manhood – he had trusted to ferry beer without spilling.

Liam remembered when men started treating him differently, how they slapped him on the back instead of squeezing his shoulder, how they shared little jokes about the mysteries of women kind, how they let him listen to their talk – still on the edge of the group but allowed to stay. After the hard work Kevin had done the night before fighting Hogan's fire, he was ready for the transition.

A breeze wafted in from the opened door cooling Liam's face. He was grateful that he was taller than the rest. The lower levels of air would be stifling. In the darkness beyond the door, Liam could make out burning embers of cigars floating in the night air like fireflies.

He was making his way to Sadie when the hard edge of something pushed into his belly. He looked down and found Eileen Hogan Gillespie looking up at him. He felt his face drain of heat. She fell back a half a step and the pressure relented.

"Have a sandwich, Liam," Eileen said, with an earnest expression. For a moment, he was confused, dazzled by the golden aura around her fine hair. He felt the nudge again and saw that she was holding a platter of sandwiches, on her way out to the dining room. "You look knackered."

"Haven't eaten," Liam said, wishing he could have come up with something clever. A man jostling through the crowd on his way back from the beer stand bumped into Eileen's back, knocking her off balance and pushed her into Liam again.

Sadie threw a dishrag at the man. "Seamus Murphy, you great lout!"

Seamus grabbed Eileen's shoulder to steady her. "Are you alright, love?"

Liam looked down at the space that had been between them and saw Eileen's protruding belly, Tom Gillespie's child. He suddenly felt violently sick. The lamb sandwich in his hand, he didn't know how it gotten there, smelled rancid. He looked for someplace to put it down.

There were round pink spots on each of her pale cheeks, flushed from the kitchen's heat. Liam had once written a poem liking her complexion to a swan's breast. He couldn't remember if he had shown it to her. What a clumsy youth he had been. Still she had allowed him to love her.

The song finished and the conversation quickly rose in volume.

"Someone take that plate from Eileen," Sadie commanded over the women's voices. The platter Eileen was holding disappeared and suddenly they were standing face to face, Liam wishing he had something inconsequential yet meaningful to say to the married woman he once hoped would be his wife.

Sadie was at their side now, shooing Eileen to the stool she had vacated. Sadie took his hand. "Are *you* alright, macushla?" Sadie knew. She knew everything. Second sight, wise woman, or because she had watched him growing up, she seemed to know more about him than he did.

Liam forced his stomach down, felt his feet planted on the floor, squared his shoulders. "I came –." Something caught in his throat. He coughed, clearing it away. "I came in to say hello."

Sadie peered earnestly into Liam's face for a long moment. "Sadness comes and goes, Liam. It's our lot to bear." Her eyes shone with tears. She steered him towards the door and gave him a little push. "Out with you now, before you fall down, and knock over some other wee lass, you great horse of a man."

Liam felt himself propelled out into the cool night air. He stumbled towards the cigar embers floating in the distance where the deep voices of men joked with one another, still lowered out of respect, but ready to be done with mourning.

S TANLEY WAS ADMITTED TO Cunningham's office by Mrs. Ramsey. The old man wasn't behind his desk or sitting by the fireplace as usual. He was standing beyond the French doors. A few moments passed as Cunningham puffed on his cigar, turning his head this way and that, noticing things in the garden. Did the old man know he was there? Stanley belched.

Cunningham glanced at him with a scowl on his face. "There you are. Join me, Captain."

Stanley meant to skirt around the desk, but instead the corner caught him in his thigh, stabbing him. He finished the few steps, certain he felt his trousers dampen with blood. His burned calves had been slathered with ointment and bandaged and he had taken a long draught of laudanum yet the searing pain was still there.

Cunningham swept his cigar-bearing hand across the vista. "Beautiful, isn't it?"

A path led to a fountain. Statues of half-dressed women lined the walkway. Stanley marveled at how an artist could make marble look like fabric falling across breasts, hips, thighs. Those wanton women aroused and disturbed him. He'd expect to see something like this in a classy brothel. Why would Cunningham show them openly in the same home his fine daughter lived? Stanley would never understand the old moneybags.

In the garden, a handful of men were finishing their day's work, loading rakes, shovels and bags of sand onto wheelbarrows, ferrying them back to the barn around the corner of the house.

"Impressive," Stanley said, for that was true.

"What news have you?"

Cunningham would be impressed when he was told about the fire. Another one of his problems dealt with. After the horse and wagon, what could be his next reward? Something big. "Hogan's warehouse burned down last night."

Cunningham frowned.

"I thought that was what you wanted."

Cunningham slapped Stanley on the back. "How unlucky for Hogan, Captain Stanley."

"You're happy then?"

The old man walked into his office without answering. He poured himself a snifter of brandy without offering any to Stanley. "That tramp Barrett arrested yesterday, what do you know about him?"

"Owen Sweeney. He was the one who took me to the dead girl's body." The tramp had interrupted his dinner. The chicken fat congealed on the platter and the blueberry pie cooled while he was dealing with Sweeney and the dead girl. His meal ruined, he had trashed it and opened a bottle of whiskey. "He was wearing a gold cross when they brought him in. I didn't see it on him Sunday. Says he found it later."

"From the sound of your voice, I take it you have your suspicions. So you're saying the same man reported the body and had the girl's cross."

"I've been thinking about that, Mr. Cunningham, sir. Say he murdered her. Maybe he pushed himself on her and she fought him off. Say after she was dead, he figured he'd take the cross. It's gold. She's got no use for it now she's dead. He could sell it later. Well, if I seen him wearing it, a tramp with a bit of gold hanging from his neck, I'd known right away it was suspicious. He'd have to explain it, wouldn't he? So he hides the cross and reports the body. It would prove his innocence because why would a guilty man report the crime?"

"You think he did it."

"There was no one else who could have. But he hasn't been charged because Barrett's convinced there isn't enough evidence."

"Why not charge him now and see if he confesses?"

"I don't like it, but Barrett's right. A judge would let him go on what we have now. If Sweeney was going to confess, he'd done it already. I'm worried Barrett's going to find more evidence, not to convict him, but to get Sweeney off like he did with that other mick, that O'Brien."

"A reasonable deduction."

Stanley didn't know what that meant, but it sounded like he agreed. The old man was always using big words he didn't understand. It made him feel stupid. He was beginning to think Cunningham did it on purpose.

"So Barrett could show up in your jail tomorrow morning with an alibi that forces you to release Sweeney. A murderer goes loose in your town. A miscarriage of justice for the family of the poor girl who was murdered. And it would look like some very sloppy police work to the Governor. Two suspects. Both released."

Why should Stanley give a damn about impressing the Governor? He'd never see the man again after this weekend.

Cunningham produced two cigars, one for Stanley and one for himself. It was the first time he'd offer Stanley anything from his own hand since Barrett showed up. Cunningham lit Stanley's first and then his own. Things were getting back to normal. Cunningham could see Barrett was useless – it was Stanley who got the job done. "I have a plan and I'd like to know what you think of it, Captain."

Finally, his reward for burning down Hogan's warehouse.

The old man squinted at the horizon. A thin flare of green hovered between the land and the sky. "This weekend, I'm asking the governor for a charter authorizing me to assemble a security force. This epidemic of workers organizing has me worried. Boycotts, strikes, shutting down industry. They don't understand how they threaten their own wellbeing. They can't make money if they're out on strike. What's the sense of it? But it's spreading across the country like wildfire. I need to protect my mills. We'll have the authority to police all of the Berkshires. I'm thinking of calling it the Berkshire Rangers."

Cunningham poked Stanley in the chest with his stubby finger. "And I'd want you to head it up. We'll give you an impressive title, something people would stand up and take notice of. They'll know you're the man in charge. How does Colonel George Washington Stanley sound to you?"

Stanley's heart flopped two times. When it started beating right again, Cunningham was still waiting for an answer.

Colonel George Washington Stanley. "Hell, yeah. I like the sound of that."

If only his sonofabitch father had lived long enough to see this.

Cunningham slapped him on the back again. "Good man. But here's the thing. If Barrett lets Sweeney go, I'm afraid I'd have a hard time convincing the governor that you're the man for the job. Are we clear on that?"

Stanley knew exactly what needed to be done. And he was happy to do it.

CHAPTER TWENTY-ONE

MAUREEN MAVOURNEEN

A s LIAM EMERGED FROM Sadie's kitchen, he found the air had a snap to it. The sky was blue-black and thousands of stars glittered. Light from the windows gave the men in the yard a flattened form.

From the house, a woman began to sing. *I dreamt that I dwelt in marble halls.* All the people were quiet again. Her voice was familiar but he hadn't heard it in a very long time. Through the dining room window, the house's interior glowed. The newsman's fiddle laid on his lap as he watched the woman sing. Taller than most, her once-red hair pulled back into a neat bun, her eyes were closed. She was lost in the lyrics. It was Mary Barrett, his mother.

She had been known for her voice. Like a linnet's, his father always said. Someone would always press her to sing at gatherings like this, the night not being complete without a song from Mary Elizabeth Barrett.

For a moment, Liam was a little boy again, curled up in his mother's lap while she sang a Gaelic lullaby and the sweet smoke of his father's pipe surrounded them.

The song was over. Mary's reverie dissolved. She looked about the room, a note of alarm in her eyes. She seemed to have forgotten where she was. Kate was beside her then, an arm around her waist, and kissed her on the cheek. She led the mother away as a long note was sounded on the fiddle. Someone started thumping a drum. A man whooped. The voices rose again in talk, the mood broken.

Liam made his way to the men congregated around the beer barrel. Finn O'Brien was closest to the spigot, drunk already, or still for all Liam knew, and he was leaning on the barrel for support. Harry Gallegher took Finn by the arm and tried to lead him away. "Here's a good lad, why don't you make room for the other fellas?" Finn threw off the arm and staggered backwards, crashing into the keg. Several men ran to brace it from falling.

"Leave me alone." Finn raised the mug to his mouth and missed. Beer poured over his face and down his shirt.

"Here now," Harry said, undaunted. "Let's find you some place to sit before you hurt yourself."

Finn tried to push Harry, but only managed to stumble into him. "You don't understand. You don't know what it's like. It didn't happen to you."

"We all loved her, don't you know," Felix Malone said.

Finn wheeled on Felix. "You're to blame," Finn shouted, jabbing at Felix with the mug, and sloshing beer on himself. "If you didn't get her that job, she wouldn't have left Adams, she'd still be alive. We'd have got married. I loved her that much. She was going to marry me. Me!"

Finn rushed at Felix before Liam could intervene, but Jack Barrett suddenly materialized and slipped between them. Jack, usurping Liam again. He held Finn with strong hands on both shoulders, forced Finn to look at him, and talked a stream about Sadie's heartbreak and how deeply everyone in Adams mourned Deidre's death. Finn began crying and Jack led him away, disappearing in the gloom.

Felix looked stricken. "Can I get you another, Felix?" Harry asked.

Felix didn't answer at first, then shook his head as if to wake himself. "What's that, Harry?"

"Can I get you another?"

"I loved her too. We all did."

"It's the drink talking," Harry said. "Pay him no mind. He won't remember what he said in the morning."

Felix handed his mug to Harry and stumbled towards the street. Liam thought to follow but a hand on his shoulder stayed him.

"I didn't catch all that was going on," Frank said.

"Finn accused Felix of causing Deidre's death. The others broke it up before I could get to them."

"That tall fella, the one steering Finn away, looks enough like you to be your father."

"Uncle," Liam said, as he slipped away. He found Jack and Finn by the chicken coop. Jack still talking. Finn huddled against the shed.

"Under control," Jack said.

"I'll take over from here. Look in on the mother, she's had a long night." Liam shouldered between Jack and Finn.

"I've got it handled."

A hen chirped.

"You're waking the chickens. You'll be wanting a word with Sadie. She'll be glad to see you." Liam, his back to the man, felt Jack draw away. He heard Jack speak from a distance. "Right you are."

When he was sure they were alone, Liam spoke again. "Finn."

Finn's head had dropped to his chest. His mug fell from his hand and what was left poured onto the ground. "Finn," Liam said again, a little louder.

Finn's head jerked upward. "Ah, Liam. How are you doing this evening?"

"Grand, Finn. What say you, we take a little walk, get some fresh air?" Liam put an arm around Finn's shoulder loosely. Finn grabbed Liam's shirt and held on as Liam guided him around to the side yard, where it was black and cold beneath an old, large tree. Liam propped Finn up against the house.

"How are you doing?" Liam asked.

Finn heaved. Liam stepped out of the way, but not fast enough. Finn vomited what seemed to be a gallon of beer, vomited again, then dry heaved a few times. He tried to pull himself to a stand, bracing against the house. His head bobbed. He swung his face up to look at Liam. There were dirty streaks of tears on his face. "I loved her. You know that? I loved her so much."

Finn's eyes rolled up into his head and he slid to the ground.

Liam knelt on one knee and checked Finn's breathing. His chest was rising and falling softly. Liam felt the back of Finn's head. His hand came away wet with blood. He'll have a nasty bump there tomorrow.

Finn's head lolled on his chest as drool poured from his mouth. He suddenly sat up and took a hard look at Liam. "I would have done anything for her. I wouldn't have cared about the bairn, where he came from. I would have married her and taken care of them both. I didn't hurt her. You know that." Then he fell over, passed out.

Liam rocked back on his haunches, watched and waited. He understood how much Finn loved Deirdre. His own Eileen had married another and carried that man's child, but he loved her still. He felt a sharp pain in his heart and he couldn't breathe.

Finn was snoring.

"Sweet dreams, lad." Liam stood, brushed grass from his trousers and walked back to the men at the keg, stopping to tell them Finn was around the corner of the house, sleeping. They said they'd check on him later. Sadie wouldn't let a drunk in the house, much less a vomiting drunk.

As Liam made his way back into the house, Frank fell in beside him. The women in the kitchen parted for the priest easily. They found Kate in the dining room.

"The look of you!" Kate said. Normally, she spoke like an American but when she was mad, she was Irish. She walked around him. "And what's that smell?"

"You'll excuse me," Liam said. He pushed his way through the crowded house. He was on the porch when he realized he hadn't stopped to say good-bye to Deidre. This was his last chance.

Father Frank came out of the house, closing the door behind him. He pulled out two cigars and handed one to Liam. "I haven't had the chance to meet your uncle."

"Best you didn't. He's nothing but trouble."

Frank puffed on his cigar and stared out into the night.

Liam heard himself talking. "I was fourteen years old. I pleaded with my father to let me go with Jack to Pennsylvania. My uncle was driving a wagon of supplies to the Irish coal miners. He convinced my da that it would do me good, to see their struggles, as I was destined to be a lawyer or a judge, or even a senator some day and would need to know about such things. My mother was worried about violence but Jack promised to keep me safe. I was a boy wanting to be a man. I idolized Jack, even more than my own father. So they let me go."

BEFORE THAT TRIP, LIAM'S only memories were of Adams. He'd read about other places but they were no more real to him than ancient Rome or Greece. Pittsfield might as well have been Athens for all he knew until they drove through it. As for Ireland, it was an abstract, a place with no concrete reality, a dreamland his people had imagined, like heaven or hell.

The changing landscape mesmerized him, how the narrow valley opened up to flat open spaces, how the lowland trees were a different color and shape than those on Mount Greylock. They drove through towns with wide streets, stately homes, and imposing business districts. Why didn't Adams look like that? Where had all that money come from? What would those people in those houses think of him if they saw the Barrett farm? If everyone worked hard, why did these people have better things than he did?

He felt lost, a lad in a wagon drifting further and further away from his mother's kitchen, with only his Uncle Jack to bring him back home again. He couldn't comprehend this ever-unrolling landscape of easier lives. There was no point to telling Jack he wanted to go home. He had made a commitment to go on this trip, practically begged his father to let him. He didn't want to look like a frightened child. He was fourteen, the same age as Kevin now, and he wanted Uncle Jack to see him as a man.

So to occupy his mind, Liam asked Jack questions about anything. Where they were. Where they were going next. What kind of tree, bird, or cow that was. Jack always knew, especially about the cattle. He talked knowingly about what they were good for, beef or milk, their dispositions, mean or gentle, and what kind of diseases they were prone to. When Liam asked him how he knew so much, he said, "Ah, it's something I picked up along the way."

At night, they stayed with friends of Jack's. Every place they visited, his uncle would task Liam with tending the horse while he walked with another man out of earshot, heads bent together, gestures tight and close, and the occasional glance over the shoulder. Then they would have dinner with a family, Jack as comfortable at that table as in the Barrett home. He'd call all the youngsters by name and flirt with the wife. Once, a little girl crawled onto Jack's lap as soon as he sat down and stayed there the entire evening. Liam had never sat in his lap. All these other children knew his Uncle Jack as well as, or better, than he did.

After the family retired and Liam bed down on the parlor floor, Jack and the man of the house would leave. "A quick run down to the pub." Exhausted, Liam lain on the hard planks in a half-sleep, vigilant for his return. When the house creaked, his eyes would snap open and it would take a few moments for him to remember where he was. He would look for Jack but the floor next to him was vacant. In the morning, when he woke, the sun would have risen and there was Jack's bedroll, tied up, ready to go.

After breakfast, he would harness the horse and notice that the tarp-covered contents of the wagon had grown and shifted during the night. If he asked what had been added, his uncle answered, "more supplies."

Jack never told him where they were going. All he knew was that it was somewhere in Pennsylvania. Later, he realized Jack had kept it secret lest Liam mention it to the other children who would say something to someone and the word would get out. Whatever you say, say nothing.

After nine days on the road, Jack drove the wagon into a shanty town. Hungry, listless children, flea-bitten and scabby, wandered narrow dirt streets. Skinny women with sunken cheeks sat in front of their plywood shacks, trading small talk. A man leaning in a doorway took notice of Jack. They exchanged nods.

They arrived at a boarding house, a two story home, so old and rickety Liam was afraid to go inside, where Jack introduced Liam to the lady of the house, a young woman heavy with child. She was only a few years older than Liam and had long yellow hair flowing about her like a halo. She looked like an angel.

She looked Liam straight in the eye, something that grown women had not done unless he was being chastised for some childhood sin. In a voice that was warm, she said, "Welcome to our home, Liam Barrett. My name is Maureen McBride. My friends call me 'Mo'."

He knew he was acting like a love-struck adolescent and would be a butt of humor to anyone who noticed. He tried to say thanks but his voice croaked and he felt Jack smothering a laugh behind him. He cleared his throat and said, "Thank you, Mo."

She brushed his cheek lightly with one hand and smiled, not like a woman smiles at a child, but like a woman in love, and he felt himself blush. For the first time, a woman had seen the man in him. Later he told himself that she couldn't have fallen in love with him, she was a married lady after all, that he had misunderstood her maternal glow. But his feelings for her were not so easily discounted.

As before, Jack told Liam to take the horse and wagon to the small barn behind the boarding house while he went for a walk. When Liam had finished currying the animal and was tossing him fresh hay, Jack returned. "We're a hungry pair of men, Liam lad, let's find some food."

Jack led him down one street and then another. Along the way, he bent over to pick a few wildflowers. Jack looked at him curiously.

"For Mo, Mrs. McBride, She's a nice lady," Liam said.

"So she is, Liam lad." Jack squeezed Liam's shoulder. "So she is."

They went into a pub and took a table near the back. Liam laid the little bouquet on the table and Jack raised a hand for the bargirl's attention. "Two drafts for your thirsty travelers." Liam was hungry but he knew better than to complain in front of a stranger.

The waitress was short with wild black hair. She was plump in mysterious, fascinating places. As she bent over their table to serve them, her top fell away exposing two swaying pendulums of flesh. Liam looked away, his face hot. Uncle Jack lifted his beer. "Sláinte!" Then he took a deep drink, hiding his smile behind the raised mug.

Liam's palms began to sweat. His pants didn't fit right anymore. He could feel her presence hovering close to him. She seemed to be waiting.

Jack jostled the table with his knee, laughing. The beer in front of Liam sloshed over the rim drenching Mrs. McBride's flowers.

"Here, now," she said. "Let me clean that up for you."

She moved Liam's mug aside, produced a rag from somewhere and wiped the table, then slid the mug back in place. She worked quickly while his own hands sat idly in his lap. He felt like a messy baby being tended by its mother. His face grew hotter.

Finally, she stood up. He dared to look at her. This must have been what his mother was worried about when she waved good-bye.

"Your young man traveled all the way from Adams, Massachusetts," Jack told the waitress. "Drink down, lad."

A wicked grin crossed her face. Her crooked teeth made her look dangerous. She placed the wet flowers in her rag and carefully pressed, then offered them to him. "Are the flowers for your girl?"

He slipped the limp bouquet into his pocket, his answer gurgling in his throat. He had meant to say he didn't have a girl but ended up choking instead.

She pulled up a stool, stepped over it like a man to sit, and took his hand. "I'll tell your fortune. I'm a gypsy. We have the gift, so."

Liam had never heard of Irish gypsies. He shot a look at his uncle.

"Aye, 'tis true, 'tis true, Liam lad," Jack said. "Back home, they travel in caravans in the countryside, with their horses and dogs. Fine breeders of both. It's a well-known fact that the Irish gypsy girls are the best fortune tellers in the world. I'm betting she can see into your future right now."

"That I can," the gypsy girl said, running a nail-bitten thumb down his palm as she peered into it. "I see a long life, a happy marriage, wealth, many sons to boast of and many daughters as well, all beautiful."

Liam leaned in. "What else do you see?"

"Come back tonight and I'll tell you." The gypsy girl tossed Liam's hand back at him. "Ask for me. Siobhan."

She walked away, going from table to table, man to man, speaking a word here and there. Occasionally she would look over her shoulder and give Liam that wicked smile again.

He turned to see what his uncle thought of the dark Siobhan. Jack's chair was empty. Gone again. From his table, Liam searched every inch of the bar but couldn't find him.

The beer was still on the table. It was not his first but that was a secret from his mother, who disapproved of drink. His father had taken him to the Black Rose for his birthday a few weeks before. As the beer hit his stomach, the room seemed to light up. He was surrounded by men slapping his back and buying him another. No longer a child, he fit in to the brotherhood of Irish expatriates.

That night, he staggered home on his father's arm and vomited along the way. He woke the next morning with a headache and spent the day working in their little patch of farm, away from his mother who would know by looking at him that he had drink taken. He suffered through the day of potato turning and animal feeding. Head splitting, knees wobbly, stomach queasy. He vowed never to drink again.

And here he was, with his hand around another mug. This night was different. The men in the pub didn't laugh and joke. They spoke in low tones and shunted looks over their shoulders to see if anyone was listening. Liam was alone and there was nothing for him to do. He lifted the beer and took a sip.

Soon, his mug was empty but the euphoria had not returned. He wanted to escape from these dangerous-looking men. He felt shame. The feelings he was having for the gypsy girl weren't holy. Would he have to confess to the priest? At the same time, he wanted to go back to the boarding house and give Mrs. McBride the flowers he'd picked for her, then home to Adams and his own bed.

Siobhan sashayed to his table. She said something he didn't understand because of the rushing sound in his ears. "What?"

She picked up the empty mug. "Another?"

If he said no, she would take the mug and leave. If he said yes, she would come back. He wanted her to both stay and leave. He tried to reason his way through his dilemma. What would Plato have done?

Jack rushed into the bar and pulled him out of the chair by his arm. "Time to go."

"But..."

"But nothing. Time to go, I say." Jack pushed Liam out the door.

The horse was hitched to the now empty wagon and waited in the street. "I thought..." Liam started. He had thought they were staying overnight before the return trip. The horse needed a rest.

"Think later, lad. We're leaving."

Angry men came down the street carrying torches. Siobhan ran out of the pub, towards them, yelling profanities. She was swallowed up by the crowd as they advanced. If she screamed, he didn't hear it. Men poured from the bar and scattered. The bar was set on fire.

Jack drove through town. The streets were empty but the distant shouting of men could be heard. When they drove past the boarding house, it was in flames. People were sprawled on the porch, their clothes burning. They were hurt, they needed help. Liam rose to jump out of the wagon. Jack jerked him back into his seat and held him in place. "Too late for them now. There's nothing you can do." As the horse quickened his trot, Liam looked back and realized all those people were dead.

One of the bodies had long yellow hair, Maureen McBride.

During the trip back, they traveled only at night and slept by day, hidden in a barn or deep in a forest. When they finally returned to Adams, Liam went straight to his room. There was an unnatural stillness in the house. He listened to the three of them in the next room, as his uncle told his parents what had happened.

The mob had been strikebreakers. They had been tipped off that Jack had smuggled guns into town. They attacked before the miners could organize an assault. Someone had betrayed Jack. One thing was certain. Jack Barrett, the uncle he had adored, caused the death of the young mother, Maureen McBride, and the others as well.

Some were lynched that night. Others arrested and later tried. Newspapers reported that an uprising had been planned by the Molly Maguires. Ridiculous, the men in the Black Rose spat, as they read the papers. A strike was planned, but not a murderous rampage. The guns were for self-defense. Too bad the Mollys got caught before the workers had a chance to walk off their jobs.

Days later, Liam discovered the small withered bouquet of wildflowers he had picked for Maureen McBride in his pocket. He took them into the yard and buried them next to the house, hoping they would take root. The following spring, he stooped and stared at the bare spot, hoping for a sign of flowers, but none ever grew.

A HEAVY SILENCE HUNG between Frank and Liam after he finished the story. They stood side by side on Sadie's porch, gazing into the night's gloom. Behind them, the wake had quieted. The fiddler no longer made music. A toddler whined. Tired voices exchanged farewells. The door opened with a gust of hot air as the people of Adams began filing out of Sadie Monaghan's boarding house.

"And the gypsy girl?" Frank asked. "What happened to her?"

"She made it out safe."

Liam's cigar had gone cold. When his uncle was in the vicinity, bad things happened to good people. "Watch yourself, Frank. Jack Barrett cannot be trusted."

CHAPTER TWENTY-TWO

A TIDE OF EVIL

S TANLEY LED THE GREY mare into the alley and stopped her near the jail's back door. Inside the wagon bed were the tools he'd need: the jailhouse keys and a long rope.

After the fire in Adams, he had found the horse wandering down the road back to Pittsfield, not having the sense to run off. He mounted her and rode the rest of the way, his burned calves abraded by the saddle stirrups. By the time he arrived home, the skin had been peeled away. He was too fat to see the backsides of his legs but he could tell by the woman's face the wounds were bad. She saw to them with ointment and bandages. Laudanum had gotten him through his meeting with Cunningham but it was wearing off. He pulled the little brown bottle from his trouser pocket and took a nip of the bitter brew.

There was still a tense truce between him and the horse. Tonight, he tied her up so she wouldn't take off again. She gave him a look which said she'd escape if she'd had the chance and next time, he wouldn't find her.

His keys jangled as he unlocked the door. He stepped into the darkness of the cell block. Silver diamonds floated across the floor, moonlight cast through cell windows.

There was only one man in the block, Owen Sweeney. He slept on his side facing the wall. When Stanley tread on a creaky board, the prisoner's back stiffened. His head lifted slightly.

"Who's there?"

"Captain Stanley. Get off your ass, you're being transferred."

Sweeney swung his legs over the cot and rubbed sleep from his eyes. "Where to?"

"Adams."

"In the middle of the night?"

"Less likely of running into a mob and getting lynched, if that suits you."

Stanley opened the cell door. The prisoner extended his wrists and Stanley locked cuffs onto them. He pushed the tramp towards the back door and then through it, leaving the door ajar.

The prisoner waited by the end of the wagon. "I can't get in with these things on my wrists."

Stanley slammed the man's head onto the wagon bed, then picked up his legs and pushed.

"You're in." Stanley picked up a loose brick the jailers used to prop open the back door on warm days and crashed it down on the prisoner's skull. The tramp's complaining could have attracted attention. Stanley was pleased with himself having found a solution to that problem. He was quick on his feet. Anyone could see that. The tramp slept through the ride out of town.

Stanley drove the wagon deep into the woods and onto an abandoned farm road that eventually disappeared into undergrowth. He went as far as the wagon could go, slung the coil of rope over a shoulder and dragged Sweeney out of the bed. The man, as heavy as a wet bag of cement, fell to the ground, groaning, still unconscious.

Walking backwards, Sweeney dragged him into the woods by the feet, frozen leaves crunching beneath him, his own breath blasting from his mouth in puffs of smoke. He began to tire. He was breathing hard. His back and elbows ached. His feet slipped. His fingers and palms burned from clutching Sweeney's trousers.

If he could find his way back following the grooves dug by the tramp in the mud, then someone might notice the trail and find the body . Next week or a hundred years from now, it didn't matter to his plan. If the body wasn't found, the prisoner had escaped and gone back to his band of thieves. If the body was found, they must have killed him thinking he had betrayed their secrets. So why was Stanley working so hard to drag him into the depths of the forest?

He dropped the tramp. He tossed the rope over a tree branch, looped the noose around Sweeney's neck and pulled. When the tramp was half off the ground, he came to and clutched at the cord tightening around his neck. Unearthly slithering noises came out of his gaping mouth. Stanley gave the rope one giant tug. He heard bones crack. There was some flinching of feet and hands. It didn't take as long as Stanley expected it would.

No last words? Stanley had forgotten to ask.

He'd get it right next time.

He tied the rope around the trunk of the tree, walked a few yards away, then checked his work. Yes, that man was dead. No one could survive with a neck bent like that. Then Stanley followed the grooves the dead man's body had left in the soil.

The mare was standing right where he left her, hitched to the wagon, tied to a tree, and wedged into an old farm road that was too narrow to go forward with no place to turn around.

∽

L IAM SAT IN A chair facing Captain Curran's desk. Curran pulled out his pocket watch, studied it, snapped it shut, and slipped it back into his vest. "They were due half an hour ago." Captain Stanley and Malcom Dunbar were late for their appointment to discuss security arrangements for the governor's visit.

Liam could not get comfortable in the wooden chair. He should be out on the street, walking. Every morning, he stopped in at the shopkeepers to make sure they found their businesses in order, exchanged greetings with mill workers on their way to their shift, and shooed wayward children toward school. He had also planned a swing past Hogan's this morning to make sure there hadn't been any more trouble.

Because his body was accustomed to walking most of the day, his leg muscles were starting to cramp. He shifted. The chair complained. He was thinking it might crumble beneath him when he heard men crashing past the young officer seated at the desk.

The door swung open. Dunbar and Stanley entered, the officer on their heels.

Liam stood. Stanley poked Liam in the chest. "Your man escaped last night. His Molly friends picked the jailhouse lock."

Liam batted the hand away.

"Stanley!" Curran was on his feet. "You will not lay hands on my officer."

The last time Liam had seen Stanley, he was beating a handcuffed Finn O'Brien. The man was a bully. In most situations, Liam tried to find a peaceful resolution but this time he pressed forward, daring Stanley to take a swing. "They aren't Mollys."

Dunbar slipped between them. "Settle down, Barrett. How could you know? The only way is if you're one yourself. It's a secret society, isn't it? Are all of you in on it?"

How was Liam to answer that? *I asked my Uncle Jack, who everyone knows is a Molly, and he told me?* Jack's arrival soon after the Irishmen suddenly appeared looked suspicious. He swore they weren't involved, and they seemed to not have known him. But his uncle had hidden the truth from him before. And he would do so again were it to suit him.

Curran stepped out from behind his desk and took a conciliatory tone. "Gentlemen, thank you for coming in this morning so we can discuss security for tomorrow's event."

Dunbar would not be derailed. "The tramps are troublemakers. Bog-trotting immigrants the lot of them, no jobs, no roots. It's no coincidence they show up days before the governor visits, the girl is killed, Hogan's burns down, and Sweeney escapes. The governor has long been set against organized labor. They're agitators, Curran, rest assured of that. His assassination would be quite the feather in their cap. Open your eyes, man! Trouble is nigh and they're at the heart of it!"

Before Liam had reported for duty, he swung by the Black Rose to check on the lads. The cellar door was unlocked. He ran down the rickety stairs as fast as he dared. The place was empty but for neatly stacked barrels and bottles. Then he heard muffled voices overhead. In the apartment above the bar, he found two men in the kitchen washing dishes while Harry and the others sat around a table playing cards. "Fine morning, to you, Liam," Harry said. "When do you suppose this whole thing will be over? The boys here aren't taking to being locked up underground."

"A little while longer," Liam had said.

With Dunbar and Stanley standing in Captain Curran's office making accusations, he was glad that he and Jack had moved the boys. He had sensed something like this was coming. Sadie Monaghan would say he had the gift of second sight. She would be wrong. All week, Cunningham had been directing suspicion away from Inverness, first to Finn O'Brien, then to Owen Sweeney. It was only a matter of time before he implicated the lads in the woods. He was protecting someone, Liam had no doubt. Most likely his son Edward.

Curran pulled a pint of whiskey and three shot glasses from a desk drawer and filled each glass. "Let's start over, shall we?"

Dunbar picked up a glass, tossed back the contents, and slammed the empty glass onto the desk. Curran, with his eyes on Dunbar, did the same, then refilled both their drinks. Stanley shrugged and picked up the last glass. "Too good to drink with us, Barrett?"

"Officer Barrett doesn't take drink," Curran said. "Have a seat, gentlemen. Let's get down to business."

Dunbar remained standing. "There's no time for chatter. We went to the Molly camp this morning. They were gone, cleared out. Stanley needs to organize a search party. Tell me what you have arranged for the ceremony and we'll be on our way."

Liam had his own ideas, but Curran was his better. He took position to the side of the room where he could keep an eye on Stanley. He could feel the man's awareness of him, radiating like heat. Liam adjusted his weight. Stanley flinched. Liam suppressed a smile.

Captain Curran gave Liam a sidelong, disapproving look. His voice was sharp. "Officer Barrett, my most trusted man, will be in attendance, roaming through the crowd. I will be there as well."

"That's it?" Dunbar shot a look at Stanley.

"Mr. Dunbar," Curran said. "Adams is a peaceful community. It's a library dedication, not a drunken horse race. The audience will be full of schoolmarms and mothers with children, families who come downtown for their weekly shopping. There's no reason why anyone would want to disrupt the festivities."

Dunbar scoffed. "Well now, laddie, that's where you're wrong. Those filthy black-guards are on the move. What reason do they have to be in the Berkshires? I'll tell you. They heard the governor's coming to the groundbreaking. For the library, I might add, that Alastair Cunningham is building out of charity to benefit your people."

The library had been the talk of the town along with how Cunningham had bought the cotton mill and planned to build another. A carrot and a stick, the workers were saying. It was only a matter of time before everyone was dependent upon Alistair Cunningham's money. The town would be trapped. What if he dropped their wages like had happened to the Pennsylvania steelworkers? Could they afford to strike? Meanwhile the town fathers were saying he was good for business, more people would be employed, the merchants would flourish, the town would grow while ever reminding the workers how generous Cunnigham was to build a library.

Captain Curran was trapped between the two factions. "I'm aware of all that, Mr. Dunbar. But as I've said, there's been no sightings of those tramps in or around Adams."

"And how are you to know that with only you and Barrett?"

"I would have heard about it. It's not only the two of us. We have Caleb Anthony, my lad behind the desk."

Caleb, upon hearing his name, appeared at the door. He was barely out of his teens and gawky in his police uniform. He had recently been hired to man the station while Liam and Curran were busy elsewhere. "Sir?"

"Him?" Dunbar laughed.

"Thank you, Caleb. I'll call you if I need you."

Caleb returned to his desk, leaving the door ajar.

Dunbar knocked on the desktop twice. "I'll tell you something you don't know, Curran. You need to keep this under your hat, mark you. The governor is making a big announcement at the dedication: his candidacy for president of the United States of America. Mr. Cunningham has made sure that the ceremony will be well-attended by the press. Reporters will be here. Photographers too. This will be national news."

"How would the tramps know about the announcement if it's been a secret all this time?" Curran asked.

"They have their ways. It's exactly the kind of thing that wretched gang of hooligans would love to ruin."

"Those men you're talking about are merely looking for work," Liam said. "They aren't hooligans."

"So says you, your own uncle a Molly."

There again. Like Cunningham before him, Dunbar knew more about Liam than should be expected. How did Dunbar know who Liam's uncle was? He'd have dug pretty deep to discover Jack, given he hadn't been to Adams in a very long time. Did he know about what had happened in Pennsylvania too? Felix Malone must have told him. How much had Felix said and why was he so talkative with this man? Was Felix's loyalty to Inverness stronger than it was to Adams? Did Felix know that Jack was in Adams now and had he told Dunbar?

If Dunbar had any idea that Victoria Cunningham was consorting with the likes of Jack Barrett, they would find Jack's body in a ditch. It was a dangerous game Jack was playing.

Dunbar snapped his fingers at Curran. "Listen here. This is what you're going to do. Stanley is rustling up some men and you will arm your own."

"What about the crowd?" Liam asked. "How are we to protect innocent men, women and children with guns being waved about? It's too risky."

Curran spoke slowly and deliberately. "If I see so much as one armed man, I will arrest him myself."

Dunbar flung an angry gesture into the air. "And you'll stand by while the Mollys take potshots at the governor? With an assassin on the loose? Who will protect your crowd then?"

Curran crossed his arms. "Violence begets violence. I will not have guns in my town."

Spit flew as Dunbar shouted. "It's not up to you, anymore, Captain. The governor is under the protection of Mr. Alistair Cunningham and it is my responsibility to make sure his visit here is a safe one."

"Then perhaps you should be working on the gala menu instead, Mr. Dunbar," Curran said, "and leave the police work to the professionals."

Dunbar stalked towards the door, then spun back around.

"Mark my words, Curran. Should anything go awry, it will be on your head."

Liam heard the bustle of street traffic as the police station door was opened and then slammed shut.

Caleb appeared at the office door. "Is everything alright, sir?"

Curran sat behind his desk, motioning his two officers to sit as well. "What was that about, Liam? I've never seen you angry much less dare a man to strike you. The reason I hired you was for your even temper."

"The man is a bully. He nearly beat Finn O'Brien to death right in front of me. I brought assault charges against him in court and he claimed it was self-defense. His sergeant backed up his story and the judge dismissed my charges. There's only one way to stop a man like that."

"Not by you, I hope. At least not while you're in uniform."

Caleb raised his hand as if he was still in school. "Sir, do you think Captain Stanley will return with armed men? What if agitators come? What will we do?"

"Not to worry, Caleb. Dunbar is the kind of man who blusters. He's said his piece and he'll be off chasing around the countryside looking for those fellows. It doesn't behoove Cunningham's man to strongarm the people of Adams. That new mill isn't built yet. If he lets thugs loose on us now, it will never get built. He knows which side his bread is buttered. Rest assured. I expect no trouble."

"Sir," Liam said. "Caleb's right. It isn't safe for all those people coming to town tomorrow. We should call off the dedication."

"Not a chance, Liam. Off with you, now. Time for us to get back to work." Curran pulled paperwork from a drawer and laid it out on the ink blotter.

Liam sat in his chair, stunned. He'd known Captain Curran all his life and had believed he was a man dedicated to the townspeople's safety. Yet here he was, acting as if he was in Cunningham's pocket, or at the least, hoping to jump in it.

Curran looked up to see Liam and Caleb still sitting before him. "Are you still here? Perhaps I didn't make myself clear. Officers, you are dismissed."

CHAPTER TWENTY-THREE

THE LOST

B Y THE TIME LIAM was back on the streets, Deidre's funeral mass was over. The mourners were clustered near the Friends Meeting House, built in the Quaker tradition a hundred years earlier, simple and plain, a tall, wood plank structure. Most Quakers had long since moved on but a few remained, including Adams' newest police officer, Caleb Anthony, who had stayed behind to care for his aging grandparents.

The sky was a thin pale blue and there was a nip in the air as Liam walked up to the pallbearers gathered around a wagon that served as a hearse. Sadie had asked six men to carry Deidre to her final resting place. Five of them, including Liam, were there: Harry Gallegher, James O'Herlihy, the newspaperman who had played fiddle at her wake, Joe Hogan, and his son-in-law, Tom Gillepsie. The sixth would have been Finn. But he was not to be found.

Frank, wearing gold-embroidered black funeral vestments, approached them from the open grave.

"Are we ready, lads?" He counted heads. "Who's missing?"

"Finn," Harry said. "No one's seen hide nor hair of him."

"I threw a blanket over him last night," Frank said. "He'd been sick so I couldn't see dragging him through Sadie's house like that. This morning, I went to check on him. The blanket was left on the grass and he was gone. I thought he had gotten up early to go to work before the funeral."

Tom Gillespie shook his head. "Haven't seen him."

"Probably in bed then," Harry said. "He'll have a mighty head on him today."

"Well then, what to do?" Frank asked. "The undertaker or his lad could step in as they did at the church."

Liam spotted Kevin with the family, caught his eye, and motioned. Kevin trotted over. "We need a hand."

"What about Finn?"

Frank said, "We can't wait any longer, for Sadie's sake."

Kevin was placed on the right side with Liam in front and Harry behind so they would carry most of the weight. They slid the coffin off the wagon, shouldered it, and carried it to the open grave.

After the coffin had been lowered into the ground, Sadie stepped towards the graveside. Her knees buckled. Kate and Eileen each grabbed an elbow. Kate spoke into Sadie's ear. Sadie shook her head.

A man stepped out from behind the Friends house. Hat in hand, bushy beard combed out, it was Malcom Dunbar. He stood away from the crowd that surrounded Sadie and her daughter's grave. Liam caught his eye. Dunbar cast that stabbing stare of his at Liam for a moment but didn't hold the gaze long. Why had he come? Paying his respects on behalf of Cunningham? They acted as if they barely knew Deirdre. When they charged out of Curran's office, he said he was going out to search for the missing Irishmen.

Father Frank said the prayers. The mourners crossed themselves and began to drift away. The men with jobs first. The women with children next.

Kevin sided up to Liam. "Can I go help Tom at the store? It's too late to go back to school."

Kevin had already missed half the school day. And, Liam was guessing, Eileen had promised to feed him. "Make yourself useful," Liam said. Kevin was turning to run after Tom and Eileen when Liam called out, "And remember to come home in time to do your chores."

The old ladies still milled about. They whispered amongst themselves, waiting for a word with Sadie, perhaps ready to offer her company for the rest of the day.

Harry began drifting with the older men back toward his tavern. "Hold on," Liam said to him quietly.

"I'll be along presently," Harry called to the men and tossed them a large key ring. "Let yourselves in. First drink on the house."

Would the Irishmen be found? "Is that safe?" Liam asked.

"The lads are in my apartment. I couldn't bear them living a hole in the ground like badgers."

Liam had planned to stay at the graveside with Father Frank until the last mourner had gone. He wanted to catch Finn if he showed up drunk again, or drunk still, and pull him aside before he wrecked Sadie's last moments with her daughter. He, Frank, and Harry stood in silence, Liam not wanting to talk about the case in the presence of a grieving mother today of all days. She certainly did not need to know that Dunbar was lurking nearby.

Kate led Sadie away, and as they left, Liam noticed Dunbar's shadow retreat behind the meeting house. After the women were well far away, Liam walked around the structure looking for Dunbar. He was nowhere to be seen. In the distance, Liam heard the sound of a horse's hooves loping away.

Liam returned to the graveside where Frank and Harry had waited. They began the walk back to the Black Rose.

"Who was that sour bugger lurking in the shadow?" Harry asked.

"Malcom Dunbar," Liam said. "He's the overseer at Inverness."

"You reckon he was sent on the old man's behalf?"

"He would have said something to Sadie if that were so."

Frank said, "Perhaps, he didn't want to find himself surrounded by a group of Irishmen, outnumbered as he was."

"He wasn't here to fight," Liam said.

"Maybe not, but things aren't much different over here. He wasn't here only to pay his respects. That man was in pain. You could see it on his face."

Liam stopped walking. Frank stopped with him. Harry kept going, shouting over his shoulder, "I'll see you lads later. I need to get back to the bar before those hooligans drink me dry."

Liam said to Frank, "Do you think Malcom Dunbar is mourning Deidre's death?"

If that was true, she was far more important to Dunbar than he had let on. Could he have been her lover, the man who had promised to take her away? Victoria Cunningham had seen them engaged in serious conversation in the days before her death. He had a bedroom on the second floor, where Deidre had been seen. If she was carrying his child, would he have killed her to protect his secret? Or had someone else killed her and Dunbar wanted Liam to find the man so he could avenge her death? It would explain how aggressive he was towards Sweeney when they found the poor man in the woods wearing Deirdre's crucifix.

"I can't tell you the reason," Frank said. "But I can tell you that I've been a priest for a few years now and I have spent a lot of time consoling the grieving. If there is one thing I know, it is Malcom Dunbar is a man in pain."

"Walk with me," Liam said. He led Father Frank out of town and turned around. They walked in on the road that the governor, Cunningham, and their retinue would take to the library dedication. Liam stopped every few yards and examined his surroundings.

"Have you lost something?" Frank asked.

"Not lost. Hidden. Malcom Dunbar and Captain Stanley were in the police station this morning, insisting that we should have armed men at the dedication. Dunbar's certain there's a plot to assassinate the governor. I want to know every possible place a marksman could conceal himself."

What Liam didn't tell Frank was that Dunbar accused the Irishmen in the woods of executing the plot. If Dunbar was right, Liam had made a critical, even fatal, mistake. He had moved them into the heart of town and had made sure they were well fed to boot. They would have no trouble fanning out and taking cover, ready to ambush the governor's party.

As a boy, Liam had played hide and seek with his friends. He wanted to revisit those places, remind himself where they all were, see which were big enough for a man to hide in.

Liam examined the trees alongside the road, those old enough to be climbed, and close enough to shoot from. Although they were bare-branched now and could not conceal a man, hiding in the foliage would not be necessary if the tree was sited so that it came into view when a traveler came around a bend.

As they entered town, they came upon brick buildings lining the road. Behind these buildings were the favored hiding spots of Liam and his childhood friends, able to dart out into the street quickly. The roofs, too, were good hiding places.

Many of the shopkeepers lived on the second story, accessible by stairs from the inside and by fire escapes on the backside. "I need to speak with all the shopkeepers, make sure they keep the fire escape door locked. We can't have someone using an apartment for a shooting blind."

The first shop on Park Street they came upon was the photographer, Parson's. Liam was reaching for the doorknob when Kevin came running towards him.

"Finn O'Brien," Kevin said with his hands on his knees, panting. "We found him. In Hogan's warehouse."

L IAM AND FRANK STOOD in wet ash, the stink of it in their nostrils, near where one of the warehouse walls had been. All that was left was charred frame. It was from a blackened rafter that the body swung. As soon as they came upon the scene, Frank blessed himself and began praying silently.

By the looks of it, Finn had thrown a rope over a beam, wrapped a noose around his neck, and jumped. The ladder he would have used lain nearby on the ground where it had fallen.

Tom Gillespie was standing some distance from the body. "I didn't know what to do," he said. "I didn't know if I should cut him down or if you wanted to see things first."

"Where is Eileen?" Liam asked.

"Inside the house," Tom said. "She was making lunch. I sent Kevin to the store for a can of beans. That's when he found him, hanging there like that."

Kevin had seen dead bodies before, but only after they had been prepared by the undertaker. This was the first time he'd seen a human die so violently that his face was bloated and purple, his eyes and tongue bulging, his trousers stained from piss and crap. This would change him, Liam thought as he felt the image engrave into his own mind. "Does she know not to come out?"

"Give me some credit, Liam. Her father is with her. He'll keep her safe."

"Did you happen by here this morning?"

"What do you think I am? I wouldn't have left him there all morning. The way that the structures are sited," he said, pointing to each building in turn, "the store facing the road, the house next to it facing the road too, and the warehouse behind the store, I couldn't see him when we left the house by the front door."

"That's not what I meant. I am trying to establish the last time you saw the warehouse before Finn was found. That way, we'd get an idea of when this happened."

"Sure, sure," Tom said, calmer. "That'd have been last night when I closed up the store."

"I must have been the last to see him," Frank said. "When I threw a blanket over him there in Sadie's yard."

Liam heard the sound of a wagon clattering up the road and supposed it was old Doc McPherson arriving. He had sent Kevin to find the town's only doctor who also served as Adam's coroner.

The doctor and Kevin came around the store and stopped beside the men. Dr. McPherson, a Scottish gent in a bespoke suit, held his black medical bag in one hand as he looked up at the body. "There's nothing I can do here but take him away," he said.

"Have you a knife?" Liam asked Tom.

"I do," Kevin said, producing a folding knife from his pocket.

"Where'd you get that?" Liam asked.

"Uncle Jack," Kevin said, then his mouth fell open as he apparently realized he'd not only revealed a secret, that he had a knife, but also a confidence, from whom he'd gotten it.

"We'll talk about this later," Liam said. "Hand it over."

Liam picked up the ladder and propped it against the rafter. He climbed the rungs as he called down, "Gillespie, you grab the legs."

Tom pulled off his Sunday best jacket, handing it off to Kevin, and wrapped his arms around the urine-soaked pants. Liam finished the climb to the top, trying not to look at Finn's face as he passed, then pulled out the knife and began sawing.

The first few threads of the rope, straining from its load, were hard to cut. Liam severed more than half the strands when the remaining started snapping. "He's coming down," Liam yelled.

"We're ready," Tom yelled back.

Liam hacked at the few remaining strands and the rope snapped. The body tumbled into the ladder, knocking it out from under him. He felt himself flying backwards, the knife still in his hand. He tossed the blade away, hoping not to land on it. He hit the earthen floor flat on his back. A light exploded in his head and the breath was knocked out of him. He was alone in darkness, the sound of his heart pounding in his ear, fighting for air. This was not his time to die. He couldn't leave his family behind, not now. They needed him.

His chest moved, slightly at first. Liam sucked for air and coughed. The first breath tasted sweet, like fresh water. Air filled his lungs, seeped out then filled again. His eyesight cleared and he saw Finn O'Brien's crumpled body.

Doc McPherson bent over Liam so close he could smell whiskey and tobacco. "Don't move, lad. You've taken a hard fall. Let's have a look at you."

Liam tried to push himself up.

"There's no urgency here," the old man said, holding him in place. "Settle down."

McPherson palpated Liam's limbs and rib cage. "No breaks, but you're bound to be sore for a few days. How's your head?"

It hurt. "Fine," Liam said.

"Try sitting up."

Liam felt hands under his arms guide him to a sitting position. McPherson was before him. Gillespie and Kevin were standing over Finn. The hands had to have belonged to Frank. As soon as he was upright, Liam felt dizzy and vomited.

McPherson felt the back of Liam's head and pulled away a bloody hand. "You have a nasty bump there, young man. Best you take it easy for a few days." McPherson stood. "Kevin!"

"Yes sir?"

"Watch your brother. If he faints or vomits again, come for me right away, you understand?"

"Yes, sir."

"Not necessary," Liam said, pushing himself to a squat.

McPherson held him down with one hand to the shoulder. "Liam, if an old man like myself can stop you from moving, you need to take it easy." To Frank, he said, "Reverend, look after your man."

"That I will."

"I don't need minding. I'm fine."

"If you won't listen to your doctor, or to me, you'll answer to your sister Kate."

"Don't go worrying her," Liam said. "She has enough to deal with. I feel fine. That's the truth of it." With that, he pushed himself to a stand.

"Let's get poor Finn into my wagon," McPherson said.

"Wait." With one hand on Frank's shoulder for balance, Liam walked to Finn O'Brien's side. Someone had stretched him out on his back. Liam bent down and rifled through Finn's pants pockets, pulling out a piece of paper. The act of bending over made his head pound. He gently pulled himself to stand and found the pain ebbing away.

He opened the folded paper. In a childish handwriting it said, "Tell Sadie I'm sorry."

He handed the note to Tom.

"Poor bastard," Tom said.

"Does this look like Finn's hand to you?"

"Couldn't say." Tom handed the note back to Liam. "You don't think someone wrote that note for him?"

Liam cocked his head, looking at the body from an angle. There were no rope burns on the wrists. Finn had been very drunk the night before. It wouldn't take much to wrap a noose around his neck and hoist him from the dirt floor into the air, making it look as if he jumped. "His fiancé was murdered. He was grief stricken. It looks like he did this to himself."

"But you don't think so." Frank pulled out his purple scarf, kissed it, and crossed himself. He knelt next to the body.

"You're not going to give him the Last Rites, are you Father?" Tom Gillespie said. The Church forbade sacrament to suicides.

Frank looked from Gillespie to Liam, to the rope still around Finn's neck, to the rafters overhead. "It looks like an accident to me, gentlemen. I have no reason to withhold absolution from this poor suffering child of God." He whispered the Latin prayers as if he was speaking them so only Finn could hear.

Liam slipped the note into his own pocket.

Chapter Twenty-Four

A Second Look

THE INVERNESS STABLE WAS large and airy with wide doors opened on both ends and half doors on each stall. It smelled of fresh hay, horse, and dung. The stalls were clean and there were no droppings in sight but that smell would linger, soaked into the wood structure. The Barrett shed was like that. Horses and cows came and went but their smell stayed behind.

Liam found Felix Malone inside a stable, currying the big black stallion that had nearly trampled Liam with Victoria Cunningham astride. The stallion's eyes flared as he approached. Horses could smell fear. The trick was not to be afraid around them. Quite a trick, if one could manage it.

The horse was hitched to a wall-mounted ring. Liam stopped far enough away that those powerful hooves couldn't reach him.

"Afternoon, Liam," Felix said, then he ducked under the stallion's neck, disappearing behind its bulk.

"Afternoon, Felix. Missed you at the funeral." Malone hadn't attended.

Felix's voice came from behind the horse. "I couldn't face Sadie. If I hadn't got Deirdre that job, she wouldn't be dead now."

Felix shuffled around the horse, murmuring and patting it on the flanks as he did. The stallion didn't twitch, only swiveled its ears to hear his voice.

"The horse likes you," Liam said.

"I've cared for Goliath here since he was a colt. He's not so bad."

"He doesn't like everyone," Liam observed. The horse's ears flicked in his direction.

"You're in his blind spot. You're making him nervous. Come closer, he'll be grand."

Liam took one tentative step closer. The horse didn't react. He took another step. The stallion's massive head swung in his direction, eyes wide.

"Stop there," Malone said. "You're right. He doesn't like you."

"I need to speak with you. Can we go somewhere else?"

"I have a job, Liam. This horse needs care. Don't get me fired." Felix began running a comb along the stallion's coat. "They're mad enough I talked to you last time. It's a good thing everyone else is afraid of Goliath or I'd be out of a job."

Liam waited for the horse to settle down. After several minutes, his head dropped and his eyes were no longer so wide.

"Sadie doesn't blame you, Felix," Liam said in a quiet voice, watching the horse. His ear moved around but otherwise he didn't react. "She thinks it was someone in the big house."

"So she would. It only makes sense. The darling girl was here six and one-half days a week. If someone from Adams wanted to kill her, and why would they – she was an angel – they would not have traveled all the way out here."

"I have some more bad news," Liam said. "Finn O'Brien was found dead this morning."

Felix turned around to face Liam. The horse woke up. "What happened?"

"It looks like he hung himself."

"God bless his soul, the poor bastard."

Liam took the note from his pocket and handed it to Felix. "Take a look at this will you? Tell me what you think."

Felix shrugged an apology and handed the note back. "I can't read. Never learnt."

"He says to tell Sadie he's sorry."

"I'm sure he was."

"It wasn't his fault Deirdre was murdered. He was with you all that afternoon, from when he got off the train until he was arrested. He didn't have enough time."

Felix ducked under the horse's neck again. Liam circled around, at a distance, so he could see Felix' reaction. "That's what you said."

"That is what I said."

"Why are you hiding from me?"

Felix concentrated on brushing the horse. "I am not hiding, Liam. I have a job to do and I'm doing it."

"Look at me."

Felix' arms dropped to his side. He steeled himself, looking hard at something inside his mind, then looked up at Liam.

"There's something you're not telling me, Felix."

"I got to thinking. Everything I told you was true. I found Finn at the train station, standing there, looking like he didn't know which way to go. I stopped to say hello. Turns out he's headed for the horse races. So I says I'd give him a lift if he helped me out with the animals and he says he was only glad to. It's only that...," Felix crossed his arms. "It's only that when I saw him, it had to be a good half hour after the train arrived."

Deirdre's body was found less than a mile from the train station. Thirty minutes was enough time for Finn to follow her into the woods, kill her, and return to the train station to be found by Felix.

Liam said, "I wish you would have mentioned this before."

"Honest, Liam, I didn't think of it. And then you caught that fella with Deidre's cross so I reckoned, there was no reason to say anything, was there?"

"Did Finn say anything to you about Deidre that afternoon?"

"Only that she threw him over. She was going off to start a new life with someone else."

Even a man like Felix Malone could lie out of misguided loyalty. If Liam had asked Felix more questions, he would have found this out before he saw Finn. He would have treated Finn differently, perhaps gotten him to confess. The truth, if he was the murderer, would have been known from the very start. Alistair Cunningham may have been right all along.

"Is there anything else you might have forgotten to tell me about?" Liam had spoken sharply. The horse pawed at the ground. Liam stepped back.

Felix murmured soothing sounds, stroking the animal, settling him again, then said. "That's the truth of it, what I told you."

"What do you know about Deidre's condition?"

"So you know." Felix squeezed his eyes shut. He rested his forehead against the horse's massive rib cage. "I found her behind the house one morning, throwing up. She told me everything. She was in love with Edward Cunningham. She said he loved her too. He promised to marry her. He was going to take her to New York City where they could start a new life away from his father. She knew it would break Sadie's heart if she married a Protestant but she reckoned when the baby came, all would be forgiven. New York's not so far away. Sadie could come visit and Deidre would bring the baby to see its grandmother. She had it all figured out. I tried telling you, Liam. But I didn't know how much you knew and I saw no reason to blacken her name, her being dead. What good would it do? You're a bright lad. I told you she had been seen on the second floor because you'd find out she had no business being there. That's where she was visiting Edward. She would sneak into his room late at night."

"But she never said anything to Sadie."

"She was waiting for Edward to set a wedding date. He said he had to tell his father and he was waiting for the right moment. She got tired of waiting so she told the old man herself while Edward was away. Marched herself right into his study, bold as you please. She told him that she and Edward were getting married and they were having a child. Old Man Cunningham blew up. I can't imagine that little girl standing there all by herself with that Scotsman bellowing at her. Such a brave girl, Deirdre was. He told her to go to Boston and get rid of it. He'd pay for everything. She said she wasn't killing her baby. Then he said she should go to a convent, have the child, and leave it there. He promised her a job with one of his friends anywhere she wanted to go. London, Paris. She refused. She believed that fecking eejit Edward was going to marry her."

"What did Edward do?"

"I don't know the lad knew about the argument, or the baby. He only returned from his trip the same day Deirdre was killed. Old Cunningham has big ambitions for Edward in politics. This party was by way of introducing his son to the governor."

"You know a lot for working in the barns."

"The staff talks."

"Mrs. Ramsey, you mean."

"She was beside herself. She'd raise the boy, his mother having died in childbirth. She was proud of Edward, for no reason in particular I could see. The boy is a wastrel."

"How long ago was this that Deirdre argued with Cunningham?"

"A week before she died."

"Did she talk to you? Did she say what she was going to do?"

"She was waiting for Edward to come home. She reckoned he'd rescue her, take her away. But they had no intention of leaving those two alone ever again. That whole week, they kept after her. All of them. Dunbar cornered her in the kitchen garden, tried to talk her into giving up the baby. He said Edward would never marry her, not man enough to stand up to his father. And Mrs. Ramsey told her the best thing she could do for the child was to give it up."

"When did Edward come back? Before or after Deirdre was murdered?"

"He wasn't here when I left for the races."

"You would know."

"I'm outside all day long, Liam. I see everyone and everything coming and going."

"**Y**OU'RE HERE AGAIN?" MRS. Ramsey asked.

Felix Malone had opened the kitchen door for Liam. They found her standing in front of the cooker, pulling a boiling kettle off the stove. Felix slipped back out, closing the door quietly behind him, and left Liam on his own.

"I have a few more questions, Mrs. Ramsey."

"Very well." She filled a teapot and took a seat at the head of the table. She did not invite him to sit.

"It's my understanding that Edward Cunningham was away until Sunday."

She did not offer a response.

"When did he leave?"

She took a deep breath and stared into the air while she appeared to calculate. "It must have been the Sunday before. Yes, that's right. I'd made lamb, Edward's favorite, but he had to leave before supper. No one warned me that he was to miss his special dinner or I would have made this again on Saturday."

"So this trip was unexpected?"

"They don't tell me what they're doing, Officer Barrett. I'm a servant. The plans could have been made weeks ago. How am I to know?"

"You've been with the family for a very long time."

"Since Victoria was a bairn I was the nanny in those days. Then Edward came along and their mother went to her heavenly reward. I raised them the best I could."

"Victoria has a mind of her own."

Mrs. Ramsey's chin jutted up. "That girl is going places."

"And Edward?"

"He's the only son of a great man and he feels the weight of that heavy upon his shoulders. Alistair Cunningham came here a poor immigrant, like so many of us, and built his empire from the ground up. He's clever, I'll give him that. Hardworking, too."

"But?"

"But he doesn't give Edward a chance to stand on his own two feet. He's ruining that boy with money. A man needs to struggle to find his destiny. With everything handed to him, he can never grow up. Not that anyone would listen to me. I'm but a lowly housekeeper."

"Did you know about his plans to marry Deidre?"

She laughed. "He never had plans to marry that silly lass. Oh, but she had plans to marry him, she did. And trap him into it. She tried, but Alistair saw her for what she was. And so he put his foot down."

"What about the child?"

"How do you know there was a child? We only had her word for it. And if there was, whose child was it? It could have been anyone's. That useless Adams boy – he followed her around like a dog. Or Dunbar, the filthy beast, I wouldn't put it past him. I caught him looking at her, you know. And they were out there in my garden, him bent over her like a suitor."

"It could have been Edward's."

She waved the suggestion away. "He's a man, like all the rest. What's he to do when a pretty girl throws herself at him? Especially out here so far from his friends, trapped with his father and nothing to do all day? What's he to do, I ask you?"

"Mind the commandments," Liam said.

"Easy enough for you to say." The housekeeper bristled. "I raised them as best as I could, but there's only so much an old woman can do when the father indulges the child."

"This trip to Albany. What time did he come home on Sunday?"

"I don't know the train schedules, young man. You'll have to check for yourself. Sunday or not, I have a job to do and it's not minding who comes and who goes. He, and those two friends of his, were here in time for supper."

"Did he walk from the station?"

She barked a laugh. "Alistair Cunningham let his boy walk a couple of miles? Certainly not! Dunbar fetched him in the carriage."

They had lied to Liam, all of them – Cunningham, his son, Edward, and Malcolm Dunbar.

"Where can I find Alistair Cunningham?"

T HE OLD MAN WAS in his study, standing by the French doors, as he smoked a cigar and gazed across the garden. "You're back here again?"

Liam seemed to be hearing that a lot lately. "I have a few more questions for you, sir."

"You're free to go, Mrs. Ramsey," Cunningham said glancing over Liam's shoulder.

She frowned, then left the room, pulling the door closed behind her.

The room felt lighter with the French doors open and the heavy velvet curtains pulled back from the windows.

"Fine day," Cunningham said.

"Indeed." Liam waited for his attention.

"Very well," Cunningham said wheeling around. He settled behind the heavy desk. "What can I do for you, Officer Barrett?"

"When did you first became aware that Deidre Monaghan was expecting Edward's child?"

"Never," Cunningham scoffed.

"You knew that she was with child."

"So she said. And she claimed Edward fathered it. But she could have said that about anyone. Edward was convenient."

"You're suggesting that someone else fathered the child and she pretended it was Edward's to pressure him into an advantageous marriage."

"Naturally. The poor boy is innocent to the ways of women."

"And who, sir, do you suggest was the true father?"

"Someone from your town. That boy, what was his name, Finn something? Maybe he was the lucky lad. But she had set her sights higher and tried to pass the mongrel off as my grandson and heir." He tapped his cigar on a silver ashtray. "Can hardly blame her."

"In the few months since Deidre came to work for you, she's only been gone from Inverness long enough to go to mass with her mother, have breakfast, and take the train back. He could not have fathered her child. He wasn't alone with her long enough."

Cunningham laughed. "It doesn't take that long, Officer. A few minutes behind a shed will do."

Here sat a man who talked about his servants as if they were animals. Yet there was no end to his compassion, and excuses, for his own son.

"I need to speak with Edward."

"Whatever for?"

"It seems he had a friendship with Deidre Monaghan."

"Bah," Cunningham said, examining the cigar gone cold. "Is that what she told her mother?"

"A number of people were aware of it."

Cunningham frowned at Liam. Rocking back in his chair, he relit the cigar. He appeared to be thinking.

The heavy door slammed open, followed by Dunbar stomping in. "They're gone! Those filthy tramps, the Mollys. We've looked all over the woods from Pittsfield to Adams and back again. They've disappeared."

Cunningham stood. "We need the area secured before the governor arrives."

Dunbar pointed at Liam. "Mark my words. There will be trouble tomorrow. If you're not going to do something about it, I will."

"Captain Curran has given orders. Any man found carrying firearms will be arrested."

"With yourself, the captain, and the boy at the desk keeping the peace? And them, twenty or more? How do you expect to do that?"

"There were only eight in the camp. You were there with me."

"That doesn't mean there won't be more. They could be sneaking into the area, garrisoned in the woods where we can't find them. You're outnumbered and outpowered, Barrett."

A grandfather clock ticked loudly in the silence that followed. If there was violence at the dedication, the Adams police would be blamed. Captain Curran, Caleb Anthony, and Liam would lose their jobs. The force would be replaced by someone in Cunningham's pocket, someone like George Stanley.

Liam saw Cunningham's plan. He had recently purchased the cotton mill. He claimed he was building another. His reputation was to take over a marginal business, cut the cost of production and increase the profits for himself. The best cost-saving move, and the most obvious one to first take, would be to lower wages. Cunningham would expect the workers to strike in retaliation.

All his complaining, all his manipulations had a purpose. To prove that the Berkshire law enforcement was inadequate. He wanted to take over policing in the Berkshires before his financial empire was threatened by a strike.

And that was his reason for the Molly hysteria. If there were Mollys, they would support a strike, bring additional men, food, supplies, and guns just as Uncle Jack and Liam had done years before.

Perhaps it wasn't a coincidence that Jack Barrett had suddenly appeared.

Chapter Twenty-Five

An Important Man

THE THREE MEN STOOD looking at each other, locked in silent battle. The bust of Robbie Burns stared at them sightlessly, no longer the bard of the working man, but now the hero of the ruling class.

The sound of horses' hooves pounding up the drive reached them and a carriage pulled into view. Two men sat in the back of the carriage: Edward Cunningham and a balding man with a handlebar mustache, Governor Greenhalge.

Cunningham tossed his cigar into the fireplace and walked out of the room. Dunbar stayed put. Liam stayed as well, still waiting for his chance to talk to Edward.

There was motion in the hallway and the sound of women's dainty shoes hurrying. Through the open door, Liam caught a glimpse of a blue velvet skirt descending the grand stairway.

"Welcome, Governor," Liam heard Victoria Cunningham say with the grace of the perfect hostess. "How good it is to see you again. Will your lovely wife be joining us this weekend?"

The man's answer was too muffled to make out the words. There was a chorus of amused laughter in response.

So this is how the other half lives? Greetings and counter-greetings, the words of which no one believed.

Dunbar continued to stare at Liam as footsteps, Victoria's flattery, and the governor's mutters approached. She led the group into the room, faltered a half step upon seeing Liam, then whisked herself to a sideboard where crystal snifters sparkled in the late afternoon light. "Drink, gentlemen?"

"Brandy all round," Cunningham commanded as he extended an arm to the leather sofa and chairs near the fireplace.

"Exactly what the doctor ordered," the governor said. "Don't mind if I stand for bit, do you Alistair? The train ride was a long one from Boston."

"I'll see to the horses," Dunbar said, ducking out of the room. His exit brought no comment from the others.

Cunningham struck a pose beside the fireplace while the governor strolled to the open french doors. Edward took position behind his father, giving the appearance of the dutiful son ready to be of service. Victoria carried a snifter to the governor and hovered beside him, more closely than was necessary. How could this vibrant woman entertain the likes of Liam's uncle and the governor with apparent equal devotion? Which one was she lying to? What would Jack think if he could see her now?

As the governor took the brandy from her, they both held the snifter for a long moment, their fingers close enough to graze. Liam felt a feathery sensation on his own hand as if Victoria had touched him.

"I hope you will save a dance for me, Victoria," the governor said.

"I am so pleased you asked. You are my favorite waltzing partner."

She pulled away to bring the second glass to her father and slid a conspiratorial smile at Liam. Who was she playing? Her father and the governor, or Jack? Maybe all three of them. Sweat prickled at Liam's collar.

The governor gestured with his snifter in Edward's direction. "And who will you be escorting?"

Edward shook his head. "Alas, sir, I will be going alone."

"A handsome fellow like you? I'm sure there are several young ladies who would be happy to walk on your arm."

"Not locally, sir. My social circle is in Boston. I've recently graduated from Yale."

"A Yale man. Of course, I should have remembered. Forgive me for not keeping up with the social page of the Globe? That's Mrs. Greenhalge's métier."

Victoria delivered the second glass to her father and then perched on one of the chairs, back ramrod straight, her ankles crossed. Edward raised his eyebrows as if to ask if she was going to serve him. She gave him a quick frown. He could get his own drink. And so he did. Cunningham pointedly ignored them both.

After the party broke up, Liam would have his chance to question Edward.

"Handsome garden, Alistair," Governor Greenhalge said.

"It's inspired by my travels in Italy," Cunningham answered. "The design is intended to have a calming effect. Care to take a stroll?"

Mrs. Ramsey slipped into the study.

"What is it, woman?" Cunningham asked.

"A message has been delivered for the governor," she said, a piece of folded paper held close to her waist.

"Hand it here," Cunningham said.

She did so. He opened it and read. "This is an outrage! Who brought this note?"

"What is it, Alistair?" Greenhalge asked.

Cunningham handed the paper to the governor who read it as well.

"I found it on the front hall table, Mr. Cunningham," Mrs. Ramsey said. "I don't know who left it there. It appeared after the governor arrived."

Cunningham lifted a brow.

"Sir," she added.

Cunningham took the note back from the governor, and crossed the room to Liam, waving it in the air. "I warned you and you did nothing. The Mollys are out there, fomenting violence."

He handed the note to Liam. Scrawled in an unpracticed hand, it read, "Tomorrow Greenhalge dies. Erin go Bragh!"

Liam took in a deep breath and held it. The note could be real or a ploy. "If someone really meant to assassinate the governor, why would they warn him? He would change his plans and spoil their attempt. It's a hoax."

"These notices were no ploy in Pennsylvania a few years ago, lad," Cunningham said. "The Mollys delivered their death threats and made good on them."

Liam was not convinced that the events in Pennsylvania were the actions of Molly Maguires. But it was the stuff of yellow journalism and readily believed.

"If you take this seriously, Governor," Liam said, "I suggest you cancel your plans."

"Absolutely not, young man," the governor answered. He seemed to notice a policeman standing in the room for the first time. "Who are you, anyway?"

Victoria rose from her perch and floated back to the sidebar. She poured a tiny glass of sherry for herself. Her father frowned at her, which she pointedly ignored. She took a sip. "He is Officer Liam Barrett from the Adams police department."

The governor frowned at Cunningham. "Alistair, why do you have a policeman in your home? Is there something I should be aware of?"

"He was leaving," Cunningham said.

"There was a murder nearby, Governor," Liam said. "I am tasked with finding the responsible party."

Cunningham whirled on Liam so quickly the wings of his coat spread like a bird taking flight. "Who is still on the loose, you might add. Through no fault of your own, I suppose? That tramp who broke out of jail last night is nowhere to be found. And that is the very reason we need our own at the dedication." Cunningham turned back to the governor. "The Adams police force is inadequate to protect you. Perhaps you should consider canceling your appearance, sir."

"Nonsense, Alistair. I am announcing my candidacy for the highest office in the land tomorrow. This nation does not elect men who bolt like frightened rabbits. I will go to the dedication. I will make my announcement. And tonight, we will have a fine gala to which I will escort the lady of the house, this lovely daughter of yours." This was the governor's display of heroism, fearless in the face of danger, and he had been shooed into it, oblivious to the machinations. Cunningham's genius was not simply visionary, he understood the hearts of men. He would make the governor feel like a great man, feared and powerful. A benevolent ruler who acted decisively for the welfare of his state, even if it incidentally enriched his friends.

The governor handed Cunningham his empty snifter and extended his hand to Victoria. She breezed across the room, her eyes upon him like a woman in love. As she passed her father, she stroked the back of his arm gently and then took the governor's hand. He led her out the french doors onto the garden.

Edward dropped into Victoria's abandoned chair and threw a leg over the arm. He drained the remainder of his brandy. "A foolish, fond old man," he said grinning at his father.

"Hold your tongue, whelp. Get out there and make sure the governor has everything he needs." Cunningham set the snifters, his and the governor's, on the mantle.

"That's Victoria's job."

"You need to be at his elbow. That is how friendships are forged. That is how you will get ahead in this world. Now, begone with you." Cunningham took the snifter out of Edward's hand and pointed him out the door.

"Very well, father," Edward said, sliding out of the chair. He adjusted his suit, his nose in the air mockingly, and sauntered out of the room. Liam would speak with him later. Cunningham couldn't hide the boy from him forever.

Edward went into the garden and approached the Governor and Victoria. They were too far away to hear what was said. Victoria smiled demurely at the Governor then took her leave, tossing a conspiratorial smile at her father as he stood watch.

Liam began walking to the door. Cunningham shouted, "Stop right there, Barrett! With this death threat, I need a policeman. 'Twould be handy if there's trouble."

If the threat was genuine, the best time to catch the governor would be in public tomorrow. The old man only wanted a uniform standing at attention for show. But remaining at the mansion would give Liam a chance to talk to Edward.

"How long?"

"Until the banquet is over, then you can go home. The mayors from Pittsfield and Adams are coming as well as several prominent businessmen and their wives. Go wait in the kitchen until Dunbar comes for ye."

W HEN STANLEY RODE UP to Inverness on the gray mare, Malcom Dunbar was driving Cunningham's finest carriage, a shiny black contraption with leather upholstered seats and red wheels, towards the barns. There was only one reason that carriage would be out today. The governor must have arrived and was inside the mansion with Cunningham, who would have no time for Stanley. He pulled alongside Dunbar and caught his eye. Dunbar nodded an acknowledgement and kept going. Stanley followed.

Dunbar pulled the carriage into a barn, climbed down from the driver's seat, and went about releasing the horse from the yoke as Stanley dismounted the grey and tied her to a post.

Dunbar took a hard look at Stanley and went back to work. "What do you know about Finn O'Brien's death?"

"Finn who?"

"The Adams scamp who was to marry Deidre Monaghan. He was found hanging in Hogan's warehouse," Dunbar said. "Did you not know?"

"The drunk and disorderly?"

"The one you arrested at the racetrack."

O'Brien had been in Stanley's jail until Barrett found him an alibi so good that Dunbar himself vouched for it. Up until then, everyone thought O'Brien had killed the girl. Last they met, Cunningham had mentioned him. And then he had talked about Sweeney which is why Stanley thought Cunningham wanted Sweeney out of the way. Did he mean O'Brien instead?

Good thing O'Brien was dead. There was no evidence that Stanley had anything to do with it. And there was no one to argue he didn't.

"God rest his soul," Stanley said with a wink.

Dunbar snorted. The horses fidgeted.

"Follow me. There's something we need to talk about." Dunbar hooked a lead to the gelding's halter and began to lead him out of the barn. Stanley untied the gray mare's reins and pulled. She resisted. He tugged until she began dragging her feet. They followed Dunbar out of the barn and into a nearby stables.

In the stables, Dunbar opened a stall door, led the gelding inside, and slipped off his halter. Stanley's mare wandered down the aisle. Another horse whinnied as she passed. She walked into an open stall that must have been hers when she lived here.

Dunbar threw some grain into a trough, then began currying the sweaty gelding, stroking him with the comb, his free hand resting lightly on the beast, muttering phrases in a language Stanley did not understand. Sometimes the horse would turn his head and look Dunbar in the eye. Dunbar would smile at the animal while they held each other in a brief gaze.

Stanley felt awkward, like he wasn't wanted there. At least by the horse.

The gelding put his head back into the trough. Dunbar came around, patting the horse on the rump. "We got a death notice against the governor. One of your typical Molly threats."

Stanley sensed that this must be important. "You figured."

"Right you are, Stanley. We knew the Mollys were amassing in the woods, ready to plant their sedition amongst the mill workers. Nothing good happens when they're around. Strikes. Assassinations. They'll stop at nothing to achieve their ends. And now they're in hiding which tells me that they're up to something."

"You think they'll try to shoot the governor?"

"I do, laddie." Dunbar thumped Stanley on the chest. "And it's up to you and me to keep him safe."

"How are we to do that? Do we know where they'll attack? Here at Inverness? Do you want me to post a guard?"

"No need for that. We have the Adams copper at hand."

Barrett, there he was again.

"I didn't see him."

"He's posted inside the mansion."

While Stanley was in the barn, Barrett was closer to danger and to glory.

Dunbar continued. "We can't be sure where they will make their move, but knowing them, they'll want everyone to hear what they've done. There will be newspapermen from all over the state at the dedication so they'll strike during the ceremony in front of the crowd and reporters. But, we need to keep on the lookout from the minute the procession leaves the estate. You understand me?"

"You promised Curran no guns."

"That was before the death notice." Dunbar nodded at the gun in Stanley's holster. "It's your right and duty as a police officer to carry a gun. So you'll be guarding the governor personally. Ride with him in the carriage. Escort him to the stage. Stand beside him or behind him at all times and keep that eagle eye of yours open." This time Dunbar thumped Stanley on the forehead. "You do what you have to do to keep the governor safe. My lads will scatter about, keeping an eye open too."

"Your men, will they be armed?"

"They will."

"How many?"

"A dozen."

When Dunbar thumped Stanley on the chest and on the head with his blunt bony finger, it hurt. But Stanley didn't react. Not now. But one of these days, he'd make sure that Dunbar knew better than to toy with George Washington Stanley.

Dunbar went on. "If you make a good show of it, the governor will be impressed. You'll get the Berkshire Rangers, no doubt about that. Money, power, a big new house if you want, all the women you can handle. How does that suit you, laddie?"

Stanley had been thinking about the Berkshire Rangers. He'd be a colonel and wear a smart uniform. There would be a big, new horse. His office would have a big, new desk and a cushy leather chair just like Cunningham's.

But as for women, he already had all the harlots he wanted in the whorehouse down the road. And he had that ragged old bird who kept his house and met his needs. They weren't what he wanted. He wanted Miss Victoria. He wanted to smell her hair. Untie her bodice. Slip his hand inside.

Right now, Barrett was a lot closer to her than Stanley was.

One thing his father told him, when the old man talked to him at all, was that you got to snap up your opportunities. That was what made the difference between rich men and poor men. Rich men saw opportunities and took them. The Colonel of the Berkshire Rangers would be a handsome dinner guest at the Cunningham table, right next to Miss Victoria.

"Suits me fine," Captain George Washington Stanley said.

"Good man." Dunbar slapped him on the shoulder. One day, Dunbar would regret that.

Dunbar ran his hand along the gelding's back on his way out of the stall. He shut the door and headed out the barn. "Be here first light. Make sure your gun is loaded. And, remember, not a word to Barrett or his captain." Then he walked towards the mansion.

Stanley had been dismissed. No chance to catch a glimpse of Miss Victoria. No fine dinner for him tonight even if it meant eating at the servant's table. He headed to the stall where the grey mare had gone. On his way, he passed that giant black stallion, the one Miss Victoria rode. The horse whinnied and sidled sidewise revealing Miss Victoria, in a man's riding habit, coat buttoned to her throat, cinched at the small waist, and trousers. She had a halter in her hands and looked surprised to see Stanley.

If she was Stanley's woman, she would never be seen in public dressed like a man. He wondered if she was one of those women he had heard of in the brothel, the ones that didn't like the touch of man, who preferred each other. If they were working girls, they'd please a man because it was their job. If Victoria Cunningham was Stanley's woman, he would be the only person, man or woman, she would give herself to.

The stallion snorted, bringing Stanley out of his reverie.

She placed a calming hand on the horse's shoulder. To Stanley, she said "Good night, Captain."

"Good night, Miss Victoria." He went to the grey's stall, took her reins, and tugged until she agreed to come out again. He didn't look in the stallion's stall on his way out. He had been dismissed, twice already. Once by Dunbar and then again by Miss Victoria. One day soon, none of the Cunninghams would dare to dismiss George Washington Stanley.

❧

L IAM WAS SITTING AT the kitchen table, a cup of tea in front of him, having been told by Mrs. Ramsey to stay out of the way. The cooks bustled about in a dance of their own.. A roasted pheasant was resting on a large platter while women heaped vegetables into bowls, piled baked rolls onto platters, and poured sauces into silver pitchers. One girl pressed butter into little molds, then popped them out again, shaped into roses. Smelling the aromas, Liam's stomach growled. The butter girl heard it and slipped him a couple of scones. When he opened his mouth to say thank you, she shook her head. It was to be their secret. Then she blushed. She couldn't have been any older than Deirdre.

After an hour, Dunbar came into the room. "You're with me, Barrett." Liam followed him through the mansion and out onto the front porch. "You'll be standing here, with your eyes peeled."

"I can only watch one door. What about the windows and the back of the house?"

"Not to worry. I have men covering all the windows and doors."

A wagon pulled up. Several musicians in black suits gathered their violins and cellos and walked up the front steps. They paused in front of Dunbar.

"You fellas, to the ballroom. Mrs. Ramsey will show you the way."

"Stay here until the last guest leaves, Barrett." Dunbar said before going back inside.

By the looks of it, it would be a long night. Liam wished he'd brought a book. He watched the sky turn color, first green, then violet, then a rim of pink, as the sun set behind treetops.

Yellow light was glowing from each window when the first carriage arrived. As if by cue, Cunningham escorted Victoria to the porch to greet their guests. He wore a black cutaway, silk vest, and a jeweled stick pin. She was in a low cut blue velvet gown, the waist impossibly small, with her hair piled in an intricate arrangement. Diamonds hung from her neck and ears.

She nodded politely to Liam. "Officer Barrett, as I recall?"

"Good evening, Miss Cunningham."

The carriage stopped at the foot of the stairs. A richly-dressed man and woman debarked. Excited greetings were exchanged and the ladies were complimented upon their beauty, then Cunningham led the ensemble back up the stairs.

As the group passed Liam, Victoria fell behind. She held back until the door closed, stepped in close and spoke quickly. "Something's being planned for tomorrow and it's meant to be a secret from you. Captain Stanley will be accompanying the governor all day. And he will be carrying a gun. Dunbar's bringing his men too, all armed."

"How many?"

"A dozen besides Dunbar and Stanley. Beware, Liam." She reached out quickly, squeezed his arm, and then the door opened. From inside, Cunningham called to her, "Come in, dear girl, you'll catch your death."

"Coming, Poppa!" She called back before she disappeared into the house.

CHAPTER TWENTY-SIX

THE GATHERING STORM

AFTER THE GALA, ONE of Cunningham's men drove Liam home. There was no talk along the way. When Adams came into sight, Liam said, "Here's fine. I need to stretch my legs." He didn't want the man observing his activities and reporting back.

The driver stopped the rig without comment. Liam hopped out and began a slow, easy stride. Once the wagon had disappeared into the night, he broke into a run and had reached Captain Curran's home, a small white two-story house on Crandall Street, in a few minutes. The house was dark. He pounded his fist on the door, waking the neighborhood dogs. Continuous barking began in the next house and soon had spread down the street. Canine voices of all pitches were joined in alarm.

Curran opened the door. He stood in the vestibule stuffing shirt tails into his trousers. "What is it, Liam?" He had to shout to be heard over the dogs.

"Malcolm Dunbar, Cunningham's man. He's planning something," Liam said in between breaths. "For tomorrow. Armed men, a dozen of them. Stanley will be armed too and guarding the governor."

"They promised us no guns. You heard them. You were right there. Has something happened?"

"A death threat was delivered." Liam pulled the note out of his pocket and handed it to Curran, who read it.

"Does Cunningham want to go forward with the dedication in spite of this?"

"The governor said he won't be scared off. He's announcing his candidacy for president tomorrow."

"Even though they're expecting an assassination attempt? If anyone shows a gun in the midst of that many angry armed men, it will set off a shootout in the middle of Adams with the entire town and everyone for miles visiting. It'll be wholesale slaughter. We don't have the manpower to stop it."

"We should cancel the ceremony," Liam said.

Curran pushed past him, took the two cement steps down from his stoop lightly. "That's exactly what we're going to do."

The two strode up Center Street and around the corner to the mayor's home, the grandest house on Summer Street, a yellow Victorian with white gingerbread trim.

Mayor John Nevin was also the hotelier. Another first generation Irishman, he, like Alistair Cunningham, had vision and he had prospered, starting with a small pharmacy. The house was built to impress, with a main floor elevated above ground so that visitors would ascend stairs to the front door.

Curran banged on a lion-head door knocker. A little dog inside started yapping.

The mayor, a tall, corpulent man, opened the door, wearing pajamas, a bathrobe and slippers. The long hairs he combed over his bald head were mussed.

"We need to call off the dedication," Curran told him. "Cunningham's planning a shoot-out."

"The last time we spoke, Captain Curran, you said everything was under control. No guns. No violence. What's changed?"

"I was tipped off, sir, by someone who overheard their plans," Liam said..

"Who tipped you off?"

Victoria had confided in Liam in secret. Not only had she betrayed her father by telling Liam, she was engaged in a clandestine relationship with Jack Barrett and there was no telling how deep her involvement in his politics was. If Cunningham and Dunbar learned that she had told Liam, they would want to know her reason. Whatever she and Jack Barrett were up to would be uncovered. As Cunningham's daughter, she would be shielded from serious repercussions, at worst she would be sent to Europe for a long tour, but there was no way of knowing what else they would do or to whom. They would not let the betrayal go unanswered. They were not the kind of men who accepted defeat.

"I can't tell you, sir," Liam said. "It's confidential."

"Can't or won't?" Nevin stepped out onto his porch. Even by the moonlight, Liam could see that his face was reddening. "Are you telling me that you have spies in Cunningham's organization?"

The little dog at the Mayor's feet, a Boston terrier, barked rapidly. "Quiet, Bella!" The dog stopped.

"Dammit, John," Curran said. "This is a matter of life and death. Tomorrow everyone in Adams will be at that ceremony. People from all around are coming as well. If – "

"I have the businessmen to answer to, Capt. Curran," the mayor said. "The ceremony will fill our streets with customers. The businesses stocked up for anticipated sales. You know nothing about commerce. These men paid for their merchandise and they need to sell it to make ends meet. Canceling the event on the mere whim of an overly-zealous officer would be irresponsible. I'd lose my job."

The mayor drew himself to his full height. "Not only that, it would be a slap in the face to Cunningham. This library is his gift to us. He paid dearly for the lot. He is building the structure and filling it with books, all out of his own pocket. He is a generous man. And not one who will take rejection well. You do understand that he recently bought the cotton mill, so he's not going away. He's someone we need to build a relationship with, for the good of the entire town."

Cunningham had bought the lot from Mayor Nevin, at an inflated price it was rumored. No small wonder Nevin refused to think ill of the man. He'd already benefitted from the Scot's largesse and expected more.

Curran leapt up the stairs and came face-to-face with Nevin, making the terrier yap. "But how am I to —"

The mayor backed into the house. "I don't believe it, not for one second. Alistair Cunningham and the men in his employ are honorable. For all we know, it's a prank. Someone is trying to make a fool of you, Captain Curran." He reached for the door. "I will see you at the ceremony tomorrow."

The little dog growled.

"Get in here, Bella."

The dog gave two sharp barks, then turned and trotted inside. The door closed behind her.

"It's settled. The dedication goes forward," Curran said. "The Mayor is right. Even if Cunningham's men come armed to teeth, if there's no Mollys, as you say, and there's no attack, there will be no counterattack. I've done everything I can do, Liam. Go home. Get some sleep."

∽

L IAM STEPPED INTO THE shed to look in on Bridget and her calf before going inside. They were asleep, the calf curled up against his mother. He had grown and fattened in the few days since he was born. Bridget woke and blinked at him a few times. Liam scratched her forehead. He settled on the nearby stool and whispered. "*Dún do shúil, a rún mo chroí.*" It was the first line in a lullaby his mother used to sing. The tune played in his head and he hummed along. The rest of the words wouldn't come to him. The song in his mind faded. He stood and stroked the cow's forehead. "Close your eyes now. The angels are looking over you." The same words his mother had spoken every night when he was a boy.

Inside the house, he shuffled through the kitchen so as not to wake the family. Other than the scones at Inverness that afternoon, he had not eaten all day. He was beyond hungry, his stomach burning and queasy. All he could find was oats steeping for the morning. Kevin would have finished off dinner. There were no leftovers with that boy in the house. In a cabinet was a pitcher of buttermilk. He poured a cup, took a seat at the table, and looked out upon the field that climbed up the Hoosac mountains. The waning moon cast enough light that he could make out Bridget's shed. Scattered around the yard were small dark lumps, the chickens bedded down for the night.

It was a good life his father had found for them in this country. A bit of land. A sturdy home. Plenty of opportunity if you worked hard.

Kate appeared in her nightdress. "Are you only now getting in? I'll fix you something to eat."

Liam shook his head. "Not hungry."

"Will you be going to bed soon?"

"Soon enough. I want to sit here for a few minutes." During the walk through town, up East Road and then up the lane, he asked himself what could be done tomorrow to keep peace in Adams town. He could try to warn the townspeople as they arrived but there would be too many to talk to even if he enlisted Frank, Harry, Tom, and Caleb. They would come in surges from mid-morning on as they did every Saturday for shopping, but there would be even more with the festivities.

Kate took the empty cup from him. "Do you want more?"

"I'm grand, thanks."

There was a knock at the door.

"At this time of night?" Kate said. "No doubt police business. You might as well answer it." She headed back to her bedroom.

Liam opened the door to find his Uncle Jack on the stoop, for a moment startling him, as it always did, seeing the image of his father.

"We need to talk."

"Come in, then."

"Outside is better."

Liam followed his uncle into the field. It reminded him of that trip to Pennsylvania and all those times when he witnessed Jack and another man standing apart, trading whispers.

Jack picked a spot and scanned the darkness.

"There's no one here but the chickens, Jack," Liam said.

"You can't be too careful. I was betrayed once before."

"Perhaps it would best be left until morning, then."

"That'll be too late." Jack stepped close to Liam. He lowered his voice. "Down at the Black Rose, the boys told me someone promised to pay them if they stirred up the old hue and cry tomorrow."

"Did they describe this man?" Liam asked.

"Your man, they said, the one you brought to their camp when you took Sweeney away. Short, bullish, big red beard, mustache."

Malcom Dunbar.

LIAM AND JACK WALKED in silence to the Black Rose, matching long strides down the lane, across town, and to the pub.

Jack led Liam up the fire escape to Harry's apartment. Inside were the two redheaded brothers, Timothy and Denny Hennessey, one a dead shot with a rock and the other who could catch a rabbit with only a bag, and the others. Four were playing cards in silence. Going around the table, each would throw a card in, then one would sweep up all the cards and throw another one down. The others watched the game.

Jack spoke first. "I told Liam here what you told me, about the man who offered you money to wreck the ceremonies tomorrow."

Liam could never be sure that anything Jack said was reliable, and someday Liam might be called to testify about what happened this night. He looked at Timothy Hennessy, the most talkative of the bunch. "I need to hear it from you. Who was this man?"

"That dour fella what was with you." The other men grunted their assent.

"Had he visited the camp before that day?"

"Aye. Not long before. A day, maybe two."

"Why didn't you say something?"

"He said if we told, the deal was off. And how were we to know what side you're on? One day you're with that fella, the next you show up with Jack here."

"Besides," his twin offered, "he doesn't look like a man you'd cross."

Liam still had the death notice in his pocket. "This letter came to Inverness this afternoon." Liam handed it to Timothy. "Did any of you write this?"

Timothy held the paper limply without looking at it. "What does it say?"

"You can't read?"

"None of us can."

If none of them could read, then none of them wrote that note.

Jack reached out his hand and Hennessey handed him the paper. "This is a fine hand," he said. "An educated man wrote it."

"And where will you find an educated man amongst the likes of us?" Timothy asked.

"Fair enough," Liam said, having already reached the conclusion Jack was suggesting. He took back the note and slipped it into his pocket. "Then someone is trying to make it look like you lads threatened the governor's life. One of you, Sweeney, is being blamed for Deidre's death. There is talk that you burned down Hogan's warehouse. And now you're being accused of breaking Owen Sweeney out of jail."

"Owen's gone?" Timothy said, an honest look of astonishment on his face. "I don't know how that happened. I will tell you one thing, Liam, the boys and me had nothing to do with it. We been here since you brought us. And sure won't your own friend Harry vouch for us? Wouldn't he know if we tramped out and came back again?"

"I'm worried about the here and now," Liam said. "There's a library dedication to-morrow. The governor will be there. It's a loosely kept secret that he's announcing his candidacy for president. Every citizen within fifty miles will be here plus newspaper reporters from Albany and Boston. If there is any kind of violence, innocent people could be hurt."

"These boys aren't planning any violence," Jack said. "They were told to show up and yell a few insults."

"He said he'd pay us," Timothy said.

"How's that to be arranged?" Liam asked.

"He was to pick us up and bring us here to a spot in the woods outside of town last night. After it was done, we were to meet back at the new camp. That's when we'll get paid."

The tramps were being scapegoated. They would disrupt the ceremony on promise of a future payment that would never be made. Once they began yelling, Dunbar and his men would start shooting. The townspeople would panic. They wouldn't know one face from another, having never seen the tramps or Dunbar's men before. For all the crowd knew, the men who were yelling and the men who were shooting were the same. That was why Dunbar was so adamant about being armed. The tramps would have to be killed to prevent them from identifying him afterwards. With the typical Molly death notice delivered and Cunningham's constant warning of Mollys in the region, Liam wouldn't be surprised if Molly pamphlets would be planted on their bodies – despite the fact they couldn't read. The boys would be accused of an attempted assassination and none of them would survive to dispute it.

Cunningham would have gotten what he wanted, proof that Captain Curran was not up to the job of keeping the peace, at the cost of these boys' lives and those of anyone else who was caught in the crossfire.

"These boys may not be planning violence, but someone is," Liam said.

"What's your plan, Liam?" Jack asked.

"Remember the old stories about the Fianna living in the forests, appearing out from behind trees when their enemies least expected it?"

"Led by the giant Finn MacCumhail," Timothy said.

"Just so. Tell me, lads, do you all throw as well as the Hennessy brothers here?"

"Better!" one shouted. And they all laughed.

Chapter Twenty-Seven

The Big Day

A S THE SKY WAS beginning to lighten, Captain George Washington Stanley spread a newspaper across the top of his dining room table. The image of Alistair Cunningham was sidewise, staring at the ceiling. Can't have that. Washington spun the newspaper around so that the old man's eyes seemed to look right into his.

He pulled the .32 Colt from a sideboard drawer and laid it on top of the newspaper, careful not to cover the picture. The gun had been a gift from Malcom Dunbar right after Stanley persuaded an old farmer to sell the property that was now Inverness. The old man had refused Cunningham's offer, saying the farm had been in his family for generations. But Stanley was able to persuade him. It wasn't a bad deal for the old man after all, he got enough money to move on.

Stanley collected his gun cleaning brushes, rags, lubricants, and solvents from a nearby cabinet and lined them up in a neat row.

"Let me show you something, Mr. Alistair Cunningham, sir," Stanley said. "Don't know much about firearms, do you? The first step is taking care of your weapon. If you take care of your weapon, it will take care of you. My daddy always said that."

The newspaper was the last Sunday edition like the one he'd been reading when the woman spilled his dinner. She must have picked up another copy. He could hear her now, shuffling from her cot in the pantry. She stepped into view, standing in the dark kitchen, framed by the doorway. Her hair was down around her shoulders and she was wearing her dingy nightgown.

"What do you want, woman?"

"I heard voices."

"Your hearing things. Make me some breakfast."

The woman moved off and Stanley gave Cunningham's picture a wink. You got to know how to talk to women. That's your problem, Cunningham, you spoil them.

In a few hours, he, George Washington Stanley, would be standing next to Governor Greenhalge on a stage with newspaper reporters aiming cameras at them. Maybe his picture would be in the paper too. It was bound to be if someone took a potshot at the governor and Stanley saved his life. He would be a hero.

Afterwards, Stanley would go back to Inverness with Cunningham and the governor. They would invite him into Cunningham's office for brandy and cigars and talk about the future of the Berkshire Rangers. There was much to be decided. Where would Stanley find recruits? Where would he want his headquarters? As the colonel, would he wear a uniform or a finely tailored suit?

Meanwhile, Malcom Dunbar would be elsewhere, excluded from the circle of powerful men, maybe tending to the horses that had pulled their carriage.

Miss Victoria would come into the office and the men would jump to their feet. She would kiss her father on the cheek. She would take the governor's hand, telling him how grateful she was that the fiend who tried to murder him had failed, a tear glinting in her eye. And she would finally come round to Stanley, lay a dainty hand on his chest – right there in front of her father – and thank him for saving the governor's life. She would stand on tiptoe to kiss his cheek. No, maybe not the hand, that might be too bold. She was a lady after all.

However it played out, one thing would be certain. Miss Victoria Cunningham would not be outside of George Washington Stanley's reach anymore. He would need money to entertain her, lots of it, as she was accustomed to fine things. Once he was the colonel, Cunningham would invite him into business dealings and he would amass a fortune. And then, someday, she could be his. If he still wanted her, that is.

The woman brought a cup of coffee into the dining room and set it on the table. When he was colonel of the Rangers, he'd resign the Pittsfield police job and move out of this house that came with it. The woman could stay behind and take care of the next police chief or go back to where she came from. Whatever happened, there was no place for her in his future.

She stared down at the floor as the smell of frying bacon reached him. She looked pale, even more so than usual.

"What's wrong with you?" he asked.

She ran out of the room. The kitchen's backdoor banged behind her. He could hear her puking in the yard. It must have been something she ate.

The first ray of morning light shot into the room, falling upon the arrangement on the table. He lifted the revolver, aimed it at the coffee pot on the stove visible through the kitchen doorway. He pulled the trigger, blowing the pot into the air and out of sight. Coffee splattered across the wall. The pot tumbled down back into view. The neighborhood dogs were already barking before it clattered onto the floor.

Today was going to be a good day.

∾

"WHEN DOES THE CEREMONY start?" Kate asked Liam as she placed a bowl of porridge in front of him.

"After lunch, why do you ask?"

"I thought I'd take the mother down to see the goings on. She was grand at the wake, don't you think?"

Liam touched a spoon of hot porridge to his mouth. It burned his lips.

"Careful," Kate said. "It's hot."

Liam blew on the porridge. "Best you stay home."

"Who are you to tell me what to do?" Kate slammed a pot onto the cooker.

"Katie." Liam caught his sister's hand as she stormed past. "There's trouble brewing. There could be bloodshed and I don't want you and the mother caught in the crossfire. Promise me."

Kevin came into the kitchen with heavy thudding footsteps. He lifted the lid on a pot. "Anything left?"

"Shoo!" Kate snapped a towel at him. After Kevin sat at the table, she handed him a bowl. "Careful, it's hot," she said before Kevin had a chance to burn his mouth.

"Are you going to Hogan's today?" Liam asked. He thought twice about warning Kevin of danger. Such a warning would only entice him.

Kevin gave Liam a dull stare. If Liam had done that to his father, he would have been smacked off his feet. "Yes, Liam," Kevin said tiredly.

"Then home to do your chores before supper."

Another dull "Yes, Liam."

"Mind yourself. I'll be home for supper."

"Sure now won't that be the occasion," Kate said turning back to the cooker to check the porridge.

"Another fine breakfast you have made for us, Mary Kathleen, and I thank you." Liam said as he rose from the table and set his bowl in the wash basin.

∾

As Liam walked to Hogan's Store, fog rolled over the land's contours, blanketing all of Adams town so that it was hidden. It reminded him of the legend about an enchanted Scottish village that was invisible to, and safe from, the outside world except for one day every one hundred years. Soon, the fog would burn off and all the evils of the nineteenth century would walk, ride, or roll their way into Adams. If only he was a magician, he'd wrap up his town in a spell, hidden from harm.

As it was, all he could do was warn people, one person at a time. Hogan's was on the edge of Adams next to the mill. He could have a word with Tom first, make sure Eileen stayed home, and then make his way back into town.

At Hogan's, Liam found Jack Barrett lounging with one elbow on a counter, eating a stick of black licorice. Tom Gillespie was behind the cash register. He didn't need to ask, he could tell by the looks on their faces that Jack had told Tom about the trouble Dunbar had planned.

"You'll be sure to keep Eileen home?" Liam said.

"She's my wife, Liam. I look out for her."

"I didn't say otherwise. I wanted to be sure. It's my job."

"Are you sure about those fellas, Liam?" Tom asked.

"They told us about Dunbar's plan. They could have done as he asked instead, hoping to get paid at the end of it."

"If you say so. It doesn't make sense to me why anyone would pay those lads good money to make a lot of noise."

"It's a diversion, Tom. The boys are meant to distract us."

"From what, that's what I'd like to know."

Tom was a good man, hardworking and responsible, but not the best mind. "Isn't it enough that we know these lads were promised money to create chaos and that Cunningham's men are bringing guns to Adams despite Captain Curran's orders? And all the time Cunningham's been insisting those boys are Molly Maguires? Any way you look at it, violence is intended."

"Whatever you say, Liam. We'll be staying well out of it. I've a store to mind." He quickly added, "And I'll make sure Eileen stays home."

"See that you do. I need to be off."

"Grand so," Jack slapped the countertop and pulled himself upright.

"Walk with me, Jack," Liam said.

Tom offered the open jar of licorice to Jack. "For the lads."

"More's to you." Jack took a handful and stuffed it into his pocket.

As they were turning to leave, Liam spotted empty burlap bags piled up on a shelf. He had an idea. "Can I borrow these?"

∽

M RS. RAMSEY TOLD STANLEY to wait in the foyer until the family finished breakfasting. That was the difference between rich and poor folks. The rich breakfasted. The poor ate breakfast. But he hadn't eaten. By the time the woman came back inside from being sick, the bacon was burnt to a cinder. He wanted to be on time and impress Cunningham so he couldn't wait for her to make more. The smell of rich folks' fat sausages and freshly baked bread tortured him. There was no reason to go hungry after all. He wasn't getting any credit for showing up early if no one saw him do it. He'd learned that from his father. Not that the old man had said it, but because Stanley had learned he didn't get credit for any work his father didn't see him do.

The soft chatter of polite people from a distant room drifted to him. Stanley crossed his arms and stood in the middle of the hallway, straining to decipher the voices and words, his stomach gnawing at him. He'd never been there. One day, when he was the colonel of the Berkshire Rangers, he would be sat at that table. Maybe this evening. And Miss Victoria would be seated near him, casting him flirtatious glances, impressed by his bravery.

A man's footsteps pounded on the porch and the front door opened. "You're late!" Dunbar said.

"How could I be late? I've been here half an hour." It was more like ten minutes but Dunbar wouldn't bother to check.

"What makes you think you're to meet me in the mansion? I've been in the bunkhouse out back waiting for you, you lout." He strode out of the house. "Look lively, Stanley."

No one had told Stanley to report to the bunkhouse. He'd always come to the mansion before. How was he to know?

He followed Dunbar. George Washington Stanley never ran after anyone, not even an escaping prisoner. He'd shoot them instead. It wasn't long before he caught up to the little Scot though, given his legs were longer. By the time they had trekked the half mile to the bunkhouse, he was breathing hard and trying not to show it.

Dunbar opened the door without breaking step. It would have hit Stanley in the face on the swing back if he hadn't caught it.

There were half a dozen bunks lining one wall. Men leapt from the upper berths and crawled out of the cots below. They were a nasty looking bunch, scarred faces and scarred hands, with hard expressions from years of doing things that would repulse softer men. All lean, all hungry looking. These were the workers Stanley had seen around the grounds. And now he began to understand why there were so many. They hadn't been brought here to garden. No, sirree.

"Now that we're all together," Dunbar shot Stanley a nasty look, "we're going over the plan one last time. I want no mistakes, got it?"

The men stared back at him.

Dunbar pointed to a pair of men with two fingers of one hand. "You two take the west flank." Then he continued pointing to different men as he gave orders. "And you two the east flank. The three of you close off retreat and you last three get inside the crowds. Your guns all loaded? You don't need any extra ammunition, you'll get a shot or two off, that's all. When the crowd starts running, drop your guns and leg it out of there. Stay with the crowds, don't get caught out. Any questions?"

"How are we getting our guns back?" Asked a man with a deep scar going from his hairline to his jaw.

"Not to worry. Captain Stanley here, our man on the force, will confiscate them and they'll all be returned to you." Turning to Stanley, he said, "There's a change of plans. You'll be driving these fellas. Where's that wagon of yours?"

"Back in town."

The night before, Dunbar had said Stanley was riding shotgun on the carriage, so he had left the wagon and rode the grey mare to the house. She was tied up in front of the mansion and it was plain to see the wagon wasn't there. Dunbar had asked this question to make Stanley look stupid in front of his thugs.

A snicker rolled through the men. Stanley followed it from man to man, giving each of them his most threatening look and getting the same stare back, some with glints in their eyes. Any one of them would be happy to brag he killed a police captain and got away with it.

"Get a move on, man," Dunbar said to Stanley. "Get that wagon and be back here in an hour."

Chapter Twenty-Eight

A Fair Day

"Where to?" Jack asked Liam. The birds had begun their morning songs, a few notes here and there. Most of the fog had burned off but a few wisps floated below knee level, swirling around the men as they walked. Not being able to see where he was stepping was disorienting and Liam stumbled more than once. Jack pretended not to notice.

"I need to take a look around and then have a word with the boys," Liam said. "Here carry these for me." He handed Jack the burlap bags.

"What's wrong with your own hands?"

"Nothing. Looked like you needed something to do."

Liam and Jack walked down Park Street to the Black Rose. Inside, the chairs were up-ended on the tabletops. On the second floor, Harry stood in the window, a mug in hand. After Liam had spoken to the boys last night, he and Jack had gone down to the bar and filled him in. He promised to keep a lookout from his apartment.

Harry pushed open the window and leaned out.

"Seen anything?" Liam called up.

"Lovely day for a picnic. No strangers in town. It's early yet, mind you. The shopkeepers are just opening now."

A pack of dogs scampered towards them. They were pets who had been let out the first thing in the morning. They came to a halt at Jack's feet.

"Friends of yours?" Liam asked.

Jack reached into his pocket and pulled out some bread crusts, tossing them in the air. They were gobbled up. He reached his hand out, the back of it showing. The leader, a sleek black lab, gave him a lick.

"I make the acquaintance of dogs in every place I visit. They don't bark at their friends."

"So you can sneak into a town without the dogs sending up an alarm?"

"Now you're learning, young Liam. We'll make a proper vagabond out of you yet."

The only time Liam had left the Berkshires was on that one disastrous trip to Pennsylvania with Jack. Liam would be content to never leave Adams again. He was happy to spend the rest of his life walking its streets, herding the young ones to school, putting a flea in the ears of men who raised a hand to their wives or children, escorting drunks to the one cell in the police station to sleep it off before they tore up a bar or frightened an old lady, catching the occasional loose bull eating its way through someone's garden. By and large, these were a law-abiding and peace-loving people. It was his job to keep them safe.

Liam and Jack said their good-byes to Harry, then made their way down Park Street. Near St. Thomas' church, in the empty lot where the library was to be built, a bandstand had been erected. It was draped with blue, gold, and white bunting, the color of Massachusetts' state flag. Two rows of chairs had been set on the stage, enough for the Governor, Cunningham, and a few more.

Shop window blinds were being raised. Door signs were being flipped from "closed" to "open". Shopkeepers scurried around inside their establishments, preparing for the day. Liam had planned to warn the businessmen until he saw Mayor Nevin in front of his grocery store, a thumb hooked in his vest pocket, a timepiece in his other hand.

"Fair day to you, John," Jack called out. They crossed the street to meet him.

"Jack Barrett," Mayor Nevin answered, "what brings you to our fair hamlet? Visiting your relations?"

"That I am. Lovely day for a party, don't you think?"

Mayor Nevin didn't answer Jack. Instead he eyed Liam. "Have you seen anything suspicious this morning on your rounds, Officer Barrett?"

"No, sir."

"As much as I had expected."

There was one last chance to avert the catastrophe. The mayor could still cancel the dedication.

"Have you reconsidered what we spoke about? It's not too late. We could send word to Inverness, tell them the dedication is off."

"And what excuse would I give? Dunbar gave Captain Curran his word there would be no firearms. I'd take the word of a gentleman over some secret informant of yours any day."

"But sir—"

"Don't you 'but sir' me. Do you have any idea how important Alistair Cunningham is to our town? He owns the mill, the largest industry in Adams. He's building another. That means more jobs, more houses, more commerce, prosperity for us all." His voice was rising. Spittle flew from his mouth as he said the word 'prosperity.' "And you want me to refuse his visit on the very morning he's to dedicate a free lending library he's building out of his own pocket, employing Adams men I might add. I'd lose my office and rightfully so. You don't know how the game is played, lad, and best you keep your nose out of it. And if I catch you spreading your sedition around town," here he pointed a finger at Liam, "I will have your badge. Don't you forget Captain Curran answers to me."

The dog pack raced down the boardwalk forcing Nevin to jump back. He was red in the face. "Now get on with your duties, Officer Barrett, and get those mutts out of here." With that, he walked back into his store and slammed the door.

"He's got his arse covered nicely, doesn't he now?" Jack said. "Bringing prosperity to the commercial class while he whores out laborers. Not a blister on his hands, mind you. That's the trouble with this country and men like him. Next thing you know, when they get that new mill built, they'll drop everyone's wages. Wring the last drop of blood from the working men to build their empires."

"Enough with the politics, Jack," Liam said. "I need to keep my town safe today. Are you coming or not?"

As they walked farther down Park Street, they came upon two teenaged boys standing on ladders, one on each end of a shop marquee. Bunting was draped between them. They pulled the decoration this way and that, taking orders from their taskmaster on the ground, Mayor Nevin's wife, a stout woman. They had already decorated one side of the street.

A wagon rattled down the street, the horse dropping fresh dung along the way. "Hurry up, boys," Mrs. Nevin called, stepping around the horse piles. "We're running out of time. We still need to put the flags up and shovel the streets." The boys gave each other meaningful looks then crawled down the ladders.

Jack and Liam reached the bottom of the street, then came back up again, looking in Liam's old childhood hiding places: behind buildings, in the alleys, in the shadows of crates and barrels, and underneath parked wagons. They found no person and nothing unusual. By the time they arrived back at the Black Rose, the street was filling with people.

In Harry's apartment, the men had finished a fry-up breakfast. A stack of greasy plates sat on a counter as the boys drank coffee. The room smelled of fried bread and sausage.

"When can we get out of here?" Timothy Hennessey asked.

"Now is as good a time as any," Liam said, passing the burlap bags around. "The best throwers on the roofs. The rest of you in the crowd."

"I almost forgot," Jack pulled the licorice out of his pocket and handed it around. "From Tom Gillespie."

The men climbed down the stairs, blinking in the sunlight. They spread out in the alley behind the bar, collecting the best throwing rocks they could find, round and fitting well within the hand, and loaded them into the bags. Liam directed the throwers to nearby building roofs, accessed by fire escapes, where they emptied their bags and scrambled back down the stairs to collect more. After the throwers reckoned they had enough to stop a hundred soldiers, the remaining men took the empty bags to the streets below, now busy with townspeople passing the time in conversation. The mood of the crowd was animated with heads flicking every so often in the direction where the retinue would shortly appear.

As Jack and Liam watched the lads melt into the crowd, Jack said, "So you're defending the town with burlap bags and rocks."

"I am."

"What about your peace loving ways? Seems to me hitting a man with a rock is plenty violent."

"We tried, Jack. You heard Nevin. It's not like we live in a castle and I could draw up the bridge. If Dunbar and his men are unarmed, then everything will be fine. But if they are carrying guns, I won't let them hurt anyone."

"I was always curious, Liam, how far someone could push you before you took up the sword."

"Send someone to find me if you see trouble." He left Jack and walked to the police station, sited one block off Park Street. Captain Curran was standing on the porch, hands in his pockets, watching the bustle.

"All's well?" Curran asked.

"At present," Liam replied.

"I want you making rounds hourly," Curran said consulting his pocket watch. "It's eleven o'clock now. The Governor should arrive shortly after noon."

"Between now and then?"

"All we can do is sit and wait."

Liam's legs twitched. "I'm going for another walk."

He headed to Sadie's boarding house. Father Frank was standing on the stoop, smoking a cigar. As Liam approached, he saw Sadie hanging laundry in the backyard.

"Fine day," Frank said.

"Indeed. What time will you be arriving at the grandstand?"

"Twelve. The mayor will lead us in the pledge of allegiance, then comes my benediction."

"Will it be a long one?"

"I've been told to keep it short. There's Protestants in the audience as well, don't you know."

"If you see a gun, or a man you don't like the looks of, I want you to signal it to the rest of us. The lads from the camp are scattered around."

"And how am I to do that standing there up on the stage?"

"In Latin."

"I'm not sure there's a Latin word for 'gun', not one that anyone would understand."

"Something from mass, then, Father." Liam patted Frank's arm. "The boys will understand."

Chapter Twenty-Nine

Secrets and Lies

D AMN IF GEORGE WASHINGTON Stanley would drive a gang of hoodlums anywhere, like he was some kind of chauffeur.

He drove his wagon in front of the mansion, pulled by a roan gelding he'd wrangled from the stable owner, his gray mare saddled and tied to the back. He passed the shiny black carriage with red spoked wheels waiting for its passengers and brought his wagon around to the back.

When he opened the bunkhouse door to announce his arrival, the man with the saber scar stared at him. Without a word, Stanley walked out and climbed back onto the wagon. The crew filed out and piled onto the bed. The wagon listed to one side and then to the other as they clambered on. The scarred man hauled himself up to the bench beside Stanley, gave him an evil look, and spat on the ground. Each man wore a holstered pistol. No one spoke.

Dunbar marched to them from the house. "Wait until you hear the carriage pull out then follow at a distance. Stay out of sight." With that, he went back the way he came.

Stanley didn't care much what Dunbar said. He handed the reins to the scarred man and climbed down from the wagon.

"Where do you think you're going?" the man asked.

"To keep an eye out."

"Dunbar said to stay out of sight."

Stanley didn't answer. He pulled a cigar out of the vest of his Sunday-go-to-meeting suit and walked around to the side yard where he could watch the mansion and the carriage – and where he could be seen. Let Dunbar spot him. After this whole thing was over, Dunbar would be taking orders from Stanley.

He pulled a match out of another pocket and struck it on the bottom of his boot. After he got the cigar going, he pressed his thumb and finger on the match's burning phosphorus the way he'd seen Cunningham do. The pain was instant. "Sonofabitch!"

The men in the wagon burst into laughter, the loudest coming from the scarred man.

Stanley had forgotten when Cunningham did that trick, he'd spit on his fingertips first. Now he remembered and it was too late. That first sting was now searing. He threw the cigar onto the ground and put both fingers in his mouth. His tongue felt the heat of his burning flesh. He'd never felt so much pain before and it got worse with every second.

From the corner of his eye, he could see Dunbar on the porch. He scanned the yard, spied Stanley, stopped and stared. Stanley's gut churned but he stared back. The thugs in the wagon were still cackling behind him like a flock of chickens. One way or another, things between them would be settled by the end of the day. Stanley had a gun too and he was a fair shot. Dunbar better watch out. That scarred man better watch out too.

Miss Victoria stepped out of the mansion, wearing a black dress with a lace collar, a little jacket with feather trim, and a tall hat, like a man's top hat, but with more feathers. She said something to Dunbar. They were too far away from Stanley to hear, but he could see Dunbar laugh.

Dunbar led Miss Victoria to the carriage, opened the door, and offered his hand to steady her. She took it, stepped a little heeled boot onto the iron step, and disappeared into the compartment, drifts of black fabric following her even after she was gone. She had never seen Stanley. She had no idea he was there.

What could she have said to Dunbar to make him laugh? Why would she lower herself to amuse him, no better than her father's henchman? Had something happened between them, a secret, that would give them a private joke to share?

Maybe she wasn't the woman he thought she was. He conjured an image of Miss Victoria disappearing into her bedroom, her hand on Dunbar's lapel, pulling him in behind her. He tried to picture her undressing for Dunbar, unbuttoning her bodice, lacy under things showing while the slathering bastard watched her, but the image faded. She would not stoop so low. Dunbar would, he had no doubt, but not under Cunningham's roof. Dunbar loved few, but he loved Cunningham best and no woman would come between them. But why would she flirt with that ugly old bastard?

The mansion door opened. Alistair Cunningham, Governor Greenhalge, and Cunningham's useless son appeared, laughing merrily, and climbed into the carriage. The crone came out last, closing the door behind her, and then she pulled herself onto the driver's seat without any help from Dunbar, taking the seat that should have been Stanley's.

Dunbar hauled himself up after her and the old bird moved as far to the side as she could without falling off. He gave Stanley one last piercing stare, then gathered the reins and snapped them. Two sleek black high-stepping geldings strained against their harnesses and the carriage began to move down the lane.

Stanley waited until they were out of sight. He spat again, then went back to his wagon, untied the grey mare, and mounted her.

"Stanley, I thought you were driving this rig," Scarred Man said.

"You thought wrong," Stanley said as he trotted his horse down the lane.

L IAM WALKED THE LENGTH of Park Street again. Judging by the position of the sun, it wasn't quite noon yet.

Denny Hennessey, the rabbit bagger, was leaning against a brick wall in an alley, talking to another Irishman, both with burlap sacks tucked under their arms. Even with his flaming red hair, he wasn't conspicuous as the street filled with townspeople, many of them Irish, with hair in various shades of ginger.

"Remember your Latin, do you?" Liam asked.

"*Et cum spirit tu tuo*," Hennessey said.

"Good lad. Father Frank will be on the bandstand keeping a lookout. Listen for him. When you hear his warning, there's trouble."

"Not quite remembering a part of the mass where the priest says 'thou shalt bag a bloody blackguard'."

Hennessey's pal snorted.

"Not to worry," Hennessey went on. "By the time he's sounds the warning, I'll be in the midst of it already."

And so Liam progressed down the street, touching base with each of the lads, warning them to listen to the priest, but not to wait – if they saw something, do something.

A wagon of musicians pulled up in front of the bandstand, wearing blue military-like uniforms trimmed in gold and carrying shiny trumpets and tubas. They unloaded, the wagon drove off, and they climbed up onto the stage, rearranged the chairs to their liking, and started tuning. A man with a trumpet stood in front sounding a single note. Another musician repeated it and made adjustments to his instrument. They went back and forth until they were apparently satisfied, then the ritual started over again with the next man in the band.

Mrs. Nevin climbed up on stage as they were going through their ritual, interrupting the band leader. Liam was at a distance so he couldn't hear her words but he saw her pointing a finger here and there. As a result, the musicians all rose and rearranged the chairs as they had been.

The food vendors appeared, parking their stands across the street from the stage. Sausages, turkey legs, ice cream, and bottles of sarsaparilla were being sold under brightly-colored umbrellas. People lined up to make purchases as the band started playing a march. The pack of dogs laid in the grass of an empty lot, their noses pointed in the direction of the food. Excited children standing in line behind their mothers began pushing each other.

Mayor Nevin appeared on the boardwalk, watching people gather. He checked the time piece tucked into his vest and looked down the road whence Cunningham's group would come. He noticed Liam observing him, put the watch away and went back in his grocery store.

A handful of boys, about nine or ten years old, came running up the street, a little dog chasing them and barking, yelling the governor was on his way. Mayor Nevin came out of his store again and started walking to the bottom of the street.

The boys ran up to the bandstand and told the conductor. He gave one of them a coin and they ran to the ice cream vendor's line. The band filed down the stage and headed down the street where they would assemble and march ahead of the governor's carriage as it entered town.

Liam followed the band. When they reached the outskirts of town, they arranged themselves in a marching order. The street was full of people now. They shuttled to the boardwalks, clearing the way for the parade. The two teenaged boys who had been hanging bunting appeared, each bearing a giant flag, one of the United States and one of the state of Massachusetts. They took position ahead of the band. The crowd quieted.

At first a dust cloud approached along the road. Then, a horse-drawn black carriage came around a bend followed by a man on horseback. Another dust cloud followed the carriage. Liam spotted Hennessey the rock thrower atop a nearby building. He climbed up the fire escape. From that height, he could see that second dust cloud was a wagonful of men. The Inverness groundsmen. They would be armed. Ahead of it was a lone rider. Even at this distance, Liam could tell by the bulk of the man that he was Captain Stanley.

"Do you see that wagon?" Liam said, pointing.

Hennessey nodded.

"There's a fallen tree on the edge of the road around the bend," Liam said. "Grab one of the lads, go through the woods, and after the carriage passes, drag that tree into the road. We need to stop that wagon. Then get away. Those are dangerous men."

Hennessey nodded. He trotted off, tapped one of the bagmen on the shoulder and they disappeared into the woods.

The carriage arrived a few minutes later. Liam hoped that the lads wouldn't be too late. Or get caught. There was nothing for it now but to stay alert.

Dunbar pulled the carriage to a stop several yards behind the band and hopped off. Mrs. Ramsey was riding alongside him and remained in her seat. Mayor Nevin emerged from the people lining the road and greeted him. They exchanged words, Liam too far away to hear. Dunbar gestured to Mrs. Ramsey who slowly made her way off the wagon. Mayor Nevin and Dunbar climbed back on, leaving her to walk the rest of the way.

The bandleader barked some incomprehensible word and the parade began. The flag bearers walked solemnly down the street in the fore. The musicians began a rousing tune and started marching. The carriage waited for the band to make its way half of a block before Dunbar shook the reins.

At that moment, Captain Stanley, a pistol in his holster, came trotting up on his gray and pulled alongside the carriage. Victoria's warning was true. Stanley was armed.

When Dunbar spotted Stanley, he looked surprised, then he turned his attention to driving the horse. Stanley tipped his hat, trotted ahead of the carriage and fell into line behind the band.

He had ridden a few yards when his horse whinnied and reared up. Stanley lost his seat and toppled to the ground. The pistol fell out of its holster and fired. Women screamed and began patting down their children to make sure none had been injured by the stray bullet. The horse took off running down the street, passing the band and flagbearers. She was out of sight in an instant.

At the same time, Liam could hear the high laughter of boys in the crowd. The loudest came from Kevin. Liam would know that laugh anywhere.

Liam tried to push through the crowd so he could get to the pistol laying in the road, but at that instant a little girl in a long white dress and bonnet, no more than two or three years old, wandered into his path and he nearly knocked her over.

"Watch where you're going!" he heard an old woman say.

A couple of men hurried over to Stanley and offered to help him to his feet. He jerked his arms away, brushed himself off, and looked around for his horse. By now the crowd was suppressing laughter.

Liam swept up the little girl and handed her over to the old woman. By the time he had turned around, Stanley had retrieved the gun and was headed in Kevin's direction. Kevin was standing across the street, elbowing his friends when he saw Stanley coming at him and took off running. The other boys scattered in different directions.

The band struck up its tune again and the parade started moving. The governor leaned out the carriage window and waved to the cheering crowd. When the carriage pulled up to the bandstand and stopped, the onlookers flowed from the boardwalks and into the street for a better look.

Liam looked down the road for signs of the wagon. There was movement in the trees, Hennessey and his friend trotting back to town. Hennessey duffed his peaked cap at Liam, replacing it without missing a step.

Chapter Thirty

Bullets Cast a Wide Net

S TANLEY HAD HELD HIS mare back for much of the journey, pacing her so that he caught the occasional glimpse of the carriage winding its way along the road. When they were close to Adams, he gave her rein and she broke into a trot. He came around a bend and saw the carriage stopped at the edge of town, a crowd of people gathered along the street. Dunbar climbed down from the driver's seat. Stanley pulled in the mare and directed her into the woods. Her hindquarters danced side to side. With each bounce, his legs crashed into her ribs making the burn on his calf sear with fresh pain.

Dunbar talked to some pompous ass and then gestured to the Ramsey woman to get off the wagon. She took her time about it, making them wait. Then Dunbar climbed back onto the driver's bench with the dandy beside him and snapped the reins. Stanley let the mare go.

She brought him alongside the carriage. He pulled her back long enough for Dunbar to spot him and shoot him a nasty look. Stanley tipped his hat and dug his heels into the mare's side. She trotted pass the carriage and fell in behind a band playing a loud patriotic song.

Stanley savored the look on Dunbar's face. Surprise, fury. He saw it in Dunbar's eyes: the Scot knew there was nothing he could do to stop him. Let Dunbar plot his revenge, it wouldn't matter. After today, Stanley would be a hero and untouchable.

Something whirled through the air. The mare whinnied. As she rose onto her hind legs, Stanley felt the sudden transition from bumping in the saddle to floating. He hung there, in silence, wondering at the sheer majesty of the animal beneath him.

Then his feet slipped out of their stirrups. He rolled off her back, slowly tumbling along her rump. As her tail brushed across his face, he tried to manage the fall, not wanting to land on his head or under her feet.

As he hit the ground, a light flashed inside his head, blinding him. When his vision cleared, clouds were floating in the sky overhead. For a moment, he wondered how he'd gotten there. Then he became aware of the mare beside him, dancing side to side, her hooves inches from his head.

He tried to push himself away from the horse, afraid she'd stomp him. His hands slipped in the dirt. Pebbles ground into his palms. The ground rumbled as the horse took off, clipping him on the thigh with one hoof. At first it was numb, then a pain settled into the leg so sharp that it had to be bleeding. Dust flew into his face and felt grainy in his mouth. His eyes burned. He sucked for air. Dirt clogged his nostrils and he was choking. He needed to breathe. He rolled to his side and gulped, sucking a handful of dirt into his mouth. His gut retched. He pushed himself to his hands and knees and puked.

His belly emptied. He sat on his heels and felt for his gun. The holster was empty. The pistol was in the dirt a few feet away. He scrambled to it and slipped it back into its holster. Before he could get his feet under him, a couple of men were at his side, strong hands under each arm, pulling him up. "You okay, mate?" one fella asked.

A few feet away, kids were laughing. He realized what had happened. Someone had thrown a rock at the mare and hit her on the flank, spooking her.

Stanley jerked away from the hands that had lifted him. He heard that laughter again. He knew that voice. It was the same kid he cuffed at the racetrack in Pittsfield. That little bastard had to be the one who spooked his horse, making Stanley fall and look like an idiot. He sensed the carriage had stopped behind him. Dunbar would have seen it all. A man who couldn't sit atop a beast was hardly a man at all, that's what Dunbar would be saying to himself.

Stanley spotted the kid snaking his way through the crowd. He was on his feet now, crossing the street. He wouldn't run. He never ran, even if he was chasing an escaped prisoner but he always caught them. Bullets cast a wide net.

⟡

LIAM RAN INTO AN alley that would bring him to the same back street where Kevin was headed. He turned the corner and crashed into a teenaged boy and girl. Her back was against the wall, the boy looming over her. Liam stopped and grabbed the kid by the collar. "Get off her."

The boy blushed, spittle on his lip. The girl's face was ashen.

Liam pushed the kid ahead of him and the boy took off running. The girl grasped Liam's arm. "Please don't tell my father!"

Liam nodded towards the crowd, indicating she should go back to the festivities. "Mind yourself." The girl walked back down the alley at a quick pace, her head bent, wiping her eyes.

The back street was empty. Liam had no idea where Kevin and Stanley had gone. He put two fingers in his mouth and whistled. Denny Hennessey's head appeared above him, peering over the roof.

"Have you seen my brother?" Liam shouted up to him.

"What's he look like?"

"Me, only younger."

"I have not seen him."

The band stopped playing. Liam ran down the street, rounded a corner and found himself behind the stage. The musicians were clambering up the stairs. The carriage was parked with the occupants piling out.

Father Frank was on the stage, greeting musicians and dignitaries alike. Kevin and Stanley were nowhere in sight. Liam scanned the crowd, hoping that a wave of movement would tell him where they had gone, but he saw none.

The assembly quieted as Victoria Cunningham took center stage, her hand upon her heart, facing an American flag held by a teenaged boy next to her. She began the pledge of allegiance. Her words were quickly drowned out by the voices of the audience. When they finished, she took her seat beside her father. The governor was seated on Cunningham's other side with Edward next to him.

Frank took a long look around the audience, then crossed himself. Most of the audience crossed themselves too and bowed their heads. The three Cunninghams and Governor Greenhalge stared straight ahead, poker-faced.

Out of the corner of his eye, Liam saw a deep, slow sign of the cross made by a white-blonde girl in the front row. Clare. She was standing amongst a cluster of children, her class. In the back of the crowd, he saw Kate's wild auburn hair, a head above the others, with the mother at her side. He should have known. Kate did what she wanted to do.

Kevin and Stanley were nowhere in sight.

Liam pushed through the crowd to Kate's side. "What are you doing here?"

She looked at Liam sidewise without lifting her prayer-bowed head. "The mother got away," she whispered. "I was hanging laundry. When I came back inside, she was gone. She must have heard all the goings-on and came to see for herself."

The mother had that vacant, happy look she always wore. Sometimes it seemed she almost understood she was out of her depth.

"Take her home. And take Clare with you. She's in the front row."

"Not until Father Frank's done. Shhh." Kate closed her eyes.

Liam spotted the schoolmistress and headed towards her. After he moved her along, he would get one of the lads to escort Kate and the mother back home. On his way, someone caught his arm. He spun around. It was Captain Curran.

Curran pulled him aside. "Where do you think you're going?"

"The children."

"Look around you. There's no gunmen. If you run the children out of here, you'll start a stampede. The mayor will have my head. And yours."

"Those men are not here, yet. But they're on their way, Captain. I saw them. We don't have much time. Stanley's armed. I saw it for myself. What I was told was true."

Kevin's head bobbed up out of the crowd. He was moving across the street, towards another alley. Stanley was standing on the boardwalk for a better view. He had seen Kevin too. He leapt onto the street and melted into the audience.

Liam pulled out of Curran's grasp and looked up at Father Frank, who was watching the exchange. Frank gave him a wink, took a deep breath and started a new prayer, "*Gloria in excelsis Deo.*" The audience gave each other confused looks and bowed their heads again.

As long as he prayed, Kate wouldn't leave. But as long as the prayers lasted, any movement would be obvious. Kevin popped up near the edge of the crowd, scanning over the heads. Stanley was only a few feet away. The big man lunged forward as Kevin's back was turned. Kevin, seeming to have sensed danger behind him, spun around, saw Stanley and ran.

∞

S TANLEY HAD FOLLOWED THE kid winding through the crowd. He'd almost had the little bastard when the kid saw him and ran down an alley. Stanley didn't run. He never ran.

As Stanley came around the building corner, a handful of dirt was thrown in his eyes and he heard the little bastard's laugh.

He lashed out, whipping a fist against anything within arm's reach. It connected with something hard. He assumed it was the kid's head, but he couldn't be sure. His eyes were watering so much he couldn't see. He heard the sound of a body slamming against a wall. He reached towards the sound, found a torso, grabbed its shirt and slammed the kid back into the wall.

The dirt scratched his eyes. He blinked fast, trying to wash the sand away. When his vision cleared he saw the boy in his grip looked a lot like Liam Barrett. The brat stared at Stanley from lowered eyelids, his head tilted back. It was the same look his father used to give him before a beating.

As the years wore on, Stanley had seen that look again on men he'd encountered. It was meant to scare him but it only made him madder. He made sure those men never looked at him like that again. Stanley bounced the kid's head off the brick wall. The boy slumped to the ground. Stanley reached for his gun.

∞

LIAM RAN ACROSS THE street and followed Stanley disappearing behind a building. When Liam rounded the corner, Kevin was on the ground, crabbing across the dirt, a wall blocking his escape from Stanley's aimed pistol.

Liam clamped a hand on Stanley's shoulder and spun him around. He balled up his right fist and plowed it into Stanley as hard as he could, nearly pulling himself over on top of the brute. Stanley's eyes rolled back in his head. Slobber and blood spewed from his mouth as his head spun from the impact, splattering Liam across the face. His body went limp. He wheeled face down into the dirt as the gun clattered to the ground.

Then all was quiet for a moment. Then Kevin let out a sob.

In the background Frank recited the final lines of a prayer. Time seemed to suspend while the assembled waited for him to say "amen." He didn't. Instead, he shouted, "*Ite, missa est.*"

That was when Liam heard the dogs barking.

"*Ite, missa est,*" Frank shouted again. Go, church is dismissed. It was in the wrong place. That phrase wasn't spoken at the end of that prayer, but at the end of the mass. Frank was telling everyone to leave.

He must have seen something.

As Liam ran back around the building, men shouted. He ran faster.

The crowd was before him, pushing and dragging, running into each other, panicked. He saw Hennessey the bagger and the other lads wading into the fray. Down the street, a couple of men lain in the dirt. Frank caught Liam's eye and leapt off the stage into the crowd.

Edward Cunningham was on his feet, crossing the stage to escape. Liam heard a blast. Edward crumpled.

A rapid series of shots burst out. Women screamed. Babies cried. Mothers and grandmothers gathered as many children as they could carry and dragged the larger ones. They were going in all directions.

The first shot had come from across the street. Liam expected to see one of Dunbar's henchman with pistol raised, but instead he saw Dunbar himself. He was the man who had shot Edward Cunningham.

Why would Malcom Dunbar shoot his boss' son? Was he aiming at the governor instead or was it an accident? It must have been a ruse, that the shots were meant to be fired into the air starting a panic. Dunbar's bullet would have passed over their heads if Edward hadn't leapt to his feet.

Edward was now sprawled across the stage with a red stain blooming across his shirt.

Mrs. Ramsey launched herself at Dunbar. She swung at him with an open hand, claws bent to rake across his face. Without glancing at her, he caught her wrist and bent it backwards. She screamed and buckled, forced into a crouch.

Liam found himself at Dunbar's side. The gun was gone. He was looking down at Ramsey, her body twisted with pain. "Let go of me, you miserable toerag. Let me go to him. He's hurt, can't you see that?"

"Let her go," Liam said.

Dunbar threw her arm away and she fell into the dirt. She scrambled to the stage and gathered Edward in her arms. Blood was smeared across her face and her hands. She pressed her skirt into his wound. With her face next to Edward's, Liam saw that they had the same Roman nose.

Because she was so much shorter than Liam, he had not seen her profile so he hadn't registered the resemblance before, a resemblance so strong that it could mean only one thing.

Mrs. Ramsey was Edward Cunningham's mother. It was so obvious now. How she doted on him. Her refusal to cow-tow to the father. Alistair Cunningham's tolerance of her rudeness. Her animosity to Dunbar, who must have known their secret. She would have killed anyone who had threatened him.

Edward groaned, his face grotesque with pain. She rocked him, murmuring into his ear.

Liam pulled himself onto the stage and crouched close to them. "It was you."

She kept rocking and whispering, taken no notice of Liam.

"It was you who killed Deidre Monaghan."

She stopped moving.

"You learned Deidre was carrying Edward's child. If Edward married her, his future would be ruined."

"He was not marrying that Jezebel."

Edward groaned.

"She thought he was," Liam said.

"She tried to trap him. Who knows if that child was his? If there was a child? I wasn't having it. Edward has a future. He will be important someday."

Edward's eyes opened. He looked about frantically. He tried to push himself away but she held on. "Everything is going to be alright. We'll take you home and call the doctor. Your father will make sure you have the best of everything."

Edward looked up into her face, soothed for a moment. Then he frowned. "Who tried to fool me?"

"She's talking about Deidre," Liam said.

Edward winced. Whether it was from the pain or the mention of Deidre's name, Liam didn't know.

"I loved her."

"You're a boy," Mrs. Ramsey said. "You don't understand the wiles of women. You were bewitched."

"I loved her. I wanted to marry her. You promised to explain it to Father and get his blessing for us. And then..."

"And then she killed Deidre," Liam said.

A hard look came into Edward's eyes. It was the same expression his father always had. Removed, calculating.

Mrs. Ramsey clung to him. "It was for you, don't you see?"

Dunbar appeared on stage. He lifted Edward into his arms as if he was a child while Liam pried the old woman's hands from her son.

Liam unhooked the handcuffs from his belt and locked her wrists. "I'm arresting you for the murder of Deidre Monaghan." Then to Dunbar, he said, "This isn't over."

Dunbar ignored him and carried Edward, now bellowing in pain, from the stage.

The crowd had gone. Father Frank was bent over a man in the street, his purple stole around his neck, praying. It was Hennessey the bagger.

The other lads were standing at a distance, caps off, heads bent. His brother came running to the scene and fell to his knees.

Stanley stumbled out of an alley. He took in the scene: men laying in the street, Father Frank praying over the dead lad, his brother at his side crying. He watched Dunbar lifting Edward into the carriage with Victoria, Alistair Cunningham, and the governor waiting their turn to board. When his eyes met Liam's, Liam had his hand on Mrs. Ramsey's arm, about to walk her to jail. Liam watched him register all these images, a dazed expression on his face. Then Captain George Washington Stanley collapsed. He landed on his seat in the dirt.

∞

L IAM ESCORTED MRS. RAMSEY down the street. She tried to jerk her arm away. "Get your hands off me, you filthy bogtrotter. I'll not have you handling me like some kind of cheap harlot."

"Mrs. Ramsey, you're under arrest. I'm taking you to the police station."

She twisted her arm in his grasp. "I'm not stupid. I know that. But I won't be dragged there for everyone to see."

Liam looked around. The few people left in downtown lined the boardwalks, watching them, sullen, not speaking. The carriage thundered past, Dunbar at the reins. Mrs. Ramsey stopped walking and Liam waited. She watched as her son, and everyone she knew, drive away, abandoning her. If she ever saw them again, it would be in court or at the gallows. Liam could give her this moment to say good-bye, even if it was only in her mind.

Sadie ran up and planted herself before them, a dishrag in her hand. To Liam, she said, "I heard you found who did it, who killed my Deirdre." Then she took in Mrs. Ramsey. Sadie's head jutted forward as she examined the woman's face.

"You," she said in a hoarse whisper.

Ramsey stared back at Sadie, then spat at her feet. Sadie didn't jump away. She ignored the glob slithering off her work boot and onto the dirt.

Harry walked up to the group. Liam was grateful to see him, not having the heart to ask the grieving mother to stand aside. "Sadie, Father Frank needs a word."

Sadie's trance was broken. She gave Harry a nod, then to Ramsey she said, "Burn in hell, witch." Ramsey snorted.

Harry and Sadie stepped aside. Ramsey began walking with Liam's hand on her arm. She entered the police station, head held high. Caleb Anthony jumped to his feet.

"Where's Captain Curran?" Liam asked.

"Helping with the wounded. He told me to stay here for when you came back." His eyebrows were raised in question.

"This is--," Liam paused. "We need your first name, Mrs. Ramsey."

"Agnes."

"Caleb, this is Agnes Ramsey. She's under arrest for the murder of Deirdre Monaghan."

"A lady?" Caleb asked.

"Who are you calling 'a lady'? See these weeds I wear? Look at these hands? Does this look to you like I'm highborn?"

"But, Liam, we've never had a lady in jail here before."

Liam pointed at the ledger on Caleb's desk. "You need to log it."

Ramsey jerked her arm away. "Where's this cell of mine?"

"Down the hall there," Liam said. She led the way, Liam behind her while Caleb filled in the station log. It was a small station with only one cell. She stepped inside. When Liam unlocked her wrists, he felt her hands shaking. She turned away. He tried to close the cell's iron door quietly but it clanged into place. She flinched at the sound.

Liam found himself staring at her back. She stood stick-straight facing the tiny barred window. He pieced together how the housekeeper's son was raised as the heir to an empire. There had been a liaison between herself and Cunningham. He had sent his pregnant wife and Ramsey back to Scotland so that his wife's child would be born on Scottish soil, perhaps not realizing that Ramsey was pregnant as well. The wife and her child died, but Edward, Ramsey's child, had lived. So she returned to America and Edward was passed off as the dead wife's baby. Cunningham may not have known at first. Or perhaps he did. But it was clear by the way he tolerated her, he now knew that she was the mother of his son. They were bonded together as parents and as partners in a lie.

Ramsey turned to him.

"Alistair made that silly girl an offer. Money and a new job in Boston. All she had to do was say that she was a widow if she wanted to keep the child. It would have been better if it was put up for adoption, of course. Or got rid of. But she insisted, she was keeping the child. She might come back claiming something later if she kept it but if she said the father was someone else first, who would believe her? And so they kept at her."

"They?"

"Alistair and that thug Dunbar. Edward came to me. This was before she said she was pregnant. He wanted to marry her. He knew I had his father's ear, so he asked me to intervene. When I told Alistair of Edward's infatuation, he sent the boy away on some errand. That's when the girl said she was carrying his child. She saw that Alistair was keeping them apart and she was desperate to get Edward back."

"Did he know that you were his mother?"

She shook her head. "Never. It was agreed that he would never learn the truth. The fewer who knew, the better."

"Dunbar, does he know?"

She sighed. Her shoulders fell. She scratched at her hairline, pulling a hair loose inadvertently from her tight bun. Turning, she examined the cell around her. Brick walls, bars, a chamber pot stashed beneath a cot with a thin mattress. "I'm bound to get lice from that," she said, bending over to examine it. She brushed it with her hand and sat down. "Dunbar. Yes, he knew. He knew from the beginning. He caught me leaving Alistair's bedroom one night. Oh, don't look at me that way. I'm no whore. It's a done thing. Maids and masters. Everyone knows. They look the other way."

"Then you cared for Cunningham?"

"A foolish young girl. I didn't feel guilty. He was a lonely man. They hadn't married for love. His marriage was a business arrangement. The missus, she didn't care. She would as soon have him crawling on top of anyone else but her. I knew it could never come to anything. One day, I would grow too old to hold his interest and he would find someone else younger, prettier. And then I'd be like any other servant. Even so, on those nights together, he talked to me about things he never told anyone else. He'd tell me about growing up back home, poor as he was. His mother died of fever when he was young. His father was a dreamer, always some new plot to make a fortune. Poor Alistair had to work since he was a wee boy to keep food on the table. We were so much alike. I believed he cared for me at the time in his own way. He may even still, not that you'd know."

"Did you speak to Cunningham on Edward's behalf? Urge him to allow the marriage?"

"Nothing of the sort. I wasn't having that tart ruin my boy's future. I tried talking to her too. I waited for her in the woods. Tried to make her see reason."

"And when she wouldn't?"

Ramsey shrugged. "She tripped and hit her head." Already the story was changing. Back at the dedication, not an hour ago, she'd admitted to murder.

Even if he misunderstood, Liam very much doubted the new story. The blow caused too much damage to have been made by a simple trip. Maybe the old lady pushed her. More likely Ramsey picked up the rock and struck her down.

Liam locked the cell door. The old woman held his gaze, unrepentant but tired.

Capt. Curran came into the cell block and took the key from Liam's hand. "Home to your family, son. It's been a long day."

CHAPTER THIRTY-ONE

THE BERKSHIRE RANGERS

A FTER DINNER THAT EVENING, Father Frank visited. The family gathered in the parlor, as they had on that previous night six days earlier. The mother in her chair, Clare beside her. Kevin excused himself and went into the yard to check on the animals. Frank balanced the teacup and saucer on his knee. Liam put his tea on a side table, his hand aching from where he had struck Stanley in the jaw. The pain in his hand was the only thing he felt. Otherwise, he was empty.

"The Hennessy lad," Frank said.

"Dennis," Liam said.

"Today, during the dedication. When we were praying, those men you warned me about came into town. They were on foot, sneaking in behind the buildings. They had guns. I told everyone to leave. They didn't understand so I told them again. They looked confused, but they knew something was wrong. Then those men came out of hiding and pulled their guns out and the crowd panicked."

Liam hadn't seen the men and the guns. By the time he came out of the alley, everyone was pushing and trying to run away. The henchmen disappeared with the fleeing towns-people, except the few that had been fallen by the Irish lads.

Frank continued. "I went into the crowd and bade everyone I met to leave quickly. I saw you there, Kate, with your mother. You were already on your way. The teacher was shepherding her students back to school. That was when the brave lad went down."

The teacup on Frank's knee rattled. He lifted it and handed it to Kate.

"He was behind one of those thugs and had dropped a bag over the man's head. Another came up from behind and stabbed him in the back. By the time I reached him, both of the strangers were gone."

"God rest his soul," Kate said.

"You couldn't have stopped it," Liam said. "You did everything you could."

"Oh, aye. I know that up here." Frank tapped his temple. "Still..."

Frank stayed long after Kate had put the mother to bed and the children had said good night. Frank and Liam sat by the fire. Liam hadn't spoken. He kept running through the events of the day, the days before, the week, asking himself what he had missed, what could he have done to prevent the tragedies that had befallen Adams.

"I never heard the ending of that story," Liam said.

"Which story is that?"

"About Deidre the Sorrowful."

"After she had traveled the countryside with her lover, they were caught by the king's men. The lover was struck down in battle and Deidre taken prisoner."

"Did she marry the king?"

"He no longer wanted her, but he had his honor to preserve. He and his guard were taking her away in a wagon to a place where she expected the king's revenge would be extracted. Believing a fate worse than death was in store for her, she threw herself from the wagon. Her head struck a rock and she died."

"Old Ramsey must have heard the same story. She's now claiming our Deirdre tripped and hit her head."

"No one would ever believe that, would they?"

"She confessed. I heard it. Dunbar heard it. Let her tell her tale to the jury. It's her right."

"You think they'll convict her?"

"If she testifies, she opens the door to the truth about her relationship with Cunningham, that she was Edward's mother, that she and Cunningham and Dunbar conspired to this fiction that his mother was dead. Jurors don't like liars. They're common sense folks. They'll see through it."

"They could acquit her, not wanting to see a woman hang."

"As long as I can remember, a woman hasn't been hung in Massachusetts. She'll be sentenced to life in prison."

SUNDAY AFTERNOON, LIAM MUCKED out Bridget's shed with his swollen, aching hand. With each forkful of soiled hay, pain shot up his arm. He focused on that pain, savored it. It proved that he was alive. It also proved that he had broken his own creed against violence. There was a limit to his high-born ideals. He was little better than

Ramsey herself who had murdered to protect her son. Liam had no doubt he would have killed Stanley to protect Kevin if he had needed.

A wagon pulled up the lane, driven by Dunbar with Captain Curran as his passenger. "Governor Greenhalge requests an audience," Curran said. "Clean yourself up, lad. We're going to Inverness."

"What's this about?"

"When the governor asks to see you, you go. We'll both know when we get there."

At the estate, Liam and Capt. Curran were led into Cunningham's study by the young maid who had given Liam scones only two days earlier.

A fire burned in the grate. Edward was propped up on one of the leather couches by pillows, a blanket covering him. He seemed to be dozing. A doctor sat in a winged back chair nearby, reading. He nodded at the men.

Stanley was shown in by the same maid just as Mrs. Ramsey walked past the open doorway. The last time Liam had seen her, she was locked up in the Adams jail. He looked at Curran for an explanation.

"Capt. Stanley called for her this morning," Curran explained. "The case is his jurisdiction."

"Why isn't she in jail, Stanley?" Liam asked.

"I dropped the charges. Lack of evidence."

"But she confessed."

"There never was a confession, Barrett."

"I heard it."

"You misunderstood."

"But everyone else heard it too."

"Heard what?" Dunbar said. Liam hadn't noticed him enter the room.

"She confessed. She murdered Deidre."

"Nah, laddie, that's where you're wrong. I was right there beside her the whole time. There was no confession."

"Edward heard it. You heard it."

Edward, lolling on the couch, lifted his head. "What did I hear?"

"Mrs. Ramsey confessed to killing Deidre," Liam answered.

Edward scowled. "I don't remember that." A tear slid from his eye.

"You heard it, Dunbar. You were right there."

"You're mistaken. All you heard was the rantings of a hysterical woman."

"She attacked you. Because you shot Edward."

"I did nothing of the sort," Dunbar said. "Edward was shot by one of those tramps, the ones I told you about time and time again. I warned you. The Mollys, those rabble-rousers. They shot at the governor and hit Edward instead. What you saw was me aiming at the assassin but he got away." Dunbar poked Stanley in the chest. "If you'd been where you were supposed to be, none of this would have happened."

Rustling of skirts brought their attention to those now entering the room. Victoria Cunningham was on the arm of Governor Greenhalge, Alistair Cunningham behind them. When Edward saw the governor, he tried to push himself up. Victoria perched on the couch beside him and rested a hand on his chest. "Keep still."

The governor patted his hand in the air, signaling that Edward should lay down. "How is our brave young man?"

"Resting comfortably," the doctor said. No doubt he was, Liam thought. He appeared to be heavily drugged. A bottle of laudanum was on the side table.

"Alistair, if your son hadn't thrown himself between me and the shooter, I may well have been killed. I'm very lucky this young man acted so quickly." He patted Edward on the uninjured shoulder. "After you have regained your strength, there is a place for you on my staff."

"Thank you, sir," Edward said weakly.

"No need to thank me, son. It is I who should thank you, every day that I draw breath." He turned to Cunningham. "You were right, Alistair I should have listened to you." Then the governor settled behind the Scot's massive desk. Cunningham, his hands loose by his side, seemed not to know where he should stand or sit.

Liam, Captain Curran, and Captain Stanley were lined up off to the side of the room. Dunbar had struck an obsequious pose, away from the others, as if he waited for instruction.

Victoria came to Cunningham's rescue. "Shall I pour drinks, Father?" As she poured, Cunningham took a seat in one of the wingback chairs flanking the fire. She served brandy to the governor, then Cunningham, then the doctor.

"Gentlemen?" she asked Liam and the two police captains. Stanley began to say something but Curran held up his hand, refusing for all of them.

"Malcolm, you'll have a drink," she said, carrying a glass to Dunbar. How odd he looked, that rough man with shaven head and full ginger beard, his stern expression, working man's clothes, holding a delicate crystal glass filled with amber liquid.

Stanley was sweating, his face bloated and red. The stank of the liquor he had drunk the night before enveloped him like an invisible cloud. Liam wondered if Stanley suspected he had been the intended target, designated as the chess piece Dunbar was happy to sacrifice in the service of his king. It could have been Stanley who was shot, maybe even shot dead, but if he had lived, he wouldn't be laying on a silk couch before a fireplace pampered by his own physician.

The governor spoke. "There was a reason why I asked you three officers here today. Captain Stanley, is that your name? You're the Pittsfield police chief, do I have that right?"

Stanley's "yes" was gargled. He cleared his throat and spoke again. "Yes, sir." His color deepened.

"And Captain Curran, you are the Adams police chief and this fine young man, Liam Barrett, works for you. Do I have that right?"

"Yes, sir."

"I'm very impressed by Barrett. I'm told that he discovered this plot, the attempt on my life and he tried to stop the dedication. I'm also told that he arrested the tramp Sweeney for the murder of a young maid a few days ago and that he discovered the Mollys' encampment. Unfortunately they seemed regrouped and made their heinous attempt on my life for which my good friend's son is now suffering the consequences."

Liam felt Stanley stirring beside him.

"Alistair has urged that I license a private police force in the Berkshires, and I have taken his suggestion with the greatest weight. He lives here. He knows the people and the goings on much better than I. Given what happened yesterday, I can only agree. Although you two captains do a fine job in each of your towns, I am certain of that, it is apparent that lawlessness can escape detection if it migrates from one town to another. There is a need for a broader authority, a centralized authority. However, with the events in Pennsylvania, the legislators have no warmth in the hearts for a privatized police force. For that reason, I am expanding the state police force and creating a barracks in the Berkshires. The man who I am appointing to this position will coordinate law enforcement efforts with and between the local police."

The governor stood. "A toast to the new captain of the Massachusetts State Police, Berkshire County." The men held their glasses in the air.

"Liam Barrett."

Dunbar raised his glass conspicuously higher than the others had. "Cheers, Barrett," he said, more loudly than was necessary, then poured the entire contents down his throat.

"Cheers," was said by the doctor and Cunningham, and they all drank. Stanley seemed to buckle, but he caught himself and stood upright again. Dunbar wiped his mustache, suppressing a laugh.

CHAPTER THIRTY-TWO

ANOTHER SUNDAY

A WEEK LATER, THERE was a Sunday dinner at the Barrett home. James O'Herlihy, the newspaperman who played the fiddle at Deidre's wake was there, helping Kate ferry dishes to the table. After dinner, Father Frank started a new story. Liam excused himself and went out to check on Bridget and her calf, Patrick.

It had been a long week. There were discussions about where the Berkshire state police should be headquartered, Captain Curran, Captain Stanley, and Malcom Dunbar in attendance. A decision wasn't made and for the time being, the headquarters was wherever Liam was.

One day, he stopped in at the Black Rose first before going home. Harry told him the lads who were living in his apartment had moved to Sadie's and all had been hired by Tom Gillespie to rebuild Hogan's warehouse.

On Wednesday, a messenger had been sent to him by the Pittsfield pathologist. A body had been found hanging in the woods. Liam visited the funeral home. What was left of the body had the look and shape of Sweeney, the tramp who had escaped Stanley's jail. Death by hanging was certain, by another or self-inflicted, the pathologist could not say.

Why would he escape jail only to hang himself? Stanley had insisted his tramp friends had broken him out, but the lads denied it. Someone else had. And that someone else was the last person to see him alive.

After dinner, Jack Barrett found Liam in the shed, sitting on a stool, watching the sun go down. He gave Liam a cigar, lit one for himself, and then passed the match to Liam. "Had a word with my friend at Inverness," he said. Liam assumed he meant Victoria. "Old Cunningham couldn't have a scandal. That's why the old lady got released. If everyone found out that Edward was his bastard, the son of a maid, all his high-born plans would go up in smoke. You understand that, don't you?"

"She confessed. I heard her. Dunbar heard her."

"Water under the bridge, my boy." Jack Barrett leaned one shoulder against the shed wall.

"Did Victoria know?"

"That Edward was old Ramsey's son? She had her suspicions about Mrs. Ramsey and her father. The old lady was entirely too familiar with Cunningham and he let her get away with insolence he wouldn't tolerate even from Dunbar. Victoria was just a wee one when the family took the boat to Scotland so her mother could bear Alistair's son on Scottish soil, too little to understand that Ramsey was with child. All she knew was that her mother had died but there was a baby in the manor. Lo and behold! Cunningham had the son he always dreamed of, to carry on his empire and his name.

"So, you see, he couldn't have her tried for murder and have the whole story come out. No choice job for Edward in politics. No advantageous marriage for Victoria. Edward's off to Boston as soon as he's well enough to travel. She's to be sent to Europe looking for a husband in the spring, preferably one with a title."

"And Ramsey gets away with murder."

"If your idea of living the rest of your life under the thumb of Alistair Cunningham is getting away. She's to chaperone Victoria in Europe and then stay on in Scotland after Victoria returns. Cunningham's bought a castle he wants modernized. She's to supervise. It'll take the rest of her days. Banished from the realm."

"And separated from her son forevermore," Liam said. "Is Victoria being sent away because they found out she warned me?"

"Not to worry. The excursion had always been the plan. Felix Malone confessed to the old man that it was he who overheard Stanley and Dunbar plotting and he had warned you. They would have fired him but he quit before they had the chance, glad to be shut of that place. We found him a job in Albany. He'll be fine."

A horse and rider, with a second horse in tow, cantered up the lane and trotted into the yard. Uncle Jack rolled off the wall and walked back to the house, his face turned away from the rider. It was Malcom Dunbar on a roan gelding, towing the big black stallion Victoria had ridden.

"A gift from Mister Alistair Cunningham," Dunbar said. "So you can attend to your duties throughout the county."

Liam hated horses. "I don't know how to ride."

"Simple, lad, hold on to the reins and don't fall off."

Dunbar dismounted. His eyes drifted to the path Jack Barrett had taken to the house and then back to Liam.

"There's something you need to understand."

"Cunningham can't have a scandal."

"What?" Dunbar looked genuinely confused but he quickly recovered. "True enough, but that's not a problem now. Poor Mrs. Ramsey passed away last night."

"I hadn't heard."

"It wasn't a police matter. She died in her sleep. The doctor was called. He said it was her heart."

"Sounds like you don't believe his diagnosis."

"I think it might've had something to do with the bottle of laudanum we found on her bedside table."

"How convenient. She confessed to murdering Deidre. Her charges are dismissed and then she dies."

"By her own hand. Or, for all we know, the doctor was right and it was her heart."

The house door banged open. Kevin ran to Liam's side, Kate, Clare, O'Herlihy and Father Frank following.

Dunbar handed Kevin the stallion's reins. Kevin's eyes widened.

"It's your brother's," Dunbar said. "I understand he's not much of a horseman. Can I trust you to take care of this monster?"

"I know everything there is to know. Currying, cleaning his hooves, checking his teeth, feed." Kevin shot Liam a look. "I learned it from my friends."

Hanging around the Pittsfield racetrack, no doubt. Liam found himself holding his breath.

"Can we keep him, Liam? Please?"

Liam felt the stares of family and friends on his back. He considered arguing there was no place for the horse, but there was an empty stall in the shed next to Bridget's.

Without waiting for an answer, Dunbar mounted the roan gelding. "His name is Goliath. He likes carrots." With that, he trotted down the road.

❧

SADIE MONAGHAN WAS SITTING on her front porch, a cup of cold tea in her lap, a shawl about her shoulders. The sun had gone down over Mount Greylock, but the sky was still tinged with pinks and pale green.

Her day's work had been done. The boarders were fed. Bread was in the oven. The kitchen was clean. The morning's porridge was steeping.

This was the first Sunday that Sadie had gone to mass without Deidre and Finn at her side. Two weeks ago, they had been with her. Last week, she hadn't left the house. Today, Kate Barrett and her mother Mary took their places on one side with Clare and Kevin on the other, Clare holding her hand throughout. Her Deirdre was gone, but she wasn't alone. But she would never feel complete again.

She had sat on that porch every evening with a cup of cold tea watching the sun go down since Deidre moved to Inverness. She knew even back then she had lost her daughter. That first night after she had left, Sadie knew that one day, her wee girl would never come back, a dark fate in store for her. She had cried herself to sleep every night, biting her pillow lest the boarders overheard.

Now she realized that when she saw the man on the bridge and sensed something had happened, she was not having a premonition. Deidre had already been murdered. What she had felt was Deidre's soul passing through her own, one last farewell, as she disappeared to her heavenly reward.

A man on horseback came down the street, the horse walking at a slow, steady pace. He stopped in front of Sadie's house, his figure a silhouette beneath the leafless trees. She recognized him and she wrapped her hands more tightly around the cold china cup to keep them from shaking.

When Deidre had first come home from Inverness on her half-days full of stories about the grand mansion, the beautiful clothes, the exotic food, the people who lived there, and the people who worked there, she had said his name. It was ironic that Deidre would end up in that household. Given his loyalty to Cunningham, Sadie should not have been surprised that he was still there. Sadie, soothing her own fears, told herself that he would look over her.

He eased himself down from the horse's back. She felt his eyes on her and now she could see the contours of his face, watching her, waiting for permission.

She had blamed him all those years for not leaving Cunningham's house when she learned the child was coming. She hated him for giving her money, as if she was to be bought off, and sending her away to lie about her past, to call herself a widow and her child an orphan. People knew. They always knew but they didn't challenge her. It was so often done in those days, a young widow with babe in tow appearing in a town where she was a stranger. They knew there had been no marriage and the mother and child had been rejected by the father.

She blamed him when Deidre came home, secretive and glowing, in love and with a bairn of her own inside her. A mother always knows. Why hadn't he watched over her, kept her safe? Did he really think that a mother could teach a girl about the dangers of the world, when she'd been forced to lie to that same child about her own birth?

And she blamed him for Deidre's murder. Where was he? All these years and on that day?

Sadie was tired now. It wasn't her job to make Malcom Dunbar miserable. He had done a fine job of that by himself. He would always live with the knowledge that he had not prevented their daughter's murder.

Her hands were no longer shaking. She put the cup down on the porch rail, and folded her hands on her lap, waiting for his approach.

Dunbar walked up the steps to her. He reached into a pocket and pulled out a package wrapped in brown paper, tied with twine. He offered it to her. While all was quiet and the last of the light was fading, Sadie unwrapped the present. It was a silhouette portrait of their daughter, Deidre.

"It is done," he said, then he walked back down the path to the horse and rode away.

THE END

Hope You Enjoyed The Sorrowful Girl!

H ELP READERS FIND THEIR next great book by leaving a review: https://www.a mazon.com/Sorrowful-Girl-Barrett-Gilded-Novels-ebook/dp/B0C7X5DGG8.

ACKNOWLEDGMENTS

This book would not have been possible without the help of numerous friends. First, my cousin, the late JoAnn Emerson, who introduced me to Adams as we explored our common ancestry. Robert Norcross, whose own family tree connects with the Barretts, greatly assisted in our endeavors and through the years, as I wrote this book, has answered my tedious questions. Elizabeth Amann, who is my source on things Roman Catholic. David Corbett, my teacher in the LitReactor online writing workshops – a great teacher. You're in luck if you take one of his classes. Cynthia Kuhn, who gave me invaluable insight in the early days of this book. Rory Bryant of the eagle eye, who gave *The Sorrowful Girl* the final review. Catriona McPherson, who assisted me in Scottish syntax and word usage. And, Joe Ide, whose critique, support, and encouragement buoyed me. If I've forgotten anyone, please forgive me.

Thanks to the authors who have encouraged and inspired me: Louise Penny, Hank Phillippi Ryan, Hallie Ephron, David Corbett, Charles and Caroline Todd, Cynthia Kuhn, Ellen Byron.

And thanks to fellow blogging partners at Miss Demeanors: Connie Berry, Susan Breen, Michele Dorsey, Marni Graff, Catherine Maiorisi, Emilya Naymark, Lane Stone, and Sharon Ward.

In 2014, I learned about the William F. Deeck-Malice Domestic Grant and applied. The grant is given to an unpublished writer to encourage that person's advancement. The following year, the grant was awarded to Cynthia Kuhn and myself. Receiving the grant was the moment when my dream of seeing this book published became a reality. If you look at the list of recipients on the Malice Domestic website, you recognize the names of many writers who went on to publish. My sincerest thanks to Malice Domestic Board of Directors, the grants chair Harriette Sackler, and the grants committee, and my Malice buddies, Bill Starck, and Adolph Falcon.

Lastly, I want to thank my family, Rory and Hardy Bryant, for their support. Without them, I would not be here.

Author's Note

The Sorrowful Girl was inspired by genealogical research. I was an Air Force brat and, as such, had very little contact with my extended family. I was curious. I knew that there was a branch of my ancestors known as the Barretts and that my grandfather had grown up in Adams, Massachusetts. After many hours of digging online, I discovered that his grandmother was Mary Barrett, who came to Adams in the 1860's with her husband, Edward Gannon, and their three small children, to join her parents and younger brothers. All were Irish speakers from Crossmolina, County Mayo.

Online, I also met my cousin, the late JoAnn Emerson, genealogist extraordinaire. Through her I connected with Robert Norcross, a great friend, who is deeply committed to the history of Adams and still lives within sight of Mount Greylock.

It was my good fortune to visit Adams in 2013, when the idea for this book was noodling around in the back of my head. JoAnn and I tromped through public and private graveyards, identifying the resting places of our ancestors. She drove me through Adams and North Adams, spotting the area of the farm where my great grandfather grew up, the inspiration for the Barrett farm. I found the bar that he owned and the apartment block occupied entirely by my family at one point in time.

By the 1900's there were more than sixty people descended from Mary Barrett's parents living in and around Adams, mostly working in the mills by the age of fourteen. The Barrett Hotel, now Barrett House, was built by great grandfather's uncle. The PJ Barrett block was named for another uncle, a man who was involved in the creation of the Mount Greylock State Reservation in 1898, the first public land for purpose of forest preservation in Massachusetts. I picture the Black Rose, the fictional pub, sited on the PJ Barrett block.

If you're familiar with Adams and its history, you'll see that I took liberties. To name one, the Adams Free Library was opened to the public in 1899. William McKinley, in his first trip to Adams as President of the United States, laid the cornerstone on September 25, 1897. I spent a delightful afternoon their combing through their collection.

While *The Sorrowful Girl* continued to cook in the back of my brain, I wrote the Maeve Malloy series, contemporary legal thrillers set in Anchorage, Alaska. The first book, *Deadly Solution,* was nominated for Agatha, Lefty, and Silver Falchion awards. After I wrote this book, I began another series, the Maureen Gould legal thrillers, set in contemporary San Francisco.

But Liam was eventually written and would not be shoved into a drawer. This is the book I wanted to write when I was just embarking on my author career. I hope you enjoyed it.

I love hearing from readers. If you have any comments or just want to say hello, shoot me an email at: Contact - Keenan Powell (keenanpowellauthor.com). If you spot typos, please point out the exact typo and page number. Much appreciated!

If you'd like to be the first to know when I have a new release or special offers, sign up for my newsletter here: Home - Keenan Powell (keenanpowellauthor.com)

-Keenan Powell

Anchorage, Alaska

May 4, 2023

About the Author

Keenan Powell is the Agatha, Lefty, and Silver Falchion nominated author of the Maeve Malloy Mystery series.

Despite being one of original Dungeons and Dragons illustrators, art seemed an impractical pursuit – not an heiress, wouldn't marry well, hated teaching – so she went to law school. The day after graduation, she moved to Alaska.

She is the author of the Maeve Malloy Mysteries, a three-book series, and numerous short stories. She belongs to Mystery Writers of America, Sisters in Crime, and International Thriller Writers. She writes a legal column, Ipso Facto, for the Guppies newsletter, First Draft, and blogs with Miss Demeanors.

When not writing or practicing law, Keenan can be found oil painting or studying the Irish language.

Follow her at:

Amazon: https://www.amazon.com/stores/Keenan-Powell/author/B0788TKBJW

Facebook: https://www.facebook.com/keenanwrites

Goodreads: https://www.goodreads.com/author/show/17008872.Keenan_Powell

Bookbub: https://www.bookbub.com/authors/keenan-powell

Also By

www.ingramcontent.com/pod-product-compliance
Lightning Source LLC
Chambersburg PA
CBHW022033240626
47154CB00007B/2383